SWEET
Surrender

Sweet Surrender – Citrus Pines Book 3

Copyright 2021 © Lila Dawes

The author asserts the moral right to be identified as the owner of this work.

No part of this book may be reproduced or transmitted in any form or by any means, including but not limited to: graphic, electronic, or mechanical, including photocopying, recording, taping, or by any informational storage retrieval system without advanced prior permission in writing from the publisher.

This is a work of fiction, and is not based on a true story or on real characters.

Dedication

This book is about a lot of things but the foundation is a story about two best friends.

My best friend doesn't read steamy romance but she is 100% my biggest supporter.
She would love it if I dedicated a book to her, she's egotistical like that haha and has definitely mentioned it once or twice.

So it gives me supreme joy to know I've dedicated a book to her and she'll never know because she won't read it…mwahahaha.

To my ride or die – thank you xx

Content Info

This book contains themes which some readers may find distressing, including:

- Abortion
- Abandonment
- Stalking
- Spanking
- Violence
- Threat of sexual assault

Please take care of yourself when reading.

Sweet Surrender

Contents

Dedication	iii
Content Info	iv
Contents	v
Chapter 1	8
Chapter 2	19
Chapter 3	33
Chapter 4	54
Chapter 5	66
Chapter 6	76
Chapter 7	90
Chapter 8	102
Chapter 9	117
Chapter 10	128
Chapter 11	143
Chapter 12	158
Chapter 13	171
Chapter 14	182
Chapter 15	194
Chapter 16	207
Chapter 17	223
Chapter 18	235
Chapter 19	250

Chapter 20	261
Chapter 21	279
Chapter 22	293
Chapter 23	305
Chapter 24	320
Chapter 25	330
Chapter 26	341
Acknowledgements	357
About the Author	358

Chapter 1

"Oh Beau, your breath smells like garbage..."

"I'm not usually a fan of receding hairlines but it really works for you!"

"Is that as big as it gets?"

Taylor snickered to herself, mimicking Beau's date as she watched the woman gushing over him. They sat across the table from each other, his date talking while Beau stared at her with open-mouthed amazement.

Ugh.

Taylor looked away before she was sick. She wrenched open the dishwasher. A cloud of steam attacked her face and she breathed in the heat, reveling in it. Pulling out a tray, she began drying off glasses, stacking them along the back bar of her pride and joy, The Rusty Bucket Inn.

Her break from the loved-up couple didn't last long as

her eyes were inexplicably drawn back to them. *God, I hate him,* she thought, staring at his stupid smug face beaming down at his stunning date whose breasts were making an enthusiastic escape attempt from her skin-tight dress.

You're just jealous your breasts don't look like that. She glanced down at her less than impressive chest and sighed before her eyes lifted to the *happy* couple again.

Unfortunately, Beau didn't have any of the things Taylor just mentioned. His hairline was damn near perfect, his thick hair a deep chocolate brown that Taylor guessed was attractive, if you liked that kind of thing. His breath was always minty fresh, like he ate mints all day long. And his dick? Well, she didn't know about that but she sure as shit didn't think it was small. The guy was a giant and he radiated big dick energy. *Ugh, stop thinking about his dick!*

Taylor hated the way women fawned over him, just because he was hella tall, tanned and absolutely *stacked* with muscle? Pssh. Okay yes, he had nice hair that was just begging to be stroked and she could admit his mouth was pretty great, his full, wide lips always smiling. And fine, she would concede that a girl could get lost in those thickly-lashed dark eyes that curved suggestively at the edges.

BUT.

None of that meant a thing when the guy's personality was a big, fat bag o'dicks and *that* she damn well knew for a fact. She just made it her mission to ensure that everyone else knew it too, like a public service. *You're welcome, America,* she snorted to herself as she hip-checked the dishwasher shut and grabbed a cloth, wiping down her bar lovingly. She sighed over every chip the cloth snagged on the handcrafted oak top, her stomach dipping each time like she was touching an open wound.

The bar itself had been what she'd fallen in love with when she first looked around the place and she'd built the idea for the Inn around it. She had put her blood, sweat and tears into this place, renovating the bar as well as the rundown cabins. She'd created a place for folks to come and let their hair down with rooms they could book into if they needed to get away. She'd been running the place for ten years now. It was her life, her passion, the thing that got her out of bed each day. There had been tough times, but she worked her ass off to bring in the customers and it was finally paying off.

On her periphery she saw Beau saunter past the bar, not even glancing in her direction, as he headed down the hall to the restrooms. Looking around, Taylor spotted only a couple of people left in the bar, the hardcore regulars who stayed until closing most nights.

Taylor rang the bell that signaled closing time and was met with the now customary boos from her clientele which she just laughed off. She began going round the tables collecting the empty glasses, stopping by Porter, one of her regulars, who was slumped over on his stool.

"Come on Porter, quit faking it or I'll call Dina to come pick your ass up. Then you'll be sorry," she said, shaking the older man.

"You wouldn't do that, would you? Not after last time," the old man replied, slurring slightly. His horrified expression had Taylor chuckling. His wife was a scary lady; no one fucked with Dina.

"Then you'd better git!" Taylor flicked him with her cloth, her Southern accent deepening with her sass. Porter grumbled at her again but slid off his barstool and patted her hand affectionately. Taylor watched as he wandered out the bar, beginning his long walk home since she had confiscated his car keys. She always took the keys of the regulars; she wouldn't have anyone driving drunk on her watch.

The last few stragglers left, and Taylor collected their empty glasses before stopping at the table next to Beau's date. She eyed the woman critically. The blonde curls bounced with every movement, as did her impressive rack, inflating with every breath.

Don't do it! Taylor's brain screamed. But she was feeling particularly vicious this evening. *Jealousy's a bitch but so am I.*

"I just want to say, well done. You're a better woman than most," Taylor gushed. The blonde looked at her, confusion tried to pinch her forehead but her vast quantities of Botox made it near impossible.

"Excuse me?"

Taylor plastered a smile on her face. "It's *so* great that you're giving him a chance. Rehabilitated criminals need love too, am I right? I mean, sure, he *killed* that guy with his bare hands, but I bet he feels real bad about it."

The blonde's face dropped. "What?"

"Oh shoot, did he not get to that part yet in his 'about me' section? Well, don't I feel like I put my foot in it. Forget I said anything." Taylor waved her hand dismissively and then headed back to the bar, trying to smother her evil grin. She stacked the remaining glasses into the dishwasher. A moment later the clack of stilettos echoed through the bar as Beau's date skipped to the door.

"Come back soon!" Taylor called after her with a little wave then laughed as the door slammed shut behind her, bathing in her triumph. Seconds later, Beau came back from the bathroom and stopped in his tracks as he took in the empty bar. His steely gaze found Taylor's and narrowed dangerously before he headed her way. His long, muscled legs ate up the distance between them. He stopped in front of her and folded his arms across his chest, covering his blue t-shirt with the Superman 'S' on the front. She gulped as she took in his expression. *Shit.*

"What did you do?" he demanded.

"Good evening to you too, Beau," she trilled.

"Don't make me ask again," he growled. That deep, hard voice of his skated across the bar, gliding over her skin and she fought off an involuntary shiver. It was like his voice was a different frequency to other men, lower and rougher too. And there was definitely something wrong with it because it always made her feel funny inside.

His scent wrapped around her. Fresh, clean cotton with a hint of mint, he even smelled like a Goody Two-shoes. Okay so it was a nice smell and she wanted to breathe it in but she wouldn't. She would hold her breath and die if she had to, just to avoid it.

"I *may* have mentioned that you murdered someone with your bare hands."

His eyebrows practically hit his hairline. "What the fuck, Taylor!"

"I think you mean to say, you're welcome. If she's going to be scared off by a little thing like that then how loyal is she, really?"

"Are you serious right now? Why did you do that?"

She shrugged. "Because it was fun."

"You're twisted, you know that?"

"Hey, your ego is so overinflated you're going to be up in the clouds at this rate. Someone needs to bring you back down to earth, and luckily for you I've made it my mission to do just that. I'm the happy pin that gets to pop you." She smiled at him sweetly, knowing that would piss him off even more. He raked his hand through those chocolatey soft locks, glaring at her.

"You're so damn lucky that you're my best friend's little sister," he muttered.

"Why? What would you do if I wasn't?" she taunted eagerly, loving and hating their verbal sparring. He was the only man who ever matched her energy. She knew she needed to pump the brakes; her mouth tended to run away with her but she liked getting under his skin far too much and hey, she had to have some flaws, right?

He stared her down, his pupils flaring until all the deep warmth was gobbled up by chilling black. "You think you've got one over on me, but I can still turn this date around. Trust me, sweetheart," he replied smugly.

Her stomach dropped at his confidence. He would do it too. Not that she cared, of course.

"Whatever, and don't call me that," she muttered, turning away. Seething as she handed him the victory in their little skirmish. She heard his boots clomp across the wooden floor towards the exit.

"Oh, and when you come to clean my room tomorrow, be sure to bring a whole bunch of fresh sheets, I'm gonna need them." He smirked at her, his luscious mouth full of spite and then he was out the door. She flung a glass at the wall in anger, the shards tinkling around her when it shattered.

Sometimes their verbal sparring gave her a crazy high, higher even than sex. But sometimes, like tonight, it left her hollow. *It's your own fault,* she chided. But she couldn't help it, it was a reflex to dig at him. To prod and poke at him and show him how little she thought of him. It had been this way between them ever since...*no, don't go there, not when you feel shitty.*

She swept up the broken glass, annoyed at herself for her reaction and wasting a glass she would now have the expense of replacing. Maybe she should add it to Beau's bill? No, she couldn't do that. She was a lot of things, but she would never take advantage of a customer like that, even if she hated him with every fiber of her being.

She finished cleaning up the bar and cashed up the register before locking up. Once outside, she stepped off the porch, the cool evening air signaling that fall was on its way. The wind swirled around her, dancing her hair across her face. The scent of citrus teasing her nostrils, so strong she could almost taste it. She loved this place, the scents, the scenery, the beauty of it worked its way inside your veins. She could never imagine leaving this town the way some of her friends had. It was home.

She walked around the side of the bar and headed for her cabin, the light on her porch calling her home. Movement drew her attention to the porch of the cabin next to hers and she saw Beau standing there, opening the door and stepping back to let his date inside.

The bastard actually did it...

When he spotted Taylor, he smiled wide, smug from his win and gave her a little pinkie wave before heading inside. The door shut with a resounding click that echoed on the breeze through the quiet night.

Her mouth dropped open and her stomach dipped. She just hoped they were quiet so she didn't have to listen to their cries of ecstasy all night. The thought tangled around her throat, halting her breath.

"Enjoy your night of boring, polite sex," she muttered to herself. Much like most things she didn't know about Beau, she assumed he was a dud in the bedroom department. He was Mr. Perfect with all those perfect manners and perfect façade, not to mention his perfect breath. He didn't exactly scream *wild nights*, ugh, not that she ever spent hours thinking about it or anything.

She should have refused to rent him the cabin. He'd been staying at the Inn for a few months now while he was having renovations done on his house. He had bought the house from Christy, Taylor's best friend, who had run away fifteen years ago, leaving town and leaving Taylor to continue life without her.

When Christy's father passed away last year, Christy had come home to clear the house and sell it. Taylor had been ecstatic that her friend was finally home after all these years, she'd hoped it would be to stay, and that Christy would decide to keep the house moving home permanently.

What no one expected was Christy falling in love with Dean, Taylor's stepbrother. Taylor had known they had a thing for each other when they were teenagers, not that they ever would have admitted it at the time. Now Christy and Dean were living together and soon to be married. Taylor smiled as she thought about the two people she loved most in the world finding happiness together.

Beau had started renovating the house, but Taylor had never asked him what he was doing with it. *Have a normal conversation with him? Never!* Still, she'd overheard a few things. It sounded like he was creating some kind of gym or spa thing for the elderly. Which was *not* a nice thing to do. Not at all.

She would have refused to rent him the cabin but Dean had stepped in and talked her into it. Dean was her only family, she loved him fiercely, would give him anything he asked for and he knew it.

Her father was a cheater through and through. He cheated on her mom so many times that eventually her mom couldn't take any more and she left, not stopping to say goodbye or even take Taylor with her. When her dad met Dean's mom, Iris, hope bloomed in Taylor: maybe she would finally have a mom again. Their parents had married, combining families like the Brady Bunch, except then her dad did what he always did: lied and cheated over and over again until Iris couldn't take it anymore and she left too.

Taylor not only lost her stepmom that day but also lost her hope that love was enough to make people stick around. Iris struggled to keep a relationship with Taylor after everything that her dad had done, but eventually they lost touch. Her anger at her father and the hurt she felt at Iris abandoning her still burned bright to this day, but her relationship with Dean had gone the distance, and that was a blessing.

Taylor shivered in the evening air, hurrying to her cabin, grateful it was only a short distance. She glanced around her, making sure no one was watching her. Her ex-boyfriend, Dale, had been hanging around lately, wanting a second chance with her and each time he didn't get it, he started causing trouble.

Dale had drawn her attention immediately. He was the ultimate Bad Boy, intense, mysterious and she couldn't deny her attraction to him. Things had been great when they were together; he was funny, affectionate and more or less adequate in bed.

But then he began to demand things from her that she wasn't able to give, so she had broken it off, hoping to save him from further heartbreak. At first he accepted it, thinking it was just some twisted game she was playing to get him to want her more. When he realized it was real, he wasn't happy and now he wouldn't leave her alone.

A twig snapped behind her and she spun around, startled. But there was no one there.

She fumbled with her key in the lock but finally got it in and ran inside, slamming the door shut behind her and sliding the bolts across the top and bottom. She had added them when Dale started hanging around more, watching her with ice blue eyes that she once thought were pretty. Now she saw they were empty. Now they scared her.

She sank against the door, waiting until her heartbeat slowed, berating herself for being silly and overreacting. When she was calm, she switched on her old TV for background noise and went into the kitchen to make herself a cup of tea.

Most people had never been inside her cabin, most people didn't know she was obsessed with pink. And why would they? She wasn't a teenager, she was an aggressive, rude, tattooed thirtysomething. Her décor was pink, her furniture was pink, her life was pink, multiple shades of pink. Her pink couch sat on her pink carpet next to her pink coffee table.

While the kettle boiled on her stove, she headed out the back door to stock up the bird feeder and throw some more nuts out for the little squirrel family she was raising. Animals seemed to flock to Taylor, she'd always been an animal lover but hadn't wanted to have any pets because of the hours she worked, thinking it wouldn't be fair. So, she developed a little wild fur family, like a freaking Disney princess. *Little munchkins won't clean my house though.*

Back inside she headed to the kitchen to wait for the kettle to finish boiling and dared a glance up through the window, already knowing it was a mistake. Her kitchen window looked directly into the next cabin and she had a clear view of Beau. And his date.

I can't believe he managed to get her back into his room, is his dick made of solid gold or something? Oh my God stop thinking about his dick!

She watched as he closed the drapes and any

remaining lights went out. Her stomach dipped again and she hated herself for it. Hated herself for finding him attractive. Hated him for the way he had ruined her life and then abandoned her like so many others. Hated him for a decision *she* made that had changed her life forever.

But most of all, she hated him for being the only man to ever break her heart.

Chapter 2

Breath sawed in and out of Beau's lungs as his feet pounded the pavement. He pushed himself harder either to beat his personal best or to drive away all his unwanted thoughts, whichever happened first.

He hadn't been able to close the deal with a woman yet again. He knew exactly why, and it made him pissed as hell. Despite his anger, he fought the urge to smile at Taylor's antics last night. Usually she attacked his physical characteristics but telling his date he was a murderer was a new twist and very creative. Taylor kept him on his toes, testing his charm skills to the absolute max, pushing him to be better. He'd barely managed to convince his poor date that he wasn't a killer, even placing a quick call to one of his best buddies, Deputy Sheriff Blake Miller to confirm he was in fact *not* a serial killer.

But by then, the damage was done and she wasn't interested in hooking up. He couldn't let her wander off in the middle of the night, so he let her wait inside his cabin for her ride home. Like a gentleman, he had waited outside on the porch as she still didn't fully trust him enough to be alone with him.

The scoreboard stood at Beau: a big fat zero; Taylor: let's face it, a million at this point. That woman had ruined so many of his dates he'd lost count. It was like she made it her mission to mess with him, trying to get under his skin and make life as inconvenient as possible for him.

"Mission accomplished," he muttered.

He loved and hated their verbal sparring. Loved it because it meant at least she still cared about him. If she was indifferent, she wouldn't bother. Hated it because it turned him into a person he never wanted to be with her. Being around Taylor transformed him into a raging sack of testosterone. All his impulses screamed to take her, put her over his knee, punish her for her sass until she was sorry, or until she was begging him for more. The image fired his blood, made his pulse pound and it *scared* him. He was known as Mr Cool, Calm and Collected, he was gentle and caring. He had never acted like that with a woman before, had never got off on that type of aggressive, dominant behavior. But with Taylor…God he never wanted it to stop, how fucked up was that?

Beau ran through the little town center like he did every day on his morning run. Citrus Pines was his home, despite both him and his family moving away, this was where his roots were. He had recently moved back from L.A where he'd been living for the past fifteen years.

He liked it in the city but the older he became the more toxic he found the lifestyle to be to himself and others. As a personal trainer to the rich and famous, he met a lot of amazing people but also people who were only out for themselves, who used him and discarded him once they had what they needed.

His last girlfriend had been the final straw. She had been so obsessed with getting the 'Hollywood' look that their relationship became transactional. If he couldn't fit her in for a training session she would accuse him of cheating on her. She only cared about the way she looked and how he could help her achieve her goals and when he ended things with her, she had tried to kill herself. He had managed to save her but he was too shaken by the incident and decided L.A was no longer for him.

He wanted to get back to helping people, he was tired of seeing people exploit each other. He'd made a fortune getting actors to bulk up or slim down and now he wanted to put his knowledge to better use.

He bought a house in order to set up a treatment and rehabilitation center. He envisaged his main clients being the arthritic elderly folks from town, or moms who wanted to socialize and keep fit, women who wanted to learn self-defense, or teenagers who wanted to bulk up for a sport or to impress their crush. But he also wanted it to be a place that people came to for injury rehabilitation, like ex-service people or athletes.

Moving back home was a big change in lifestyle but he had never been about the L.A scene. He had been about helping people and he could do that anywhere. He wasn't leaving anyone behind in L.A except for his friend and business partner Will Crawford. But Will had already visited Citrus Pines a few times and Beau knew that their friendship was strong enough and they would make the effort to see each other.

Beau loved his hometown and was pleased to be back,

even though his parents had retired to the south of Florida last year to be closer to his sister. He knew plenty of people in town and everyone was like family.

He waved to Justine as he saw her car pulling up outside her office. She was a psychiatrist and the fiancée of his buddy, Citrus Pines' deputy sheriff, Blake. But Beau didn't stop to talk to Justine today; he was in the zone. That sweet spot where his muscles burned like hellfire and his adrenaline was sky high, pushing him on.

As the ground switched from concrete to dirt and pine needles, he pushed himself harder, drawing on reserves of strength to get him back to the cabin where he was currently staying. He ran across the empty parking lot of The Rusty Bucket Inn, the breeze caressing his sweat-slicked skin. *Nearly there, keep going.* When he hit the porch of his cabin the endorphin rush he got from running evaporated. The door was wide open and *she* was there.

Taylor.

She was inside, bent over, emptying the little trash can by his bed. Her hips and ass swaying to the dirty beat of whatever song she was listening to. He stopped in the doorway, leaned against it and permitted himself to do the one thing he tried to do as little as possible: watch her. A mix of emotions rampaged through him. Anger, hurt, and regret mingled with lust.

Taylor shimmied her shoulders and stood upright, belting out the lyrics to the song. His throat ran dry when he realized it was *S&M* by Rihanna. She shrieked the words to the chorus, pelvic-thrusting her way across the room to her cleaning supplies and he tried to keep the smile from his face.

She let out a loud *woo* and nostalgia cracked his chest open and memories poured out. All the times he'd heard that sound, all the times they had made that sound together. Pain lanced through him at the reminder of all the times he had missed. People say that certain scents could trigger a memory, well this sound did it for him and it was agony.

"Jesus Christ!" she shouted, ripping her ear buds out when she spotted him, her scowl snapping into place. "Creepy stalker much?" Her good mood was all gone the second she registered his presence, as usual.

Annoyance flitted through him. "How long are you going to be?" he snapped, like the asshole he was. Guilt instantly ate at him, he started to apologize but her withering glare had his lips folding inwards. Taylor was effectively the maid service at the Inn. He'd told her that he didn't want her cleaning his room but she'd taken that as a personal challenge, *typical*, and she cleaned his room every day, with relish and a dash of spite.

Taylor drew herself up to her full height, 5'8" with long, slender legs that he definitely had *not* pictured wrapped around his waist a thousand times. She flipped her flame red hair over her shoulder with all the sass she could, the gold hoop through her nose caught the light and her emerald eyes flashed at him.

"I'll be done when I'm done. It's not my fault you're messy as fuck."

He snorted. He wasn't messy at all; everything was as neat as could be. *She* was the messy one. He remembered the number of times he'd been in her room as a teenager. Tripping over all her crap scattered on the floor, getting tangled in the clothes strewn about the place like a hurricane had hit it. Tornado Taylor, that's what he'd called her. He shook his head at the memory, trying to dislodge it.

He grabbed a towel from the clean stack she had placed on an armchair, and wiped his sweaty face then the back of his neck.

She scowled at him and turned away. "You stink."

"Leave then so I can shower," he grumbled.

"I will as soon as I change the bed." She looked at it now, her cute nose wrinkling. "I can't believe I have to change your gross sex sheets," she complained.

"Oh sweetheart, we didn't have sex in the *bed,*" he purred. It was technically the truth, he and his date hadn't had sex at all, but he refused to admit that her little stunt last night had succeeded. He watched her closely for a reaction and saw her face flush, adorable red covering up the smattering of freckles that ran across her cheeks and nose. Freckles he used to fantasize about licking until...*nope, not going there.*

He couldn't believe she was blushing. That he rendered that motormouth of hers speechless, with a *sex* joke no less. She was the queen of dirty jokes but she wasn't used to him making them. The Beau she knew from years ago would never have made a dirty joke to Taylor, he would have stuttered and stumbled and stared at his feet, tongue-tied and blushing.

"Unless you're moving out then I need another two weeks paying up," she interrupted his thoughts.

He nodded. "I'll get you the cash later today."

"Are you sure you wouldn't rather move out? I wouldn't mind at all." She shot him a smile full of teeth and snark. Unfortunately for her, he wasn't going anywhere.

"I'm sure."

She cursed and turned back to the bed and began pulling the sheets off. He stepped forward to stop her, he couldn't watch her do this, like she was his damn maid. She sensed his intentions and shot him a look that would have turned a lesser man to stone. As it was, Beau was so used to that look, he was immune. She glared at him as she wrenched a pillowcase free and dropped it to the ground, shaking her head and arching her eyebrow in challenge, a challenge she won.

He stormed into the bathroom and slammed the door, trying to shut the feelings out. He felt like he was suffocating in this twisted game they were caught in.

Things hadn't always been like this between them. At one point she had been the most important person in the world to him. They had been the best of friends; she was the reason he jumped out of bed each day. She was…God there weren't words for what she had meant to him…

Back then he'd been such a fucking cliché. The geeky, fat kid in love with the beautiful, popular girl. Only the beautiful popular girl had become his best friend's new stepsister. The time he spent hanging out at Dean's house, around her, had brought them closer together and soon she became his other best friend.

At first he was so shy and tongue-tied around her. When she paid him attention, he didn't trust that she was genuine. He'd been used by the popular girls at school who pretended to be his friend or acted like they wanted to date him when really they wanted him to do their homework or to use him to make another guy jealous.

He hadn't been under any illusions, he was a nerd, he was fat and awkward as hell with zero confidence. No way would those girls be interested in him. Eventually he realized that Taylor genuinely wanted to know him and be his friend. He managed to put his *awkward* aside and have conversations with her.

They talked about everything. Music, movies, books and TV, politics sometimes, and even pointless crap like if you had to choose between having dicks for fingers or testicles for toes which would you pick? Dick fingers all day long, FYI.

Taylor would always come and grab him for lunch at school and they'd walk to the cafeteria together, past all the other overweight, nerdy kids who watched open-mouthed as this goddess picked Beau. Every damn day she picked *him*.

They would sit together, sometimes with Dean, and people-watch, making up stories about strangers, getting more outrageous with each person they picked. As well as random discussions about dick fingers and testicle toes, Beau liked to challenge her. Taylor had this silly belief that you could fit a *woo* into any song, so he spent his time testing her on songs of all different genres. So far, she hadn't proved him wrong.

Taylor had been magnetic. Hell, she still was. She had a vibe and an energy about her that was addictive, you always wanted more. And damn his soft, naïve teenage heart but he had wanted more. He wanted *everything*.

Who had he been kidding though, there was no way she was interested in him like that. Plus, she already had a boyfriend, Bobby, who treated her like shit. Taylor had an amazing bullshit detector and kept her circle small; it was something Beau adored about her. She wasn't fake, she didn't need the world to love her and care about her, just her close friends. Which was why Beau could never understand how Bobby had snuck into her circle. He was a fucking moron.

Twice their football coach had to break up fights between Beau, Dean and Bobby after Bobby had opened his mouth in the locker room and overshared his and Taylor's sexcapades. Why the fuck would you share that information with her stepbrother and best friend in the vicinity? That's what a fucking moron he was. Not that

Beau had minded, he relished having an excuse to beat the shit out of him.

Sometimes it was difficult being such good friends with Taylor. The more time he spent around her, the more he fell for her and had to put his feelings aside. Beau had become perfectly content with wanting her and settling for friendship, hell, he would take what he could get.

Until one evening after school, Taylor had burst into his room, ranting and raving about what a dick Bobby was. This was a regular occurrence, but Beau always listened, he never bitched about Bobby and he was never disrespectful. Any comments he wanted to make would only be borne of jealousy and not fit for her ears.

But this time when she had finally finished ranting, she flopped down onto his bed and sprawled there, staring at him. He had to look away, her fiery hair flared around her head, her cheeks flushed from her rage and her eyes beseeching him did funny things to his insides and made his seventeen-year-old body want things it couldn't have.

He needed a moment to pull himself together, so he went and made her favorite drink. Her love of pink was well known to him by then so of course it made sense that her favorite drink was strawberry milkshake. When he came back to his room she was, mercifully, sitting up on the edge of the bed. She smiled when she saw what he had.

"Thank you, my *Teddy Beau*, you always know what I need." She took the drink from him, taking a big gulp and closed her eyes, savoring the taste. He wrinkled his nose at the nickname but didn't say anything. He sat on the bed next to her, his mattress dipping with his weight and she slid closer to him. Embarrassment heated his cheeks, he really needed to do something about his weight. He was at least two hundred pounds heavier than he should be.

She turned to look at him, her eyes wide and gentle. Her cinnamon scent crept over him and he discreetly inhaled.

"You're such a good listener," she murmured, putting her hand on his thigh. He met her stare, her eyes sparkling in the soft light of the room, bewitching him. Something about this evening was different, tension lit the air around them as they sat in silence. His mouth ran dry and he swiped his tongue over his lips, her eyes tracked the movement and her breath hitched.

She raised her hand from his thigh and stroked it down his cheek affectionately. His breath heaved in and out of him, his body pulled tight with tension. He was too scared to move in case he broke whatever spell she was under. She stroked his cheek again, then swiped her thumb across his bottom lip. Her hand continued its exploration, traveling into his hair and caressing the strands. Beau had never been more terrified in his life. Terrified this wasn't really happening, that she wasn't real, that his most *desperate* fantasy wasn't coming to life right before his eyes.

Taylor settled her hand on the nape of his neck and before he could say a word, she pulled him towards her. He didn't close his eyes, didn't dare to miss this. His heart beat like a drum in his chest, trying to escape his body with every enthusiastic pound. He watched her eyelashes flutter, hiding those dazzling eyes from his view and then his fantasy became reality.

Her lips touched his. Silky soft. The pressure so light, but he felt it everywhere. She pulled back hesitantly before she leaned in again. This time he returned the kiss, his lips meeting hers and a blissful sigh slipped out of him. He felt like he'd come home.

She moaned softly, the sound jolting him and he hardened beneath the fly of his jeans. Her tongue was at his lips, stroking the seam, begging him to open up and let her in. He opened tentatively as though he still couldn't believe that he was lucky enough to be *kissing Taylor Done-Campbell*. Her tongue stroked his and rockets went off behind his eyelids. She tasted like strawberries, and he was addicted to the flavor. The zing of their tongues touching had him gripping her waist tightly. He huffed out a breath and felt her smile against his lips, he could picture that smile now in his mind. Just as he was about to surrender to her kiss, she pulled back, gasping.

"Oh my God, what am I doing?" She looked at Beau, her face twisted in horror and she leapt away from him like she could barely stand to touch him. Confusion replaced his joy as he watched her cover her mouth with a hand, like she was stopping herself from vomiting. Her expression burned itself into his brain as her eyes dropped down to his pelvis where she could see just how much he had enjoyed his first kiss.

Humiliation lashed at him, cutting his heart open and letting him bleed out in front of her. This wasn't his fantasy; this was his worst nightmare. So why the *fuck* wasn't he waking up?

"This was a mistake…" she murmured, wiping at her mouth like she couldn't stand his taste on her lips a moment longer. Mortification and hurt swirled through him and bled together, creating something new: hate and anger. Of course she didn't want him, he knew he shouldn't have pushed his doubts aside but he was too desperate to believe it was real and that desperation made him a fool. How could she ever have been interested in him? It was just a game to her and she was just like all the other girls at school.

"You played me! I can't believe it, *you* of all people!" he sneered, and her face dropped.

"No, Beau I…"

"Get the fuck away from me, get out and don't ever come back."

She tried to reach for him but he shook her off. "Bobby was right about you; you are a slut!" he shouted and then snapped his mouth shut before any more poison slipped out. Her face twisted at his words and then she was gone.

Beau paced up and down his room, fists clenched tightly. He punched the wall but it didn't make him feel better. He spotted the glass that still held her favorite pink drink. The one he made her, always taking care of her like some pathetic lovesick puppy. He picked it up and threw it against the wall, watching the glass shatter around him like his heart. Then he sank down on his bed and cried.

He didn't sleep that night, his hurt burned so brightly he didn't think it would ever dim. He didn't understand why she'd done that, how could she be so cruel?

He had dreaded the next day at school. He looked like shit from lack of sleep and crying but he went anyway, nausea churning in his stomach the whole time. He was hurting badly, the backs of his eyes prickling as he walked the halls. But he'd said something horrible last night and even if he and Taylor were finished, even if she didn't give a shit about the little fat boy who doted on her, he owed her an apology.

He and Dean stood at his locker at lunch, normally the time Taylor would meet him and they would go and people-watch. Maybe if she turned up now, he would know it was all a misunderstanding, they could make up and everything would go back to normal. But as he stood listening to Dean moan about how snooty Christy was, he didn't see Taylor.

"Maybe she's not coming today? I saw her with Bobby earlier," Dean said, looking around. Beau's nausea increased as time ticked on. The bell rang for class and it felt final. She wasn't coming. Then the familiar prickle ran along the back of Beau's neck and he looked up.

There she was. Striding down the hallway towards him, on Bobby's arm. Popular, muscular, attractive Bobby, the complete opposite of Beau.

Taylor caught his eye, something sharp spiked in the emerald depths and her lips lifted in a cruel smile he'd never seen before. She pulled Bobby to her and kissed him, aggressively, hungrily, watching Beau the entire time. It was the biggest *fuck you* of all time, and bitterness threatened to consume him. The hope that had bloomed in his chest died a strangled, agonizing death.

When Taylor and Bobby pulled apart, Bobby smacked her ass loudly and she giggled before shooting another one of those new, cruel smiles at Beau and brushed past him. Beau's apology froze on his lips…

Trying to break himself out of his most painful memory, Beau stepped under the spray of the shower. *Why the fuck did you decide to go down that rabbit hole?* He wasn't that sad little boy anymore. He was a grown man. A successful, strong man. Nothing like the boy he had been before L.A. He had moved on and it was pathetic to hold on to past resentments.

But he owed Taylor an apology; he still felt remorse for what he'd said when he was an idiotic teenager who didn't know how to control his emotions. Call him oversensitive but he'd had enough insults hurled at him in his time to know that once something was said, it couldn't be taken back. He couldn't take back his words, but he could apologize.

The problem was he and Taylor never had a civil enough conversation for him to work it in, and they were definitely never alone together. They hadn't said a kind word to each other ever since that night. He needed to bridge this gap between them, especially now he was home for good and would see her all the time. She had been his best friend at one point and although they would never get back to that, they could let go of the animosity and be civil again, right?

He needed to grab the cash to pay for the cabin so he would try later to get her alone and then he would apologize, once and for all.

Chapter 3

"I'm pregnant!" Justine blurted out, absolute joy pouring from her. Christy screamed and flung herself at Justine before pulling back at the last minute as though Justine were as delicate as glass.

Justine's words echoed in Taylor's mind, words Taylor knew she would never say herself. A rushing sound filled her ears and she struggled to catch her breath. She wanted to cry, scream, throw a tantrum like a child. Instead, she swallowed the lump in her throat and blinked away her tears.

"Congratulations, babe!" she cried, trying to pass off her emotion as happiness. Which it was, absolutely. She was so thrilled for her, it had been Justine's dream to be a mom for as long as Taylor had known her. Guilt stabbed at Taylor's gut that her first thought when her friend shared such incredible news was for herself.

She enveloped Justine in a bear hug and pulled back to stare into Justine's whiskey eyes filled with so much happiness. "You'll be the most amazing mom, I cannot wait to watch you do this," Taylor said, her voice husky with emotion before squeezing Justine again and kissing her cheek.

"And Blake! He's gonna be the most amazing dad. No one will mess with your kid, they'll be too terrified of him," Christy said, and the three of them laughed.

"Oh God, my poor child," Justine joked, cradling her still flat stomach protectively and Taylor's heart squeezed in her chest.

"Let's celebrate," she said, distracting herself. She looped around the bar and grabbed three shot glasses and a bottle of Patrón but only filled two of the glasses.

"No fair, you know Patrón's my favorite," Justine whined.

"And you can absolutely have some, when the little one is out," Christy teased. Taylor poured fruit juice into the remaining shot glass and handed it to a pouting Justine.

"To Blake, Justine and Bump," Taylor said, raising her shot glass. Christy repeated the toast and Justine giggled before they all clinked glasses and downed their shots.

Christy began asking a million questions while Taylor secretly had three more shots of tequila. She listened in to every detail of pregnancy life that Justine shared, drinking it in and savoring the knowledge until it started to hurt again. When she couldn't take anymore, she made an excuse about needing to go and do some paperwork. She hugged her friend again and when she pulled back, she cupped Justine's cheeks.

"I'm so happy for you, *mi corazón*."

Justine sniffled. "*Te adoro.*"

Taylor patted Christy's arm before slipping away and into her office. She shut the door and went over to the window and stared out at the trees. A sob rose in her throat that she couldn't stop.

Just one, no one will know.

She would not allow more than that. A single tear slipped over her lower lid and snaked a path down her cheek but she didn't wipe it away.

She cupped a hand over her stomach. Grief and longing swept through her for what she'd lost followed by anger. She had been an idiotic teenager and now as an adult, she was paying the price.

Some days she could pretend it hadn't happened. But other days, it was shoved front and center in her mind. Especially after an announcement like this. Taylor had been expecting it though, her friends were pairing off and getting married. Soon it would be Christy announcing the same news. She needed to get used to it, needed to stop finding the pain in it and embrace the joy.

A smile twitched at her lips at the thought of her being a cool aunt. At the idea of her stepbrother, Dean, being a dad. He would be the best dad, looking out for his child the way he'd looked out for her all these years.

She tried to steer her thoughts towards other things, but it seemed her brain was determined to pick over this and torture her with her most regrettable mistake. How could one kiss have such devastating consequences?

Her mind drifted back to that night. It always took her back to the most painful and humiliating moment. It was as fresh today as it was all those years ago…

She sprawled on Beau's bed, watching him watch her, with that look in his eyes that made her feel truly desirable. Yes, her boyfriend Bobby wanted her, but he was a horny teenager who just wanted a body, he didn't want *her*. The way that Beau watched her? Unparalleled.

He was her best friend; he knew more about her than anyone. Knew her deepest, darkest secrets, her thoughts and fears, and yet he still looked at her like she alone hung the moon and dotted the night sky with every single star. It was addictive.

She had turned up at his house that evening, ranting about what an *asshat* her shitty boyfriend Bobby was. As usual Beau just listened, he didn't interrupt to give his opinion, didn't hurry her along when she went off on a tangent. He just listened patiently and when she was finished, he went and got her favorite drink: strawberry milkshake. He always knew what she needed.

When he came back and sat next to her on his bed, the mattress dipping until she slid closer to him, it was like fate itself was trying to orchestrate what would happen next. Taylor had always excelled at hiding her feelings for him, not wanting to ruin the most important friendship she had. But tonight, something was different. The air around them was charged and heavy, expectant.

He looked over at her and she stared into those warm, dark eyes that made her insides twist into knots.

"You're such a good listener…" she murmured, placing a hand on his thigh like it was the most natural thing to do. They had hugged before; she was used to touching him but her hand on his thigh was deliberate. A statement. The air between them thickened and she couldn't draw enough breath. His tongue peeked out and swiped across his full bottom lip. She was dying to know if that lip was as soft as it looked.

Her arm lifted as though she were the puppet and someone else was pulling her strings. She stroked her hand over his cheek, her knuckles brushing his soft skin. Warm and silky, the lightest rasp from his facial hair. Before she could stop herself, she stroked his lip, his hot breath coasting over her thumb as it explored the place that fascinated her most.

He didn't stop her.

Her boldness increased.

She slid her hands into his hair, desperate to know how it felt, she'd fantasized about it enough. When he still didn't move to stop her, she settled her palm on the back of his neck and made her boldest move of all. She pulled him towards her, and he came willingly.

Her lips sealed over his.

She was used to kissing but this was something else.

Bobby ate at her, forcing his slavering tongue into her mouth, practically gagging her. But Beau was hesitant, he was *reverent*. He sipped her lips gently, lovingly and it broke her. She half-sobbed, half-moaned and tears welled in her eyes as he let her inside and when their tongues touched her whole world ignited. It was beautiful. Why couldn't this have been her first kiss? Why hadn't she been bold enough to tell him how she felt? Why was she with Bobby when she wanted Beau?

And just like that, it was as though someone had thrown a bucket of water over her. What the hell was she doing? She had a boyfriend; she had broken her cardinal rule and *cheated*. Disgust at her selfishness ripped through her. Her stomach churning with the realization that she was just like her father, the man she swore she would never become.

"Oh my God, what am I doing?" She pulled away from Beau, horrified at her behavior. She stood up, trying to put space between them. She didn't want to look at him, too horrified of what he would think of her for cheating on Bobby. Beau was good, a genuinely kind and decent person, she didn't think she could stand to see him disappointed in her.

"That was a mistake…" she said, wiping her mouth to try and remove the wonderful feeling of his lips still pressed to hers.

She wanted Beau too much. She needed to break up with Bobby. She was only with him because he was safe, there was no danger that she would develop deep feelings for him and be hurt. The strength of her feelings for Beau scared her, he had the power to break her and she knew it, had always fought against it. But now, after what they just shared, she was ready to give in. Yes, that's what she would do, she would go and see Bobby now and end things and when she came back, she and Beau could pick up where–

"You played me! I can't believe it, *you* of all people!" Hurt lined Beau's words.

She looked into his stricken eyes and her stomach flipped. Played him? She would never. Terror filled her at the idea of him thinking she was like all the other girls at school that used him. Girls Taylor usually threatened for daring to treat him in such a way.

"No, Beau I-" she started, reaching for him and he batted her hand away.

"Get the fuck away from me! Get out of here and don't ever come back."

She reached out to him, wanting to end this misunderstanding but her friend was no longer here. An angry stranger had taken his place.

"Bobby was right about you; you *are* a slut!"

His words lashed at her and she recoiled as they hit their mark, whipping across her heart. Is that really what he thought of her? The one person who knew her best?

Her heart shattered at the way his lip curled in disgust. His eyes held no affection for her now, just hatred and anger. She couldn't stand it, couldn't watch the way his face twisted before her.

Her legs turned to jelly as she fled from the room, from that look, from her crumbling heart. She ran until she found herself at Bobby's house, on his front porch pounding on the door.

"Hey Babe, what are you doing here?" he said, stepping back to let her inside. Their earlier fight completely forgotten. He was a good-looking guy; tall, blond, all angular features and solid muscle. Not soft and gentle like her Teddy Beau. She blanched at the thought of Beau, she needed to forget what had happened tonight. Needed to forget that she made a move on him and the look of disgust on his face. Needed to forget the helplessness that clawed its way through her veins, she just needed to forget.

"Let's have sex," she blurted out. She knew Bobby talked a lot at school but the truth was they hadn't had sex yet. It was what half of their arguments were about. Taylor cared about him but something had been holding her back. Beau. *Well, not anymore.*

Bobby grinned and the next thing she knew, she was naked in his bed. He grabbed at her breasts and pawed at her. His touches hard and desperate, not gentle like Beau's had been. Taylor bit her lip to keep from crying as Bobby shoved himself inside her, the burn running through her entire body. He thrust into her, clumsy, not caring if she enjoyed it, he was just using her. He tried to kiss her and she turned her face away, no way could she handle one of his empty, sloppy kisses after what she'd experienced with Beau.

Beau...

Mercifully, it was over quickly. Inside she felt hollow and lonely, so lonely. She cried and Bobby just assumed she was happy and left her to it. Humiliation and shame were her companions as she walked home alone. She didn't speak to anyone, just went straight to bed, the thought of school the next day already weighing on her mind.

She didn't think she could face Beau tomorrow. He had thrown her affection in her face like what she'd offered him hadn't mattered but he was wrong. It was her heart and soul she had handed to him. Resentment burned inside her and she decided she would show Beau that she didn't care about him anymore.

The next day she walked through school with Bobby and he paraded her about like some trophy he'd finally won. Down the hallway she spotted Beau. As soon as their eyes met she was transported to that moment in his room, to that look of revulsion on his face.

Taylor's pride kicked in and she pulled Bobby to her, kissing him aggressively before she could realize her mistake. Now her last kiss wasn't the one she and Beau had shared, it was this kiss with Bobby. A kiss full of revenge and spite.

She watched Beau the entire time, desperate to see jealousy, pain, regret, goddammit just *something!* But his expression hardened, and she knew then that they would never be the same again. Now she was too heartbroken to care.

Unfortunately, her actions had consequences. That night with Bobby she had been too distracted to think about appropriate contraception, and soon she realized she was pregnant. She didn't know what to do, who to talk to. Christy had left town and abandoned her, and she certainly couldn't tell her father. She tried to talk to

Bobby but he made his feelings clear, he didn't want to be a dad and he wouldn't have anything to do with the baby or her if she decided to keep it; he abandoned her too.

Justine was away and in any case, she was so family-oriented that Taylor felt like she couldn't have the honest conversation she needed to have. The only person she could turn to was Dean. Just because their parents had now divorced didn't mean a thing, they still loved each other the same. Except when she went round to see Dean to tell him, Beau was there. She could have waited until Beau left but the scornful look he gave her the moment he saw her, made her insides shrivel and she left. She had gotten herself into this mess, she could damn well get herself out of it.

Taylor wasn't ready to be a mom, she could barely look after herself at this point and her father's health was deteriorating so she was spending her time looking after him. What kind of life could she give a child?

So, she made the only decision she felt she could.

As she sat in the waiting room at the doctor's office, she went back and forth in her mind. Tears slipped down her cheeks, guilt strangled her, but what could she do? She had only just turned eighteen, what did she know about anything? It was better this way. She cried all through the procedure, she cried for weeks after. She cried when she got the infection, she cried when the doctors said they couldn't get it under control and she cried when they said they would have to remove her womb...

The sound of her office door closing snapped Taylor back to reality. She swiped at her wet cheeks, surprised more tears had leaked out. She had cried enough in the past to last a lifetime and only permitted herself a few tears when she was sad. It had been so long ago now that she was over what happened, truly she was, but Justine's announcement had brought it all back. She turned towards the door to see Beau standing there.

"What do you want?" she snapped, mortified that he'd caught her in such a weak moment.

He held up a wad of cash. "The money for the cabin?"

"Just put it on my desk and leave." She knew she was being a bitch but she couldn't help it, she hadn't buried her hurt yet.

He had caught her crying because she couldn't have children. Because she got knocked up and had an abortion. Because she slept with her useless boyfriend and didn't use protection. Because she was too miserable and heartbroken to notice. Because Beau had broken her heart. Logically she knew absolutely none of this was his fault. They were *her* actions, *her* choices and she was owning them and living with them.

But right now, in this second, she felt like she didn't owe this man a goddamn thing.

*

She turned back to stare out the window, dismissing him like she always did. Beau sighed and dropped the cash down on her desk and headed for the door, but something stopped him from leaving. She was different.

Sure, she was her usual snarky self but something else too. There was a sadness about her, a vulnerability that he hadn't seen for so long it made his chest ache. Clearly she'd been crying, her cheeks slightly splotchy like she used to get. He never could stand to see her cry. He watched her, lost in another world as she brought her hand to her mouth, her knuckles brushing across her lip and she nibbled absently on them, he knew what that meant.

He sighed again. "Stop picking."

She jolted at his words, as though he shouted them at her. She slowly turned to face him.

"What?" she asked, almost breathless.

He couldn't quite fight back his smile at her expression. "You heard me. Stop picking."

"I wasn't, I was-" she spluttered.

"Don't lie to me, Tay. Whatever old scars you're poring over, scratching and picking at until they bleed all over again, leave them alone."

Her brows flew together and his words hung in the air, an uncomfortable reminder of the closeness they had once shared. Pain briefly flashed across her face before her expression shuttered. He balled his fists, tamping down the instinctive urge to go to her. To pull her into his arms and soothe her, like he would have done fifteen years ago. But he didn't. He wasn't that person to her and they didn't have that relationship anymore.

He waited, expecting her to hit him with some sarcastic retort but nothing came. Instead, she shocked him by nodding her head. So softly that if he wasn't still so in tuned to her body, he wouldn't have noticed.

Hope bloomed in his chest and his apology pushed to the forefront, but he held it back. It didn't feel like the right moment. He didn't know what just happened between them but he knew bringing up their history, no matter how much he wanted to apologize for his words, would ruin this moment of peace.

He nodded at her then slipped out of her office, closing the door softly behind him, still in awe at what just happened. He felt raw and exposed in sharing that moment with her. That was the first time that either of them had acknowledged what they'd had.

"Dipshit!" A deep voice shouted, and a solid arm banded around his shoulders. He turned, putting the moment with Taylor out of his mind, to pore over it later, as he came face to face with his friend, Blake.

"What's your sorry ass doing here?" Beau asked, slinging an arm around him.

"Come sit down, I've got something to tell you," Blake said cryptically and led him over to a booth where Dean was sitting. As they passed the corner of the bar Beau waved to a beaming Justine and Christy. *What the hell is going on?*

"'Sup dude," Dean said with a wink.

"What's going on?"

"Beats me, he's being cagey as hell." Dean punched Blake gently on the arm.

"You're okay right?" Beau asked, concerned. He knew Blake was at the tail end of a big battle with his mental health and was worried that he'd suffered a setback.

"I'm more than okay, man," Blake replied, sitting down opposite Beau and sliding a beer across the table to him. There was a pause as Blake looked between Dean and Beau before he unleashed a wide smile.

"Justine's pregnant!" Blake exclaimed.

"What? That's amazing!"

"Wow, congrats bro," Beau said, clinking their beer bottles together.

"Thanks guys, we're over the moon," Blake gushed, glancing at Justine. The sheer adoration on his face made Beau feel like he was interrupting a private moment between them. He felt his throat tighten with emotion. He knew how much Justine had wanted children and he was so pleased that her dream was coming true.

"Holy shit, I'm gonna be a dad," Blake said suddenly

and went slightly pale.

"You're gonna be a fucking awesome dad. I have zero doubts at all, my friend," Dean said seriously, putting his arm around Blake's shoulder.

"Ditto, man. Your kid is so lucky to have you two as parents, they'll be the most loved, protected and cherished child in all of Citrus Pines," Beau added.

The guys talked a bit longer before heading over to Justine and Christy. Beau and Dean both enveloped Justine in a giant but gentle bear hug. They all chatted about the exciting news, guessing weight and gender and soon baby talk slipped into Christy and Dean's wedding talk. But the whole time Beau's eyes kept flicking to the closed door of Taylor's office.

*

"Get in the effing bag, you mothereffer!" Taylor grunted, shoving a final pair of jeans into her wash bag to take to the laundromat. It was her night off from the bar, she only got one a week and what excitement did she have planned? Laundry and paperwork. *I'm so rock and roll.*

She surveyed her bedroom: clothes strewn everywhere, pink pillows on the floor and shoes scattered about. She was a messy person but hell she was the only one living here, she didn't need to keep it tidy for anyone. And even though it was messy, she still knew exactly where everything was.

She rummaged through the floordrobe to see what needed washing and spotted a pair of pink panties hiding under her bed and crammed them into the bag. When she didn't think she could fit any more clothes in there and still carry it, she left her cabin and walked into town.

The laundromat was quiet, apparently people other

than her had better plans for a Friday night than doing laundry. A row of washers lined one wall and dryers along the other with a bench separating them. There was a row of wooden seats by the window, although no one sat there unless they wanted an ass full of splinters. Next to the seats was a small table with ancient magazines on it. The one she read last time had a fascinating article about the wedding of Charles and Diana.

Taylor filled a machine with her clothes and checked the timer. She could pop across the street to Ruby's Diner to grab a late dinner and do her paperwork there then come back for her clothes when they were finished.

In the diner, the addictive smell of coffee and sugar hung heavy in the air. Nostalgia smothered her as she remembered all the good times she had here. Times with her mom before she left, times with Dean when they were teenagers just hanging out, or the times she came here with Beau and they always split a slice of cookie dough cheesecake. She hadn't had the dessert since the last time she came here with him, couldn't bring herself to though she knew Ruby still sold it.

"Evening gorgeous," Ruby said, standing by the register.

"Hey Ruby, how's it going?" Taylor called, glancing around at all the red Formica and mirrored surfaces that blinded you when the sun caught them. Ruby had been running this place for fifty years. Taylor had been coming for nearly thirty and had gotten to know the old bat well.

Ruby had become something of a surrogate grandmother to Taylor. A really rude, zany grandmother. The woman was in her seventies but still sported bright purple hair which clashed horrifically with her scarlet red lipstick. Her dark eyeshadow peaked out around the rim of her electric-blue-framed glasses as she peered at

Taylor, looking her over from head to toe, making sure she was okay.

"Much better now I've seen that pretty lil' face of yours," Ruby replied before a hacking cough rattled her petite frame.

Taylor frowned. "Did you go to that doctor's appointment I set up for you?"

Ruby began to vigorously wipe down the Formica counter. "He won't be able to help me, he's nothin' but a quack! I tell you I used to see that fool runnin' around town with no clothes on, why would I trust him?"

Taylor pinched the bridge of her nose, holding back a frustrated sigh. "Rubes, he was seven years old when he did that, and he hasn't done it since."

Ruby waved a hand dismissively.

"Please go and see him, for me?" Taylor batted her lashes innocently.

Ruby stared at her over the rim of those bright glasses and sucked her false teeth sharply.

"I want to make sure you're healthy. What would I do if I came in one day and you weren't here? That you'd left me too?"

"Oh, hell enough! I'll go goddammit, make me a new one for this week."

"Third time's the charm," Taylor muttered under her breath.

"You sassin' me, girlie?" Ruby snapped.

"No ma'am. I'll let you know the time and day." Taylor unleashed her Cheshire cat grin at the old woman. Ruby harrumphed but patted Taylor's hand affectionately.

"Take a seat and I'll bring you some dinner," Ruby said. Taylor didn't even need to order anymore, Ruby always knew what she wanted: pancakes with bacon, maple syrup and a scoop of vanilla ice cream with a

Sweet Surrender

strawberry shake. Taylor had the biggest sweet tooth, and Ruby's sweet treats were the stuff of dreams. Taylor thanked her and headed towards her usual booth in the corner.

"Hey Bear," she called as she walked past the gentle giant who worked as a mechanic at Dean's garage.

"Evening," he grunted, and she doubled back to chat although Bear was never one for words when grunts would do.

"How's your mama doing?" she asked. Bear's mom had been really sick for the last few years and Bear had moved home to take care of her. Taylor didn't know if it was the kind of sick someone would get better from and didn't feel like it was appropriate to ask.

His brows knitted together. "About the same," he replied gruffly before running a hand over his thick beard.

"Sorry to hear that. Give her my love, will you?" she said, and he grunted in assent. Taylor looked him over. He was a good-looking man under all that hair and flannel, giving off real lumberjack vibes. He was sweet and so caring to look after his mom the way he did.

"Are you single, Bear?" she asked, a gleam in her eye. He narrowed his dark eyes at her but didn't respond. She already knew the answer though.

"You should come by the bar; we do a singles night and I bet the ladies would just love to get their hands on you." She winked at him, and she could have sworn a blush filled his cheeks under all that facial hair.

He cleared his throat. "I'll think about it."

She smiled, that was enough for now. "Enjoy your evening, Bear."

"You too, and Taylor? I appreciate you asking after my mama like that," he said and then turned back to his food. She headed to her booth, settling in and spreading her paperwork out on the table but her mind wouldn't focus. She wondered if Bear would be a good match for Taylor's barmaid, Kayleigh, or if he would just terrify her. Maybe someone else for Kayleigh, the girl needed some excitement in her life. *Oh yes because your life is sooo enthralling isn't it? At the diner on a Friday night doing paperwork? Party. Animal.*

She was enjoying her quiet life for once. Usually she would have a new man on the go but ever since her ex, Dale, she had decided to take a break. She needed someone who could deal with the fact that she just wanted casual and nothing more.

Taylor didn't do commitment. She had issues with abandonment after seeing her father's behavior. To him and most men she witnessed growing up, women were disposable, and she never wanted to be that girl, so easily tossed aside and forgotten about. That's why she always got out first before feelings developed.

She didn't want romance, didn't want flowers or chocolates or kisses in the moonlight. She didn't want kisses full stop. She hadn't kissed anyone since that time with Bobby in the school hallway. After such a mind-blowing kiss with Beau, the revenge kiss with Bobby the next day had felt hollow and bitter and she never wanted to feel that way again. So, like Vivian from *Pretty Woman*, she didn't kiss on the mouth.

It had driven Dale insane. He was convinced it meant she didn't care about him which wasn't true. Taylor hadn't realized how much Dale had grown to care for her, otherwise she would have ended things sooner. When he told her he wanted to get serious, she had broken things off hoping to avoid hurting him more.

Determined to get her back, he kept showing up at the bar trying to talk to her then a few times he got angry and refused to leave. One time Beau had kicked him out, dragging Dale from the bar when he got too forward and damn if her lady parts didn't enjoy Beau's display of alpha male aggression, something she'd never seen before from *Mr. Goody Two-shoes*. Taylor had deputy sheriff Blake to help her out a couple of times but she didn't think Dale had gotten the message yet. Hopefully he would soon and just leave her alone.

Ruby interrupted Taylor's thoughts, placing her overflowing plate of pancakes in front of her. The old woman had even added rainbow sprinkles in the shape of a heart.

"If you tell anyone, I'll deny it," Ruby muttered.

"I love you, you old crone," Taylor replied, and Ruby snorted a laugh before heading back to the counter. Taylor attacked her pancakes like she hadn't eaten in a year, moaning at the flavors exploding on her tongue. *Savory, salty, sweet perfection.*

She finished her food and got lost in her work. She didn't know how long she had been working when the prickle of awareness had her looking up. She could feel eyes on her. She looked around the diner but no one was watching her. She looked out the window but couldn't see anything. She must be imagining it; she was all out of sorts this week.

First Justine's baby announcement, then the weird moment with Beau in her office that had completely thrown her. His acknowledgement of their friendship had her thoughts spinning. He'd been sweet with her, and her walls had crumbled slightly before she could reinforce them.

As though her thoughts alone had summoned him, the door to the diner opened and the man walked in. His eyes bright and cheeks pink from the cool air. Taylor took in his black sweatshirt with the Batman signal on it and sweatpants and heat coursed through her. *How did he look so good in casual clothes?* She had been obsessed with him when he was a teenager, his weight never bothered her, it was *him* she wanted. But she couldn't deny that hard bodied, muscular Beau wasn't just as attractive to her.

Gah, you don't find him attractive, shut up!

He strode over to the counter and Taylor watched as he dropped a kiss to Ruby's papery cheek. *What the fu-*

"Well, if it isn't my favorite personal trainer," Ruby cooed, fluttering her eyelashes.

Is she actually flirting? Beau huffed out a deep laugh that hit Taylor down in the lady parts region.

"How are you feeling after our session this morning?" he asked.

"Like a new woman," Ruby purred.

Taylor couldn't believe what she was seeing, her pancakes nearly reappeared.

"A few more sessions like that and you'll be the fittest in the class." He was doing that horrible thing where he was nice and charming. Ruby giggled and Taylor looked around for the hidden cameras. This had to be a fucking joke, she had never seen Ruby behave like this before, not even with her husband, Roger, God rest his soul.

"Now, what can I get you, young man?"

"Just the usual please, Ruby," Beau replied, taking out his wallet and pulling some bills from his wad of cash.

His usual?

HIS FUCKING USUAL?

He hadn't even been back in town five minutes, okay fine for nearly a year, and he had the audacity to have a *usual*? It had taken Taylor ten years to earn a usual from Ruby.

As though he could feel her fury growing, he turned

those dark, seductively curved bedroom eyes that promised untold wicked delights on her.

Taylor's skin prickled as his stare stroked over her, hot and questioning. He unleashed a small, hesitant smile and it made her feel things she hadn't wanted from him since she was a teenager. And it was for precisely that reason that she ignored his smile and went back to her paperwork. She could feel his eyes on her though; she couldn't breathe under the weight of his probing stare.

Come over here, no don't fucking come over here! Her mind screamed, at war with itself. God, what was wrong with her? Eventually she felt his gaze leave her and she sucked in huge lungfuls of air. Ruby came back with his *usual* and he flirted with her some more, the bastard, before he left the diner. Taylor packed up her paperwork and stomped over to Ruby to pay her bill.

"What's Beau's usual?" she growled before she could stop herself, not even trying to rein in her temper. The old biddy could handle it.

"Cookie dough cheesecake," Ruby replied.

The air choked her as it left Taylor's lungs and she couldn't breathe. She hadn't been able to eat it since they were last together, but he had it so often it was his fucking *usual?*

"You know, maybe you could make him one sometime," Ruby said.

Taylor's eyes narrowed to dangerous slits. "Why on earth would I do that?" she spat.

"Because then maybe he would realize you've been in love with him since the day you met him."

Taylor spluttered angrily, heat suffusing her cheeks. Where the hell had Ruby gotten that ridiculous idea from?

"Deny it all you like, girlie, but I remember the way you used to look at him."

"Make your own damned doctor's appointment!" Taylor snapped before slapping down her money on the counter and storming out of the diner.

"Maybe he could give you a good seeing to as well, you might be less cranky!" Ruby shouted after her. Taylor flipped her the bird and Ruby laughed so hard she had a coughing fit.

Chapter 4

"Damn fool woman, what does she know?" Taylor muttered to herself as she stormed back to the laundromat. She was so caught up in her indignation that she didn't immediately spot that she wasn't alone.

"Oh, hi," she said, smiling at Rebelle who was digging through the lost and found box in the laundromat. Rebelle leapt away from the box, clutching a garment behind her back, her cheeks turning scarlet.

"Hi there." Rebelle's smile was sheepish. Taylor went over to her machine, ignoring the pang of sympathy for Rebelle which tried to consume her. Even though they'd both lived in the same town and gone to school together, Taylor didn't know the woman very well, but she knew Rebelle and Christy had been close.

The only things Taylor knew about Rebelle was what

she heard from the town gossips. She didn't know the details of what had happened with Rebelle's husband, the now deceased Sheriff Black, but she didn't for a second believe that this tiny, quiet-as-a-mouse, slip of a woman could have murdered him.

"Christy said you're coming to the wedding?" Taylor asked, turning back to face Rebelle who was no longer holding whatever item she had taken from the box. Her doe eyes were wide, her cheeks still flushed.

"Oh yeah, um, I'm not sure if I'm gonna go after all."

"Really? I know she'll be super bummed if you don't," Taylor said, then felt crappy when she saw the guilt in Rebelle's eyes.

"It'll just be so *fancy* is all." Rebelle shuffled her feet. Taylor's gaze ran over her. Her shorts had a tear in them and her sneakers were held together with some duct tape, her shirt was in good condition but had a large ink stain on the bottom.

"Well, the ceremony is only going to be at their house in the garden and the reception will be at the Inn. They just want to get married around their friends and family, it'll be about as fancy as my little pinkie. But if it's a date or an outfit you need, I can help you with both?"

Rebelle started grabbing her clothes from the washer and stuffing them into one of the dryers, not meeting Taylor's gaze.

"Thanks, I'll, uh, think about it."

Taylor knew when she was getting the brush-off so she dropped it and turned back to her own laundry.

"Oh shoot! I thought I had more quarters but I'm out," Rebelle said, scanning the change in her hand.

"Ruby will make some change for you if you need it," Taylor said. Rebelle nodded and then scurried out of the laundromat, jumping when the door banged in its frame.

Taylor turned back to her machine but saw the door was slightly open and her clothes weren't inside.

"What the-" She looked in the machines either side but they were empty. She turned to the opposite row of machines and opened up one of the dryers, and there were her clothes inside it. There was no way she had put her clothes in there, that was why she had come back now. She hauled them out, hugging them to her chest, eyeing them suspiciously as she absorbed the heat from them.

It must have been Rebelle. An idea struck her and she laid her clothes on the table, rummaging through them until she found the navy cotton dress she was looking for. Taylor folded it up and shoved it inside Rebelle's laundry bag with the other clothes she must have taken from the lost and found box. The cute dress would do nicely for a casual wedding although it might be a little big on Rebelle judging by how slim she looked but it should fit her fine. Now at least if Rebelle decided to come to the wedding, she would have a dress.

Taylor went back to her own clothes and began folding them as Rebelle returned. They moved in silence, Rebelle putting her quarters into the machine and setting the timer while Taylor continued folding clothes that would probably just end up in a heap on the floordrobe again.

"Thank you, by the way, that was really sweet of you," Taylor said, facing Rebelle.

Rebelle's dark brows pinched in confusion. "For what?"

"Moving my clothes into the dryer?"

Rebelle shook her head. "I didn't move your clothes."

"Well then who-" A shiver ran down Taylor's spine, cutting off her words. *No, it couldn't be Dale, could it?* She'd thought she felt someone watching her earlier. Could that have been him?

"Everything okay?" Rebelle echoed Taylor's words from earlier.

Taylor pasted a smile on her face. "Oh yeah, I must have forgotten I did it." She smacked her hand to her forehead and rolled her eyes theatrically.

"I do that a lot too," Rebelle replied with a slight grin.

Taylor finished packing up her clothes, her thoughts running into overdrive. As she headed out she decided that walking home this late would not be a good idea. She had a weird feeling and she knew to trust her gut so she called a cab and waited. When it pulled up outside, she made her way to the door, lugging her clothes behind her.

"I'll see you later then," she said to Rebelle who was sitting reading a battered magazine with Bill Clinton and Monica Lewinsky on the cover.

"Bye," Rebelle replied softly with a small wave.

"Please come to the wedding. I know it'll mean a lot to Christy, to all of us actually. And feel free to stop by the bar anytime for a chat," Taylor added. Rebelle nodded at her but didn't say anything, so Taylor just left.

On the ride home Taylor was on edge. She kept expecting Dale to leap out in front of the car. By the time she arrived back at her cabin she had worked herself into a state. Should she report it to Blake? Was she just being ridiculous? It's not like Dale had *threatened* her, he'd just put her clothes in the dryer, it was actually a nice thing to do. He had done her a favor and she had no proof that it was even him.

As she climbed the porch steps she glanced over at the cabin opposite, like she did every time now that *he* was staying there. It was becoming a habit and she hated that she actually felt comforted when she could see he was there.

Was he alone?

The idea snapped her out of any sentimental thoughts that may have tried to rear their ugly head. She didn't give a shit if he had fifty women in there and they were all naked, handfeeding him cookie dough cheesecake. And she never would.

She let herself into her cabin and felt along the wall for the light switch, relaxing when the place was bathed in light and she could see it was empty and untouched. She stepped inside, her feet crunching over something on the doormat. She shut the door, sliding the deadbolts across the top and bottom then dumping her clean laundry in her room to put away later. Or not. Yeah, probably not.

She went outside to feed her squirrels, sad that she hadn't seen them for a few days due to her working hours. Then she came back inside and went over to pick up the slip of paper on the doormat. She flipped it over, reading the words scrawled in red ink:

You're welcome.

*

Beau walked into The Rusty Bucket Inn and immediately felt like he was home. There was something about the place that called to him and he couldn't stay away. *Could that be anything to do with its owner?* He gritted his teeth at the thought.

He was here to meet Dean for a drink but he wanted to come a little earlier to see what kind of mood Taylor was in. They were well overdue a conversation and he'd wanted to speak to her at the diner last night but her expression had, not so kindly, told him to *fuck off*.

Beau headed over to the bar, surprised to see that Dean was already here but so were Blake and Justine, and all were talking to Taylor.

Taylor's curls were pulled back into a bun on top of her head, showing off the piercings running down her ears. She wore a simple pink cotton dress but the light color did amazing things for her fair skin, making her tattoos stand out even more.

She'd gotten a number of tattoos over the years and he'd discreetly tried to map them all. The collection of roses down each of her forearms, the skull and butterflies on her upper thigh he spotted once when her shorts rode up, the colorful splashes and shapes across her left shoulder and back. But his favorite one was just behind her left ear, the letter B inside a small heart.

It was her first tattoo and he'd gone with her to get it. He remembered how tightly she gripped his hand as she sat in the chair, keeping her eyes locked on him the whole time. He could still hear the harsh sound of the tattoo gun vibrating as the needle punctured along her skin. He was still able to picture her forehead pinched in pain but she didn't cry out, just sat there and took it, as long as he held her hand.

"B for Bobby?" Beau had asked through gritted teeth, like he was the one in pain.

"Yep," she murmured, nibbling her lip until it turned a deep red.

"Then why isn't he here with you?" he grumbled, annoyed she was marking her skin over that asshole.

"Because it's *you* I want with me." *Then why aren't you getting my initials tattooed on you!* he wanted to scream, but then she offered him that soft smile and all his anger disappeared.

He was pulled out of his memory as he neared the

group and the conversation filtered through.

"-can't prove it's him," Blake was saying.

Beau slapped Dean on the back in greeting.

"Hey man," Dean nodded at him and they bumped fists.

"But it is him, I just know it!" Taylor cried, huffing loudly as frustration poured off her in waves.

"I know Tay, I *know*. But without proof my hands are tied," Blake said, shaking his head.

"What's going on?" Beau asked. Taylor's eyes flicked to him, then away again, her lips pursing. As usual he permitted himself a quick glance and then looked away before he lost himself in her.

"Fucking Dale again," Dean hissed, and Beau's blood ran cold. He didn't know what had happened between Taylor and Dale and for obvious reasons, he didn't want to think about it. He didn't like the guy, but didn't like him even more when he had come to the bar months ago and harassed Taylor, making Beau's legendary hold on his temper snap and he escorted Dale from the bar. He would love to get his hands on Dale again...

Beau pulled himself out of his uncharacteristically homicidal thoughts. "What's he done now?" He directed the question to Taylor, not expecting her to answer but she surprised him.

"He messed around with my clothes at the laundromat and slipped a note under my door," she replied.

"Last night?" Beau asked, trying to keep a leash on his temper as it was fraying at the seams.

"Yep. You didn't happen to see anything did you?" she asked, her stunning emerald eyes brightening with a hope he hated to dash.

"No sorry, after I got back from the diner I went straight to my cabin and stayed there all night."

"Alone?" The word whipped from her as though she had no control over it.

He narrowed his eyes at her, her brow furrowing under his scrutiny, and she nibbled her lower lip. He forced himself to look away. *Why is she always so interested in my love life?*

"How is that your business?"

Tension thrummed between them.

"If there's potentially another witness we can ask, then hell yeah it's my business." A smug look crossed her face, she knew she had him there. *Dammit.*

"I was alone," he gritted through clenched teeth and his gaze flicked to her long enough to see triumph shine in those dazzling eyes, setting them aflame. The triumph was short-lived though as he watched her realization that it meant there was no witness to what happened. He could hardly bear to see her disappointment.

"I'll swing by again and see him, Taylor. But in the eyes of the law, until we have a witness or evidence, I can't do jack shit. You know I would otherwise, I'm sorry," Blake said.

"I know, B, I understand," Taylor replied.

"I just don't get it, why is he so obsessed with you?" Dean burst out, struggling to keep his temper under wraps as well.

"Because she's a really amazing person, that's why! Who wouldn't be obsessed with her?" Justine cried defensively.

"It's okay sweetie, you don't need to defend me, it wasn't an insult," Taylor said gently, patting Justine's hand and Dean snickered.

"I'm sorry, it's the hormones," Justine said tearfully. Beau smirked as Blake sighed before pulling his wife-to-be into a hug, catching Beau's eyes and shaking his head before smiling.

"He just wants me back and won't get the hint that I'm not interested," Taylor shrugged.

"What if we can prove you're not interested?" Dean asked softly.

"What do you mean?" Beau replied.

Dean began pacing up and down, shoving his hand through his blond hair.

"He thinks you haven't moved on, that there's still a chance you could get back together because you haven't been with anyone else."

"So?" Taylor asked, her brows furrowing.

"So…" Dean stopped pacing and snapped his fingers. "We need to make it look like you've moved on."

"That's interesting, you might be onto something there," Blake chimed in. Beau looked back and forth between them. *What are they on about?*

"Can you stop speaking in code?" Taylor's waspish tone had Beau smiling: finally it was directed at someone other than him.

"You need a boyfriend," Dean said.

"Oh great, I'll just pop to the store and buy one, thanks." Beau fought another smile at Taylor's sarcasm and the adorable way she stomped her foot in anger. The urge to smile disappeared as a spark of jealousy flared in his chest at the idea of her with another man. *Weird.*

"No, really. He needs to think that you've moved on and you're madly in love with someone new and not interested in him," Dean said.

"That's not a bad idea," Justine sniffled, raising her head from Blake's chest.

"What? Are you both insane? That would take *months!*"

"Not if you had someone pretend."

"Oh yeah, are you gonna do it?" Taylor scoffed.

Dean blanched. "Gross, obviously not. He knows we're brother and sister."

"*Step*brother and sister," Taylor glared at him. "And lucky if we're still that by the end of this conversation!"

Beau smothered another smile as he realized just how much he had missed watching them bicker.

"Blake could do it?" Justine volunteered.

"No honey, he's seen us together already and besides we're getting married and having a baby," Blake said gently like he was talking to a small child, probably scared to set off another round of tears.

"No, it needs to be somebody he knows isn't attached but someone who knows you well enough to sell it," Dean said. "Like Beau!"

Suddenly, as everyone's eyes settled on him, Beau wished he'd never come into the bar today.

"Yes! Beau could do it, you've known him for years. And he's single. Dale has seen you with him before. Remember that time that Beau kicked him out of the bar? It's perfect!" Justine cried. Dean nodded in agreement and Beau felt Taylor's piercing gaze slide over him. He shoved his hands into his pockets and rocked on his heels, smiling at her sheepishly.

"That is a really great example of a shitty idea," Taylor deadpanned, shaking her head violently.

Beau's pride prickled as she began shouting at Dean, the shouting increasing when Blake agreed it was a good idea. Beau tuned out the argument as his thoughts went frantic. Unfortunately, he agreed. He *was* the perfect candidate. He was staying in the cabin next to her so could keep a close eye on her; he knew her better than anyone, and knew he could sell it, hell it wouldn't be hard. But it would be painful to tap into all those old memories, remembering how much he had cared for her. But... If it meant keeping her safe, he would do it.

Dean had ducked out of the argument, leaving Blake to fend for himself against the rabid lioness.

"Man, are you sure you'd be okay with this?" Beau asked.

"What? Watching you get all snuggly with little sis?" Dean snorted and Beau went hot all over. *Shit.* He hadn't even considered that. Would they have to hold hands and shit? Hug? *Kiss?* Someone must have sucked all the oxygen out of the room because suddenly Beau couldn't breathe. The memories of their first kiss tried to overtake him. For a moment he let them, until the memory of her horror appeared, followed by those hateful words, and he had to shove the rest of the scene out of his mind.

If they did this, then he would spend a serious amount of time with her, he would have plenty of time to have *the chat* and apologize to her, to set things right and move on. Was this actually a blessing in disguise?

"Besides, you'd only be pretending, right?" Dean interrupted his thoughts.

Images of him and Taylor tangled in his sheets, sweating and moaning filled his mind. *Fuck, this was a terrible idea.*

"Exactly. Just pretending," Beau rasped, clearing his throat. Dean clapped him on the back and jumped back into the argument, sensing Blake needed back up.

Beau watched Taylor, gesturing wildly, her bun jiggling with each indignant movement, her eyes flashing angrily.

Man, she really is something.

"I'll do it," he said and the noise in the bar immediately stopped, like when Frodo volunteered to take the ring to Mordor, although Frodo's chances of survival were greater than Beau's.

Taylor's eyes snapped to his. Her look scorched him,

promising him a painful death. Her mouth opened, then closed. A look of raw pain crossed her face, and he felt its echo in his gut. He knew what he was doing, knew it would be difficult, but he also knew they both needed this. Of course, she didn't seem to agree.

"No." Her tone left no room for argument. Her word was final. And with that, she walked into her office and slammed the door, leaving them all standing in silence.

"She'll come around," Dean said, confidently.

"It'll work one way or another. Either Dale will get the hint and leave her alone. Or it'll push him to do something stupid and we'll get him," Blake agreed.

Only Justine was silent, her honey eyes on Beau and her head cocked, assessing him. He tried to look away, he didn't want her psychologist brain analyzing him right now and putting things together. But he was trapped. She must have seen something she liked because a smirk split her face before she nodded.

"Taylor will come around, just let her cool off. I think this will be for the best, in more ways than one," she added, staring pointedly at him.

Fuck.

Chapter 5

The bar was heaving tonight, plenty of bodies crammed inside and Taylor was *loving* it. Being busy meant more success for the bar but also meant she didn't have time to think about the Dale situation or rage over Dean's ridiculous suggestion.

Pretend to be Beau's girlfriend, pfft! She let out an unladylike snort and Kayleigh, her barmaid, shot her a questioning look.

But really, what the hell had Dean been thinking? *That boy's been inhaling too many car fumes lately.* Taylor stepped to the end of the bar to take a moment to pull herself together. She ran her hands through her hair, snagging her fingers on the intricate braid crown that ran along the top of her head, the rest of her hair in a high ponytail.

She had decided to make an effort tonight, thinking

maybe that would make her feel better. She'd taken extra care with her makeup, put on gold hoop earrings then paired a strapless pink lace top with her favorite black leather pants.

She took a breather, shaking off the crazy thoughts that had been spiraling around her brain since the idea of her and Beau pretending to be in *love* had been suggested by Dean. When she felt calmer, she dived back into serving the customers currently three deep at the bar. She worked her little butt off and only took a break a couple of hours later when her girls turned up.

"Oh heeey!" Christy called, coming over to her, Justine close behind. They all hugged and Justine tapped Taylor's gold hoop earring. "You know what they say don't you?"

"The bigger the hoop, the bigger the ho?" Taylor replied.

"Exactly!" Justine laughed.

"Kayleigh, are you okay for ten?" Taylor shouted over the music.

"Yes, ma'am," Kayleigh replied, bobbing at Taylor.

"Why does she always curtsy at you?" Christy giggled.

Taylor pinched the bridge of her nose. "Jesus, I have no idea but the girl needs to stop."

"Have you told her to stop?"

"Hell no! She looks up at me with those Bambi eyes and I lose all power to scold."

"Aw, Tay's gone all soft!" Justine taunted, tucking her dark hair behind her ears.

Taylor flipped her off and gestured to a free booth in the corner. The girls took a seat as Taylor made Christy a cocktail and grabbed Justine an apple juice.

"How's my lil' pregnant mama?" Taylor asked, placing the drinks on the table. Justine didn't answer, she was too busy drooling over Christy's cocktail before Taylor nudged her apple juice closer. Justine scowled at the drink.

"Fine really, no morning sickness yet but my emotions are *loco*."

"I'm aware after the incident this week," Taylor replied, arching her eyebrow.

"Speaking of, what are you gonna do about that?"

"About what?" Christy asked.

Taylor sighed as Justine began filling Christy in on the meeting and Dean's stupid-ass idea. When Justine reached the crucial part in the story, dropping Beau's name in, Christy spat her drink out.

"No way! Oh my *God*, that's perfect!" she shouted with glee.

"I know, right?" Justine added and they shared evil grins.

"Hello!" Taylor called, clapping her hands to get their attention. "This is not perfect and it's not happening!"

"Why not?"

"Because…because it's…. just because!" she spluttered.

"Look, it might be a little awkward at times, but you'll get past it. There are worse men to pretend to be in love with," Justine said.

"Absolutely!" Christy agreed, enthusiastically slurping her drink.

"No, it's not a good idea, trust me."

"Question, why do you hate each other so much?" Christy fixed her piercing blue eyes on Taylor.

"We just don't get on, that's all. He's too nice, our personalities just clash."

"He isn't *too* nice, he's a great guy," Justine defended him, sounding slightly emotional.

"Can we just drop this? Please?" Taylor begged.

"Okay. For now. But we need you to consider this because it seems like Dale's getting bolder and he needs to be stopped. We're worried about you, and Beau could actually keep you safe and it could end this whole ordeal," Justine said, giving her *mom* eyes.

"We want you safe and happy. Would you really risk that just for your pride?" Christy added and Taylor felt like she was being scolded.

Taylor shrugged. "I'll think about it, I promise."

"Thank you, boo."

"Now, tell us more about your pregnancy. Any weird cravings?" Taylor asked Justine.

Justine shot them both a coy smile. "Oh yes, but not for food." She waggled her dark eyebrows and Christy cackled.

"That's my girl," Taylor smiled, shaking her head. After a few more minutes of chatting, she went back to the bar and saw Dean, Blake and Beau come in and sit with Christy and Justine.

She kept her head down, the girls' words playing on her mind. She knew they wouldn't understand her resistance to the idea but maybe they were right. She threw herself into work and the more customers she served the more she realized how many good-looking men were here tonight. Maybe she could find another man to use instead of Beau? It was worth a shot. Hell *anything* was worth a shot.

Taylor turned her charm up to the max and flirted shamelessly with every man who crossed her path. Serving them smiles and compliments with their drinks which earned her plenty of appreciative looks but none of them took the bait. *What gives?*

"What can I get you, handsome?" she said, turning to the next man in the queue and found herself face to face with Beau. His huge arms were folded over his chest, his black muscle tee with another colorful logo that she assumed was something to do with superheroes, pulled way too tight, highlighting each bicep to a scandalous degree. He really was a man-mountain, but one she had no intention of climbing. He raised his eyebrows and his mouth quirked up in that annoyingly sexy way.

"I'll take another Blowjob please; the last one you gave me was just too good." His voice trekked over her, tantalizing her like it always did. *Okay, does he do something to deepen it on purpose because this isn't natural!*

"Really, Beau? Immature sex jokes? Okay, how about a Slippery Nipple? Or a Screaming Orgasm?" she snapped, annoyed that he'd already gotten under her skin by being…annoying.

"If you're giving away Screaming Orgasms, I definitely won't say no."

"Aw, you probably need all the help you can get with giving those."

A lazy smirk lifted his lips again. "No sweetheart, I really don't."

Grr, damn him! "You know what word comes to mind when I look at you? *Crymaxer.*"

She was trying to hit a nerve but he surprised her by bursting out laughing, a deep rumble from his chest that made her feel all tingly.

"If that's what you think sweetheart, then fine. But if you fancy putting in the time to find out then I'm definitely open to that." His voice dropped low, pitched for her ears alone. The heat in his eyes inviting, the dark depths stroking over her, taking her all in, memorizing her. She fought a shiver at his blatantly sexual perusal.

What the hell, is he flirting with me? She loved to flirt as much as the next woman, but she couldn't with him. This was one battle with him she would always back down from because he made her *feel*. And she didn't like it.

She spun away and grabbed three bottles of beer which is what she figured he actually wanted. She took the tops off and when she turned back a petite brunette was leaning all over him, fluttering her lashes so aggressively Taylor was sure she felt a gust of wind.

Beau was staring down at her, returning her flirtatious smiles. A lance of hurt spread through Taylor when she realized Beau had only flirted with her to get under her skin and win yet another round of verbal sparring. She ignored him other than to slam the beer bottles down on the bar top, suds flying everywhere. She turned to the next man waiting, pasting a big ol' smile on her face and got right back to flirting.

Except none of the men were giving her anything. At this rate she would never be able to persuade them into a fake dating situation. When it was clear she wasn't going to have any luck, she turned her attention to her favorite hobby: Beau sabotage.

Each time he went to the bathroom, or to the bar, or just turned his back she made a beeline for the woman he was talking to. *Consider it revenge for being a flirty douchebag.*

"I'm sure it still works after his accident, but if not then thank God for vibrators, right?"

"Fingers crossed all his crabs are gone!"

"He and his mom are like, super close. He called out her name one time when we had sex."

"He has some weird fetishes; did you know he can only get a boner if you bark like a dog?"

She actually saw the last woman bark at him. His face was priceless, and Taylor couldn't contain her laughter. Unfortunately, her glee drew his attention. His dark eyes swiveled to her and narrowed dangerously. He downed his drink, slamming the bottle on the table before stalking over to her.

Shit.

She tried to escape but he moved quicker than she anticipated, his hand curling around her upper arm.

"Not so fast."

"Get off me!" she snapped.

"Not a chance," he growled, but loosened his grip.

"You don't scare me, I eat guys like you for breakfast!"

"Really? Lunch and dinner too? Could you be any cornier?"

He started pulling her away from their friends and she struggled against his hold.

"Come on, we're going for a little chat," he said and dragged her over to her office door. She called out to Christy and Justine but they just turned away. *Traitors.* She spluttered the whole way until he shoved her inside and shut the door, blocking out all the background noise of the bar.

"Congratulations Taylor, I didn't realize you were running for cock-blocker of the year," he said, letting her go. She huffed and smoothed her hands over her outfit.

"I don't think I did a very good job, you've successfully eye-fucked every woman in here tonight."

"Nearly every woman." He smirked at her and she bared her teeth in return. "Is that the come-hither smile that's sent every man running for the hills tonight?"

"Fuck you!"

"No thanks, sweetheart."

She had only a moment to be shocked at the sting of rejection she felt at his words before he started again.

"Why do you keep interfering?" he asked, stroking his hand over his jaw. The rasp of his stubble against his palm was so loud in her silent office it had her mouth running dry. She bolted for the door, needing to be away from him before she did something stupid.

"Oh no you don't, Princess, you don't get to walk away right now."

She opened the door but he was right behind her, raising his arm above her head and easily batting the door closed, caging her in.

"Get out of my office," she said, her breathing ragged.

"Why do you keep chasing women away from me?" He lowered his voice until it was a gentle rumble and it affected her as though he'd whispered right in her ear. Heat pooled low in her belly as he stepped closer. Muscular, lethal grace coiled and ready to strike but she wouldn't be intimidated by him, wouldn't show weakness.

"Get. Out."

"Make me," he growled.

It was dangerous being this close to him. She felt perfectly safe around him, but her body was thrumming with anticipation, and she wasn't sure what would happen next. *I know what I want to happen next,* her vagina piped up. She reached up to grip his bicep, whether to draw him closer or push him away she couldn't say but he was quicker. His hand snapped out, circling her wrist, his thumb sliding over her pulse pounding away beneath her skin.

He pulled her to him, her palm flattened over his chest, the muscle bunching under her touch, reaching for her. Her eyes drifted over his face, his eyes heated, probing her and they stayed like that for the longest time. Her feeling the steady beat of his heart, him stroking the pulse in her wrist, tingles branching out from where his skin caressed hers.

Tension hummed between them. She couldn't explain what was happening, it was like they were stuck in a crazy game of chicken. Neither of them willing to make the first move and strike but neither willing to back down.

His warm, sweet breath fanned across her face like a lover's caress, her mouth drying at the intensity in his eyes. Her tongue swiped across her lips and his eyes followed the action.

His head dipped.

Yes…

No!

She ducked her head away, his breath trekking over her ear. *Shit.*

They both froze.

For the first time in her life, she was too scared to look at him. He'd tried to kiss her, she'd ducked away and rejected him. She swallowed hard and forced herself to look at him. His eyes which had been so warm and inviting became cold, lifeless and so familiar to her that nausea churned in her stomach. She was suddenly transported back to that night in his bedroom all those years ago. The hurt flooded her all over again.

His eyes slammed shut, squeezing tightly. "Shit, I've had too much to drink," he muttered.

"It's fine," she whispered.

Then he was wrenching himself away and yanking the office door open. The laughter, music and clinking glasses rushed in, bringing her back to reality. Kayleigh called to her for help, but she was too shocked to react.

Beau had tried to kiss her.

She had nearly let him. What did any of it mean? She had never let anyone be that close to kissing her, not since…

"Taylor!" Kayleigh called again. A glass smashed and snapped Taylor out of her haze. Hurrying into the bar, she pushed her thoughts away, dismissing the incident.

She walked past Christy and Justine who looked pretty pleased with themselves.

"Did he give you a tongue lashing?" Justine smirked.

"Yeah, or did you just want him to?" Christy added, and they cackled like the evil banshees they were. Taylor flipped them off and then threw herself into work. She didn't see Beau again for the rest of the evening.

She closed up the bar at the end of the night, not even feeling proud of how well they'd done tonight. She just wanted to curl up in bed and forget the evening had ever happened.

Make me...

Beau's words trampled through her thoughts again. She shook herself and headed to her cabin, glancing across at Beau's like she did every night. Only now it didn't hold comfort, it held questions.

She unlocked her door and went inside, breathing a sigh of relief when she found the cabin empty and her doormat free of *love* notes. She slid both bolts into place and put the kettle on to boil, then grabbed the squirrel food. She would feed them now as she didn't plan on being out of bed until tomorrow afternoon at the earliest.

She unlocked the back door, flicking on the porch light and stepped out onto the deck. Something on the ground caught her eyes. She looked down and her breath snagged in her throat. The food fell from her grasp, scattering everywhere. She opened her mouth and screamed.

Chapter 6

Beau had gone back to his cabin and straight to bed, wanting to put the whole evening behind him. His pride was stinging so much from Taylor's rejection that it even followed him into sleep. He dreamed that he and Taylor were in a boxing ring, gloves up and ready to rumble only he was his teenage self, his insecurities clearly at the forefront of his mind. When the bell dinged to start the round, she knocked him out with one punch.

A scream penetrated the dream, jolting him awake before he realized what was going on.

"Taylor?"

He leapt out of bed and ran to the cabin door, yanking it open and found her on the other side. Her chest heaving, her skin so pale that her freckles stood out in stark contrast. They stared at each other for a moment. Then she lifted her arm and pointed towards her cabin.

"T…The b…back porch."

"Stay here," he said, stroking down her arm to comfort her before going to investigate.

He tried to keep his eyes focused in the pitch black, his ears listening for any foreign sounds. His breath slipped out as quietly as possible, he didn't want to alert anyone to his presence if there was anyone around. Only now did he realize he had no idea what he was looking for. He crept around the side of the cabin, prepared for anything, when heat at his back had him spinning around, fists raised, primed to attack. Her mouth-watering cinnamon scent hit him just in time.

"Goddammit Taylor, I nearly hit you!" he hissed in the darkness.

"I didn't want to be alone." Her voice, so small, pierced his chest. She was shivering, her teeth chattering from shock. He took her hand and folded it between his, linking their fingers, trying to ignore how well they fit together.

He drew her close behind him as he walked around the porch, scanning the dark line of the trees surrounding them. An owl hooted, scaring the shit out of him but he didn't see anything else.

"There," she said, pointing to the deck of the porch. Then he saw it.

Five dead squirrels, arranged in the shape of a heart.

He cursed under his breath. "Okay sweetheart, let's get you inside."

He maneuvered her past the tiny corpses, keeping her view of them blocked as he led her inside the cabin and closed the door. Once inside, he took her to the pink two-seater couch and gently eased her down. Goosebumps covered her skin and her teeth still chattered so loudly he thought they would crack.

He grabbed the baby-pink throw blanket that felt as soft as her skin and wrapped it around her, tucking in the sides so she was swaddled like a child. Then he moved over to her kitchenette, looking for some mugs. He finally found them crammed in a random cupboard, none of the designs matching, typical Taylor.

He discreetly took in the details of her home, eager to drink them in. It was wall to wall pink and the textile of choice was fluffy. Nothing at all like the snarky, sarcastic ballbuster that Taylor appeared to be, but he knew the real her. He had seen her bedroom as a teenager and it looked exactly like this: fit for a princess.

Silence filled the small cabin as he made her some tea and brought it over, helping free her hands to hold the steaming mug.

"Drink this and I'll be back in a few minutes, okay?" he asked, unsure if she was really *here*. Her eyes were glassy but still magnificent in their deep color. Eventually she nodded.

He stepped out onto the porch, surveying the scene. This was definitely Dale's handiwork, *the sick fuck*. There was a ton of blood. The squirrel feeder was broken and there was food scattered everywhere. Beau swept up the food that had been spilt, probably by Taylor as the bag was on the porch too. She had obviously been feeding the little guys for a while if Dale knew about them. *Why would he take the thing she loved away from her? What the fuck is wrong with him?*

Beau found a little storage shed next to the porch and after rummaging around inside he grabbed a shovel, bucket and some rags. He set to work digging a little grave by the row of spruce trees that lined the back of the property. Once the animals were all buried, he filled up the bucket from the outside faucet and cleaned down the deck, getting rid of every trace of blood so she wouldn't be reminded every time she looked at it. The squirrels were obviously important to her. No wonder she was so deeply shocked.

He went back inside, washing his hands in the kitchen sink before he turned to face Taylor again. She had fallen asleep, curled up on the couch, the blanket thrown off her. He watched her, her face softened in slumber. Her sassy mouth puffy from being nibbled on. God, he nearly kissed her tonight, what the hell had he been thinking? Once again, she had rejected him. When was he going to get it into his thick skull that she wasn't interested in him?

He had gone to the bar once again in the hopes of getting her alone so he could apologize to her. He didn't want her to feel pressured about the whole pretend relationship ruse that Dean came up with, and he wanted to tell her not to worry about it. But as soon as he saw her charming the pants off every man in the bar, every man except him, he'd turned defensive again.

Watching her slink around the bar, her hips swaying seductively as she walked, designed to draw his attention to her and make him want the one thing he couldn't have, had set him off. He flirted his way round the bar, like he did all the time, desperate to prove that she didn't affect him anymore. *Because you think she doesn't? You're a fool.*

When she served him at the bar and her expression immediately hardened from the flirty temptress she was, his stomach sank. His walls slammed back into place and his confidence disappeared.

After all the work he had done on himself. The workouts, the diets, beating the tests of his willpower, the cravings he'd ignored. Followed by surgeries to remove excess skin that left small scars he was super conscious of, let alone all the stretchmarks across his shoulders, back and hips. Yep, he felt like that sad little fat boy who had doted on her all over again and his attitude had kicked in. God knows why he had tried to flirt with her tonight. He knew better than that.

Then he'd tried to talk to her and instead of just having a normal conversation, he'd cornered her in her office. Being so close to her had turned him into some horny neanderthal trying to tamp down the intense need to dominate which only ever flared to life around her. When she got all sassy with him, he just wanted to put her over his knee.

Except something about the way she stared at him and the tension mounting between them had made him think…ugh never mind, what was the point? Why did he keep fucking up with her?

He moved over to her now, slid one arm under her knees, the other around her back and lifted her into his arms. She was a tall woman, but she felt tiny in his arms and that old urge to protect her roared to life. Her head fell perfectly into the crook of his neck. Her warm breath fanned over his skin and had him biting back a moan whilst his cock eagerly sprang to life at exactly the wrong moment. *Jesus, really? Just from a bit of air on his neck?*

She stirred as he carried her into the bedroom and began muttering, trying to fight his hold. *Always rejecting me.*

"Beau?"

"Go back to sleep sweetheart, we'll talk in the morning," he murmured. He shoved loads of clutter from her bed and onto the already messy floor.

"No, I-"

"Yes Taylor," he commanded, leaving no room for argument.

"So bossy," she muttered, and a smile split his face.

Sassy even when she's sleeping. But for once, she agreed with him and immediately fell back to sleep as he tucked the quilt around her. He brushed a strand of hair behind her ear and she sighed in her sleep. With a final glance at her, he left the room.

He made himself a drink then sat on her tiny couch and tried to watch some TV.

*

Taylor awoke in the morning, reluctantly pulled from a deliciously sinful dream about her and...

"Beau?"

Last night came flooding back to her. Trying to find a man to be her fake boo, followed by the confusing scene with Beau in her office, then coming home to find the massacre on her porch. She squeezed her eyes shut, tears stinging but she refused to let them fall. Dale had killed the little squirrel family that she'd been feeding, rearing and loving for years. He'd taken his obsession to a whole new level last night.

"The sick fuck," she muttered, suddenly wondering what the hell she ever saw in him.

He had arranged her fur babies in the shape of a heart, that was how she had known this was him. There was no doubt in her mind but once again, where was the evidence? Taylor tried to push the image of their little furry bodies, twisted and covered in blood, out of her mind. It was an image she would never forget.

Beau had been great, helping her out, treating her shock with sweet tea, just *being there*. He remained calm throughout the whole situation and looked after her like she was someone he cared for, their bitter hatred for each other pushed aside.

Sweet Surrender

When she discovered the squirrels, she'd been truly terrified. It meant things with Dale were far more serious than she imagined. The realization that Beau was the only person she wanted to comfort her had her stomach twisting into knots.

Taylor swung her legs over the side of her bed, noticing that she was still in last night's clothing. She padded into the adjoining bathroom, the only bathroom in her little cabin, and stripped off, taking a quick shower. Once she was done, she threw on a graphic tee that read *"Surely not everyone was kung-fu fighting?"* and a pair of sweatpants, piled her wet hair on top of her head and swiped moisturizer over her face. It wasn't much but she felt a little better already. She opened her bedroom door and stopped in her tracks.

Beau was squeezed onto her little couch, making it look like toy furniture under his giant body. Her fluffy pink blanket covered him, somehow making him look even more masculine. Taylor rolled her eyes. The TV remote was balanced in one hand, the TV still on but playing softly in the background.

He must *have stayed here all night to make sure I was okay…* definitely *not* sweet. *Not at all.*

Her spine tingled at seeing him here in her home, surrounded by all her belongings, looking perfectly at home. Pink really suited him. She took the remote from his grip, fighting the weird urge to climb into his arms and burrow down. He stirred and sat up, the blanket falling into his lap and she was relieved to see he was still wearing a t-shirt. Completely one hundred percent *relieved.*

"Morning Tay. Sorry, I must have drifted off." His voice was gruffer than normal from sleep. The deep timbre raking over her nerves, leaving her practically panting. *Imagine that voice deep in your ear, commanding you to...* she spun away as heat flooded her cheeks and arousal pounded through her. God, how long had it been since she'd gotten laid? *Too long,* her brain answered.

"It's fine, Beau," she muttered. Her default Beau-Bitchiness tried to surface until her eyes landed on the back door leading to the porch and the reminder of last night hit her. She unlocked the door and stood in the doorway, not sure if she wanted to face the scene or not. She felt his heat at her back, too familiar, too comforting and too painful.

"Do you want me to show you where they're resting?" he asked softly.

She nodded, her throat catching at the fact that he said *resting* and not buried. She must have blocked out what he did last night. She didn't remember a lot except that he made her tea. She nodded and he took her hand, his warm palm enclosing hers and she didn't pull away.

He led her over to a patch of dirt by the tree line, the soil dark and fresh against the sun-scorched pine needles.

"Are they all together?" Taylor asked, hating the hitch in her voice that belied her emotions.

"Yeah sweetheart, they're all together," he said, his thumb stroking her skin. A lump rose in her throat and she released his grip, emotions overwhelming her at the endearment, his care and the fact that he kept her little family together.

"The two rocks either side are so that you'll always be able to find them. I'll be just inside," he added. Then he was gone, like he knew she needed a moment alone. She didn't care if it was stupid that she was so devastated. After feeding them and talking to them for years, watching the family grow, they were her little fur babies. Taylor scanned the ground and saw a group of wildflowers and picked a few, sprinkling them over the squirrels' resting place.

"I'm sorry you guys got caught up in this. But I bet you're all in complete nut heaven right now, aren't you?" She bit back a sob and tried for a watery smile. After a few minutes she blew a kiss to them she went back inside where Beau was making a drink.

She stood at the other side of the kitchen counter, just watching him. So much hung in the air between them, she didn't even know where to start.

"Thank you for burying them and for cleaning off the porch," she said.

"No problem," he replied, gruffly. She watched him a moment longer before she sighed inwardly. She'd been thinking a lot and there was only one way out of this situation with Dale that she could see, she had fought it, tried to find someone else but she had to face facts.

"I'll do it," she said.

"Do what?" he asked, rummaging in her cabinets for a clean glass.

"I'll be your fake girlfriend."

He stiffened; the wide expanse of his back tensed at her words. She couldn't tear her eyes away from it. *Fine, I'll admit I want to see him shirtless, is that such a crime? I mean all that muscle being covered up, surely that's the true crime here?*

Finally, Beau shook his head. "It's not a good idea."

"Beau, I really think it's the only thing that will work."

"No, Taylor. Find another guy."

"I tried last night!" she cried. "It'll take too long to make it convincing with a complete stranger and we need to do something now. Look what he's done, God knows what we'll be burying next!"

He leveled a look at her. "That's not exactly convincing me." His wry smile had her heart beating wildly.

"I...I'll owe you big time, anything you need and I'll do it, I promise," she said. She knew she needed him. She was being stubborn before, her hatred of him getting in the way but this incident with her fur babies had set her priorities straight.

"You'll owe me what? A favor? A boon?" he asked, eyeing her closely.

She shifted under the intensity of that stare. "Y...yes," she stuttered. He continued making a drink. "You're the best man for the job," she added when he didn't say anything more. He set the drink down on the counter, a strawberry milkshake. *He still remembers, after all these years.*

"Oh yeah, what makes you say that?" He planted those big hands on the counter and leaned towards her.

She pointed to the drink he just made. "Because of this. Because you know me."

He stared at the glass for a long time, then dragged his eyes to hers. "This is a mistake, Taylor."

"I know that. But help me Obi-Wan, you're my only hope," she replied, trying to appeal to his inner geek.

He swiped a hand over his mouth, groaning. The sound punching her in the gut, leaving her breathless. "Jesus, don't say shit like that to me."

"Sorry," she nibbled her lip, and his eyes followed the movement.

"I'll do it, for a favor."

"What do you want?"

He ran a hand through his hair, her eyes following the way his bicep curled and flexed. "I don't know, nothing right now. Maybe in the future though, to be named at a later date."

She felt like she was being led into a trap only she didn't know what the trap was, and she didn't really have any choice except to follow blindly. She nodded in agreement and a breath whooshed out of Beau.

"If we did this, you would actually co-operate?" he asked.

"We'd need rules. No kissing, no touching and absolutely nothing sexual, obviously," she said, narrowing her eyes.

"My, my what a convincing couple we'll make." His sarcasm had her fighting a smile, *damn him!*

"Okay fine, we can hold hands, casual touching but absolutely no kissing." She definitely didn't want to go there. *Yes, you do…*her brain taunted. She told herself, *shut the hell up!*

"Kissing on the cheek at least, I wouldn't greet the girlfriend I *loved* with a fist bump or a snappy high five," he snorted.

"Fine, but cheeks only," she growled.

"Then you have yourself a fake boyfriend in exchange for a favor to be named later, agreed?" He held out his hand and she stared at it, hesitating a moment. She had possibly just made a deal to sell her soul but right now she didn't know another way. Her palm slid into his, the heat skating up her arm.

"Agreed," she replied, and they shook.

"Holy shit, we're actually doing this." His words hung heavy in the air between them. She reached for her drink, but he swiped it out from under her and downed it in one.

"Get the others here, we need to update Blake on Dale's recent activity, and let them all know the plan so they'll be ready," he said. Her eyes were drawn to the muscles on his forearm as he swiped the back of his hand across his mouth. She swallowed hard.

"Meet me at my office in one hour," she said, already grabbing her phone and messaging the others.

An hour later everyone was gathered in Taylor's office staring at her expectantly. Beau sauntered in last, his hair damp from a shower and swept back from his tanned face. He looked like a goddamn movie star. He'd changed into a brown sweater that matched the deep color of his eyes, and black jeans which molded to his solid thighs in a mouth-watering way. *Keep your thirsty thoughts to yourself, lady!* Even though he'd only seen her an hour ago, his eyes roved over her, cataloging her and she tried to ignore the shivers that coursed through her.

She explained to the group what happened with the squirrels but before she could move on to the next point, Blake came over to her and wrapped her in a big hug. She stood there, shocked. She and Blake were close, but this was uncharacteristic behavior. *Maybe approaching fatherhood is changing him?* Taylor shot Justine a quizzical look over his shoulder, but Justine just smiled at her.

"If you cared about them the way we care about Penny, then I know how much this must be hurting you. I'm sorry for your loss," Blake said quietly, for her ears only, before pulling away. The soft look in his gray eyes and his words pricked her emotions. *Goddamn him, I was not expecting that.* Penny was the wild fox that he and Justine had adopted after Justine had accidentally injured the animal. Blake had nursed her back to health and been a great fox daddy. Taylor was beginning to see what a big softie this badass deputy sheriff really was.

She cleared her throat. "Thanks B, I should've known you would understand."

Beau took over and filled their friends in on the rest of the plan. As expected, Christy and Justine shrieked with joy.

"Oh em gee! This is going to be so amazing!" Christy cried.

Blake looked between the two women. "Am I missing something? They can't stand each other, right?"

Christy and Justine just snickered like a pair of schoolgirls.

Beau cleared his throat. "We'll just have to put down our weapons, call a ceasefire," with a pointed look at Taylor, "and learn to get on for the next few weeks," he added.

"You know, I could do a couple of sessions with you as, like, couples counseling? Work out some of these issues, build your connection etc, confidentially of course."

"That's a great idea, she's an amazing psychologist," Blake nodded.

"Thanks *mi amor*," Justine said, blowing him a kiss and if Taylor wasn't mistaken Justine looked like she was about to cry.

"No! We definitely don't need that," Beau said, and Taylor nodded in agreement.

"So, just to be clear, as soon as we leave this room, we pretend you guys are a couple and madly in love?" Dean asked. Taylor and Beau shared a heavy look.

"That okay with you, man?" Beau asked him.

Dean slapped Beau on the back good naturedly. "Of course, bro. It was my idea, remember?"

"I cannot *wait* to see this!" Justine said, glee dripping from her words and Christy nodded eagerly.

"Try and contain your excitement," Taylor muttered.

"When's the first live show?" Blake asked.

"Ooh tonight, please be tonight! We're all meeting up for drinks again, aren't we?" Justine asked.

Taylor looked towards Beau, raising her eyebrow in question and he gave her a clipped nod.

"Tonight it is," Taylor said. Everyone was on board

but as they all filed out of her office, Beau hung back.

"You sure? Last chance to back out?" he said when they were alone. She could be wrong but there was an edge of what sounded like hope in his voice.

"I'm sure, just remember the rules. Also, to be clear, this changes nothing between us."

He clenched his jaw. His nostrils flared. "Then I'll see you tonight...my love." His voice dropped seductively at the end and her whole body responded, readying itself. Feeling like she couldn't wait for tonight and like she never wanted tonight to come.

It's just anticipation for this whole thing to be over, that's all.

Even she knew that was bullshit.

Chapter 7

That afternoon Taylor had to duck out of the bar to take Ruby to her doctor's appointment. She sent her a message letting her know she was leaving.

Taylor: Rubes, I'll swing by the diner to pick you up in 15.

Ruby: Not at the diner. I'll drop you a pin, sweet cheeks.

Taylor: Stop calling me that. You better not be miles away because if we miss this appointment, I'm not booking another one. I felt like an idiot calling them again the other day!

Ruby: Kisses.

When the pin came through for Ruby's location Taylor died a little inside. She walked into town and headed for Justine's office. Taylor had sold her car recently seeing that she lived and worked at the same place, it didn't make any sense to keep paying for one when she could use that money to put towards the bar. Justine and Dean said she could borrow their cars any time she needed to, like today.

She got inside Justine's little Toyota and turned the radio up, blasting her favorite rock station and hit the road. She pulled up outside the house, ready to collect Ruby but of course the old bat wouldn't make this easy on her. She wasn't waiting outside so Taylor had to go looking for her.

Taylor made her way past the stylish new black and white *Beau's Bodies Spa and Gym* sign, which also shouted about being a rehabilitation and fitness center where he taught yoga and was available for personal training sessions.

The house had changed a lot since the last time Taylor was here. Beau had added a ground floor extension on the side of the house which looked to be the new gym. Large square windows ran along the side, flooding the room with natural light. She could hear workmen shouting and construction noise coming from behind the building presumably where the swimming pool and spa were going.

She opened the door to the gym, peering inside and she couldn't believe her eyes. Nearly every woman from the town and even some from the next town over were crammed into the room. Bright lycra lit up the place in a sweaty rainbow. The women stood in various stages of the same yoga position, some perfected, some not so much.

"And deep breath in…" The deep timbre of his voice echoed around the room and shivers stole through her. She looked through the throng of ridiculously sexy workout gear to find Beau at the front of the class in some sort of torturous yoga pose. His sweatpants pulled tight across his thighs and ~~biteable~~ ass, a red tank top exposing those toned biceps. The damp half-moon in the material at the base of his throat caught her attention and kept it.

"...And out. Well done ladies, we're done for the day. Apologies again for the noise, hopefully the work will be finished soon, then you can all take a dip afterwards to cool off," he said and the women tittered like schoolgirls. That snapped Taylor's attention away from his sexy man-sweat. The women all hastily gathered up their mats, pushed their tits up as high as they could and converged on the man *en masse*. Taylor fought an eye-roll.

She found Ruby amongst the raging pheromones and stomped over to her.

"Really? I couldn't have met you anywhere else?" Taylor grumbled as she watched Beau fight through the crowd of women. Of course, he was too nice to tell them all to get lost. He placated them all with compliments and sweet smiles that he'd never given her. Not that she wanted them obviously.

"Well, hello to you too, Miss Grumpypants, are you my escort for the day or is Taylor coming back at some point?" The old woman sassed her like she wasn't wearing a bright yellow leotard that showed *everything* Ruby had. The hot pink legwarmers really made the outfit pop.

"I needed to get in my weekly yoga class with the Beautiful Beau Thompson, it's not to be missed." Ruby eyed Beau up and down, licking her lips lasciviously. A few of Ruby's friends came over and they all started gossiping about their sexy instructor.

"I nearly spat my teeth out when he went into that

downward dog, did you get a look at that ass? I could bounce quarters off of it!" One of the women said, not bothering to lower her voice.

"Damn Gladys, it was all I could do to stop myself from launching over these other bitches to bite it!" Another with white hair streaked with hot pink highlights cackled. *Bitches? How gangsta were these old biddies?*

"He's trained in CPR too. I might need to fake me a heart attack just for some mouth-to-mouth action."

Taylor looked around Ruby's coven, not believing her ears. Did Beau know the effect he had on all these women, and the disturbing things they wanted to do to him? Did everyone love Beau and want a piece of him except for her? Apparently.

You also want to do disturbing things to him Taylor's brain piped up. *No, my vagina does, we're very different people!* She snapped back, annoyed she was arguing with herself.

"Ladies, you had a great session today. Gladys, your hip doesn't seem to be as stiff at all," Beau said when he reached them.

"I wish something else was stiff…" Gladys murmured, and the coven guffawed. Even Taylor had to admit that was a good one. Ruby put her arms around Beau's waist and drew him into their inner circle, fluttering her lashes at him innocently. *Gag.*

"How did I do today, Beau?"

"You did amazing as always, Ruby. Just keep working on your flexibility and you'll be able to hold some of the moves for longer," Beau replied.

"Can we put in some one-on-one time to work on it?" Ruby asked, adoration pouring from her.

"For you? Of course, just say when." He smiled down at her, squeezing her to him affectionately and Ruby looked like she was about to eat a tasty snack.

"I wouldn't mind him giving me a one-on-one," Pink Streaks said.

"Yeah, I need a private work out too, you know what I mean?"

"Keep it in your pants, Gladys!" Taylor snapped, drawing Beau's attention for the first time.

"Ooooh!" and "Someone sounds jealous!" They tittered. *Sweet Lord, give me strength...*

"Aw, she's just looking out for me, isn't that right, sweetheart?" Beau said, mischief sparkling in those deep brown eyes as he bent his head towards her and waited. Taylor looked around awkwardly. *What is he doing?* Then it dawned on her and she tilted her head reluctantly and he pressed a very quick, uncomfortable kiss to her cheek. She had already forgotten what they were supposed to be doing.

"Yes!" she shouted, feeling so awkward she wasn't able to control the volume of her voice. "I needed to make sure you weren't all over my...my man," she said unconvincingly and uneasily patted his shoulder.

"Are you a couple then?" Pink Streaks asked, and every pair of eyes in the entire gym swiveled to Taylor, silence echoing so loud you could have heard a pin drop.

"Yep, all loved up now," Beau replied enthusiastically and put an arm around her, pulling her into his body so her face ended up caught between his chest and armpit. *God, even his sweat smells sexy, for fuck's sake!* She elbowed her way free before she ended up burying her face in him and licking his damp, salty skin.

Ruby eyed her sharply and raised a suspicious eyebrow that said she definitely would have questions later.

"Come on, we need to get going," she said to Ruby, needing to get away from all those unfriendly eyes staring at her like she wasn't nearly good enough for their precious personal trainer.

"See you tonight, I can't wait," Beau called, his voice managing to be sickly sweet and rich with promise all at the same time. Every woman in the gym sighed deeply.

Jesus, how did he do that?

Taylor grabbed Ruby's hand, dragging the pensioner from the gym. They made it to the car and Taylor managed to avoid any interrogation until they had buckled their seatbelts.

"What the fuck was that?" Ruby asked.

"Language, missy," Taylor scolded.

"Well pardon my fucking French, I'm too in shock from the fuckery I just witnessed. Care to explain that at all?"

"Absolutely not," Taylor replied evenly, pulling away from the curb and heading towards the doctor's office.

"Ouch!" Taylor shouted as Ruby pinched her arm. "What the hell?"

"Tell me or I'll do it again," Ruby threatened. Taylor pressed her lips tightly together and shook her head, scowling at the road.

"I don't know about you, but I feel a little nippy in here," Ruby said, then the old bat reached over and began pinching Taylor all over with both hands.

"Ow, ouch okay! I'll tell you," Taylor cried, half in pain, half laughing at her crazy antics.

"Spit it out then, I ain't getting any sexier."

"Beau and I are pretending to be in a relationship to get Dale to realize I don't love him, that I've moved on and we won't be getting back together."

"It won't take much pretending with that one," Ruby snorted.

Taylor bristled. "What does that mean?"

"That man is perfect for you. Why you're so mean to

him I'll never know!"

"Me?" Taylor cried indignantly.

"Yes you! If you didn't push men away all the time, I wouldn't worry so much that you'll end up alone!"

"Well that man, that you love so fucking much, is the reason that I probably will end up alone. He's the reason I can't have children!" Taylor shouted.

Ruby was the only person who knew she couldn't have children, but she didn't know the full story. Ruby's sharp intake of breath sent guilt crawling through Taylor.

"Okay so that's not strictly true. It's my fault, I know what happened is my fault."

"Do you? Because it sounds to me like you're blaming someone else for something that happened to your body."

"If it wasn't for Beau breaking my heart I never would have gone running to Bobby and gotten knocked up!"

"So that's it, is it?" Ruby said, folding her arms over her luminous leotard. "He broke your heart?"

Taylor clamped her mouth shut. Silence once again filled the car as she pulled up at a red light. She could feel Ruby's gaze burning into her but she wouldn't meet it. Her emotions were simmering far too close to the surface. From seeing how much all those women loved Beau. From Ruby picking at her wounds that suddenly still felt so fresh.

The rest of the drive was silent and as Taylor parked up at the doctor's office, Ruby didn't make a move to get out. "You need to forgive that man," she said quietly.

"I know it's not his fault. I don't really blame him."

"Don't lie to me. You do blame him; you can't help it. But listen to me real clear now, Taylor. It's. Not. His. Fault." She clapped, punctuating her words. "That shitstain Bobby? He's got eight kids now, if it hadn't been the time you went running to him after Beau hurt you, it would have been the next time that he knocked you up, or the time after that. But it's not Beau's fault and you need to forgive him, for yourself."

Taylor opened her mouth to protest.

"Hush it! I ain't done. Now, I love you like you're my own, as far as I'm concerned, you are. And I don't want to spend my days, however many are left, watching you hold onto pain and anger and push every man away. There are other ways to have children and there are good men out there. He's one of the best, so *forgive him*."

"I can't, I hate him," Taylor shook her head.

"No sweet cheeks, you really don't." Ruby's stare penetrated her.

Maybe Ruby was right, maybe in her mind she did need to forgive Beau. It wasn't Beau's fault but her hurt hadn't gotten that message yet. It had reached out and latched on to someone else to blame for what happened, because how could she live with herself otherwise?

Ruby opened the car door and Taylor made a move to follow her but Ruby held up a hand to stop her.

"You don't need to come with me, you can stay here and think about things."

"Yes ma'am," Taylor joked.

"I won't be long anyway, unless you think I can convince him to give me a pelvic?" Ruby's eyebrows wagged and Taylor snorted. Then Ruby was heading inside the doctor's office, her vivid yellow leotard shining brighter than the sun.

Ruby was right, Taylor would have to forgive Beau for what happened, but could she be civil with him? There was still a lot of murky history between them, tonight would be a big challenge.

Sweet Surrender

*

That night at the bar, instead of being the boss ass bitch she usually was, Taylor was deep in her thoughts. The doctor had referred Ruby to a specialist and booked in some tests. He wasn't able to say what was wrong with her and that was what panicked Taylor the most. She didn't think she could lose anyone else and be okay.

She was drying glasses, lost in her thoughts when an arm banded around her waist and squeezed. Startled, she pulled away, dropping the glass in the process and it smashed on the floor.

"What the hell!" Taylor shouted, her heart rate returning to normal when she realized it was Beau.

He held up his hands defensively. "Shit, sorry Tay. That's my bad."

"What in the Garth Brooks were you doing?" she snapped.

He rubbed the back of his neck, meeting her eyes hesitantly. "Being your boyfriend?"

She sighed and pinched the bridge of her nose. "Sorry, I didn't mean to-"

"No, it's fine. It'll probably take us a few tries to get used to this," he said.

"Maybe just announcing your presence would be a good start. When a man grabs a woman in a bar without her permission, it's not usually a good thing." She began sweeping up the scattered glass.

He nodded. "You're right, that was stupid and insensitive."

"And stop agreeing with me, it's annoying!" she snapped again, his goody-goody behavior setting her temper flaring. She moved around him to dump the glass in the trash and he stood there watching her with his giant hands wedged in his pockets.

"Can I help you with something?" She tried to soften her tone but failed miserably.

"Can I greet you properly?" he asked, raising an eyebrow.

What is he on about? Oh shit, he wants to kiss your cheek. Her pulse thudded.

"Uh, yeah, I guess so," she muttered. He leaned forward but couldn't quite reach her. They both stepped forward at the same time and rebounded off each other. She swayed back, grabbing the bar to keep herself upright. He mumbled something and dipped his head, placing a very quick kiss on her cheek, so quick she barely felt it. When he pulled away, she noticed his cheeks had a rosy tint to them. *Is he blushing?* Her annoyance softened slightly.

"So, we're over there, are you joining us?" he asked. She scanned the bar, there were only a few customers wanting a drink, nothing Kayleigh couldn't handle. She nodded and he gestured for her to lead the way as she did the same thing. *God why was this so awkward?* She moved past him, ducking out of reach, afraid to touch him, even accidentally.

Christy, Justine and Dean were all sitting around a table but there was only one chair free.

"We thought you might like to, uh, sit on my lap?" he said, flushing again. When he was like this it reminded her of what he was like when they first met. As usual the memories and the hurt barreled into her, stinging her.

"You thought wrong," she replied, pulling a chair from another table. Besides, Christy wasn't sitting on Dean's lap so it would look weird if she sat on Beau's. That was the reason why, it had nothing to do with not wanting to be close to him.

"Where's Blake?" she asked Justine, pulling her chair up next to her.

"He's checking in on Rebelle," Justine replied with a sunny smile.

"Really?"

"Oh yeah, he does it a lot. He's very protective of her, acting like he's her big brother."

"That's nice that she has someone looking out for her like that," Christy said.

"Yep, ever since that scary night at the shelter he's been doing it. Stops him worrying about her."

"I worry about her too," Christy frowned.

"We spoke briefly at the laundromat the other night. That was nice," Taylor added. Beau pulled her chair closer to him, the metal legs scraping against the wooden floor making her glare at him.

"Hopefully we'll all talk to her more and she'll feel like she can hang with us."

"Because who wouldn't want to hang out with you, darlin'," Dean teased Christy, putting his arm around her and kissing her.

"Exactly!" Christy squealed before their lips met. Beau shot Taylor a questioning look and she shook her head, no. She didn't want his arm around her, pulling her close to him, soaking in his heat and squeaky-clean nice guy scent.

He leaned in so only she could hear him. "You said you would co-operate," he murmured, his breath trekking over her skin, goosebumps rising to greet it.

"I will but we don't need to be the King and Queen of PDA," she hissed. His jaw clenched but he said nothing.

"Sis, we were saying it would probably be a good idea for you to take some self-defense lessons, given everything that's happening," Dean said when he pulled himself away from Christy.

"Absolutely, so if you do find yourself in a position where you need to defend yourself, you can kick ass!" Justine added.

It wasn't a bad idea actually; she loved the idea of being able to beat the crap out of someone. She had a lot of pent-up rage that needed to go somewhere.

"Say, doesn't Beau teach self-defense?" Christy's innocent tone wasn't fooling anyone. Taylor glared at her.

"I can teach you self-defense. I would be happy to," Beau said.

"I can't afford you."

"I wouldn't charge my *girlfriend* for lessons on how to protect herself," he said, giving her that *play along you idiot* look.

"True, but I really can't-"

"You owe me, remember? I'll get payment for it one way or another." His voice dipped low, sounding like a promise. She couldn't speak, just nodded her head like one of those stupid bobbing dogs.

"Great." He smiled wide, white teeth flashing and her stomach fluttered in response which immediately had her scowling again.

Chapter 8

The next week was a nightmare. Every time Beau tried to act like he and Taylor were a couple it was awkward, clumsy and extremely unconvincing. They'd had numerous arguments, and insults were thrown around like confetti. One night they were at dinner with their friends and during a particularly spiteful argument Beau realized just how badly their poor relationship was impacting the group.

"You gravitate towards each other just so you can hurl insults and spit mean barbs, and I for one have had enough!" Justine fumed at them.

Taylor's eyes widened. "We don't gravi-"

"Oh my God, you're so obsessed with each other! Can you please just go and bang it out so we can have some peace?" Christy cried.

Dean plugged his ears. "Whoa! That's my sister."

"I'm sorry, darlin', but you need to accept what's going to happen," Christy soothed. But it did nothing. Dean glared daggers at Beau who shook his head all, *Dude, I don't wanna bang your sister* even though all he thought about recently was doing exactly that. *Man, hate is a powerful aphrodisiac.*

"Hear, hear!" Blake added, smiling ruefully, not helping in the slightest.

The worst part about all of this fake boyfriend shit was he'd become so awkward that he felt like he had zero game at all which was absolutely not true. It was killing him having her see how unsure of himself he was, but she tied him in knots and always had. He had changed a lot since high school, his confidence with women had grown. But this was a nightmare.

They needed to do better at being a fake couple, so far it wasn't working and at this rate he and Taylor would be stuck like this for months. No way would anyone believe they were together.

By the end of the week, he was ready to ask Justine for some couples counseling. They needed to be more comfortable in intimate situations and show a certain level of affection that didn't look forced or uneasy. Every time he touched Taylor she jumped out of her skin. It didn't look natural.

The week *dragged*. Finally it was Friday night and he was getting ready to go to The Rusty Bucket Inn. Tonight, everyone would be there. Justine was singing and that always drew a crowd. With the bar being packed full of regulars and a few folks from out of town this would be the perfect opportunity to showcase their 'relationship'.

He finished getting dressed and headed out to the bar,

arriving in seconds thanks to how close he was at the cabin. He paused outside the door to take a deep breath. He had to stay calm. He noted all the cars parked in the packed lot. Tonight was the night to take this to the next level.

Showtime.

Anticipation fired his blood as he pushed the door open. Music blared from the jukebox, the crack of cues hitting balls on the pool table rang out. Bodies crammed into the bar, sending the temperature soaring, laughter and conversation filled the room, ringing in his ears. He spotted Christy and Dean by the bar and was headed their way before flame-red hair caught his attention.

Taylor rushed around behind the bar, her long corkscrew curls trailing after her. His eyes roved over her, not even trying to pretend he wasn't checking her out. Besides, he didn't need to pretend anymore, it would be expected now. He took in her royal blue sequinned jumpsuit with its deep vee, emphasizing her cleavage that he suddenly wanted to dip his tongue into. The contrast of the blue against her opal skin was breath-taking and he had to tear his eyes away.

"But I don't mind if you want a stripper, darlin'. It's fine," Dean growled as Beau approached.

"Yes, your growly tone really suggests you're fine with it," Christy pouted.

"I don't want someone else putting their hands all over you, that's all. But if that's what you want then honestly, I'm fine with it."

Christy grinned at Dean. "That's the correct answer. But you know I don't want anyone but you touching me."

Dean grinned back at her, and Beau's chest ached at the love pouring from them both. He couldn't believe that only a year ago he had been the one dating Christy.

He'd been attracted to her way back when they were teenagers, but over the course of a few dates a year ago nothing more had sparked between them, and they agreed to be just friends. Which worked out well considering she and Dean had been fighting their attraction to each other since they were fifteen. Fate had intervened and given Christy and Dean their happy ending.

Beau had never really thought about the kind of woman he wanted to settle down with. He wanted a person who challenged him in the best ways, a person that excited him. A soulful connection, a deep friendship, and only one woman had ever come close. Beau's eyes flicked to Taylor again of their own accord and he bit his lip before greeting Christy and Dean.

"We've booked the bar by the way, for my bachelorette. Sorry not sorry, you need to find another venue," Christy said, hugging him hello.

"Ah man. No problem, I'll find something else," Beau said, bumping her shoulder affectionately.

"You mean didn't book anything yet?" Dean raised an eyebrow.

"Uh, absolutely I have," Beau lied.

Dean shook his head in disbelief. "I knew I should have trusted Blake with it."

Beau laughed. They both knew Blake had his hands full right now with his bid to be Citrus Pines sheriff, a baby on the way and trying to plan the perfect wedding for Justine.

"Relax bro, I got this."

"You've invited Will, right?" Dean asked.

Last year Beau had recommended Dean's garage, Iris Motors, to Will who needed some work done on his latest sportscar. Will had actually taken him up on it, and when he'd dropped his car in for detailing, he and Dean had gotten chatting about business, life and cars, and become fast friends.

"Yes, and after the wedding he's got a break in his filming schedule so he's gonna hang around for a little while," Beau added. Will was the head of the panel on one of those entrepreneur reality shows. He was the leader, an aggressive, no-holds-barred, cutthroat businessman, and it made for amazing TV.

"Awesome, can't wait!" Dean gushed, excitement pouring from him.

Beau nodded and once again his eyes were drawn to the bar.

"I better go and say hi to the old ball and chain," he joked then headed over. He watched Taylor pouring drinks, emptying the dishwasher, joking with customers and helping Kayleigh. Her energy zapped around her, giving him a crazy second-hand high. It bolstered his confidence to walk behind the bar and straight up to her. She frowned at him for invading her space but offered up a tight smile.

"Evening sweetheart," he said, and bent down to kiss her cheek. Lingering slightly and inhaling the cinnamon scent that turned his brain to mush and his body to steel.

"Hi," she gritted out.

"You got a few minutes, for us to put on a performance?"

She looked around, surveying the bar. "Just give me five to get through this lot."

He nodded and went back to Christy and Dean. They chatted until Taylor eventually came over carrying two beers and a fruity cocktail that none of them had ordered. But that was what she did, she anticipated what people wanted and did nice things for others without being asked. The one thing he could never fault her on was the way she cared for people.

He tried to get her attention but she refused to meet his gaze. How was he going to get her to relax and let him in? He had known this would be difficult, but they needed it to work and he felt like she was purposely fighting it. He decided to speak to Justine when she and Blake turned up to see if she could fit some time in with them.

"I'll be back," he muttered, not sure if anyone heard him as he headed to the restroom. While he was in there, Porter, one of the bar regulars cornered him.

"I've heard about you and my girl Taylor, is it for real?" Porter said. It was sweet that Porter was looking out for her, but Beau's main takeaway from that was that news of their relationship was spreading, just as they'd hoped.

"Yes Porter, it's for real."

"If you hurt her, I will end you," Porter said, his smile replaced by a scowl. Beau didn't feel threatened in the slightest, hell he was more scared of Porter's wife, Dina.

"Don't you worry 'bout a thing," he said, clapping Porter on the shoulder then heading back out. When he rejoined them, Taylor was staring at something behind them, her eyes wide, her shoulders drawn in.

"What is it?" he asked.

Her eyes didn't move to him, but she replied:

"Dale's here."

*

Taylor watched as Beau spun around and scanned the bar, looking for Dale. She expected him to march over there and drag Dale outside like he'd done in the past but instead he turned back to her, anger flickering in the depths of his eyes.

"Are you okay?"

She tilted her head, surprised that this time he was focused on her. She wasn't okay. It unnerved her more than she expected that Dale was there after what he had done to her squirrels. Fear skated down her spine but she just nodded.

"I'll just go and tell him to leave," she said, taking a step forward but Beau's massive body blocked her path.

"Like hell are you going over to that motherfucker," he growled. Heat sparked through her. Did she like the possessive alpha thing he had going on? Yes, wait, no. She usually hated it when guys got all macho and started measuring their dicks, but on Beau? She could get used to it. Then she remembered he was only doing his job as her fake boyfriend. It was just pretend.

"No, Tay, you can't. It's exactly what he wants, and it defeats the whole purpose of the evening," Christy said.

"And what is the purpose of the evening?" Taylor grumbled.

"To show him how in love you are," Dean said, then shoved her face-first into Beau's chest. The hard wall of flesh didn't give way beneath her cheek and Beau's arm came around her shoulders, keeping her in place. As annoying as he was, Dean was right. That was exactly what Dale wanted. He wanted her to seek him out and give him attention when she was meant to be showing everyone how in love she was with Beau.

Taylor gritted her teeth and leaned into Beau, trying to relax the tension in her shoulders but not quite managing it. She still couldn't let go of their past and give herself over to what she was meant to be doing. Couldn't relax into it and let him touch her, kiss her.

It was too much, too painful because she had started

to think about what it would be like if he really did touch her, really did kiss her. Because he wanted to and not because it was pretend. She shook him off, needing to keep her guard up and protect herself.

"Let's go and relax," he said and gestured to the one table in the whole bar that was free. Christy and Dean sat down but when Taylor grabbed the back of the chair to sit, Beau snatched her hand and tugged her towards him. She fell unceremoniously into his lap, elbowing his ribs and he let out a startled *oof* before he righted her.

"Your ass sits right here," he commanded, for her ears only, and traitorous tingles erupted at his demand. She brushed said tingles aside and settled in, his powerful thighs cradling her ass perfectly. She sat ramrod straight and his hand came up against her back, rubbing soothing circles. His thumb found the edge of the split in her jumpsuit and stroked across her exposed skin. Thankfully her sharp intake of breath was covered by a particularly loud guitar solo blaring from the jukebox.

This is perfectly normal, it's what a normal boyfriend would do, completely acceptable behavior. She chanted it over and over, willing herself to relax but she just couldn't. *No, this isn't happening!* She bit her cheek and leaned forward out of his grip which pushed her ass back into his lap and he jolted.

She tried to throw herself into the group's conversation, but her heart wasn't in it. She kept slipping forward on Beau's thighs but every time she tried to resettle herself, he pushed her slightly further forward.

She scowled at him over her shoulder the third time she slipped forward. *What the hell is he doing?* He had been the one to pull her onto his lap in the first place, but then wouldn't actually let her sit on it? He also wouldn't meet her gaze. She slipped forward and resettled herself a few more times, trying to focus on the conversation but the last time her annoyance took over. She stood up and pushed his arms out of the way then dropped herself back down in his lap before he could maneuver her.

That was when she felt it.

His long, hard, *thick* erection against her ass. Her hands gripped her knees and she stilled. It took all her energy not to brush against it.

"You okay, Tay?" Christy asked.

But she couldn't speak, just nodded, too enthusiastically, shaking her whole body. Beau hissed in her ear and his hands clenched her hips to stop her from moving. His breath tickled her neck as she turned to stare at him and the noise in the bar around them seemed to fade.

His lip was caught between his teeth, his eyes screaming an apology at her as he shifted her forward off his hard cock. At least now she knew why he wouldn't let her sit properly.

Did I do that?

She couldn't tear her eyes away from his, the arousal written all over his face drawing her in. Her breathing deepened as his eyes roved her features. He lifted his hand and tucked a stray curl behind her ear. She longed for him to touch her, to cup her cheek, to stroke her jaw.

His eyes dropped to her mouth. "Beau…" she began, not even sure what she was going to say.

"Hey guys, that looks great! Way to go on the acting," Dean hissed, breaking the spell as he nudged them both.

What the hell was she doing? It was too much, it was all too much.

"Excuse me," she muttered, getting up and heading back to the safety of the bar.

*

Not long after the incident that went around and around on a loop inside her head, Blake and Justine turned up. Taylor immediately pulled Blake aside and told him Dale was here, although she couldn't actually see him right now.

"Has he done anything?" Blake asked, scanning the crowd with his laser focus.

"No, he's actually stayed away."

"That's good, then I agree with the others, let him stay here. Let him see you and Beau together, you stay close to Beau, and I'll keep an eye on Dale," Blake said. Her stomach sank at the whole 'stay close to Beau' thing. She really didn't know if she was strong enough to do this after all.

"I'm gonna set up Justine's guitar and then she's ready to start," Blake said and ducked away, pausing to greet the others on his way to the stage. Her eyes landed on Beau and stayed there, that deep red sweater clinging to his biceps like a needy bitch. Accentuating his muscles too nicely for her comfort. The color was great against his tan skin, dark hair and eyes. Eyes that drifted to her now. She turned away before she could get lost in them.

"Get your shit together, remember who he is to you," she whispered. She served a couple of customers then saw Blake signal to her that everything was set up for Justine. Taylor grabbed the microphone from under the bar, switching it on.

"Good evening gorgeous ladies and tasty menfolk. Welcome back to the best bar in the South!" Whoops and cheers abounded the room. "I know you're all here to listen to our very own Justine so without further ado, please welcome her to the stage!"

Applause rocked the bar as Justine took her seat,

glowing under the stage lights. The crowd surged forward to get the best positions, but Blake emerged and headed for the bar. Taylor didn't usually serve drinks during Justine's performance, but she poured a whiskey now and slid it down the end of the bar to him. It had become tradition that she and Blake stayed back at the bar to watch Justine together. He didn't like crowds and Taylor loved to people watch.

As Justine began to sing, a smile split Taylor's face. Her voice really was something else. She usually sang eighties classics with the occasional nineties tune making an appearance. Tonight was a bit of Sade. Halfway through the first set, Taylor started to feel antsy so began tidying up and restocking the fridges, cleaning glasses ready for the intermission, anything to ignore the feel of Dale's eyes on her. She was drying some glasses off when she saw Beau approach the bar and head around. She felt his delicious heat first then his arms wrapped around her, and his head bent to whisper in her ear.

"I didn't say anything to alert you to my presence as I figured you saw me so you can't be mad this time," he teased.

She snorted but didn't say anything, just willed herself to relax.

"He's by the jukebox. Come on sweetheart, we need to show the town that we're in love." That voice right in her ear had exactly the impact she feared it would, she didn't know what was wrong with her tonight, but she didn't fucking like it.

He pulled her back so she was flush with his chest then he swept her hair back over her shoulder. His head dipped and he placed a soft kiss on the space between her neck and shoulder. Tingles shot through her so forcefully she rocked forward slightly. God, she hated how he made her feel, hated that her brain took her to that night when he kissed her, how his lips had felt then, and she tensed.

"I told you, cheek kissing only," she hissed.

"Which cheeks would that be?" he murmured against her hair. She tried to hold back the shiver that moved through her but failed miserably. This man oozed confidence, nothing like the boy she had known, and she struggled to marry the two parts of him in her brain.

"I swear to God, Beau," she growled.

"Relax, sweetheart," he laughed. "I'm just trying to get you to relax. Come and dance with me?" He pulled away from her and she finally felt like she could breathe again.

"I don't dance."

"Now we both know that's a bear-faced lie," he said, spinning her to face him and taking the glass from her hands to place it on the bar. Once again, his hand found the parting of her jumpsuit at her back and his fingers brushed over her skin, followed by heat.

"Fine, but just one dance."

Triumph flickered in his eyes as he led her out from behind the bar and into the dancing throng. She ignored Dale watching them, his intense eyes boring into her. After all, she was meant to only have eyes for Beau now.

Justine slipped into a slow ballad just as Beau pulled Taylor into his arms.

"Perfect," he grinned down at her. She swallowed past the lump in her throat and tried to ignore what was happening to her body. Maybe it was just sex-starved and that was why it was overreacting to everything Beau did. His arms wrapped around her waist and her hands automatically ran up his chest and locked around his neck. It felt…natural.

"This is nice," he murmured. The way he was looking at her sent alarm bells clanging in her brain. She didn't like it one bit and got ready for a bit of self-sabotage.

"Do you hear that?" she asked.

"Hear what?"

"If you listen closely, you can actually hear the sound of my skin crawling," she hissed but instead of hurting his feelings he actually barked out a laugh.

"There's my feisty girl."

"I'm not yours."

He dipped his head, kissing her cheek. "Oh yes, you are." He punctuated his words with a nip to her earlobe and she fought a moan as sparks of pleasure glided through her veins. *Fine, if that's how he wants to play, I can play this game with him.*

"Managed to control yourself yet?" she asked innocently, before brushing her pelvis against him and raising an eyebrow. He huffed as she made contact and narrowed his gaze at her.

"You were writhing in my lap."

She scoffed. "Writhing? I can assure you I wasn't writhing! I have never writhed in my life."

"No wonder you're still single then. You were writhing more than anyone has ever writhed in the history of writhing, it's like you *wanted* to turn me on," he said with a smug smile.

She spluttered. "Bitch please, I couldn't think of anything worse."

"I've got a lot of built-up sexual frustration that's not been released since *someone* keeps scaring off my dates," he snapped, and she was pleased she had managed to get under his skin and put them back on a normal footing. This was familiar, this was comfortable territory.

"And now you won't be able to go and relieve yourself with any poor woman who agrees to have sex with you, thanks to our deal. This has more benefits than I realized," she said, feeling pretty smug herself.

"Kiss me," he said suddenly, gripping her tightly. She blinked, shocked.

"Kiss me, Taylor," Beau said again, his tone urgent. She laced her hands at his neck and pulled him down to her, tension mounting between them before she veered to the side and her lips met his ear.

"I'd rather be waterboarded than kiss you," she whispered. She pulled back, feeling rather proud of herself until she saw his face.

"Dammit Taylor! Dale was right next to us. He would have seen us kissing but you were too busy trying to sabotage this to notice," he hissed, his eyes flashing angrily at her. She stood on her tiptoes and peered over his wide shoulders. She spotted Dale about to leave the bar when he stopped at the door and looked back, their eyes connecting. He shook his head, laughing at her. Dale blew her a kiss that turned her stomach, that vile smirk taking over his face, and then he left. He hadn't fallen for their act; he didn't believe it was real.

Taylor's stomach dropped. Beau was right, she'd fucked up. She'd been too busy putting Beau in his place and sniping at him to remember what the goal was. She had completely sabotaged the evening.

"Jesus, we need serious help," Beau said.

"He doesn't believe us."

"Yeah, no shit." Beau's arms dropped from her waist and a chill immediately swept through her as he moved away. "We can't keep doing this, or it'll take forever. Justine's right, we do need to go and see her for help. We're not believable like this, we need to be more natural with each other," he said.

"No, I can't," she said, shaking her head. She was terrified of what a session with Justine would reveal.

"Taylor, this shit is serious. This is more than just our history. Think about what I had to bury last week. Think about how much worse it could get. We're going and that's that," he said and then walked away, leaving her alone on the dancefloor.

He was right. She was being selfish and spiteful; this was too important to mess up but she just couldn't let go of her hurt and anger. She made her way back to the bar and began prepping for the intermission.

During the interval Blake came over to speak to her. "Beau said that Dale's left. I've done a search inside the bar and the parking lot, and I can't see him."

"Thanks, Blake," she replied. He frowned at her but didn't say anything. Then Beau came over, his face still like thunder.

"Justine said she'll see us. She's going to have a look at her schedule and let me know when she's free."

She opened her mouth to reply but no words came out. How could she tell him she was scared? His eyes hardened when she didn't say anything, then he just shook his head and walked out of the bar.

Chapter 9

Beau stared out the window of his cabin like some obsessed creeper as everyone filed out of The Rusty Bucket Inn at closing time. Some sober people were going to cars, some not so sober people were getting into cabs as they'd had their car keys confiscated by Taylor. Dean had mentioned to Beau a few times that intoxicated customers hadn't been as appreciative of her efforts as they should and the thought of her facing the wrath of drunk people made his blood boil. It was just another sign of her big heart and how much she cared about people.

The woman was tying him in knots. One moment she was writhing in his lap, her lush ass rubbing against him so perfectly he'd had to fight to stop a moan slipping out. The next she was so snarky with him that the only way he envisioned getting her smart mouth to stop running was to put her over his knee. He wanted to bite her head off but mostly just bite her. These aggressive urges were getting out of hand. He had nearly reached for her earlier, then had to tear himself away before he made a move he regretted.

He needed to get control over his instinct to dominate her, but he had no idea how to handle it. He'd never had this problem with anyone else. Taylor was the only woman who pulled all kinds of impulses from him; he was all over the place tonight. When he spotted Dale slithering closer to them, his protective instinct had roared into life, and he had been ready to tear the man apart. Only he couldn't do that, he was supposed to sit back and play the doting boyfriend to an unwilling and resentful girlfriend.

Her refusal to kiss him had sparked something in him. He couldn't deny that he wasn't going to take full advantage of the opportunity. He *wanted* to kiss her. His memory was well-worn and patchy but he remembered how their first kiss had felt, even if she had been faking it at the time.

He hadn't had a kiss like that ever since, and tonight, with the tension boiling between them, he felt like he needed that kiss more than air to breathe. He'd tried to force her hand, knowing Dale was watching them so closely but she hadn't gone for it, choosing instead to belittle him and insult him, shoving them back into their destructive pattern.

They needed help, fast, or this whole thing would come crashing down. Justine's therapy was the best chance at getting them more in sync with each other and maybe even finally resolving their past.

He watched until the customers had all left, followed

by Kayleigh, which meant Taylor wouldn't be far behind. He waited. And waited. He was reaching panic-mode, ready to go into the bar to look for her when her red hair caught his eye even in the dark. She strolled around the side of the bar, the blue sequins on that sexy outfit glittering in the moonlight. A sharp ache pierced his chest.

Then she stopped in her tracks, staring at her cabin.

"What's she doing?" he murmured, trying to look out of his window to see what she was staring at. He couldn't see anything so he moved across the cabin to peer out of the window that looked directly into hers. Then he saw the glow of light coming from her kitchen. There hadn't been any lights on when he'd come back. A shadow was moving inside the cabin.

"Fuck!"

He raced for the door, wrenching it open. Glancing across the empty parking lot, his eyes met hers for a split second, then he ran across to her porch.

"Beau, no!"

Her door was ajar, a light shining inside. He kicked the door open, and there was Dale. Fear flashed in the man's eyes briefly as he took in the towering frame of Beau, not the slight redhead he was waiting for. Beau took advantage of his surprise and grabbed him by the shirt, hauling him out the door and across the porch. Dale grunted and swung for him, but Beau ducked. He shoved Dale, watching as he tripped over his own feet and fell backwards into the dirt. He popped up quickly and swung for Beau again, his face twisted with rage.

"Beau, stop!" Taylor cried, wrapping her arm around Beau's bicep, trying to pull him away but she couldn't move him. Dale tried to duck around Beau to get to Taylor, but Beau blocked his view with his body.

Sweet Surrender

"Get the fuck out of here!" he shouted.

Dale laughed. "Seriously baby, this meathead is my replacement?"

"Sweetheart, let's go inside." Her gentle voice couldn't penetrate his anger, her hands were fisted in his sweater trying to tug him away, but Beau refused to move until this asshole was gone.

"I guess I knew you wouldn't wait long to welcome someone else into your bed. Gotta get through all the men in town like the little slut you are," Dale sneered.

Rage detonated inside Beau's mind and he lunged for Dale, drawing a fist back and letting it fly at full force. Dale's head whipped back from the impact, blood pouring from a split in his cheek. Before Beau could strike again, Taylor stepped between them.

"Beau, please, stop! Let's just go inside," she begged, and his rage cooled at her fear. Dale spat a mouthful of blood on the ground then grinned up at Beau before hauling himself up. Waving at them both, he sauntered off like he hadn't a care in the world. Beau let Taylor lead him back to her porch.

"I'm sorry, I just got so angry. I'm usually more controlled, it's just that... When he called you *that*, I saw red."

"Excuse me?" she said, her tone hard. He looked at her, her expression so blank he couldn't read her at all. She stepped towards him, not stopping until she was pressed up against his hard body. She ran her hands up over his chest, his muscles bunching under her touch. Muscles that he knew hadn't been there the last time she touched him like this. Muscles he had built with the shallow hope that one day, this would happen between them.

Her emerald gaze pierced him, her hands trailing all

over his body, setting him alight, his adrenaline still rocketing through him. He could hardly breathe as she stood on tiptoes and brought her mouth to his ear.

"Would you like me to thank you?" Her voice was husky, her hot breath teasing over his skin had his eyes rolling back into his head. He had to lean a hand against the wall of her cabin to keep himself upright as arousal tore through him.

"Should I thank you for protecting me?" Her voice had an edge to it that he couldn't bring himself to analyze in this moment. Too overwhelmed at being so close to her, at having her hands all over his body.

His cock hardened beneath the fly of his jeans for the second time that night, desperate for her touch. Her hot, tight little body plastered to his, her curves fitting him like a puzzle piece that had been missing his whole damn life.

Her lips brushed against his ear and he grunted, wrapping his other arm around her waist pulling her even tighter to him. Needing to be closer, to fade into her, drown in her.

"Should I thank you for defending my honor? For saving me from the big, bad man?" she purred, running her tongue along the shell of his ear and he shivered. *Fuck yes.* His mouth ran dry as he considered all the ways she could thank him and it would never be enough. He realized he would always crave more.

Taylor pulled back to stare at him, and his passion-fogged vision cleared as the moonlight shone down on her face. He blinked in surprise. A snarl curled her lips, her eyes glittered up at him violently. Her face twisted into a cruel mask and her mouth split into that nasty smile she had given him all those years ago and he was transported back to that pathetic boy, in that hallway, watching his heart get broken by her all over again.

"Thank you, Beau, for defending me against a man who called me a slut. You would never say such a thing, would you?" Venom dripped from her words, each one punching him in the gut. He had no words, didn't know what to say.

"How can I ever repay you..." Her eyes flashed at him before dismissing him and heading towards the door.

She'd done it again. She'd played him. She had brought him to his knees yet again and he'd let her. Anger and pain coiled inside him, so familiar now it was almost a part of him. Before he could stop himself, he called after her.

"I'm naming my favor."

She stiffened then turned slowly to face him, her eyes blank.

"A kiss."

"Fuck you!" she spat.

"No, not yet. I want a kiss first," he said, giving her a devilish smile.

"Fine, we'll do it now," she said and made her way towards him. But he didn't want her to give in. Not so easily, he wanted her to *earn* it.

"Oh no sweetheart. Not only do I want a kiss, but I want you to ask me for it. I want you to *beg* me for it. And only when *I'm* ready, will I give in."

Her mouth twisted again. "I hate you."

He smiled sadly. "I know."

His statement hung between them, painful, like an open wound. "But you need to forget about that tonight, I'm staying here."

Her eyes widened and she started to protest. "No way!"

"Yes, Taylor. Think about it, he was in your home. Even with all of our mountains of bullshit I'm not leaving you alone. So put a pin in your hate tonight, you can let it all out when we go to therapy," he said, brushing past her and stepping into her cabin.

She came in behind him, still sputtering, spitting rage at him but he ignored her, locking the door behind them and sliding the bolts into place. When she realized he wasn't going anywhere she stomped off to her room, slamming the door.

Beau called Blake to let him know that Dale hadn't left after all and that he'd been inside Taylor's cabin, also that he and Beau had an altercation.

"Be careful man, the last thing I want in all of this is to have to arrest *you* for assaulting this asshole," Blake growled down the phone. Beau could hear Justine calming him in the background.

"I will be more careful, I promise. I just…my anger got the better of me," he replied.

"Man, that isn't like you. But don't worry, I'll go and pay him a visit tomorrow and have a chat with him. I'll keep you updated."

"Thanks Blake. Take it easy," Beau said and hung up then turned his attention to trying to get settled on her tiny couch for the night.

Had he been an asshole to her tonight? Absolutely.

Did he regret it? Absolutely not.

Sometimes you had to play dirty to get what you wanted. He wasn't always the good guy.

*

"Rise and shine, Princess."

His deep voice penetrated her dream and pulled her from it kicking and screaming. Taylor pushed back her covers, confused and there he was, in all his muscley glory.

God I just hate his face! She glared at him as memories of last night came back to her. "Why exactly are you waking me up?"

"We've got a counseling session in thirty minutes."

"What!"

"Yep, crazy I know. Get that booty out of bed." He stood there, arms folded across his chest like the bouncer of her bedroom.

Her glare deepened. "Can you leave my room?"

"Not until you're up. I know you, you'll fall back to sleep." He grinned down at her. She wanted to slap it off his face, especially after his stunt last night. Of course, this asshole was a morning person.

"But I'm naked under here."

He narrowed his eyes, scrutinizing her face before his smile widened. He gripped the corner of her quilt and yanked it back.

"Beau!" she shrieked, covering herself.

"Cute unicorn jammies, who knew they came in adult sizes too? I know all your tells, sweetheart. Don't bother lying to me again," he said. She grabbed a pillow and heaved it at his stupid smug head. He ducked unfortunately but she was already grabbing another, ready to go again.

"Pillow fight!" He threw a pillow at her and hit her in the face. She cursed and stood up.

"God, I hate you," she huffed.

"I know, you told me last night. Twenty-eight minutes left, you don't wanna keep your best friend waiting for you when she could be seeing other *paying* clients." He pushed her towards the bathroom. She flipped him off and his dark chuckle snaked over her as she slammed the door.

She seethed under the spray of the shower. When she had agreed to a therapy session she hadn't expected it to be less than twelve hours later. After the incident with Dale last night and what followed with Beau she was feeling a little raw.

A kiss.

The bastard wanted a kiss. Not just any kiss, he wanted her to ask for it, to beg him for it. *Fat chance of that happening*, she snorted as she lathered herself aggressively. She would be on her deathbed before she accepted one kiss, let alone begged him for it.

Her mind turned to Dale and his little visit. Seeing him in her cabin had been a shock. The only people who had a key were Dean and Justine. Which meant Dale had stolen hers and had a copy made at some point. The thought turned her stomach. How many times had he been into her place? Was last night the first time or just one of many? She needed to call a locksmith after this stupid therapy session.

She finished showering and dressed in a floral-patterned blouse and pink jeans. She applied a little makeup wanting to look nice for ~~Beau~~ Justine.

"We gotta go!" Beau's voice interrupted.

"Damn, he's still here?" she muttered, trying to ignore the way her heart skipped at the idea of him hanging around her home. Last night had been difficult, being so close to him and flirting with him had flared to life the old attraction she felt for him. It was dangerous territory when she was meant to be pretending to be in love with him.

She brushed her hair and headed into her living room. "Why are you still here?" she groused at him, trying not to notice how his navy t-shirt clung obscenely to his biceps.

"I figured you needed a ride."

She grunted at him in response.

"Coffee's in the car, I know you're about as useful as shaving cream to a Wookie without it," he drawled.

"Trust you to make a *Star Wars* reference in the first thirty minutes of the day." She grabbed her bag and opened the door to the cabin, stepping aside to let him pass. He stopped in front of her and bent down, putting them nose to nose. Her breath hitched as she stared straight into those warm eyes and arousal unfurled in her stomach. No, not arousal. *Never* arousal. His pupils expanded, chasing away all the deep chocolate color.

"Say what you like, Princess, but geeks are cool now. You're the loser here," he said and then booped her nose, walking off and leaving her mouth gaping open. When she finally snapped out of it, she locked her cabin door and ran after him to the sleek black car parked in the lot.

He didn't bother to wait for her, just got in and started the engine. She ran up the side and went to grab her door handle as the car rolled forward a few feet out of reach. She growled and skipped after it and when she reached for the handle the same thing happened again.

"Beau, I swear to God!" she shouted, and the car stopped abruptly. This time she was able to open the car door and get inside. She sat down and glared at him. *That fucking smirk.* He held a coffee cup out to her with *Ruby's Diner* emblazoned on the side.

"Uh-uh, seatbelt," he said, wagging his finger at her when she reached for it. She was so close to losing her shit. She knew he was being an ass on purpose to distract her from worrying about their session, but it didn't make her hate him any less. She clicked her seatbelt into place and snatched the coffee cup from him, taking a big gulp and moaning enthusiastically when the liquid hit her tastebuds.

Beau cleared his throat, shifting in his seat and then they were off. The ride was smooth, she relaxed against the cool leather seats that smelled like him, fresh and minty. She watched him out of the corner of her eye, his forearms flexing when he changed gears, his big hands wrapped around the steering wheel like they were wrapped around her-

She swallowed. "This is a mistake, Beau."

He sighed. "I really don't think things between us can get any worse than they are, do you?"

She stayed silent. She didn't know what would happen today, but she felt like after this session everything would change.

"Besides, we need this. Dale didn't fall for it last night. We're not convincing enough. We need to be better, do better and then this will all be over with, and we can move on," he added, pulling up outside Justine's office. He switched off the engine and looked at her. He must have seen the apprehension on her face.

"Good things will come from this, trust me," he said.

It was ridiculous but after all this time, and with all the shit between them, she did trust him. His willingness and commitment to this whole ruse was impressive. If he was okay with this then she could be too, right?

She nodded, took a deep breath and got out of the car.

Chapter 10

Beau's nerves were in pieces. Outwardly he projected a calm demeanor but inside he was a mess. He opened the door to Justine's office and stepped back to let Taylor enter first. She didn't thank him as she went through, probably still annoyed at him. Rightly so after his behavior last night and he had totally overcompensated this morning by being the asshole she expected him to be.

He was ashamed at the way he'd behaved the previous evening. The anger, the aggression and then demanding a kiss as payment. What kind of man did that make him? Not the kind of man she needed him to be, that was for sure.

He followed her inside, walking through the cloud of cinnamon that seemed to follow her around. Ignoring how good she smelled had been the only reason he managed to get them here without crashing the car; his attention was shot.

Justine was ready and waiting for them. It looked like they were the only people in the building today and he was grateful for the privacy. She gestured for them to go into her office and came in behind them, closing the door. Taylor made a beeline for the armchair that sat facing the leather couch, probably so she wouldn't have to sit next to him.

"Nice try, move it," Justine said, pointing to the couch. Beau grinned at her as Taylor huffed and flopped down onto the couch next to him. He glanced around the room while Justine got her notepad and sat down. The office was brightly lit with luscious green plants which, coupled with the dark wooden furniture, created a soothing zen ambiance.

"Okay!" Justine clapped her hands together and looked at Beau and Taylor expectantly. "I think we're going to do something great today. By the end of the session, we'll have had a long chat and focused on some intimacy exercises to help build your relationship so that when you're faking it, it feels as natural as possible," she said.

"Thanks for taking the time out of your schedule to see us," Beau said sincerely.

"Suck up," Taylor tutted, and he rolled his eyes.

"Anyway," Justine began, taking control of the conversation again. "Anything discussed here will stay between the three of us. As far as I'm concerned, you're both clients and will be treated with strict confidentiality. Now, let's begin!" Justine eyed them both before speaking again. "My own observation, having known you both for a long time, is that something between you has fractured. I remember how close you used to be, so what went wrong? Did you just grow apart?"

Beau's stomach dropped. *Yep, this was a mistake.*

"Well, I guess it was-" he began.

"Why do you get to go first?" Taylor interrupted.

Beau sighed deeply. *This was going to be fun.* "By all means Taylor, take it away."

"So Beau decided to-"

Beau snorted. "I see, it's all my fault? God, you're the most spoilt, inconsiderate-"

Taylor cut him off again. "See how he dotes on me? It's suffocating, isn't it?"

"Let him speak, Taylor," Justine reprimanded.

"Thank you, Justine," Beau replied, flinging a shit-eating grin Taylor's way.

"This isn't about point scoring, Beau," Justine admonished.

"Ha ha!" Taylor laughed, wagging her finger in his face.

"Back to you Beau. You just called Taylor spoilt and inconsiderate. Is that really how you feel about her?"

Beau shook his head.

"If that's not how you feel then why are you attacking her like that?" Justine's stare probed him, and his bravado slipped.

He could feel himself unraveling and suddenly he was exhausted with pretending everything was okay, so he decided to let it happen. His palms began to sweat as he realized he had been given the opportunity he was looking for to get it all out. Say his piece somewhere safe where Taylor couldn't run away; he'd finally apologize and set things right between them. Then the weight he had been carrying around since he was seventeen would finally be lifted.

He twisted his hands in his lap, not looking up. "I'm

hurt," he said quietly.

"I'm sorry?"

"I said I'm hurt. She hurt me," he repeated, finding his voice. He felt Taylor stiffen next to him.

"And when did this happen?" Justine asked, her voice painfully soft.

He laughed, the sound hollow. "A really fucking long time ago."

"How long ago are we talking?" Justine asked.

"When we were teenagers."

"How did I-" Taylor began, but Justine raised a hand to silence her.

His gaze swiveled to Taylor in shock, his eyes wide. *Seriously? Did she honestly have no idea what she had done?*

"You used me! We were friends. I was your *person* and you used, then rejected me. I know I was fat and geeky and not the most attractive guy at school, but you *knew* me. You knew my personality and I thought you of all people could look past all that crap, but you played me. Just like all the other girls at school. To get what you wanted, which was…I don't fucking know, some kind of humiliation or some shit. Or just for kicks? Just because you could? Did it make you feel powerful? You did exactly what they did, only you were worse because you *knew* me." Beau didn't hold anything back. This could be his only chance to say how he truly felt. Taylor's mouth hung open, and he couldn't bear to see the pain in her eyes.

"I know what I said to you, what I called you. I know it was wrong. I regretted it the instant I said it. I've regretted it ever since; it still haunts me, and I've wanted to apologize to you a thousand different ways. But we can't be around each other long enough without the insults flying, can we?"

"What did you say to her, Beau? What did you call her?" Justine asked.

Beau looked down at his hands twisted in his lap. Now he understood Taylor's anger at him last night, which made his demand for a kiss even fucking worse. How could he react like that when someone else called her the same thing he had? He was a goddamn hypocrite.

He faced Taylor, looked her straight in her jewel stone eyes.

"I called her a slut," he said, and he saw Justine's mouth pinch in disapproval. It must be hard for her to hear this but at least now she knew what happened between them.

"I'm so sorry Taylor. I didn't mean it, I never should have said it. I was lashing out because I was hurt and angry, but I *never* meant it," he said. He felt that weight easing from his shoulders although it didn't go anywhere, it just hung in the air between them.

Taylor's face didn't change. Her cold stare didn't soften and the tiny flame of hope he had for today flickered and died. He pushed out the breath he had been holding.

"Do you have anything to say, Taylor?" Justine asked. The silence in the room felt loaded. He was on the edge of his seat waiting to hear what she had to say, yet dreading it. Would she save them or would she pour gasoline over the smoldering remnants of their relationship and let them burn?

"You're a fucking idiot," Taylor spat, and his gaze snapped to her again.

"Taylor," Justine admonished.

"Sorry. But he is. Fat? Geeky? Unattractive? You think I gave a shit about any of that? You honestly thought I was that low that I would do that? You weren't any of those things. You were my best friend, my ride or die, you were *my person*! I kissed you because, shock horror, I wanted to. You didn't even give me a chance to explain, you just jumped to conclusions and said the worst thing anyone has ever said to me." Taylor's lip wobbled, only briefly but he saw it and his heart caved in on itself.

"I pulled away from you because by kissing you I had just cheated on my boyfriend. If you were truly my best friend you would know what that really meant to me, that I would do that, for you. I was ashamed of my behavior and terrified that you would think so little of me for breaking my ethics. I *cannot* condone cheating, not after my father." Taylors chest began heaving, her eyes frantic. He tried to reach for her hand, but she batted it away. "All I was thinking about was breaking up with Bobby so I could be with you! But you were too busy calling me a slut to let me get a word in. You knew me better than anyone and that's what *you* assumed? But it's fine, Beau. I got what was coming to me. You know I fucked him that night? I was so devastated by what you'd said that it drove me straight to him for comfort. I let him use me."

Beau squeezed his eyes shut, trying to block out the words coming from her.

Taylor's breathing was growing more labored, like she was having a panic attack.

"Taylor, just take a minute to catch your breath," Justine said, gesturing to Taylor to try and moderate her breathing. If anything, it became worse. Her eyes swung to him, a wildness in them that wasn't there before.

"I guess I owe you an apology too," Taylor said, laughing humorlessly. He didn't like where this was going but he had committed to this session. As painful as it was, he had no choice but to see this through.

"For what?" he rasped.

"I've been blaming you for something that happened for so long and it wasn't your fault at all. But my stupid brain and heart were too hurt to do anything other than attach the blame to you as a way of protecting myself. It made me *hate* you, which was so much easier. If I hated you then I wouldn't hurt anymore, I wouldn't miss you..." she trailed off and silence filled the office.

His heart pounded so loudly in his chest that he was convinced they would hear it.

"What was it, Taylor?" Justine prompted when she didn't elaborate.

Taylor shook her head, a tear slipping down her cheek, that tear flayed him.

"I can't," she whispered.

Justine took control again. "Taylor, I think in order for you to move on, for both of you to move forward and start with a clean slate, you need to be honest. It's just us here, we both care about you, you're safe here."

Beau swallowed thickly, not sure if he could take much more. He reached out a shaky hand to take hers and this time she let him.

"I was so upset and wasn't thinking straight, contraception didn't even occur to me. I got pregnant but I couldn't keep it. You have to understand, I was just a kid. So I had an abortion."

Whatever he had been prepared for, it wasn't that. His stomach contracted and goosebumps mottled his skin, tears pricking the backs of his eyes.

"My womb got damaged in the process and then I got an infection, a really bad one. It's not very common. I guess that was my punishment, huh? I was scared, too scared to tell anyone and to have to explain what had happened so I hid it. It got worse, until I couldn't cope anymore. I finally went to the doctor, but it was too late.

They couldn't get it under control and the damage was too severe. I had to have a total hysterectomy and now I can't have my own kids," she said the last on a gasp and out of the corner of his eye, Beau saw Justine's hand grip her stomach.

"And you weren't there Beau, you left me. You *abandoned* me when I needed you most," she whispered, shaking her head, her tears falling like rain. He felt his own slip down his cheeks.

"I know," was all he could say.

"You left me all alone, Beau." She was sobbing, huge gut-wrenching sobs that he had never seen before. He didn't know what else to do to make the pain go away, so he pulled her into his lap.

He rocked her back and forth and let her cry it out, just repeating over and over again how sorry he was. He would never forgive himself for abandoning her. No wonder she hated him, he fucking hated himself right now.

He'd been upset because she'd hurt his pride and rejected him, which she actually hadn't done at all. He was the biggest piece of shit. He didn't need her apology, didn't damn well deserve it. He buried his face in her neck and cried for his guilt and what she'd lost, what they'd both lost all these years.

"I'll never leave you again."

*

When her sobs finally subsided, exhaustion swept in to claim her, but she also had a sense of calm she hadn't felt before. Taylor had told her story, told *him* her story. It was out, and no longer bottled up inside her and festering away. It was devastating to face it head-on, but cathartic too. She felt safe cocooned in his arms and was reluctant to move but she made herself. She pulled back, his t-shirt damp with tears and very likely snot. She had never been a pretty crier.

"Sorry," she mumbled.

"Do not apologize to me," he rasped. He had cried too. His emotion had astonished her.

"Well, I'm not going to lie to you both, I was not prepared for that," Justine said, breaking the spell. Taylor scrambled off Beau's lap, immediately missing his warmth. She untangled their fingers and folded her hands in her lap.

"I'm sorry for what you've lost," Justine added with a pointed look at Taylor. "Both of you," as her eyes then flicked to Beau. "It sounds like there's a lot of hurt here caused by misunderstandings that have gone on too long, and it's torn you away from each other for nearly two decades."

Beau stood up abruptly and went to look out the window, his hands on his hips as he faced away from them. Despite his relaxed pose, the rigid set of his shoulders gave him away.

"Thank you both for sharing your hurt. It might not feel like it, but it was a good thing. You understand now what went wrong between you. There was nothing malicious in it, it was just a sad incident that spiraled. What you need to decide now is if you can move forward from this. Taylor, what do you think?" Justine said.

Taylor glared at her, hating that she had to go first. Her eyes swung to Beau who was still staring out the window, his shoulders hunched, his back tensed.

She put on her big girl panties. "We need this fake couple thing to work. I need Dale gone so I can move on with life so I guess I want to work on this."

"And you, Beau?" Justine asked.

"I'll do whatever you need me to do, Taylor," he said, still not facing her.

"You've both had a very emotional morning, so we won't try any exercises today as I think you're both a little too raw for them right now. But you can do them as homework, over the next day or two," Justine said. Taylor rolled her eyes. *Homework? Yuck.*

"If you want this to work then you need to work at it. Neither of you is afraid of hard work so put the effort in. I'll start with something simple, an eye gazing exercise."

Taylor scrunched her nose up. "Eye gazing?"

"Yes. Eye gazing is a simple but very intimate practice. Your eyes are your most expressive feature, you communicate a number of emotions and social cues through them. They're the window to your soul and maintaining eye contact builds intimacy and trust. You need to sit close together, embracing is always best but it's not necessary, and stare into each other's eyes for five minutes."

"That's it? That's easy enough," Taylor scoffed.

"Then you'll be surprised. I think we should leave it there for the day unless either of you want to discuss anything?" Justine asked. When neither of them had anything, she continued. "Are you okay to leave together?"

Beau glanced over his shoulder at Taylor, his expression unreadable. She nodded at him, then he nodded at Justine in confirmation. When they stepped outside Justine's office, she pulled Taylor into her arms and squeezed her fiercely.

"I'm so sorry, *mi corazón*. I would have supported you, always. Please tell me you know this?" Justine whispered, then pulled back, peering into her eyes.

"I know, I was just too scared," Taylor replied and kissed her friend's cheek. Justine nodded and squeezed her again before she moved to Beau and enveloped him in another bone-crushing hug. She saw Justine whispering in his ear but couldn't make out what she was saying.

"I'm here for you both, as your friend and your psychologist," she said, glancing between the two of them.

They both thanked her then they were getting in the car and heading back to the bar. The air between them thick and heavy, but it wasn't hostile.

"I meant it," Beau said, the first to break the silence. "I will do whatever this takes. Let me make this up to you."

"Beau, I told you, I should never have blamed you and I'm sorry I did. It was never your fault. You don't need to make anything up to me."

His jaw clenched at her words but he didn't say anything more. She just wanted to move forward now. Didn't want to be dictated to by past hurt and resentment.

Only now, she didn't know how to act around him. She was feeling more awkward by the minute at the thought of what faced them. She wore her snark and spite as armor to keep him at arm's length with her hurt always burning inside her, keeping her warm. Her walls were used to being up too, to guard her. Now, what the fuck did she do around him?

They pulled into the parking lot of the bar and as she headed towards her cabin, he took the lead.

"Let me go in first," he said, taking the keys from her hand. She didn't bother arguing with him, not when alpha-mode had been engaged. Normally she would be rolling her eyes over an unnecessary display of male dominance. Only from him she didn't mind so much, she knew it came from a good place. He unlocked the door and swung it open wide. When there was no movement from inside the cabin, he gestured for her to enter and headed off to scout her bedroom.

She sighed deeply, dropping her purse on the kitchen counter. *What a morning.*

"Taylor, did you do this?" he called from her bedroom.

"Do what?"

He was standing by the bed, pointing at her pillows. She looked down and saw her panties laid out across her pillow. Her stomach dipped. Dale had been inside again while they were out. The realization that he was watching them had nausea burning her throat.

"I take it you didn't do this?" he asked.

"What do you think?" she sassed, trying to cover up her fear, not wanting Beau to see how upset she was. Beau's fists balled as his sides.

"I think that sick fuck is playing a game with us," he said, snatching up the displayed underwear and waving them around. "But we're gonna show him. Let me call Blake and we need to get a locksmith out here, now!"

The sight of her lacy panties fisted in his giant hands made her squirm. She made a discreet grab for them but he moved his hands out the way. He took out his phone and called Blake, updating him on what had happened.

"Oh, he says she gave him a key, huh?" Beau said, facing her. She shook her head and made another grab for the panties. *Why was he still holding them?*

"No, she didn't give him a key, the lying bastard. Yeah, we'll get a locksmith out now," he said into the phone. They spoke for a few more minutes while she made ineffectual grabs for the panties, her cheeks flushing. Beau gestured so much when he talked, when had that started? Was he doing it on purpose? When he finally ended the call, she tried again.

"Beau, can I-"

His attention was elsewhere. "What's that?" he asked, heading into her bathroom.

"Beau!" she snapped. "Can I please have my panties back?" She held out her hand. He looked at her, then down at his hand, a sly smile creeping onto his face.

"What, these panties?" He held them out, she moved to grab them but he lifted them just out of her reach.

"Nah, I think I'll hold onto them," he said and tucked them into the back pocket of his jeans. She opened her mouth, about to unleash war like she normally would. But then she saw the warmth in his eyes, the way they crinkled in the corners. He was *teasing* her. No malice, no snide curl of the lip. He was trying to keep things light between them so she rolled her lips inwards instead.

He turned back to the bathroom and pulled the cord for the light. Then she spotted it. The message scrawled on her mirror in her favorite red lipstick:

Who are you saving all your kisses for?

She stared at the scrawled, mocking words and she knew Dale realized she and Beau were faking it. They needed to step up their game.

Beau's words last night flung themselves across her mind, his favor. A kiss. No, she couldn't, she *wouldn't*, they would just have to convince Dale another way.

"He's watching us," she said.

"What does he mean?" Beau asked.

Taylor squeezed past him and began scrubbing at the mirror. "How should I know?"

"Last night he said something similar."

"Beau, please just drop it?"

He was silent as she scrubbed the lipstick off, when she turned around, he was sitting on the end of her bed, watching her.

"I'm moving in," he said.

She snorted. "Hell no!"

"Taylor, be reasonable. He can get in here, he got into your bedroom!"

"And I'm changing the locks."

"You don't get a say in this." He waved his phone at her. "Dean agrees it's the right thing to do."

"You ratted me out? To my own brother?"

"Yeah, get over it." He shrugged, every inch the commanding alpha, and damn if her lady parts didn't do a little cheer.

"It's not a good idea, Beau," she said, hoping he caught her drift. After their session with Justine, she didn't think being shoved into close proximity was the right thing for them.

"It's the best idea. It shows Dale that we're a serious couple." His features softened. "I get your worry, Taylor. But we've been through a lot, we'll be fine. Trust me."

She spluttered more protests, but he ignored every single one. When she was all out of excuses, she hung her shoulders in defeat.

"Fine, I'll make some space for your clothes," she grumbled.

"Really? You'd think your closet would be empty with how many clothes are on the floor," he teased. Then his teasing tone was gone. "I'll, uh, sleep on the floor in here. That way if he gets in again, I'm right here."

She swallowed. "You don't need to sleep on the floor, I have a king-sized bed." *For your king-sized body...* "Plus he's watching us, so it makes sense for you to be in the bed, um, with, um, with me." She thought she saw something flare in his eyes but when he blinked it was gone.

He nodded. "I'll grab my stuff and start moving in today. Will you be okay on shift?"

"Yeah, Kayleigh is with me all day."

"Great, I'll swing by at closing and walk you back."

"Great."

Things between them felt strangely polite and tense. She really didn't know what to do with it.

He cleared his throat. "And we'll start your self-defense lessons later this week too."

She smiled, genuinely excited. She had a lot of rage and…tension to get out.

Chapter 11

Beau packed away the last set of dumbbells from his bodypump class, watching as the ladies filed out of the gym slowly, still shooting him sweaty, lingering smiles over their shoulders. He cleaned up and then locked the gym. Next he headed around the back of the house to meet the construction crew to get an update on how work was progressing on the swimming pool and sauna.

This was the precise reason he had bought this house. He needed the land that came with it so he could expand and build his own fitness center. He gazed around and pride bubbled in his chest for the first time in a long while as he could see his plans all coming together. He truly loved what he was creating here, more so than the last gym he owned in L.A. His classes and PT sessions were already a hit with the locals, and the elderly residents were loving the yoga and stretch classes to help with their aging joints. Business would only grow even more once the pool and sauna opened.

He said goodbye to the crew and headed into the house to grab some extra clothes, and if he was moving into Taylor's place then he was definitely bringing his TV. He couldn't believe she had accepted his demand to move in, let alone offered to share her bed. He wasn't sure how he was going to find sleeping next to her each night, especially now they had laid down their arms, so to speak.

He felt like an even bigger ass after their therapy session. Demanding a kiss as his reward for carrying out this charade with her; he certainly wouldn't hold her to it now. He had done it out of spite towards the person who hurt him the most in his entire life. But after that session with Justine, it turned out she hadn't meant to do that at all, and his heart ached at the realization. He was consumed by shame at his behavior towards her, and not just from one but from multiple encounters. Add to that this new knowledge of what his actions had led to: her inability to bear her own children. Guilt twisted in his gut. He didn't know if he would ever forgive himself.

When he'd cradled her in his lap, wrapping his arms around her like he had done so many times as a teenager, he'd felt something shift inside him. It was as if all the animosity had just left him, replaced by something else, something he couldn't name. *Sometimes our deepest hate stems from something else entirely...*

He wasn't sure how they would cope living together but he would do what he needed to and put aside his feelings to keep her safe. Though he couldn't help but dwell on the words he discovered scrawled on her bathroom mirror. Was she saving all her kisses for someone? She made 'no kissing' one of their rules and even when he had tried to get her to kiss him, she refused. Did she not like kissing at all? He thought at the time that she was ignoring him or using the moment to snipe at him, and maybe she had. But was she also using it to avoid kissing him?

It wasn't like they hadn't kissed before. She'd been his first kiss and if he was honest that was still the best kiss of his life, though it pained him to say it, given how much experience he had since then. He still dreamt about it; that kiss haunted him. So yeah, if he got the opportunity, he could admit he would go there again. But what was the big deal? Surely she had kissed loads of guys over the last fifteen years?

He shook his head and loaded up his car with his clothes and TV then grabbed some more protein powder. He was doing a final sweep of his house, checking he wasn't forgetting anything when his phone pinged.

Taylor: Can you be at the cabin in an hour?

Beau: Sure, everything okay?

Taylor: Locksmith coming. Kayleigh's sick, can't leave.

Beau: No worries, I've got this. *Thumbs up emoji.*

He finished his final check, grabbing the last item he wanted and locked up. He headed back to the cabin and the locksmith arrived soon after. Beau positioned the new TV, putting Taylor's old one in his cabin next door. While there, he emptied the place of his belongings as it might be a while before he was back. Once the locksmith was finished and gone, Beau began to unpack the rest of his stuff.

Taylor had made some space for him in her drawers, so he put his clothes away next to hers. She had even made an effort to tidy up, which he appreciated. Once he was finished, he lingered, looking around her room. He inspected the picture collages on her walls, ran his hands over the white veneer of her dressing table, felt the soft texture of her make up brushes, the weight of her perfume bottles.

He knew he was being intense, but he just couldn't help it. He hated to admit it, but she still fascinated him like no one else. He had a burning desire to immerse himself in her life, to fill the void of all the years they'd missed. He needed to get to know her again. Eventually he snapped out of it, unpacked his toiletries and then grabbed the last thing he'd brought with him from home. He stood in her room and looked around for the best place to display it. He rearranged some of the scented candles on her dresser and slid the picture frame into place.

Riddled with anxiety over the picture frame, he watched TV until closing time at the bar when he went to fetch her. She stepped outside into the cool air, her whole body sagging, her expression one of complete exhaustion.

"Tough day?" he asked, tucking his hands into the back pockets of his jeans as she looked up.

"Uh huh."

"Was it busy?"

"Uh huh."

Okay, noted, she's too tired to talk. They walked back to the cabin in silence. When they went inside she trudged straight over to the couch, ignoring the giant TV or just not seeing it in her tiredness, and dropped down, letting the couch swallow her into its cozy cushions.

"The locksmith came, there's only two keys for this lock now. Yours and mine," he said, dangling both sets in the air.

"Uh huh," she mumbled, her mouth covered by

cushions and her eyes drifted closed. He smiled to himself. *A tired Taylor is a docile Taylor, I need to remember that.* She'd had a tough day before she even started her twelve-hour shift alone at the bar. She wouldn't have eaten properly today so he padded into her modest kitchen and rummaged through the cupboards. Her little snores soon reached him, and he smiled again, looking over his shoulder at her, her sassy mouth parted in slumber.

He found some instant mac and cheese then frowned. Her cupboards were pretty much empty except for strawberry milk powder and his protein powder, as was her fridge. She really didn't have any food in and that just wasn't going to work. He was Mr. Food Prep, no way could he live like this. He heated their dinner and set her little bistro dining table for two, clearing it of her crap first. He made her usual drink then went and shook her gently.

"Dinner's ready," he said softly, not wanting to startle her.

"It is?" Her tone was so hopeful that his chest hurt. He wondered how many proper meals she ate. It was no fun cooking just for one, he only did it because his diet required it.

Her jaw cracked with a huge yawn and she sat down at the table, rubbing sleep out of her eyes and he tried to ignore how freaking adorable she looked. He really did try, because it would do them no good if he noticed stuff like that too often.

She inhaled her food, then licked her fork clean which he forced himself to ignore. Her tongue sliding between the prongs was one of the most arousing sights he'd seen. She let out a happy sigh. "Thank you for that, I usually don't bother."

"Well, that's something you'll get out of this arrangement then: a fake boyfriend slash chef. You're very lucky." He smiled at her and she blushed. She finished her drink, her tongue darting out to catch a stray droplet in a way that had him clenching his hand on his thigh. *Jesus, stop.* It felt strange to be polite to each other, yet normal and nice. But the physical desire it was creating was hell.

He cleared his throat. "I've got some ideas for things we can do to be 'seen' together."

Trepidation lit her eyes briefly before disappearing with a flutter of her lashes. "Oh yeah?"

"We'll do your self-defense training, but I was thinking we could go for a, uh, couples run each morning?"

She made a noise like a game show buzzer and narrowed her eyes. "Taylor doesn't run."

"A jog then?"

"Nope."

"A brisk walk?"

She shook her head.

"I go for a run every day, I kind of need to and I would feel better about it if I didn't have to leave you alone then worry the whole time," he tried again.

"And I would feel better if I didn't run," she quipped, raising a cocky eyebrow that fired him up.

He clenched his hands on his thighs to keep from reaching for her and pulling her into his lap, flipping her over and bringing his palm down on her ass. How satisfying would that feel? An animalistic sound rose in his chest at the image, and he had to fight to keep it down. Man, she really did turn him into some kind of beast.

"Are you okay?" she asked, peering at him, a strange expression on her face. He cleared his throat again, his cheeks heating at his fantasy and he adjusted his jeans which were suddenly very constricting.

"Fine," he conceded. "We'll circle back to couples running. We can do some more hangouts at the bar. Justine's performing again soon so that will be a good opportunity."

She nodded. "Agreed."

Bolstered by her pleasant attitude he continued. "Me and the guys play basketball on Sundays, you could bring Christy and Justine and cheer on your boo," he teased.

"What, like your lame cheerleader?"

"Yeah, and don't pretend you didn't want to be a cheerleader when we were at school. I know your secrets, remember? I know you tried out for the squad."

"Bitches didn't let me on the team though, did they?" she sulked, and he fought a laugh at her still being wounded over the snub.

"Well look at it this way, they can all suck it because Taylor's finally getting her shot."

She smirked and then rolled her eyes. "So if I'm your personal cheerleader does that mean I get to hang with my girls *and* make fun of you?"

He nodded, momentarily distracted by the thought of her in a cheerleading uniform.

"Then yes this is acceptable," she replied.

He decided to push his luck a bit further. "Actual dates out somewhere?"

"Maybe," she shrugged.

"We can take it in turns to plan what we do. Fake relationships also need to be fifty-fifty so I'll go first then you can plan to take me somewhere nice, sweetheart. I wanna be wined and dined too."

Taylor rolled her eyes again but said nothing, so he continued. "I think we should also try to act like a couple while we're at home as well as when we're out," he said and waited for her protest. When she began, he held up his hand. "You said it yourself, he's watching us. There's a lot of windows in this cabin and it's better to be safe than sorry."

She huffed. "Fine."

"And finally, I was thinking we could go to Christy and Dean's wedding together, like as a couple. Best man, maid of honor, everyone will love it."

"Hopefully this will all be over by then, that's still a couple of months away. But if it isn't, then fine, I agree."

"Good." Negotiations complete, a strong sense of accomplishment filled his veins with a victorious high. Then an arrogant smile lifted her lips and his high dipped slightly. Uh-oh.

"Now it's my turn." Her sharp eyes pinned him in place. "*Free* self-defense lessons, beginning Friday on my day off and lasting as long as I want."

"I already said they would be fr-"

"If strangers ask you about us then confirm but politely tell them to mind their own business," she interrupted, pointing her finger at him in warning.

"Already done, Porter threatened to hurt me already."

She clasped her hand to her chest. "Really? That's so sweet of him."

Beau snorted.

"We share the bed, but you stay on your side, and I'll stay on mine."

He snorted again and rolled his eyes. These were really easy; he had been expecting much worse from her.

"And no other women while we're doing this." She smirked at him when she dropped that little bombshell.

"But this could last for months!" he cried. She shrugged, still smirking.

"Fine, no other men then," he retorted, and her smile slipped slightly.

"Not a problem."

"Likewise!"

They glared at each other across the table. "We need to do Justine's exercise," he reminded her.

She winced. "Not tonight please, I just need sleep."

"Tomorrow then," he agreed. She made a move to tidy up their plates, but he put his hand over hers, the contact zinging up his arm.

"I'll do it. Go on, get to bed," he ordered. Something odd flickered behind her eyes before she looked away.

"Okay, thanks again," she said and got up from the table and headed into the bedroom.

He was on edge while cleaning up, expecting her to come storming out from the bedroom yelling at him once she spotted the picture, and wrecking the first peaceful evening they'd shared together in nearly two decades. But she never did. He sat down at the table and made a grocery list and meal plan before he decided to go to bed.

He crept into the room, not wanting to wake her but nearly ruined it by laughing when he saw the giant pillow fort she had erected down the middle of the bed. Normally he slept in his boxers or sometimes, nothing. But with the possibility that she could wake up before him and catch a glimpse of the imperfect body he worked so hard to fix and spent so long trying to hide, he wasn't taking any chances. He kept his t-shirt on and changed into his sweatpants.

He got under the Barbie-pink quilt and settled down into the comfiest bed he'd ever been in. Her scent immediately made a beeline for his nostrils and he tried to ignore it. Soon he would be so used to it that he wouldn't notice it anymore and he hoped that day would hurry the fuck up.

He waged a war with his libido, convinced he was actually winning until he heard it. The soft moan from next to him.

Then another.

The sound punched a bolt of lust straight through him, his cock immediately reacting. She moaned again, longer this time and breathier than before.

"Sweet Jesus," he muttered, biting his lip to keep from reaching for her or himself.

She was right, this whole thing was a mistake.

*

Taylor awoke the next morning feeling fully refreshed. Yesterday was so exhausting both emotionally and physically that she was asleep as soon as her head hit the pillow and she had the best night's sleep ever. Which had nothing to do with who she was sleeping next to, not that she could see him over the pillow fort. Sitting up, she saw she was alone in bed, which was just as well because she knew that if Beau had been laying there, she would have been tempted to watch him sleep like a creeper.

Since the revelations and apologies yesterday morning, which seemed like so long ago, she felt her resentment towards him already easing. She felt lighter and a fraction—but only a fraction—less rage-filled than usual.

Then he had to go and take care of her last night, making her dinner; immediately her walls began to crumble like someone had taken a wrecking ball to them. The care he'd shown reminded her of how they had once been together, the bond they'd shared. She needed to refortify. She had built those walls for a damn good reason. She didn't want to slip back into old feelings. She could already feel the fire rekindling but she had learned from her mistakes, she knew this fire came with pain.

The bathroom door opened and he stepped out, steam billowing behind him like from a movie scene. His hair damp from his shower but annoyingly, uh, *thankfully* he was fully clothed. Most men with the kind of Adonis body that Beau had would have been walking around shirtless, all their muscles on display. So why wasn't Beau? *Why didn't he walk around shirtless, dammit!*

"Morning," she said, rubbing sleep out of her eyes.

"Morning," he grunted and turned his back, rummaging in the dresser.

She took in the rigid set of his shoulders. "Everything okay?"

"Mhm."

"Sleep well for your first night?"

He turned and faced her. "No."

"Oh really? Was the bed not comfortable? Was it the pillow fort? Maybe we don't need it?"

"No, let's keep it in place," he answered quickly and then disappeared out of the room.

What's crawled up his butt? Maybe he's not a morning person after all. She heard him filling the kettle with water. Maybe he's regretting the living arrangements. She frowned, her anger spiking. *Well, it was his bright idea, I didn't want it to happen so if he's not happy he's only himself to blame.* She lay back against her pillows, worrying. Ugh, since when did she worry about him? Her eyes swept the room before landing on the dresser. Her body jolted as she took in the new addition. She swung her legs over the side of the bed and grabbed the photo, peering down at it.

"Oh my God," she whispered, stroking a finger over the picture. It was an old photo of her and Beau on

Halloween. He'd dressed up as Chewbacca and she was Batgirl. They had their arms around each other, grinning like idiots. She remembered that night, the two of them had gone trick-or-treating together, ending up at Ruby's Diner. They had split a slice of cookie dough cheesecake while counting out their treats and swapping each other for their favorites. He liked chocolate, she liked candy, the perfect Yin and Yang.

It wasn't long after that they'd had their big fight. Taylor stilled herself for the anger that usually followed when she took this particular trip down memory lane, but it didn't come. She stared at the photo, amazed at how retro it looked. Ruby had taken it on one of those disposable cameras that Beau had taken out that night, wanting to make memories.

She heard him banging around in the kitchen and stood in her bedroom doorway, staring at his back as he measured out protein powder into a bottle.

"How long have you had this?" she asked softly.

His back stiffened and the powder spilled over the counter then he turned to face her.

"Since the day after Halloween. I got all the photos developed the next day."

"Were there more?"

"No, they were too overexposed, too blurry. That was the only one that survived."

She peered down at the photo again, stroking her finger over the image of the two of them, so happy. He kept the photo all this time? The man was tying her in knots she didn't know how to untangle. He came over to her now and tried to take the frame.

"It's stupid. I thought if Dale was peering in windows and saw it then he would realize how long we've known each other. How close we are. Were," he corrected. "I'll put it away."

"No!" she cried, keeping a firm grip on the frame. "Leave it, it was a good idea."

They stared at each other, both gripping the frame. Then he gave her a clipped nod and let go, heading back into the kitchen. She swallowed and went back into the bedroom, replacing the frame.

"I've got an early PT session; will you be okay while I'm gone?" he called. She padded back over to the doorway, watching him move around her little cabin like he'd been there forever. So natural in her space.

"Yeah, Kayleigh's still out sick so I need to head over soon and open up, maybe try and do some paperwork before the masses descend."

"Cool, I'll get us some food in as well," he said, stuffing a zip-up hoodie in his backpack and grabbing his protein shake.

"You don't need to do that," she said, feeling guilty about her lack of food. She never cooked for herself, it was too boring and depressing.

"Actually, I do," he replied, patting his stomach. His t-shirt molded obscenely to the eight-pack she could see. *Trust him to be so disciplined to have the extra two-pack.*

"Okay, well thanks then."

"I'll see you tonight, let me know if you need anything." He came over to her, brushing a very quick kiss on her cheek. So quick that the tingles barely had time to form before he was leaving.

"Lock the door behind me," he said over his shoulder and then he was gone. She did and then quickly showered and dressed, trying to make sure she left things as neat as possible, knowing she couldn't be a slob now they were living together. *Wow, me and Beau living together, who would've thought?*

Sweet Surrender

Work was crazy busy, and she decided at ten to close up. She needed food, then bed, in that order. When she stepped outside The Rusty Bucket Inn, Beau was waiting for her.

"Hey sweetheart, don't you look beautiful?" He pulled her into a hug, his warm body enveloping hers and she surprised herself by snuggling in. He was still just like hugging a bear. She used to call him her *Teddy Beau* like teddy bear, because he was so good to hug, he always made her feel safe. Did he really think she was beautiful? *No moron, he's pretending, remember?*

"You hungry?" he asked, his voice tight. He pulled back but took her hand in his, entwining their fingers. *Why is this affecting you so much today?* Her brain quizzed but didn't reply.

"Starving," she sighed.

"Dinner's on the table," he chuckled as he let them into their cabin.

This was how things went for the next week. Barely seeing each other in the day, only seeing each other when he came to take her home, then every night he made her dinner. He liked to food prep she noticed, she enjoyed seeing all the little containers in the fridge with different, colorful foods in them. He probably needed to do it when he lost weight and the habit has stuck with him. She was too tired to quiz him on it.

It was her own fault she was so tired. She had done such a good job driving customers into the bar that she hadn't spent time thinking about how to handle all the extra business. She was too tired to even be proud of how much her hard work and grind had paid off. She had accomplished something amazing as a businesswoman; now she ought to enjoy it.

She hadn't hired anyone since Kayleigh last year and

business had tripled since then. When she had gone in early this morning to do some paperwork before the crowds started pouring in, she placed a job ad. Fingers crossed she had some decent applicants. Last time the only one good enough was Kayleigh, and although she loved the girl now, training her had been *hard*.

Hopefully Kayleigh would be back in action by the time Taylor's day off came around this week. That was when she had her first self-defense session with Beau, and she was really looking forward to kicking his sexy ass.

Chapter 12

Beau didn't think he'd ever been more sexually frustrated in his life. All because of one woman. That woman was currently strutting into his gym in barely-there workout gear that displayed her long legs and all that creamy, flawless skin with the skull and butterfly tattoo he'd glimpsed before. His eyes devoured the intricate design, traveling up until it disappeared beneath her shorts, desperate to know how high it went. A muscle ticked in his jaw.

She had spent so long cock-blocking him that he honestly couldn't remember the last time he had gotten laid. Now he had to spend his nights listening to her heavy breathing and sultry moans while she slept. When he managed to ignore those unforgettable moans, he finally entered his own dreamland where he and Taylor did all sorts of deliciously dirty things together. He got the added bonus of waking up achingly hard each morning.

His self-restraint had reached new levels. Nuns would be proud of him. Fuck, he was proud. Proud that each damn night, the second she let out one of those moans, he didn't demolish that fucking pillow fort and pull her on top of him and pour all that frustration into her. That goddamn pillow fort was his new best friend, because like a true best friend, it kept him from making all kinds of stupid mistakes.

Taylor came towards him and dazzled him with a bright smile. She shocked him by bouncing onto her tiptoes and kissing him on the cheek. He felt his cheeks heating, he had to clear his throat, suddenly feeling flustered. She had always been able to do that; get under his skin and drive him insane like no one else could.

Something had occurred to him last night while he'd lain awake, picturing all the ways he could make her moan for real. When she had kissed him all those years ago, when she had made the first move, it had been because she *wanted* to. She had wanted *him*. She wanted to dump that shit-stain Bobby for him. There was a time when she could have been his and that thought had tortured him all night long.

Did she still want him? No, not with the way that she'd been behaving towards him for the entirety of their adult lives. Did he want her to want him? So much had happened between them and while they had laid their ghosts to rest, it was all still too fresh.

He wanted to try and get back some form of friendship with her, but more than that? Was it even on the table and did he want it to be? Part of him wanted to find out how she felt but the other, more sensible part of him was terrified of another rejection from her. He honestly didn't think he could take it.

"Morning!" she trilled, pulling him from his thoughts.

"Wow, someone's in a good mood," he said, folding his arms over his chest. She flashed him another one of those dazzling smiles that he hadn't been the recipient of since he was a teenager. She ran her hands up to her hair, smoothing the strands down and pulling her ponytail tighter. His eyes lingered on the elegant slope of her neck. He'd spent last night imagining trailing kisses there.

"Hell yeah, I'm in a good mood today. I get to learn how to kick some ass!" Her enthusiasm was contagious, especially when she poorly executed a few karate moves then shouted, "Hi-yah!"

He snorted. "Okay, calm down Bruce Lee, and come with me." He took her hand, tingles skating down his arm at their touch. He brushed it off. He needed to keep himself under control today, there was about to be a whole lot of touching. It wasn't appropriate or professional to get a boner and he was nothing if not professional.

He led her over to a stack of mats, past the two teenage boys he'd just been talking *Game of Thrones* fan theories with, who now stopped to gawk at this goddess walking among them. He couldn't blame them, she was electric. He gestured for her to take a seat on the mat then he sat opposite her. She folded her legs, her bare knee pressing against his and even that set off sparks inside him. He scooted back a fraction.

"Why are we sitting? This doesn't help me kick ass," she moaned, crossing her arms over her chest and pouting. The action, sticking that plump bottom lip out and pushing her breasts together, had him struggling to tear his eyes away. *Get a grip and stop ogling her tits.*

"I thought we could talk about your self-defense goals," he said, when his voice was working again.

"My goals? To kick ass, duh."

He fought the smile trying to work its way onto his lips. "I get that, but I was thinking something more specific?"

"Right, I get ya." She pondered for a moment. "Have you seen *Avengers*?"

"You're asking if the geek has seen a Marvel movie?" he asked, sarcasm his new best friend.

"So, you know that move that Scar-Jo does where she runs at that guy and wraps her thighs around his head and then flips him?"

She lost him at *wraps her thighs around his head*. His brain taking him to a very dirty, very beautiful place that had his pulse, and his groin, throbbing wildly. Images of him showing her that move over and over again but she wasn't wearing clothes and was screaming his name took up residence in his mind.

"I want you to teach me that," she said, dragging him out of the captivating new fantasy that would now live rent-free in his brain for the rest of his life.

He cleared his throat. "You want to wrap your legs around my head?" He dropped his voice flirtatiously, back to playing the role of fake boyfriend and savoring the opportunity to flirt with her intensely.

She did not enjoy it.

"Not like that," she replied, scandalized.

"Exactly like that," he smirked. She gave him a withering stare that would have confirmed exactly how she felt about him if it wasn't for the flush staining her cheeks. Was his little Princess imagining wicked things too?

"Exactly like *Avengers*. Like Black Widow, and then I

throw you to the ground," she clarified.

He groaned theatrically and bit his knuckle. "Sweetheart, you're killing me."

"Jesus Christ, are you done?" she hissed and he barked out a laugh.

"Nearly. I think that sounds a little too advanced right now given that she's a world class Russian spy. Oh, and fictional. Why don't we start with some basics?"

"Fine," she sulked.

"It'll just be for a session or two. I'll show you some of the easier, quick-to-master moves to incapacitate an attacker so you can escape. Then we'll go on to ways to break certain holds and situations where *you* can be incapacitated."

Disappointment lined her face. "So, nothing too extreme today?"

"Sorry sweetheart, but even the majorest of ass-kickers have to start somewhere."

"This is very true," she nodded wisely and this time he didn't try to fight his grin.

"Come on, let's stretch out. Then I'll show you the heel palm strike, elbow strike and a hella nasty groin kick," he said, pulling her to her feet.

"I get to kick you in the balls?" The glee on her face was too much.

"You do not get to kick me in the balls," he deadpanned, and she pouted again. "Now bend over."

The heat in her stare had him exhaling slowly to fight another wave of arousal.

"You need to stretch out, I will get absolutely zero pleasure from this, at all. I'm a complete professional," he lied.

*

Taylor's hands shook as she worked at the clasp of her necklace, trying to get the damn thing to open.

"God, get a hold of yourself," she muttered. She was getting ready for this stupid date Beau was insisting they go on. She really didn't think it was needed, they were acting like a couple everywhere they went, so this was total overkill.

Also, she was petrified.

How was she more nervous about *this* date than any other date she had ever been on? Because it was Beau and even just thinking his name had her traitorous lady parts squealing with glee.

She needed a break from him. She'd spent all day around him, being touched by him and watching that cute crease appear between his dark brows as he put his hands on her, demonstrating self-defense moves. When she wasn't focused on him touching her, she watched the way he worked. She loved seeing his passion and dedication to teaching. His enthusiasm was infectious.

When they had gotten home, she made him leave and get ready in the cabin next door. She just needed some time apart. Her mind and body taking all his gestures and compliments at face value instead of remembering he was faking it. She was getting too confused about what they were doing. He didn't mean the things he was saying, he was playing his part. But her mind and *definitely* her body acted like he meant it. She was feeling things for him that she hadn't felt since she was seventeen.

She finally managed to secure her necklace and added a pair of pearl drop earrings. Smoothing her hands over her deep green satin dress, she padded over to her dresser and spritzed some perfume on her wrists and neck. She added some more gloss to her lips then teased her hair into some form of style, the curls refusing to be tamed.

When she heard a tentative knock at the door that sent her heart rate through the roof. She left her hair alone, terrified she would make the frizzy mess even worse.

She stood upright. "Come in."

There was a brief pause before her bedroom door opened and there he was. He was dressed in a simple black sweater, black slacks and black formal shoes but despite the simplicity the overall effect was breathtaking. His dark eyes roved over her, so aggressive in his inspection that she felt as though he were stripping her naked.

"You look beautiful."

She swallowed around the lump in her throat. *Faking. It.* She reminded her brain. "So do you."

He smiled briefly and looked away. "You ready to go?"

"I just need to put my shoes on," she said and went over to the sky-high heels placed by the door. She stepped into one, wobbling slightly and he gripped her arm, steadying her so she could tighten the strap.

He opened her car door in true gentleman fashion, and they drove in a comfortable silence to the restaurant. When they arrived, he opened her door again and held her hand as they walked into the restaurant. She rarely had any chivalry from men on dates, she was lucky if they even put on clean clothes. She wasn't usually a fan of it, being too independent to enjoy people doing things for her, and she believed chivalry worked both ways, but she couldn't deny the little thrill that leapt through her whenever he took charge.

While the hostess looked for their reservation, he dipped his head to her ear. "I meant what I said earlier, you look beautiful," he murmured. Little butterflies took flight in her stomach which gave her pause. Instead of responding nicely, she decided her fake girlfriend persona was a brat.

"Am I the most beautiful woman in the room tonight?" she simpered at him. His gaze collided with hers, his eyes turning molten.

"You're the most beautiful woman in every room," he replied fiercely, his intensity stirring something inside her and she floundered for a reply. *Whelp, that shut me up.*

"This way, please." The hostess led them to their table. Beau pulled out her chair and eased it under her with finesse as she sat down. His attentiveness was definitely working its way under her skin. The specials were read to them, they ordered wine and scoured the menus then once they ordered their food they were alone.

Beau laid his arm across the table, palm up. "Give me your hand," he commanded. A thrill running through her once again, giving her pause. *Okay, alpha commands are apparently your kink now.*

"Hand-holding was on the list of acceptable behaviors. So gimme," he said. She smirked but placed her hand in his warm palm and he stroked his thumb over her knuckles.

After a moment he spoke. "I'm not sure how you're feeling, after…everything so I'm just gonna put this out there."

Her stomach dropped. *Is this it? Is he feeling all this torturous tension and tingles too?*

He took a deep breath and let it out in a puff. "You were my best friend. We fucked up and lost a lot of time together. We can't get that time back, but we have a chance now to fix this so we don't miss anymore. And I want to, Tay. I want to get back what we had. If we even can," he finished.

Disappointment flooded her. *Okay so he just wants to be*

friends, it is just you feeling all this weird energy. Wait, did she even want something more with him? No of course not, it would only lead to someone getting hurt. Then his words registered, he wanted to go back to what they had, which meant he still cared about her. After all their shit, it must have taken a lot of courage for him to admit that to her. She watched him take a long sip of his wine, his throat working as he swallowed, waiting for her to answer.

She nibbled her lip. "I'm scared we can't."

His hand tightened in hers and his eyes dipped away briefly as disappointment drew his luscious mouth downwards.

"But I want to try," she added.

His head shot up, a bright smile pulling across his lips, and it teased her own into place.

He nodded, wide smile not faltering. "In that case, what have you been up to these last million years?"

She laughed. "You know what I've been doing."

"I don't know the details though. Tell me about the bar, what made you buy it and how did you turn it into the success it is? I remember how that place was," he said, shuddering dramatically.

"It wasn't that bad!" She took a sip of wine, the flavors bouncing off her taste buds. She nearly groaned when she caught a hint of vanilla. *This is good shit, I need to find out who their supplier is and get some for the bar.*

"I had a few jobs out of school but never really knew what I wanted to do. I worked at Ruby's Diner for a bit until she got fed up with me sassing her all the time."

Beau snorted. "I don't think she could ever get fed up with you."

"You're probably right but her sass and my sass combined? We over-sassed and customers started complaining. It was her livelihood after Roger died and I didn't want to jeopardize what they had built together so I took a job as a secretary. I didn't enjoy that either, and Daddy got sicker, so I started looking after him. But I couldn't do both so I quit working." She took another, larger sip of wine.

"I felt like I was suffocating. I was so young and having to take him to the toilet, help him shower, keep him medicated and clean up after him just felt too much. Then the guilt at feeling like that about looking after him started to eat at me. One day we had a fight and I went for a real long walk and stumbled across the bar. I went inside and Bob was there, we got to talking and he mentioned he wanted to take a step back and I saw my opportunity."

Beau's eyes were fixed on her, giving her his full attention and she couldn't deny she loved having all that attention focused only on her.

"Bob hired me as a manager and I took over doing all the books and staffing, dealing with the suppliers. I spoke to Dean to learn more about the business side of things, and he offered to loan me the money."

"So we both owe our successful businesses to your brother? Damn," Beau joked.

Taylor squirmed; she didn't cope well with praise. "I wouldn't have said the bar was a success exactly."

"Are you freaking kidding me? I said I remembered how it used to be, did you not see the shudder? What you've done with that place is incredible, don't put yourself down at all. I'm proud of you, sweetheart," he gushed.

Taylor's cheeks flushed. *He's proud of me.*

The waiter interrupted them to drop off their appetizers and Taylor reluctantly removed her hand from

Beau's; she'd almost forgotten he was even holding it.

"Well, Dean gave me the help when I needed it and I've paid him back in full already," she said.

"You're amazing," he said, shaking his head in awe.

She shrugged. "Anyway, I hired a nurse to look after Daddy and she kept demanding more and more money from me. I didn't want to give in to her demands but there was no one else available to look after him and he refused to have anyone but her." Of course, now she realized what an idiot she had been back then. They ate in silence for a moment, his eyes finding hers again and again, waiting for her to finish her story.

When the waiter came back and removed their plates it felt like the most natural thing in the world for them to hold hands again, both of them reaching across for each other without a second thought.

"They ran away together. They'd been trying to get as much money out of me as possible to finance their future so they would have a nice nest egg." A wave of sadness at her only flesh and blood, *her father*, treating her in such a way distracted her.

"Assholes!" Beau spat bitterly, squeezing her hand in sympathy.

"It was the final nail in the coffin. I've never heard from them. I choose to assume they're happy somewhere. It's better than worrying about whether he's alive or not."

"I can't believe he would do that to his only daughter," Beau said. "I'm so sorry, Tay."

"It's okay," she smiled at him. "I'm not surprised, we never had a good relationship after the way he treated women and he was never Father-of-the-Year material. Anyway, now I'm not paying for his care, I've managed to save more money and I'm nearly ready to buy the other half of the bar from Bob, then she'll be all mine!" she said gleefully.

"I'm impressed, truly. But I always knew you would do well." His soft smile played at his lips before he took another sip of wine. "We should make a note of this supplier and see if we can get this in at the bar because this shit is good."

She smiled at his use of *we,* the word settling over her warmly.

"Anyway, what about your love life? You left that out of your History of Taylor 101. I mean, before now. I know how your last foray into romance ended up," he said pointedly.

Other than randomly fantasizing about climbing you like a tree, you mean? Her brain interrupted.

"Well for start, let's not call it my 'love life', you know how I feel about that and why there will never be anyone special," she said.

Beau scoffed. "You can't tell me you still don't believe in love?"

Taylor nodded as the waiter appeared and placed their main meals in front of them.

"But, how? I mean, I know what shit representation your parents were, your father really out-did himself in that area, but surely Christy and Dean changed your mind?" he asked, cutting into his steak. Taylor shook her head.

"Blake and Justine?" His eyes widened with dismay when she shook her head again.

"I'm sure they care about each other very much and believe they're in love, I just don't trust that love is enough to make people stay. I've never seen it work and it's all I've ever known."

Beau chewed, his jaw working away as he pinned her with his stare. They ate in silence, just him watching her, trying to figure her out. She didn't want him to.

"Anyway, let's talk about you, Mr. Hollywood. What have *you* been up to these last million years?"

Chapter 13

He watched intently as his thumb grazed over her delicate knuckles, thinking about what she had said. She didn't believe in love, like, at all? She had never felt it for another person? Very interesting. He knew her dad had been a cheating asshole, never settling with one woman, leaving a trailing of broken hearts and vows. But how could she not think that their friends were truly in love?

After they finished eating, they reached for each other across the table again, like they couldn't not have a connection, having missed out on it all these years. Her question broke through his thoughts.

He said, "I went to college, got my diploma, started my business and here we are."

She fixed him with a sharp look. "I see how it is. I tell you about my life but get nothing in return?"

"What do you want to know?"

"I think you left something pretty big out, a big change you had?" she said.

Embarrassment heated his cheeks and he felt his walls sliding back into place. His weight loss was a prickly topic, especially given that it was her rejection of him that spurred him into action. He had always wondered what she thought of the way he looked now but was too scared to find out.

"And what's that?" he gritted out, his palms starting to sweat.

"Why didn't you go to culinary school? I thought you wanted to be a chef?" She blinked at him innocently and he felt like an ass. He always jumped on the defensive with her, never stopping to consider what she was really saying.

He willed his body to relax. "I guess it wasn't as much of a passion as fitness turned out to be. I got work experience in a gym, trained various clients and discovered a new passion for helping people. I got investors for a gym; Dean saved the day again."

Her warm chuckle trickled over him. He continued, "And my friend Will as well. He started out as a client and when I got him in shape, he saw the potential in me. Will was already something of a celebrity so he hooked me up with a few influential people and then came Hollywood."

Taylor leaned forward, drawn deeper into their conversation. Her eyes sparkled up at him. "What made you give up all that glamor to come back to Citrus Pines?"

He laughed. "L.A. does have a dark side. A toxicity. I got my fill of it. It was getting in the way of my passion to help people. Not help people to become unhealthy by living up to unrealistic beauty standards."

She smiled softly at him again and he wanted to hold onto this moment forever, the thought surprising him.

"So, what about your love life, anyone special?" She tried to sound casual but he heard an edge creeping into her tone. An edge he wanted to explore but couldn't right now.

"Not since Tracy."

"Tracy?"

He rolled his neck, getting ready to go over a painful memory. "She was the last woman I was seeing in L.A. and one of the reasons I left. She became obsessed with her weight and her looks. She demanded I help her lose more and more weight. It became unhealthy, and when I refused, she went ballistic, accusing me of cheating on her. I tried to end it and…" he broke off, getting flashbacks of that night. He pressed his eyes shut, trying to block them out. The heat from Taylor's palm penetrated his, soothing him.

"It's okay, Beau. I'm here," she murmured gently. His eyes popped open and took in her face. So beautiful, so comforting.

He cleared his throat. "She tried to kill herself. Locked herself in the bathroom and swallowed a bunch of pills, washing them down with alcohol. I eventually broke down the door and got her to throw everything up. Then the paramedics arrived and that was that."

Her grip tightened around his. "I'm sorry that happened to you."

"I'm fine. It was Tracy who-"

"Beau, don't try to diminish the impact it had on you. Yes, it was horrible for her and I hope she's okay, but it was traumatic for you too. I'm sorry you had to go through that."

He smiled. Of course she would call him on his

bullshit. They stayed like that, just staring at each other, small smiles playing at their lips and as he took in the details of her face he felt like he was staring at her for the first time. When the bill came, he got his credit card out and Taylor didn't make a move to stop him.

He arched an eyebrow at her. "Really? You're not even going to fake offering to pay?" he teased.

"Absolutely not. You're a famous Hollywood personal trainer. You probably have *millions* stashed away."

"Famous, huh?" he grinned at her. "I guess you did follow my career a little more than you let on."

"No! I just..."

"Just what?"

"Dean's a little gossip queen, so I heard a lot," she finished. He thought for a second. Yes, she was right, Dean was a gossip queen.

He paid the bill and they got up to leave, his hand on the small of her back as they walked through the restaurant. He held the door open for her and as she walked past, he dipped his head to her ear.

"And not millions, plural. Just the one," he teased.

She gasped and fanned herself dramatically. "Why, sir. I do believe you just became a *million* times more attractive." Her Southern Belle voice drove him wild. She fluttered her lashes at him, and he laughed loudly.

He drove them back to their cabin, listening to the radio, challenging her to find the *woo* in every song, like he used to when they were teenagers. And just like she did then, she managed to pull it off every time. He pulled into the parking lot, laughing as she managed to fit one last *woo* into an extremely depressing Country song. She looked far too smug when he was forced to admit that her *woo* actually made the song better.

He opened her door to let her out and took her hand,

lacing their fingers together. As she unlocked the cabin door, his eyes did a quick sweep of the area, making sure Dale wasn't watching them or hanging around before they went inside. The moment they stepped inside the cabin, the evening's happy bubble burst, seeming to take all the air out of the room with it.

They faced each other, and he could feel the tension mounting before Taylor broke it.

"I think I'm gonna go to bed, I'm wiped from this week," she said.

But he didn't want the night to end and was so eager to spend more time with her, he couldn't get enough.

"How about we do Justine's homework?"

Trepidation skipped across her beautiful face. "I don't know, Beau. I'm really tired."

"I know Tay, but it's only five minutes."

"Okay, let's get this over with," she huffed.

They both settled on the couch but she sat right up against the arm, as far away as she could get. The whole point was they needed to be close to stare into each other's eyes.

"I don't think so, sweetheart," he said and then gripped her hips, sliding her over to him so she was practically in his lap, not that he minded one bit. She squealed and placed her hands on his shoulders to balance herself, her sweet vanilla breath huffing over his face.

"Now what?" she grumbled.

"We just stare into each other's eyes, for five minutes," he said, setting a timer on his phone.

She rolled her eyes. "And what is it meant to achieve?"

"It'll get us to develop a level of intimacy to help us seem more realistic as a couple," he said, his eyes capturing hers and refusing to let them go.

"Oh…" was all she said.

She began to talk again but he shushed her. "I think this is meant to be quiet time."

Her eyes flared, pupils dilating. He noticed her eyes were two different shades of green. The dark emerald was a thick outer ring, thick enough that it hid the lighter swirl of jade that sat inside. He hadn't noticed before but then again last time he was this close to her, her eyes had been closed and she was kissing him.

He wanted to count each of the adorable freckles sprinkled over her cheeks and nose but couldn't tear his eyes away from hers. At first it felt uncomfortable, and they both kept grinning and giggling awkwardly.

Then it happened.

Awareness trickled down his spine and his lips snapped shut. Time seemed to slow as Taylor gently pushed out the breath she had been holding and her eyes softened until her wariness melted away.

Suddenly it felt almost painful to watch her so closely. To have her see right into him with no barriers, no shield. What would she see? Her hands gripped his shoulders, her fingers plunging into his tissue, teasing his muscles and he bit back a groan. He fought to keep the passion out of his eyes, trying to hide the image of him wrapping her legs around his waist and arching his growing erection between her thighs. He thought he had succeeded until her eyes went molten, the two shades of green swirling together to form a new shade. *Lust.*

He saw it and knew he was in trouble. Desire burned its way through his veins with nowhere to go, like an addict who had his vice right before his eyes but was unable to take what he desperately needed. He wanted her, ached for her. Her tongue wet her lips, his eyes didn't move from hers but he still saw it. Seeing that pink tip darting out had his fingers tightening on her hips.

The tension between them built with each breath, reaching an agonizing crescendo just as his alarm blared, signaling that their five minutes were up. He squeezed his eyes shut, willing his legendary self-control back into his body. Their heavy breathing was the only sound in the room, filling up the space between them. He wasn't sure how long they stayed like that until he heard her dress rustling and she extricated her limbs from him.

"Great, uh, we can tick that off the list." Her voice was all husky gravel, raking over him.

"Yep, we sure can."

She leaned forward and unbuckled her shoes and he used her distraction to rearrange himself.

"Well, now that's done, I'm going to bed. It's been a long day, week, month," she joked.

"Cool, I'll be in a bit later." He grabbed the remote and flicked on the TV to try and distract himself. Taylor stood and walked towards her room, heels swinging in her grip.

She paused in the doorway. "I had a nice time with you today." Her words were sweet, hesitant. She lingered in the doorway, staring at him, her hands playing with the straps of her shoes. Her expression seemed to be asking him, *was this real?* He wanted to scream, *yes!*

He needed her to leave. He was two seconds away from launching out of his seat and shoving her against the wall, tunneling his hand under her dress and between her thighs to find out whether she was as turned on as he was. Jesus, who was he? So damn aggressive, it wasn't like him at all.

Yep, he needed her gone. "Goodnight Taylor," he said resolutely, turning back to the TV. He held his breath, waiting to see what would happen, and only let it out once he heard the bedroom door close.

"Fuck," he hissed, wiping a hand over his face.

He switched onto the channel that aired *The Great British Bake Off* around the clock, the real reason he had brought his TV in the first place. Her old TV didn't have all the good channels. Taylor was right that he had wanted to be a chef when he was younger, but now he preferred baking to cooking and this show from the U.K was pure perfection.

But even that couldn't get his mind off Taylor and their day together. After an hour he finally gave in and put the TV off. He checked the windows and doors before he went into the bedroom, praying she was asleep. He grabbed a t-shirt and sweats and changed in the bathroom like he normally did. He got into bed, his favorite pillow fort still in place, thank the Lord.

He tried not to look at her, tried to just will himself to sleep. He eventually drifted into dreams but they were short-lived.

He woke with a start, his heart pounding in his chest. Sweat drenched his t-shirt. What the hell had woken him? Then he heard one of those little moans coming from the ball of heat next to him, through the pillow fort.

"Jesus, please no. Not tonight," he begged, praying to whoever was out there to just give him a break. He couldn't cope with this tonight, his self-control was already stretched to the max. Thankfully there was silence. Relief at his answered prayer was brief when another, much louder moan hit him. His cock responded instantly, not that it had really gone down since their little stare-off.

A husky gasp from next to him had him gritting his teeth and tucking his hands under his head to keep from doing something he shouldn't. He needed to get some noise canceling headphones or some shit if this kept happening. The moans continued, increasing in volume and frequency.

"Mmm, Beau," she moaned.

His whole body jolted, going on high alert. *Holy shit, this is a game changer.* Was she having a sex dream about him? His cock throbbed in his sweatpants, begging for some attention. Attention it hadn't had for a loooong time. His hand ran down his stomach but stopped. There was no way he could do that right now, what the hell was wrong with him?

He tried to block out her moans, blowing out deep breaths, but he couldn't do it. He reached breaking point and he needed to get out of there. Needed a cold shower to calm his body down. Perfect.

He got out of bed as quietly as he could, and padded into the adjoining bathroom, closing the door softly. Once safely inside he braced his hands on the sink and took a deep breath, looking at himself in the mirror. Wild eyes stared back at him. His shirt was damp so he stripped it off and turned on the shower, not even bothering with the hot tap, he wanted it ice cold.

He tugged down his sweatpants and boxers, ignoring his hard dick. His mind replayed her moaning his name and his cock jerked at the memory.

"Stop it," he hissed to himself and stepped under the spray.

He released a string of curse words as the ice-cold water pummeled his shoulders and down his back. He ducked his head under the water, tilting his face up to the spray. The water felt like little ice picks stabbing at his face. Before long, his body adjusted to the temperature and the shock wore off. He stood there, trying to think of anything he could to try and deflate his arousal but it wasn't working.

He hung his head, giving into the inevitable. Hating himself but eager for release. He gripped his hard length, a hiss of pleasure escaping him. He fisted himself again before grabbing his shower gel and squeezing some out onto his palm before he stroked over his hard cock, slowly.

"Oh, shit," he grunted, before he began working himself in earnest. He stroked up and down, faster, then slower. Teasing himself as her moan played over and over in his mind. He imagined waking her up, talking her through what he wanted her to do to herself.

"Slide your fingers inside yourself. Deeper."

Little moans would flow from that playful mouth as her hand disappeared between her legs, doing exactly what he said.

He worked himself faster, his hand slipping and sliding over his length, bumping over his thick head. In his mind the sound of her wetness consumed him as he watched her hips arching into her hand.

"Beau, I need you Beau," she moaned in his fantasy. He gripped his balls and tugged firmly as he quickened his pace, breathing like he was running a marathon. He slid his thumb over the sensitive head, stroking the slit there.

"Touch me, Beau, please," she begged him, beautiful eyes glazed with need. He felt heat coil inside as he thrust his hips, fucking his fist. Heat raced up his spine as he came hard, biting his arm to stop from crying out with his release. He slowed his strokes, teasing the last drop from himself and watching it swirl down the drain.

He leaned against his arm, catching his breath. He was surprised he'd come so quick, just from picturing her touching herself but it had been the hottest fantasy of his life. His knees were like jelly as he finished showering and toweled off. He hadn't brought any clean clothes in with him in his hurry so he put his sweatpants on and tossed his t-shirt in the laundry hamper.

He was a little uneasy at the thought of going back in the bedroom with no t-shirt on. He didn't want her seeing his body, it wouldn't look how she thought it would. But he reasoned that he would be awake before her for his run so she wouldn't see him. He opened the door, flicking off the light and saw her lying there, so still.

Guilt at what he'd just done swamped him. She was asleep, surely she hadn't she heard him? He hadn't meant to be loud but he couldn't help it, he was too worked up to be quiet. He tiptoed over to the bed and got back in, only relaxing when he heard her soft snores.

Chapter 14

Taylor bustled around the heaving bar, restocking the fridges, collecting dirty glasses and making sure she was getting to each customer, keeping everyone happy. Anything to forget about the way her heart had stumbled in her chest last night when she and Beau had done their intimacy exercise. At first it was awkward, but then something in the air changed between them. She had seen the moment his eyes softened, gobbling up her vulnerability greedily, like he couldn't get enough. Like he liked it and wanted more, like he wanted it *all*.

She thought her cup of lust was already full to the brim, until she saw the heat in his eyes. Then that damn cup overflowed. All sorts of naughty fantasies stormed her mind. Fantasies she almost suggested they act on, too drunk on their newfound intimacy to think straight.

Clearly being around him all day yesterday had taken its toll on her sanity. In a moment of madness she had hinted, but had not been brave enough to actually say the words and offer herself to him. But she had hinted in other ways, only for him to ignore it.

Unfortunately, uh, *luckily* Beau wasn't interested in anything like that, and didn't pick up on any of her *come fuck me* vibes. So those damn vibes had followed her into her dreams. *And what delicious dreams they were*, she thought, smiling to herself. She had woken up feeling ten kinds of frustrated and alone in bed. She couldn't take matters into her own hands, so to speak, because he had gone for a run and could be back any minute and she would actually die if he caught her doing that. She had to have a cold shower to calm herself down.

So here she was at work, trying not to think about the fact that she had the best date of her life and it was with someone who was only *pretending* to be her boyfriend. Except it didn't feel like pretend to her. Not when they talked, not when they comforted each other, not when they joked around, and certainly not when they gazed into each other's eyes. She couldn't help but want him, and now she was more confused than ever. But they were finally getting their relationship, their *friendship* back on track, so did she really want her stupid hormones messing that up? The problem was she had wanted him since she was a teenager, and she didn't think she could ever stop wanting him.

"Evening, sweetheart."

His voice had butterflies taking flight in her stomach. She tried to shove her happiness down.

"You're early," she said, looking at him over the bar. His warm brown eyes sparkled down at her, his mouth tilted up on one side in amusement. He folded his arms over his wide chest. A chest she still hadn't seen bare and was dying to. She hadn't managed to catch him shirtless yet, even after showering or getting dressed, she always caught him fully clothed. All her previous partners had paraded around shirtless and the one time she was desperate to see a bare chest, he had the audacity to keep it covered up. *Why won't he let me see it, for fuck's sake!*

"I missed you too much," he said, penetrating her thirsty thoughts.

Tenderness flared in her before she realized once again, he was just playing the part of the doting boyfriend. He did it too damn well. Taylor was saved a response when Justine and Blake joined them. When Blake left to set up her guitar, Justine turned to them, her honey eyes bouncing back and forth between them.

"Did you do your homework?"

"Yes, we did it last night," Taylor replied.

"And? How did it feel?"

There was a heavy pause that Taylor sure as shit wasn't going to fill.

"Very...uh...intimate," Beau said, rubbing the back of his neck.

Taylor's eyes caught on his bulging bicep, her mouth running dry.

"Perfect," Justine purred in her husky voice. "We shall see tonight how well it worked."

Beau raised an eyebrow at Taylor but she turned to grab a water and began getting a beer for him, a whiskey for Blake and a mocktail for Justine.

"I've not heard a peep from your *fan*, have either of you seen anything?" Blake asked when he joined them again.

"Nope, thank God. And Taylor's started self-defense lessons now too," Beau said.

She slid the whiskey to Blake who caught it with a slight smile.

"You kick him in the balls yet?" Blake asked her.

"No, he won't let me," she pouted, leaning on the bar.

"Dude, she needs to practice an effective kick to the balls, stop being a bitch-baby," Blake scoffed.

"By all means, Big Daddy, you first." Beau fixed him with a facetious smile.

"Don't you dare!" Justine growled and Blake laughed, kissing her scowling face before leading her to a table. Taylor snickered as Justine glared at Beau over her shoulder, muttering under her breath in Spanish, calling him a *puta* and threatening his appendage. More customers came up to the bar, so Beau followed Blake and Justine and left Taylor to serve them.

The crowd got busier, but thankfully Kayleigh arrived to help out. After a while Taylor looked over to Beau's table and saw Christy and Dean had joined them. She watched Beau and Dean talking. The way Beau threw back his head when he laughed had her smiling and her insides clenched as he caught her eye and blew her a kiss. Blushing, she turned back to pulling pints.

Later that night, she leaned against the bar, listening to Justine singing a slow love song and watching couples swaying romantically on the dancefloor. She spotted Beau standing off to one side, watching her with a heat in his eyes that bordered on dangerous. How could he fake it so easily? Her breath hitched as he headed over.

"Come on sweetheart, it's our turn."

Before her brain could process his words, her feet were moving and she was standing in front of him. His hand held hers, his arm wrapping around her waist and his masculine scent fogging her senses. She burrowed closer, knowing that later she would regret not putting some distance between them but struggling right now to care.

"I meant what I said earlier. I missed you," he murmured, his timbre causing a shiver to roll through her. She didn't say anything, didn't trust herself to speak. Justine slipped into a slow, sultry cover of *Addicted to Love*, her husky voice filling the room, demanding to be heard.

"I've been thinking," Beau began.

She leaned back to look at him, a sarcastic quip locked and loaded, ready to push them back to their old ways but the look in his eyes wouldn't let her.

"About the incident that pushed us apart. Something finally occurred to me. You weren't using me."

"Duh," she interrupted.

"You actually *liked* me," he said.

Ah. She had been hoping he wouldn't pick up on that. Heat flooded her cheeks and when she didn't respond he prompted her.

"Yes, fine. Okay, I liked you," she sighed.

"Interesting development..." he rumbled.

They continued to sway and when he didn't elaborate any further, tension rolled in thick and fast. It was too hot in this place, she wanted to escape to get some air.

He bent his head to her ear. "I still think about our kiss."

Her eyes flared and her stomach completed a series of somersaults and she tried to get her rampaging pulse under control. *Shit, he did?* He pulled back and she quickly smoothed her expression. He tucked a strand of hair behind her ear, his touch lingering.

"I've been thinking about something else too," he said.

Like how amazing it would be if we went back to the cabin and didn't leave my bed for forty-eight hours? Yeah, me too...

"What's the deal with you and not kissing?" he asked,

his voice slightly breathless. *Or not.*

She didn't answer, couldn't get her tongue to work properly to respond and she saw defeat settle in his eyes.

He said, "Don't worry about my favor. I didn't realize you would be afraid to kiss me so let's just drop it."

Her pride rankled, hard. "I'm not *afraid* to kiss you!"

"Tell your sweaty palms that."

"I'm not afraid and I don't back down when I owe someone something. Taylor doesn't owe anyone shit so if that's what you want then that's what you get!"

"I'm just teasing you, sweetheart," he spoke softly, trying to calm her rage.

"No, if that's what you want then come on let's do it now," she challenged. Too late did she see the flare of satisfaction in his eyes. He pulled her closer, his mouth against her ear again.

"Fine, we'll stick with it. But don't forget sweetheart, you have to *beg* me for it."

She swallowed her groan and buried her face in his sweater to stop from doing exactly what he wanted. *God, what's wrong with me?*

Beau swayed them back and forth, slowly, intimately. He let go of the hand he was holding and wrapped both his arms around her, pulling her flush against him, her body melting into his. His palm rubbed up and down her back, then into her hair. His thumb caressed the nape of her neck and her eyelids fluttered closed. The whole bar disappeared and there was no one but her and Beau, swaying to the beat of the music.

He nuzzled into her neck, drawing her hair away from her shoulder. His mouth pressed to her sensitive skin, in that place where her neck met her shoulder. His soft lips closed together agonizingly slowly and a current shot through her entire body. Her breath whooshed out of her and he gripped her tighter, pulling her hard against him, impossibly closer as he repeated the kiss. This time a moan slipped from her lips as she felt the barest flick of his tongue over her hot, damp skin. She was on fire, burning from the inside out as flames of desire devoured her. Desire more intense than she'd ever felt before.

She was shaking, moaning softly, ready to beg. Ready to beg for that kiss she owed him. That she secretly wanted to give but couldn't admit. His tongue swirled against her skin, his teeth nibbling gently and she wondered what it would feel like between her legs.

The sound of applause broke through the lust haze he had wrapped her in, just from kissing her neck. She leapt away from him and he raked a shaky hand through his thick, chocolate hair then down over his face and across his swollen mouth. His eyes blazed with arousal, telling her everything his kiss just had. *I want you.*

"I'm, uh-" she began, not having an end to her sentence.

"Tay, I-"

"Excuse me," she interrupted. She needed air. Now. She headed for the door but was stopped by his grip on her upper arm.

"Tay, we should talk."

"No!" she shoved him off. She grabbed the door handle, pulling it open but he batted it closed, forcefully, his body pressing in behind her. Why wouldn't he let her escape, she didn't want to be around him right now. She whirled on him but he held up a hand.

"I don't want to be that toxic-masculinity guy, but I need to know if you're going somewhere," he said.

"I don't answer to you," she hissed.

"You don't, but it's not safe for you right now and I don't want to leave you alone."

"You can see I'm right here and perfectly safe!" she snapped.

"Goddammit Taylor! When you get snippy like this it makes me just want to-" He cut himself off, rolling his lips inwards and looking away.

"You just want to *what*, tough guy?" she sassed. He looked away, refusing to meet her defiant gaze. "Come on big man, you just wanna what?" she goaded.

His eyes flicked to hers, hot and hard.

"Spank you."

*

Fuck what was he saying? He shouldn't have said that, this wasn't like him at all. He couldn't deny it was the truth though. He had way too many fantasies lately about his palm slapping her bare ass. Every snide, cheeky comment, every insolent look had his palm twitching, itching to dole out a sexy punishment. His every primal instinct screaming at him that she would enjoy it just as much as him.

"Sp...spank me?" she stuttered. He saw her delicate throat bob as she swallowed hard. Her voice quivered but her eyes gave her away. They screamed *do it* at him so defiantly, so loudly and the semi he'd been sporting upgraded to a full hard-on.

"You wouldn't dare." She was provoking him. Laying down a challenge she didn't think he would accept. He knew she loved pushing his buttons. She got off on driving him crazy and shoving him to breaking point but he wouldn't back down this time, not when her eyes were begging him to do it. He was determined, stubborn as fuck and wanted her any damn way he could get her. He took a step towards her, closing the distance and tilted his head down, putting them nose to nose.

"Wanna bet?"

She didn't flinch, just stared back at him, not giving an inch. He'd given her an out and she wasn't taking it. His jaw clenched hard. God, she drove him insane.

"Get in your office," he growled.

She didn't move but her eyes didn't lose that sparkle, that need that was calling to him.

"Now."

Her eyes flashed at him but she shocked the hell out of him by strutting into her office. Well, shit. He made his bed, and he couldn't wait to lie in it.

He went after her, anticipation firing his blood. Once inside, he closed the door and turned the lock, the sound of the tumbler clicking into place echoing around the room. He turned to her, his heart pounding in his chest. She stood there, wide-eyed, shifting her feet and nibbling on her lip, a mixture of nervous anticipation.

He walked over to her messy desk with the lamp on it the only light in the room. His movements slow, dragging it out as a power play. He pulled out the wooden chair and hauled it into the middle of the room before settling himself onto it. He rolled up the sleeves of his sweater, flicking his eyes to her, watching him. Her eyes widening as they caught on his forearms.

"Lay yourself across my lap. Ass up." When she hesitated he dropped his voice. "Now, sweetheart."

Her breath faltered and he nearly moaned at the heat in her eyes. She definitely responded well to this dominant, commanding side of him. She bent down and lay herself across his lap, ass up like a good girl. Her compliance sent another wave of arousal shooting through his veins like a drug, giving him the most intense high. To have his feisty Princess become putty in his hands, to dominate her and have her *let* him was a rush like no other. Because she was choosing to let him do it, trusting him. To have this hard, strong woman surrender to him, that was sweetest of all.

He flipped up her dress and stilled his hand when he saw her round, white lace panties-covered ass. *Of course she's wearing white lace,* his brain short-circuited as another wave of desire plowed through his body.

He pulled her panties down and stared, torn between wanting to spank her, nibble her cheeks and just sink inside her until she clenched and quivered around him.

"Beau…" she began, a nervous edge in her voice. The magnitude of what was happening wasn't lost on him. He didn't want to rush anything though. He wanted to savor and he couldn't help but feel this moment was long overdue.

She shifted like she was going to get up so he palmed her ass and squeezed, *hard*. Her breath hitched and she stilled. He squeezed her other cheek before sliding his finger down the seam between them. Another hitch of her breath had him smiling, especially when she raised her ass ever so slightly into his touch.

He slid over that seam once more and followed it under to her damp slit and she moaned, gripping his thigh. Her moan was the perfect sound, the one he had been dying to hear. She tried to twist her lower body, to get him to touch the heart of her, where she wanted him so he removed his hand.

"No, that's a bad girl. You know what happens to bad girls, Taylor?" His voice rasped from him, deep and guttural. These words, surely they were not coming from him?

"What?" she asked breathlessly.

He waited, silent. Then lifted his palm and brought it down hard.

Crack.

She groaned and a curse slipped from her lips.

Oh fuck. He shouldn't have started this, it was a mistake, he could see that now. How was he ever going to look at her again and *not* remember that groan? The sound alone was nearly enough to finish him off. He brought his palm down again, squeezing her cheek as he did to take the sting out of it. She tried to raise her ass into it again and started writhing in his lap.

"Beau, please," she breathed.

"What did I say?"

He watched her clamp her lips shut then spanked her again. And again. And again. Her moans the soundtrack of this monumental moment. It felt so right to be doing this with her. So natural and he was astounded.

He spanked her one last time and she moaned so loud he was sure they could hear her out in the bar. He needed to end this before it went any further between them. Needed to end it now while it could just be some power play that got out of hand and that would be forgotten in time and not a bewildering sexual encounter that they never mentioned again but was always in the background. Like someone waiting to butt into a conversation, it would mar their friendship, no best to end it now. He pulled her panties back up and flipped her dress down, patting her ass.

"Now get back out to the bar and stay where I can see you. No more running off alone."

She stood on shaky legs, her face flushed and her lower lip swollen from being nibbled on. She didn't make a move to leave and every second she stared at him, his control frayed a little more. *Control? Ha, what control?* He just fucking spanked her in her own damn office.

"Taylor, get back out to the bar, now."

If she didn't go he was likely to flip that dress up again

and pound inside her slick heat. Thankfully, she snapped out of her spell and moved towards the door, unlocking it before heading back out to the bar.

Beau stayed put, trying to get his fierce arousal under control. God, she brought out such a crazy side of him. He needed to wait until the tent in his pants went down but he didn't think it would go anywhere soon. He wouldn't be fully satisfied until she was under him, begging for him to make her scream.

Chapter 15

Pay attention, pay attention, pay attention! Taylor's mind chanted but she just couldn't. She was too busy thinking about what the hell just happened. Her body still humming and pulsing with needs that had been left unmet. Her ass still stinging slightly and she was shocked at how much that was turning her on.

Beau *spanked* her.

Beau.

Spanked.

Her.

And it had been the hottest thing any man had ever done to her. Who would've thought that the *gentleman extraordinaire* liked to get down, dirty and dominant? Taylor hadn't thought he was serious when he said he wanted to spank her. She thought he was trying to shock her and never for a moment thought he would go through with it. But the second they were in her office, when he dragged the chair across the floor and sat down on it, rolling his shirtsleeves up like he had all the time in the world, she was a goner. She was suddenly very excited about being spanked.

She wanted more, wanted to push his buttons and see what else he had to give her. She could tell he was holding back and she wanted to push him, to make him snap whatever restraint he had and unleash.

She snapped out of her daze when the door to her office creaked open and time slowed down as Beau sauntered out and joined Dean and Blake like nothing had happened. Like he hadn't just shaken her world to its core.

His eyes met hers, all that hot intensity hitting her as he rolled down the sleeves of his sweatshirt, covering those mouth-watering forearms. He arched an eyebrow at her as he did it, a small smirk playing at his lush lips like he knew exactly how close to coming she had been as she lay across his lap and he relished refusing to let her fall. She nearly started panting. She just needed two minutes alone with him and then she would–

"Earth to Taylor!" Christy waved her hand in front of Taylor's face, drawing her attention away from Beau.

"Yeah?" Taylor replied.

Christy and Justine exchanged a knowing look. "Everything okay?"

"Yes! Great set, Justine, as always!" Taylor shouted. *Jesus woman, try to control the volume of your voice and pull yourself together.*

"Oh yeah? What was your favorite song?" Justine asked, smirking at her.

"Uh…"

"I think she was a little busy," Christy hissed loudly.

"What do you mean?" Taylor's eyes widened.

"Are you really gonna act like we didn't see you and Beau sneak off to your office?" Christy said. Justine snickered as Taylor's cheeks grew warm.

"Shit, our girl's blushing. What did he do to you in there?" Christy asked, leaning closer.

"Nothing!"

"Bullshit, don't lie to me, *mamacita*," Justine said.

Taylor's eyes flicked back to Beau, watching him talking to the guys like he was a perfectly normal human male who didn't secretly enjoy spanking women. She suddenly wondered if he had done it to other women and rage at the thought consumed her. She realized she had no idea and she suddenly felt like she didn't know him at all.

"I-" Taylor cut herself off.

"Please tell us, you know all our secrets!" Christy cried.

Taylor sighed then leaned forward so no one else could hear them. "He…spanked me," she murmured.

Christy whooped so loudly that nearly every eye in the bar turned towards them.

"I guess that intimacy homework really worked. I'm such an awesome psychologist!" Justine high-fived herself.

Taylor tugged both the women away and into a quiet corner of the bar to discuss. "This isn't funny," she hissed.

"It's fantastic is what it is! And I totally get it, we've dabbled in spanking before," Christy said.

"You have? No fair, Blake's never spanked me," Justine whined.

"Oh no, I'm the spanker, not the spankee," Christy winked.

Taylor groaned. "Now I need a time machine so I can go back and *not* have this conversation where I learned that my stepbrother likes to be spanked. Thank you very fucking much. Ugh, I'm gonna hurl."

"At least you know it runs in the family," Christy laughed.

"You're sick."

"Ladies, pay attention!" Justine clapped. "Why won't Blake spank me?"

"Probably because it's kinda wrong to hit a pregnant woman?" Christy offered, patting Justine's still flat stomach. Then she grabbed hold of Taylor's hand and squeezed. "So, what does this mean?"

"I don't know," Taylor answered truthfully.

"Do you want it to mean something?" Justine asked.

"I don't know. We used to be so close but we've spent the last bazillion years hating each other. We agreed we would try to get back what we had but, I guess I've always had a little thing for him," Taylor nibbled her lip nervously.

"No way," and "Get out," they deadpanned.

Taylor rolled her eyes at them.

"Look, yes you and Beau have had a lot of turmoil between you but that's in the past now," Justine began.

Taylor saw Christy shoot Justine a confused look and knew she would at some point have to fill Christy in on their history. "Maybe this whole fake boyfriend and girlfriend thing is a blessing in disguise? It can give you the opportunity you lost all those years ago to explore what you could be. So, my advice, *chula*? *Explorar*."

"What if he doesn't want to explore?"

They cackled. "Darlin', if he's spanking you, he *definitely* wants to explore, trust me."

Blake appeared at Justine's side, holding her guitar

case. "You ready to go, honey?" he asked, kissing Justine's forehead with a tenderness that Taylor felt in her soul.

"Blakey, why won't you spank me?" Justine whined.

Blake leveled a look at Taylor and Christy before pinching the bridge of his nose. "Thank you so much for that, ladies," he sighed, leading Justine away, promising that as soon as their baby arrived safe and sound he would spank her to her heart's content. Taylor and Christy were still laughing as Dean and Beau joined them.

"Can I grab you for a minute, Christy?" Beau asked, wrapping an arm around her shoulders, and leading her away.

"Come here, sis," Dean said.

"Step-sis," Taylor clarified as he pulled her into a big bear hug

"Still my sis," he said. "I've missed you, we still on for dinner next week?"

She and Dean had regular dinner dates together. It was a little tradition the two of them had and it meant the world to her. He might not be related by blood, but he was her only family left and their bond was stronger than ever.

"Yep, looking forward to it," she smiled up at him.

"Me too."

He went to pull away but she wouldn't let him just yet. "What are we having?"

"Whatever you want," he said, ruffling her hair.

"Yay, that's my favorite," she replied, shoving him off and he laughed, his dimples flashing and she tried to poke them while he fended her off.

"Listen, I've been wanting to ask you something," he began, shifting his feet and not meeting her eyes.

"Why am I suddenly worried?" she joked.

"I wanted to see if you would give a speech at our wedding?"

If Taylor had been drinking she would have spat it out. Her give a speech? About *love?* She would literally be the last person to ask.

"You're the person who loves us both the most and you've been there for our journey. You're my family and it would mean the world to me." Dean said. *Well shit, how can I say no now?*

"Of course, I will. I'm honored you've asked me," she replied, pulling him into another hug but when they parted, her stomach was in knots. *What the fuck am I going to write?* Christy and Beau returned. Christy's grin was wider than it had been all night.

"What's got you smiling so much?" Dean asked, tucking her into his side where she slotted in perfectly.

"You," Christy replied.

Normally Taylor would have rolled her eyes and shouted "Gag!" at their lameness but instead she watched the interaction, taking in the detail of their faces as they looked at each other.

"How long until you close up?" Beau interrupted her thoughts.

"Half an hour."

"I'll wait here until you're done and then we can go home."

Anticipation had her stomach clenching sharply at his words. When they got home would they finish what they'd started? God she really hoped so.

Christy and Dean left and her last few customers trickled out. She was glad she hadn't had to take many car keys tonight. She cashed up the register and put the money in the safe in her office, ignoring the chair in the middle of the room and the memories of what happened.

Beau collected up the glasses and stacked the dishwasher for her.

"Thank you," she said shyly. He smiled in return and then they were at the door locking up. He took her hand, his warm palm covering hers and gripping tightly. Her step faltered as she thought about the way his palm had gripped her ass. She was so on edge, what would happen when they got home?

The walk back to the cabin was short but also the longest walk of Taylor's life. She fumbled the key in the lock, her hands shaking from anticipation.

"You need some help?"

"No, I got it. New locks, amiright?" she said, trying to laugh off her nervousness while mentally scolding herself. She went inside, flicking the lights on and Beau came in behind her, shutting the door and locking it. She turned to face him, expectant. Eager to see if they would pick up where they left off. If he gave her any sign, she would throw caution into the wind and go for it. Surely after the moment in her office he wanted this as much as her?

He clapped his hands, rubbing them together and fixed her with a bright smile. "Well, I'm gonna head to bed. I've got an early PT session, goodnight." He headed into the bedroom and closed the door without a backwards glance. She stood there, flabbergasted, her mouth opening and closing like a fish.

What. The. Fuck?

Was he serious? She paced the kitchen for ten minutes. Their date night had changed things between them. Her nerves had been charged all night watching him, wanting him. Her hormones were all over the place, and the heat in the air between them couldn't be denied. She was terrified she would lose control and throw herself at him, giving him everything she could but would that wreck their relationship? She didn't think she could handle that again. *Unless he gave you everything right back…*

What should she do? She had been attracted to him for most of her life no matter how hard she fought it, was this her one opportunity to have him and get him out of her system? If she went in there and something happened, then they were crossing a line. Their relationship was complicated, but they were in a good place right now, could she take that risk? She wasn't looking for anything serious and how could this not change things between them?

Maybe he was just messing with her, waiting for her in bed even now. Decision made, she headed for the door, opening it a crack. A shaft of light from the living-room illuminating her dark bedroom. Beau was in bed, on his back, already snoring softly. Definitely not waiting for her to come in and finish what they started.

That motherfucker!

*

"How late does he want to keep her out?" Beau grumbled, checking his watch for the thousandth time. It was barely ten. He tried to forget about Dean and Taylor and focus on the episode of *GBBO*, groaning as yet another contestant produced a cake with a soggy bottom. Could no one bake properly? He hadn't done any baking in forever, maybe he should try that to take his mind off things.

It had been a week since the moment he lost control and had his little foray into spanking and he had barely seen her since. Although Kayleigh was back at the bar, Taylor seemed to be spending a lot more time there. He was busy at the gym so they had only been together a few minutes each day.

Sweet Surrender

Things were strained between them. He knew he shouldn't have taken things as far as he did but he couldn't help himself. There was so much built-up tension and frustration, and he was almost certain she had enjoyed the moment. Now he was stuck in this stalemate of wanting to make a move and see if she reciprocated but also being too scared to make it. He wasn't sure if it was worth potentially ruining everything they were rebuilding. So, he hadn't made a move and tension just continued to simmer, suffocating them both.

"Come on, Bethany, you should know not to attempt spun-sugar decorations this early in the competition!" he shouted at the TV. He heard Taylor's key in the door and quickly switched channels, not wanting her to catch him watching a baking show like an old biddy; she would definitely have something to say about it. She came in, waving goodbye to Dean who had dropped her off after their dinner date as agreed.

"Good news, *Teddy Beau*. We've got a barbecue next week at Dean's to celebrate their-" She started but her voice faded away when she turned and looked at him. Her mouth dropped open.

"What the hell are those?" she demanded, a slight growl in her tone. Her anger surprising him and *shock* turning him on.

"What are you talking about? What's what?"

She stomped towards him, whipping her arm out and jabbing an accusatory finger at his face. "What are those on your *face*?"

"What? Oh, my glasses?"

She nodded vehemently. He pulled them off, studying the thick square black frames.

"When did you start wearing those?" she spat.

He shrugged and pushed the frames back up his nose.

"I've always worn them?"

She snorted, her nostrils flaring angrily. "I've never seen them!"

"I wear contacts?"

"Unfuckingbelievable," she muttered.

He stood up and came towards her. "Is everything okay?"

"Oh God, what are *those*?" she gasped.

"I'm wearing sweatpants. Taylor, what's going on with you?"

"Gray sweatpants?" She shook her head.

"Why are we playing twenty questions?" he asked.

She laughed, the sound hollow. "I know what you're doing buddy, and I'm not going to fall for it!"

He reached for her but she darted out of the way.

"No, I'm not gonna be the one to give in, that's for damn sure!" she shouted and stomped away from him and into the bedroom. Mumbling something about *damn Clark Kent* before slamming the door shut.

"Give in?" he muttered. "What the hell just happened?" He shook his head and then began his food prep for the next day. When he'd filled up his various containers and packed his gym bag he sat back on the couch. He glanced at the closed bedroom door and shook his head. Sometimes he thought he knew her and other times he had no idea what was going on in her head.

She never finished her sentence, but her mention of Dean reminded him of something he had been meaning to do. He took out his phone and created a new group chat:

Beau added Dean, Blake and Will to Boy's Night.
Beau: 'Sup, ladies?
Dean: Boy's Night, is that for me?
Will: Is this bachelor party chat? Fuck yes!

Sweet Surrender

Dean changed the group name to Dean's Bachelor Shenanigans.

Beau: Shenanigans? Really, bro?

Blake: Don't masculinity-shame him.

Beau: Dude, you've been reading too many of Justine's Psychology for Douches textbooks.

Blake: *Middle finger emoji.*

Will: *Laughing crying face emoji.*

Beau: And yes, this is for bachelor party info. This is the info: It's at The Apple and Duck in two weeks, be there by eight.

Will: I'll have my assistant update my calendar.

Beau: *Thumbs up emoji.*

Blake: @Will, looking forward to meeting you man.

Will: Ditto. Also, is there an airfield nearby?

Beau: The fuck?

Dean: Dude, you're so extra.

Will: Am I extra, or are you just #basic? Never mind, my assistant already found it. I'm booked in to land.

Beau: There, that's all the info so let's talk about something else.

Dean changed the group name to Basketball Badasses.

Dean: Yo, how come we've never done a group chat before, this is sick!

Blake: Because we're not teenage girls?

Will: Yeah, what he said.

Blake: I can tell we're gonna be good friends Will, once I've done a full background check of course.

Blake changed the group name to Four Men And A Little Lady.

Blake changed the group picture.

Will: Who's the fox? *Laughing crying emoji.*

Blake: This is Penny, my fur baby.

Dean: *Eyeroll emoji.*
Will: Cute, I love animals.
Blake: Aaand now we're besties.
Beau: WTF? Did you guys trade in your balls and testosterone?
Blake: Don't bring your toxic-masculinity shit into this group.
Dean: Yep, definitely reading Justine's textbooks, he wouldn't have learned that big word on his own. *Laughing emoji.*
Blake sent a picture.
Dean: Is that you and Penny cuddling?
Blake: Yep, masculine as fuck, dickhead.
Will: This was fun but I gotta run, filming just started again. Catch up later. *Waving emoji.*
Blake: Me too, pregnancy hormones just kicked in, the hella good ones if you catch my drift. *Winking emoji.*
Beau: Gross.
Dean: I am also required by my lady, don't wait up, haaaa!
Beau: You're all douchebags.

Beau chuckled and dropped his phone down on the couch, sighing. As if he'd been ditched for their women. Well, not Will, he would always stay single but the other two were big fat Judases. His eyes flicked towards the bedroom door again.

Man, he missed Taylor this week. They'd gone from hardly speaking to each other to living together and seeing each other every day. She had settled back into his life so seamlessly it was like they were never apart. Now he was back to hardly seeing her, it didn't feel right.

He was looking forward to their next self-defense lesson, where he could finally get his hands back on her, uh, spend time with her. *Just have to get through a few more days* he thought, getting up and heading to bed.

But why was she so mad at him earlier? Just because she didn't know he wore glasses? And because she'd caught him slobbing around in his sweatpants? He shook his head, not attempting to try and work her out. He opened the door and saw she was asleep so quietly got changed and slipped under the sheets. *Is the pillow fort larger than normal tonight?*

Taylor's soft moan echoed around the room.

Here we go again.

Chapter 16

"Oh, I see how it's going to be," Taylor muttered under her breath as she stalked into Beau's gym and spotted him. Wearing his glasses. The square black frames perched on the end of his nose like that wasn't the sexiest damn thing she'd seen *ever*. No, wait, if he took them off and cleaned them with the hem of his t-shirt. Oh mama, *that* would be the hottest thing she'd ever seen. God, when did she get such a thing for nerds? Trick question. She'd always had a thing for *him*.

She had no idea he wore glasses, had never seen him in them before and had been totally unprepared. Her knees had gone so weak she could barely walk. To say she reacted calmly would be an absolute lie. Her horror had only increased when he stood up and she noticed the gray sweatpants that clung to his muscular thighs and left very little to her imagination. And boy had her imagination run wild after seeing the bulge he was hiding in his stupid jeans all the time.

But she wouldn't give in. Wouldn't make the first move, *hell naw*.

He acted all innocent but he knew exactly what he was doing. He was a sly fox, but she wouldn't let him win. She just hoped she could keep it together today when they were getting handsy.

"You're late," he frowned at her over the top of said glasses, that little crease forming between his brows. Her knees nearly gave out. *For fuck's sake, this is war!*

"Hello my love. How nice to see you," she simpered, then lowered her voice to a husky drawl. "I've missed you." She pressed herself against him. The elderly ladies around the gym all turned and glared at her as she dared put her hands on their beloved personal trainer. She patted his ass trying not to notice how firm it was, and he frowned down at her again. She squeezed hard and he jumped.

"Really?" he croaked.

"Just gotta make sure these ladies know who you belong to," she said.

His eyelids dipped seductively. "You could always just kiss me?" She pursed her lips at the reminder, and he chuckled. "That's what I thought."

"Do I get to kick you in the balls today?" she asked, her smile all spite.

"No. I'm going to show you how to flip an attacker over your shoulder," he said.

"Oh, goody. Come at me, bro!" She smacked her hands against her chest aggressively.

His frown slithered back into place. "Yes, that's the whole point? I'm going to."

Okay, take it down a notch. She followed him over to the mat, her eyes glued to his glutes. Then stood facing him as he explained what they would be doing. Her eyes lingered over his tanned biceps as they flexed with each gesture.

"Huh?" she said when she realized he'd stopped talking.

"Try and focus, sweetheart." He gave her a knowing smirk and her cheeks flamed. He grabbed her arms and spun her around, pulling her against him so her back came up against his solid chest. His arms and heat wrapped around her, making her feel small and delicate for the first time ever. Desire ricocheted through her.

"So, first we'll try and get you used to escaping from a bear-hug hold and then progress to you throwing me over your shoulder," he said, his hands settling at her hips.

"I'm going to throw you over my shoulder?"

"Yep. Why?"

"But you're just so…big?"

His stubble rasped over her cheek as he spoke into her ear, amusement lightening his tone. "Sweetheart, that's never been a complaint before." Her vision swam as images of him in those sweatpants flooded her mind, her mouth running dry. *Ain't that the truth.*

"Grow up," she scoffed and was treated to another of those dark chuckles. She tried to pull away, but he snapped her back against him. His aggression sparking pleasure like lightning in her veins, and she bit back a moan at memories of the last time she'd witnessed that controlled aggression.

"Now then. What you want to do when someone comes up behind you and grabs you is, first, don't panic. That may be difficult, it may feel hard, but you can get out of the hold. So, bend forward at the waist," he said, and his palm settled against her back and he pressed her forward. This proceeded to push her ass back into his groin and she thought she heard a muffled curse over her shoulder.

This could get very interesting, the devil on her shoulder chipped in. She wiggled her hips slightly and he gripped her firmly, holding her still.

"Everything okay?" she asked innocently.

"Of course, why wouldn't it be?" His voice was all hard edges and gravel. He cleared his throat, "This stance makes it harder for your attacker to get a good grip on you to pick you up," he said.

She tried to straighten up but his firm hand on her back kept her in place and another of those little thrills shot through her at the way he dictated her movements. He leaned forward and wrapped his arms back around her, speaking right into her ear.

"From here it gives you a better angle to get your arms free and use either your hands or elbows, preferably elbows, to attack. Let's try it a few times." He released her, taking all his warmth with him.

He attacked her again and again, surprising her with his strength, and each time she had to try to break free. After an hour she held up her hand for a break and he took pity on her, grabbing her a bottle of water from a mini fridge. She drank it greedily then rubbed it all over her face and neck, trying to cool down. Her eyes flicked to him; the bastard wasn't even winded. She watched his eyes track a drop of water as she felt it slide down her neck and into the top of her sports bra.

She smirked when he realized she had caught him. "Something I can help you with?"

"Let's go again," he growled. He demonstrated how to throw him over her shoulder and she tried but he barely moved. She wasn't convinced she was strong enough to do it. She grunted in frustration when she failed again.

"Gah! Aren't you even going to try and go easy on me? Because ya know, I'm a weak little lady?"

"Nope, there's nothing weak about you at all, Taylor."

Pride suffused her at his words, renewing her energy and she tried to use the feeling to motivate her muscles but it didn't work. "I can't!" she whined as she collapsed on the mat in exhaustion, throwing an arm over her face dramatically, giving into her theatrics now they were alone in the gym. The sun had set during their sparring, and now it was just the two of them.

"You can, Tay," he said, grabbing her flailing arm and heaving her up. He spun her around and wrapped his arms around her, tight. Caging her in.

"Maybe you just need a different kind of motivation," he said, then grabbed a handful of her ass. She gasped in surprised arousal.

"I can't wait to feel all this feisty passion wriggling around underneath me, I'm gonna give you something you're never gonna forget." His voice was dark and menacing. She knew what he was trying to do but unfortunately it was having the complete opposite effect. Heat spread through her and her core throbbed for attention.

"Um, Taylor?"

"Hmm?"

"You're meant to be throwing me over your shoulder?"

I'm trying but you keep turning me on instead! With an almighty grunt, she put all her force into it, using her body weight and drawing forth all her rage over what Dale was doing to her. Beau flipped over her shoulder and thudded to the ground. She leapt on him, cheering triumphantly, peering down into his shocked face.

"Take that, evil attacker!"

"Holy shit, you did it!" Awe filled his voice as his hands fell to her waist.

"Damn right I did." She did a little celebratory wiggle and his hands flexed on her hips. She felt him harden underneath her and she looked down. Her body froze, no longer light and jubilant, now heavy with want and need. She dragged her eyes back up to his. Her hands on his chest rose and fell with his hurried breaths.

"Taylor," he began.

"Beau?"

"Taylor, you need to get off me now." His jaw clenched so hard she heard it crack.

"Then let go of me," she murmured. His hands flexed again but then slowly released. Disappointment curled inside her. She was sure he would give in, take this opportunity to give them both what they wanted, what he started in her office nearly a week ago. For days she had waited in exquisite agony.

Her body cried out in denial as his hands dropped to his side. Maybe he had made the right decision for them, maybe keeping them just friends was for the best.

"Thanks for the session," her voice wavered slightly as she got off him, her body screaming out in betrayal. She grabbed her stuff. "Don't wait up for me, we're having a sleepover at Christy's," she rambled on.

"Taylor..."

She could already hear the apology in his tone.

"See ya." She pinkie waved and then ran out without a backwards glance.

*

Later that week, Beau took her hand as he led her around the side of Dean's house towards the backyard.

"You think he'll be watching us here?" she asked, glancing around. The moonlight shone down, glinting off her gold heart earrings, drawing his attention.

"A few times we've been together I've felt like we're being watched so I wouldn't put it past him. This is a big open space with lots of trees for coverage so I'm not taking any chances," he said, pulling her closer and stroking his thumb over her knuckles to reassure her.

"I just want him to make his move, I just want it to be over." She sighed, frustration pouring from her. He paused to look at her and she stopped next to him, shifting her feet which were tucked into faded pink cowboy boots that looked adorable paired with her white sundress. That sundress was playing havoc with his libido but he pushed that aside for now. He rubbed his hands up and down her arms.

"I know, sweetheart. I want him to make a move too, but only when I'm around to kick his ass."

She snorted, his words having the desired effect and he pretended to be affronted. "You don't think I can kick his ass?"

"You can totally kick his ass. I'm just surprised at how bloodthirsty you are these days. You're much more aggressive than I remember."

"Only where you're concerned."

He smiled down at her, pleased that their teasing had wiped the worry from her beautiful face. He patted her ass to move her along and she turned to stare at him, heat in her eyes.

"Do that again, but harder."

Shit. She definitely enjoyed the spanking he gave her. He'd been trying to avoid flirting and any verbal sparring that could lead to another spanking. But he mainly stayed away from her because she terrified him. She was the one woman above all others who mattered and meant more to him than any other. What if he wasn't what she wanted? What if he wasn't good enough? What if crossing that line broke them for good?

How was he supposed to respond to her? *Every time I see you, I think about dragging you off somewhere and fucking you until neither of us can think, but I'm so scared.* Hell no!

The other morning in bed he had considered waking her up and giving them both what they wanted. But he stopped when he spotted the two photo frames she had added to the dresser. Both were pictures of them as teenagers. When he asked her about them, she just shrugged and said she randomly found them when she was cleaning. Taylor, *cleaning?* Psh.

Seeing the pictures was the reminder he didn't want. He never dreamed that they could go back to how things were. That they could gain back the trust, the easiness, and the affection but they were well on their way to it. Only he wanted more, but at the risk of ruining everything? His body said one thing, but his brain was more considerate.

He was saved from responding to Taylor by Christy spotting them through the open gate and cheering loudly.

"You're here!" she yelled. *How could someone so tiny make so much noise?*

"Now it's a party!" Justine shouted as they made their way into the back yard and over to the firepit where Blake and Justine were sitting while Dean and Christy worked the grill and poured drinks. Taylor let go of Beau's hand as she followed Christy into the kitchen, Justine jogging after them. Beau scanned the trees, looking for any sign of someone who hadn't been invited.

Blake clapped him on the back. "Already patroled the area my man, he's not here."

They went over to accompany Dean at the grill, and he tried to get lost in their banter but his eyes kept cutting back to Taylor. He watched as she talked to the women, his lips lifting in a smile as he took in her animated expression, her wild gesturing. She was one hundred percent the Taylor he'd always known and nostalgia stole his breath.

"How's things going with you two?" Blake interrupted his thoughts and Beau pulled his eyes away from his enchanting woman.

"Yeah, uh, good I think."

"You're sure keeping a close eye on her," Dean said, a heavy undercurrent in his tone that made Beau's pulse trip.

"Just looking out for her is all," he said, trying to sound casual and suddenly feeling like he'd jumped onto the grill with the rest of the meat.

"Anything you need to tell me?" Dean said, clicking the meat tongs a couple times and somehow managing to make that look menacing.

"Dude, I don't think you want to know," Blake stage whispered. Beau shot Blake a dark look that screamed *not fucking helping*, and Blake returned his look with one that said, *I wasn't trying to*.

"Nah man. Just playing pretend, like you wanted." Beau took a long sip of his beer, trying to act cool. Dean held his stare, then dropped his shoulders.

"Dang it. I always thought there was something between you and that you would get together eventually. I kinda hoped this would push things along a bit."

Beau choked on his beer, the bubbles fizzing his nose and Blake pounded him on the back, not stopping until

Beau glared at him. Blake just gave him an infuriating grin.

"You...you would be cool with that?" Beau asked tentatively.

"I mean, I would be all over your ass if anything happened to her and I would want *zero* information on your sex life but yeah, it'd be pretty darn special if it worked out that way."

Beau released the breath he didn't realize he'd been holding, and Dean gestured to pass him the plates. He hadn't really considered how Dean would react if something developed which was shitty considering Dean was his best friend. He stared at the guy, amazed that his friend would be so cool with it.

"All done, come and get it!" Dean shouted and that was the end of the conversation. Blake winked at him before going off to fetch Justine.

They all ate around the outdoor dining area and when they finished, they gathered around the firepit, talking, drinking beer and looking up at the stars. Taylor had tried to sit in her own chair but Beau grabbed her and pulled her into his lap.

"Do you think you can control yourself this time?" she asked, arching a haughty brow at him.

"Let's find out," he murmured, wrapping his arms around her and pulling her back against his chest where, after a glare, she reluctantly snuggled in.

His mouth at her ear, he whispered, "Don't fight it, we both know you like it when I'm in control." She stiffened and a satisfied smile split his lips.

Christy signaled that she wanted to make a toast. "We wanted to invite you here to say thank you. With our bachelor and bachelorette parties tomorrow night and how busy we are with the new garage opening and my book tour in the next few weeks, we just wanted some down time together."

Dean was looking at Christy like she held the answer to all his questions. Longing clawed at Beau's chest. He couldn't wait to experience that, having never even come close with another woman. His chest thudded when he realized the woman he had cared about the most his whole life was Taylor, and hell they'd hated each other from the age of seventeen up until last month.

"Yes, and thanks to Beau and Taylor for organizing them. We know we're going to absolutely love them," Dean added.

Christy shot Beau a knowing smirk, Beau had something special planned for Dean alright.

"So, here's to our wedding, our group expanding with the new arrival and…" Christy's eyes locked on Taylor and Beau, "New love."

They all clapped and cheered then Dean asked Justine how pregnancy was going.

"We had our first ultrasound yesterday and so far everything looks fine." Justine and Blake shared a look full of love as Justine pulled out a scan picture from her pocket and handed it around the group. Christy and Dean cooed over it before passing it to Taylor. Beau felt her withdraw as she stared at the picture.

Although she had nodded along enthusiastically, asking questions and though he knew she was happy for the couple, he knew this must be hard for her. He kissed her temple and stroked her arms, comforting her.

"Your feelings are valid and acceptable. I know you're ecstatic for them, but I know this is also a painful reminder for you. I just want you to know that I've got you and I'm here for you," he murmured, and she nodded imperceptibly before handing the scan picture back to

Sweet Surrender

Justine and Blake. She snuggled back against Beau's chest and he continued to stroke her arms until the subject changed to tomorrow night's events.

"So, strippers all around then?" Blake said.

Christy whooped loudly, getting a frown from Dean and a laugh from Taylor.

"I couldn't get two in the end so you're just gonna have to settle for the one," Beau teased and Dean looked horrified.

"No, dude! I didn't want any!" Dean exclaimed. They ribbed him some more before Justine gasped, "Oh no!" and clapped a hand over her mouth as she leapt up, running inside the house. Taylor made a move to follow but Blake stopped her. "It's all right, I'll go. She might be a while."

Taylor resettled against Beau and he twirled one of her curls around his finger, bringing the lock of hair to his nose and inhaling her spicy scent.

"Well, I can't cancel Candy Cane now or I'll lose the deposit, she wasn't cheap," Beau said.

"Tell me you're kidding?" Dean's face was a picture. Christy stifled a laugh and Beau couldn't keep eye contact with her without losing it.

"Darlin' I didn't ask for one, I swear," Dean said to Christy.

"It's okay, I don't mind you having one," she replied sweetly.

"Ugh, I do," Taylor muttered quietly.

"Something you'd like to share with the class, sweetheart?" he said when Christy and Dean got drawn into their own conversation.

"I don't want to think about you watching a bunch of strippers, getting all worked up then coming back to my cabin and taking your frustration out on yourself, manually, if you catch my drift."

He laughed, then nipped her ear, her sharp intake of breath making him smile. "What makes you think I haven't already done that in our cabin?"

She turned slightly to face him, her eyes tangling with his. "Have you?"

All her twisting in his lap was hell on his control, his body began readying against her ass and he fought the urge to rub against her. He pulled her tighter against him, the arm holding her waist shifted slightly so he could stroke the side of her breast and another sharp intake of breath had him biting back a moan.

"You have a lot of dirty dreams, don't you Taylor? Laying in bed, listening to you moan has been a special kind of torture I never knew existed."

Her eyes went wide, her breathing quickening. "Especially when I discovered the star of your dreams was me. You moaned *my* name," he murmured. His lips brushed against her ear and he felt the shiver that rolled through her.

"Beau…"

"Mhm, just like that. What was I doing to you in these dreams?"

She glanced over to Christy and Dean who were still deep in their own conversation, not paying them any attention.

"They can't hear us. Tell me, what itch did I scratch for you?" He pressed against her breast harder, the fall of her hair hiding what he was doing. He swiped his thumb over the hard peak of her nipple and she shifted in his lap, rubbing her thighs together. He felt a new level of arousal at watching her under his mercy. He liked being in charge, controlling what she felt and when, seeing her get off on what he was saying.

"Did I lean over in bed and slide my hand down into your wet panties then deep inside you?" He pinched her nipple and a breath shuddered out of her; she gripped his arm tight.

"Or did I let you play with yourself while I told you what I wanted you to do? You'd like that wouldn't you, if I whispered all kinds of dirty commands in your ear?"

She nodded and pure, undiluted pleasure sparked through his veins. He pinched her nipple again, rolling it between his fingers and she arched her back slightly, a silent beg for more.

"You've touched yourself while thinking about me, haven't you? Stroked inside yourself wishing it was me?" She nodded again but it wasn't enough, he was greedy for more. "Use your words, Taylor," he growled.

"Yes," she moaned softly.

"That's a good girl. I've thought about you too," he admitted. He saw Christy and Dean out of the corner of his eye, they seemed to be making up after some kind of argument and would soon be ready to interact again, but he wanted Taylor's attention fixed on him. He wanted her all to himself. Wanted to finally cross that line with her. He was ready.

"Go inside, to the bathroom and wait for me. I'll be there in a minute." He dropped a kiss on her temple. At first, she didn't move, just turned to stare at him, those emerald eyes ablaze with unrestrained lust.

"Now, Taylor."

She leapt up and disappeared inside. Beau discreetly rearranged the pulsing erection in his jeans and went after her. The effort to act casually and not race after her was immense. When he got to the bathroom he spotted Taylor hovering outside, an embarrassed look on her face.

"What is it?" he asked and then he heard it. Retching.

He peeked in the doorway and saw Blake holding Justine's dark mane aloft and rubbing her back while she puked.

Justine spotted them. "Sorry guys, I'll be done in a minute."

"Don't be silly *mí corazon,* are you okay?" Taylor asked, concern etched on her face where lust had been only moments before.

"Yeah, the baby just isn't loving meat right now. What are you guys doing here?"

Beau looked at Taylor, his cheeks heating. "Oh, uh we-"

"Oh my God, you were sneaking off to hook up, weren't you?" Justine cried, flushing the toilet and rinsing her mouth.

"No, we totally weren't, we were-" Taylor started but Justine's squeal interrupted.

Justine clapped and then burst into tears, gesturing between the two of them. "That makes me so freaking happy, you guys!"

"Okay honey, I think it's time to go home," Blake sighed, steering a sobbing Justine around them.

Mood. Killed.

Maybe it was a sign, maybe it was for the best. Fate had intervened and stopped them yet again and maybe they should listen. But Beau couldn't shake the feeling that it felt wrong to stop.

Blake and Justine left and then shortly after that Taylor started yawning so they called it a night. They didn't speak the whole ride home and when they got inside Beau decided once and for all to put himself on the line, to make it clear what he wanted. They'd had enough miscommunication in the past.

He reached for Taylor, his eyes searing into hers with

hot need. He saw the hesitation in them, knew he needed to give her an ultimatum, to make her pick.

"Tomorrow night. You can think about this until tomorrow night but then time's up and you need to decide what you want. If you come near that bedroom door when you get back tomorrow, then you're mine."

Chapter 17

You're mine.

His words echoed around in her head. The memory of his touch on her body played havoc with her hormones. She wanted him but what if, after all this time, it wasn't good? What if he was a dud? God, what if *she* was? What if it ruined everything and they couldn't claw their way back from this?

All she'd done since last night, other than simmer in unmet need, was worry. And remember the way he comforted her when Justine's sonogram picture was passed around. His comfort had wrapped around her, nestling under her skin like a soothing balm to her wounds. Protecting them. Sealing them. A lump formed in her throat at the beauty of the feeling yet it terrified her. Because as much as she wanted him back in her life, to rekindle their friendship, she also *wanted* him with a deep ache that wouldn't be eased.

If you fuck him, it could fuck everything up! her brain screamed, not helping her at all. She was fully aware of the magnitude of this decision. Were they mature enough to deal with the fallout of sleeping together? One time couldn't hurt, could it? Just to get it out of their systems and then move on. If it was bad then that would work, but shit, what if it was good? Surely that was worse because then she would want to do it again and that's when feelings got involved, shit got messy and then Taylor was out.

Do you really think you can sleep with him and not *have your feelings involved?*

"No, hence the fucking dilemma," she muttered to herself. Shit, her evil brain was right. She needed to talk it through with someone. She opened her chat with Christy and Justine but paused. Taylor was biased and couldn't form an objective opinion but they were also biased. They wanted this almost as much as she did. She needed to speak to someone who wasn't on her side. She opened her chat with Ruby.

Taylor: Should I sleep with him?

Ruby: *Shocked emoji.* You haven't already ridden that horse????? I didn't raise you right.

Taylor: You didn't raise me at all.

Ruby: Keep telling yourself that, girlie.

Taylor: I think it'll make things too complicated.

Ruby: Too complicated? Isn't it just 'insert part A into part B'? Or has it changed in the last decade?

Taylor snorted as her fingers flew over the screen.

Taylor: You know what I mean, it could get messy, feelings-wise.

Ruby: Because it could lead to something more?

Love? Happiness? Everything you ever wanted? Yeah, sounds fucking horrible.

Taylor: You know how I feel about relationships, feelings and love etc.

Ruby: No, I know how you THINK you feel about love. But that man will give you everything you need.

Taylor: What's that supposed to mean?

Ruby: It means, saddle that horse before some other filly does #giddyup.

Taylor dropped her phone on the couch, annoyed at Ruby. Why did no one understand how she felt about love and relationships? Her phone pinged and she saw a barrage of horse, cowboy and eggplant emojis coming from Ruby followed by another message.

Ruby: I want all the dirty details once you've taken that stallion for a ride.

That woman is too damn thirsty for her age. Taylor switched off her phone and put on the TV to escape. It came on to the same show it always did, some random British baking show that she was now addicted to. *Just a few minutes,* she told herself and then two hours later she was crying out in horror as Maureen's showstopper cake collapsed and fell to pieces on the way to the judges' table. She heard Beau's key in the door and fumbled with the remote, switching the TV off and jumping up.

"Hey," she called when he came in. Her eyes were immediately drawn to the patch of sweat on his t-shirt running along his collarbone. His dark hair curled at the edges, his cheeks were flushed from the exercise, and she suddenly understood exactly why Ruby was so thirsty.

"Hey sweetheart!" he boomed, before taking his AirPods out of his ears. "I won't kiss you, I'm all sweaty," he said and closed the front door. She knew he was faking for Dale's sake in case he was watching but she hadn't seen or heard from Dale for weeks. Maybe he was gone?

"So I see," she said, her tongue so heavy in her mouth that her words slurred slightly.

Get a hold of yourself!

"I thought I'd grab my stuff and get ready in the cabin next door as we'll probably just get in each other's way," he said, putting his gym bag on the table.

"Sounds good," she replied. He went into the bedroom to grab his things and she followed him, watching him move around the room. Tonight, was the bachelor and bachelorette parties and she was excited to let her hair down.

"You have a plan for tonight?" he asked.

"Yeah, Christy wants to stop off somewhere first and then we'll be back in the bar," she said, leaning against the doorway. She wondered if he was going to ask for her decision. Her eyes darted around the room, landing on the picture frames she added to the dresser. She had stored them under her bed for years, unable to get rid of them even at the height of her misplaced hatred for him. Now there was a small collection of pictures, a little shrine to their youth and friendship. Seeing it there put the doubt back into her mind about whether they should cross that line or not.

He turned to her, grabbing his overnight bag. "Well, I guess this is it. Have a good time with the girls and I'll be back here tonight…" His eyes followed her gaze to see what she was staring at.

"So, when you're back later…" Her voice trailed off, she didn't know what the end of that sentence was. He stepped closer, dominating her space and firing her senses.

"Let me make things real clear, sweetheart. When you

get back tonight, don't come near this room unless you want to take things further. I'm warning you. This room is off-limits." He ran his thumb along her jawline, his touch leaving tingles in its wake. He hooked a finger under her chin and tilted so her eyes met his, clashing heatedly.

"Because if you come near that room, I'm going to fuck you. Hard. Just the way you've been dreaming about." A desperate sound slipped from her lips as he pressed a soft kiss to her forehead that she found herself leaning into.

Then he was gone.

*

"I can't believe you're making me go to another bar! How do you know I won't combust as soon as I walk inside?" Taylor complained as Justine pulled the car into the parking lot of The Apple and Duck.

"Relax Tay, I've just gotta do something quick and then we'll be gone, half an hour tops," Christy said as they got out. She grabbed her bag from the trunk.

"What's in that?" Justine asked, pointing to the bag.

"This? Oh, er, the owner is a big fan of my books, so I said I'd drop some off for him and sign them," Christy said, not making eye contact.

"Cool, I need a drink," Taylor said as they headed inside. Loud music immediately assaulted them. Taylor glanced around the place, unable to help but compare it with The Rusty Bucket. The bar here was laid out nicely but had tiled flooring which in Taylor's opinion clashed dramatically with the brick walls. Unfortunately, this bar had the one thing Taylor had been coveting: a mechanical bull. It earned the bar an extra point, but overall the place was cold and impersonal. *Nothing like my baby*, she thought

Sweet Surrender

smugly.

"I'll be back in a sec," Christy said and scurried off. Taylor and Justine headed to get a drink.

"What do you want, boo?" Justine said, scanning the selection.

"Patrón, a whole fuck ton of Patrón," she muttered, needing to take the edge off as Beau's words circled her mind.

"Let me get this round." The deep voice reminded her of smoke and whiskey and she turned, coming face to face with an absolute mountain of a man. Tall, tattooed and stunning. Strawberry blond hair, stubborn jaw and a straight blade for a nose. But it was his eyes that caught her attention. One blue and one green and framed by thick lashes.

He raked a hand through his hair and a crooked smile took over his face, making him only slightly less terrifying. She scanned his tattoos peeking out from the rolled-up sleeves of his white Henley, coveting the intricate designs. *We've got matching roses on our arms.* Though his crooked smile said, *I'm the shy boy next door,* his eyes and whole demeanor screamed *lady-killer* and she doubted he had spent a night alone in his whole adult life.

"Oh my God, it's you!" Justine cried. Practically jumping up and down. Lady-killer's expression closed off a fraction before he nodded.

"Three shots of Patrón?" he asked.

"Just two and some apple juice for me thanks," Justine said, patting her little baby bump. Her eyes wide as saucers as she stared at him.

"What's wrong with you?" Taylor hissed.

"I'm totally fangirling right now and not even trying to hide it!" she squealed.

"And what are the names of the prettiest ladies in the

bar?" Lady-killer asked, and Taylor fought an eyeroll when Justine giggled coquettishly.

"I'm Justine and this is Taylor," she replied.

"No shit? Well pleased to meet you both. I've heard so much about you, especially you," Lady-killer winked at Taylor.

Taylor frowned. "Do we know each other?"

"Taylor! Are you kidding me? You don't know who this is? It's Will Freaking Crawford!"

Will Freaking Crawford gave her another crooked smile but she was drawing a blank.

"You better be buying my girl a drink because you're just being friendly." Beau's voice sent a shiver rolling through her, barely banked aggression lining his tone. She turned and there he was, her heart skipping in her chest and her lady parts singing like the Hallelujah Chorus.

"Shit man, you know how it is. Only just found out who she was," Will said, looking bashful. Then he and Beau did one of those cool guy handshakes that ended in a hug and lots of back slapping and it all clicked into place, this was *Will*. Beau's bestie and celebrity businessman from whatever that show was called that she never watched.

They pulled apart and Beau put his arm around Taylor, drawing her possessively into his side.

"Message received, not that I needed telling after I caught her name," Will said and winked at Beau.

"It's great to see you man, and there's someone else who's been looking forward to meeting you," Beau said, pointing behind them.

"Honey, what are you doing here?" Blake said, coming up behind Justine.

"Why are you here?" Justine asked.

"Bachelor party," Blake shrugged.

"Deputy Sheriff Blake Miller meet Will Crawford," Beau said, making introductions.

"My new bestie!" Will cried, opening his arms wide and Blake barked out a laugh as they hugged.

"Great to meet you, bro," Blake introduced him to Justine again who then fangirled all over him to an embarrassing degree. Dean appeared behind them and stopped when he saw Taylor.

"Uh, no offense but why are you here?" Dean asked.

"Your fian-"

"Let's get the man a shot and then it's time for your lap dance!" Beau shouted, interrupting Taylor. Will shoved a shot into Dean's hand then tipped it towards his mouth.

"I said no strippers!" Dean shouted.

"Did you? I didn't hear that, did you Blake?" Beau said.

"Nope, Will?"

"Nah, definitely didn't hear that."

The lights dimmed and *Cherry Pie* by Warrant began blaring from the speakers as Beau pushed a protesting Dean onto a chair in the middle of the bar. "Just trust me!" Beau shouted over the music.

"Stay!" Blake commanded, then joined Justine and Will at the bar. Beau came to join Taylor and spun her around so her back was plastered to his chest.

"You smell incredible," he murmured, kissing her shoulder.

She shivered, leaning into him. "I feel like you're buttering me up."

"You're right. I need some brownie points because you're about to see something that will haunt you and it's all my fault. Your stepbrother is about to get a lap dance that is going to drive him wild."

She tried to pull away, but a firm arm banded around her stomach and kept her in place.

"That's disgusting and I doubt he'll get turned on by a random stripper," she scoffed.

"Well, I warned you." His words had her drifting back to that moment in her bedroom where he said something similar and her brain nearly short-circuited. She was pulled from her thoughts by the lights in the bar dimming as the stripper appeared.

She was a little on the short side and a lot curvy. *Strange choice of outfit,* Taylor thought as she took in the mechanics overalls that covered the stripper's ample curves and a welding mask shielded her face. She was only wearing a bra underneath the overalls, her blonde curls bouncing around her shoulders and Taylor burst out laughing as she recognized her best friend.

"He's going to love you forever," she said, looking up at Beau.

He grinned down at her. "Damn straight."

Christy slinked over to Dean and twirled around him, stroking a hand down his chest before grabbing the hem of his shirt and tearing up the middle. Justine whooped loudly as Christy began unsnapping her overalls then let them fall to her waist.

"Uh, ma'am. I don't mean to be rude but…" Dean's words rose over the music but stalled when she straddled his lap and pushed her breasts into his face. After a moment a smile split Dean's face.

"I fucking love you!" Dean shouted to Beau, then he wasn't able to talk as Christy shimmied and shook in front of him and his eyes were glued to her chest. Christy stepped out of the overalls to reveal a matching bra and panty set. The crowd cheered but Dean didn't notice them, he couldn't take his eyes from her. Christy whipped off the helmet to more cheers and brought a finger to her mouth, licking it and running it down over her body. The growl from Dean echoed around the room and then he lifted her into his arms. Her legs wrapped around his waist and they kissed hungrily. Taylor turned away as they disappeared down the dark hallway of the bar.

"Whelp, that's something I never want to see again," she groaned.

Beau laughed. "I think they might be a while, let's get some drinks in."

They all chatted while waiting for the love birds to finish something Taylor didn't want to think about. They finally reappeared, Christy fully clothed and glowing with happiness, and a sharp pang pierced Taylor's stomach at the sight of it. *That was weird.*

"*Chica,* you're amazing and that was fucking hot. I was *so* turned on," Justine said, wrapping Christy in a hug.

"This feels weird to say after what I saw you do to my brother, but I'm proud of you," Taylor said. Christy had worked really hard to gain her body confidence after years of tearing herself down so to see her come out and do a performance like that was truly impressive.

"Now that's out of the way, we can leave and start my bachelorette party!" Christy squealed.

"Just need to go to the bathroom," Taylor said, heading off and leaving Dean and Christy to say an emotional farewell, like they weren't going to see each other at the end of the night. *There's that damn pain again, what the hell?*

When she came back from the bathroom she spotted Beau at the bar but he wasn't alone. Some perky blonde was draped over him, walking her fingers up his arm to his chest. Something dark exploded inside Taylor and she stomped over to them, barely containing the growl rumbling through her as she grabbed the girl's arm and pulled it away from Beau.

"Hands off, he's taken."

The blonde's eyes widened but a catty smile appeared on her perfect face.

"You sure about that, Red?"

"You heard her, he's taken," Beau said, his voice hard as he curled his arm around Taylor's waist and pulled her against him. The blonde rolled her eyes and walked away to try her luck with Will, but Beau didn't release his grip.

"Christ, Taylor. That was hot as hell," he rumbled in her ear and then spun her to face him. "Remember what I said. I know what I want and I damn sure hope you want the same."

The fierce possessiveness in his eyes left her speechless. She nodded and then she was leaving with Christy and Justine, throwing one last look at him over her shoulder. Their eyes met again and, in that moment, she had never wanted anyone more.

They made their way back to The Rusty Bucket Inn, had a lot of champagne and played some traditional bachelorette party games, including blindfolded 'pin the penis on the stripper', which ended up with them all cackling loudly at the random places the penis was pinned.

"I love Dean, like, soooo much. I hope you know that," Christy slurred. Taylor had got them some more shots, she needed alcohol to give her the courage that Sober Taylor needed to make her decision. To give her body what it wanted, *who* it wanted. If she was Sober Taylor then her mind would be thinking about silly things like consequences and the morning after. Drunk Taylor was like Daffy Duck: *consequences schmonsequences.*

Taylor nodded at Christy and then started drunk

karaoke. Justine kept insisting that she was the only one who could actually sing but to her ears Taylor sounded perfect and only half of the bar disagreed. Justine decided to call it a night when Christy shredded all the paper penises from their game, announcing dramatically that she had found the perfect one and didn't need these. They waited in the parking lot, watching Taylor get home safely, making sure stupid Dale wasn't around and then Taylor waved goodbye and Justine drove off to take Christy home.

Taylor's pulse thudded in her ears as she went inside the cabin and spotted the light shining under the closed door from her bedroom. She paused for a moment before she tiptoed over and pressed her ear against the door, listening.

"What did I say, Taylor?" His voice came through the door and she gasped, leaping back.

After a beat, she replied. "You warned me."

"And what are you doing, Taylor?" His voice was calm but there was a layer of anticipation in his tone that caused her own to spike. "I'll give you until I count to one. Five…"

Was this what she wanted?

"Four…"

Absolutely it was. There was no denying it anymore.

"Three…"

Consequences, schmonsequences.

She reached for the door handle but it flew open and there he was. Facing her down, all need and hot aggression.

"Get in here," he growled. "This game we've been playing ends tonight."

Chapter 18

He pulled her into the bedroom, slamming the door behind them.

"How drunk are you?" he asked, decency belatedly kicking in.

"I tried real hard but I'm not very drunk at all," she nibbled her lip. He looked at her skeptically but her eyes were clear and she wasn't swaying or slurring. She looked at him from under her thick lashes and ran her hands up his chest.

"I want this, Beau, are you gonna let me have it?" Her nails scraped him through the thin material of his t-shirt, heat rippling up his spine.

"Fuck yes." He wrapped his arms around her waist and twisted them, falling back onto the bed and pulling her on top of him. Her hair tumbled around them, a red curtain he buried his face into and inhaled. "You always smell amazing, that scent has driven me crazy for weeks." *For years...*

He brushed the strands over her shoulder and peered up into her face, capturing her eyes with his.

"It's just this once," she said, her breath coming in a rush. He watched her for a moment, thinking. Once was better than never. Maybe it was for the best if it was just once, to get it out of their system.

He nodded then cupped her jaw and rubbed the pad of his thumb across her plump bottom lip, wishing it was his tongue instead. Her warm breath coated him before her lips puckered against his skin in a soft kiss. His stomach clenched, her lips were like silk, just as he remembered. God, he wanted to kiss her but he knew if he pushed it, it would only ruin things. His cock hardened underneath her and she hit him with a devastating smile. *Christ, this is really happening...*

She leaned back, placing her hands on the bed, pressing her full weight on him. The pressure on his arousal had him biting back a groan of pleasure. He ran his hands up her thighs, squeezing them, moving to her ass and plumping the round cheeks in his hands.

She stripped her leather dress over her head, leaving her in just a pink bra and panties. His eyes drank her in, memorizing her creamy skin and the slight swell of her breasts, big enough to fill his palm, the nipped-in waist and the flare of her hips. Tattoos scattered across her skin, flowers adorned her, an anchor hidden between the petals. His eyes were drawn to the watercolor hummingbird wrapped around her ribcage and the gold ring through her belly button winked at him in the light. She was exquisite.

"Now you," she said. His stomach dropped. He didn't

want her to see the body he'd damaged, didn't want her to stare at him in disgust, ruining this moment that had been building between them for so long.

"In a minute," he stalled and pulled her down to him, running his hands over her back. He didn't know what to do with his mouth, his instinct was to kiss her but not being able to was a new kind of torture. Especially when he had done it before, he knew how she felt, how she tasted and he was dying for another hit. He settled for her neck, sliding his tongue over the pulse pounding away and gently sucking. A curse slipped from her off-limits mouth and she rolled her hips, grinding down on him. He thrust up to meet her, their moans filling the room.

Her hips settled into a slow, teasing roll that had him seeing stars and meeting her with a lift of his hips each time. Fuck, he couldn't take much more. He'd imagined this moment a thousand different ways but this was so much better than any fantasy he could conjure, because tonight, even if it was for one night only, she was finally, blissfully *his*.

Beau nibbled her neck and unsnapped her bra, drawing the straps down her shoulders. She sat up again, her lips swollen, her eyes glazed with pleasure. She drew her bra away and his eyes dropped to take her in. Creamy silk and mouth-watering blushed nipples that he needed to taste. He sat up, his hands pressed into her back, pulling her to him and he flicked his tongue over the tip of her breast.

She gasped and plunged her fingers into his hair, holding him to her. He licked and sucked as she squirmed in his lap but he needed more. He tunneled his hand into her panties, hissing when he discovered how hot and wet she was, just for him. He stroked over her damp curls and slid a finger inside her. She cried out, her body clenching around him like it never wanted to let him go. *I could stay like this forever.*

"My beautiful princess," he murmured, watching her face twist with pleasure. He dipped his head and licked her other nipple. When her grip on him finally relaxed he slid another finger inside and curled them, hitting the spot that had her head dropping back, her mouth open as little moans slipped out.

He lifted her, pulling her panties down her legs, ripping them slightly in his haste but he didn't care, they were stopping him from getting to what he wanted. He watched as he slid his fingers in and out of her, then slicked his thumb up over her clit.

"Beau..." she moaned.

"That's not the first time I've heard you moan my name but goddamn it's the best time."

"Shut up and take your clothes off," she muttered, grabbing for the hem of his shirt. Panic consumed him but he couldn't stay fully clothed and apparently she wasn't going to let him.

"Okay, turn off the light," he said, fear clenching his stomach.

"What? Why?"

"Because."

"Hell no! I've been dying to see you shirtless for *weeks* and I'm not missing out now," she pouted.

Shit. He reached over and snapped the bedside lamp off. She got off his lap and his hands went to the hem of his shirt and started to lift, then the light snapped on.

"Taylor!" he growled.

"I want to see you, Beau."

He snapped the light off again and removed his sweatpants.

"Why don't you want me to see you?" Her voice

sounded small and insecure in the dark. Christ, he didn't want her doubting him.

"It's not you sweetheart, it's me. I'm not very…confident," he gritted out, hating his weakness being exposed.

"Seriously? But you're ripped as fuck. Well, I assume."

"Taylor, I lost a shit-load of weight. I have stretch marks and had lots of loose skin removed so there's a couple of small scars and a bit of my abdomen that won't ever be completely flat…I just don't look how you might expect." He couldn't meet her eyes.

There was silence, then her hand was on his chest, pushing him back until he was laying on the bed. She slowly raised his shirt and trailed her fingers across the skin on his abdomen. Goosebumps flared to life at the sensation, the muscles bunching under her teasing touch.

"Taylor…" he warned.

"Beau," she replied and stroked higher. "I want you. I've wanted you for so long. You leave me breathless," she whispered in his ear, her tongue stroking over the shell. His eyes rolled back and his hand curled around her hip possessively, gripping tight enough to bruise.

"It's you I want, Beau. It's your personality and your looks and all the pieces inside that define you and make you, you." Her hand moved higher, stroking over his pecs, kneading the flesh. She pinched his hard nipples until his breath stuttered out of him.

"I'm not going to lie and pretend I don't find you attractive. You're the most beautiful man I've ever seen. You were back then, and you are now, I've always thought so." She placed a kiss to his stomach.

God, she was killing him. Her actions, her sweet words like soothing balm to his pride, unmanning him with every moment. Giving him something he knew he needed but never thought he would get: her seal of approval.

He was meant to be the one in charge, he instigated this. He'd made a lot of noise about the things he wanted to do to her but she had turned the tables on him, surprising him as always and keeping him on his toes.

She tugged down his boxers and straddled him, placing her hot, wet pussy over his aching length. His hands snapped to her hips and he cursed as she glided over him, back and forth like she couldn't wait for him any longer.

"Beau, don't you know how much I want you? How much I've always wanted you. *Always*."

His heart thumped in his chest and then she was laying down over him and suddenly, he needed to be shirtless. Needed to feel her skin against his, her bare breasts pressed against him. He whipped his shirt over his head and held her to him, the hard points of her nipples abrading him in the most perfect way.

"God, Beau," she gasped as she continued to rock her hips, rubbing herself over him. He thrust up, unable to help himself. He needed to get a condom quickly or this would be over before it began at the rate she was going.

She bit his ear and he groaned in response.

"I've been dying to know how you taste, how you look when you come." Her breathy words riling him up like never before. Her hips moved faster and faster. "How it would feel to know I made you come. I think about you when I touch myself."

"Shit, Taylor, don't stop," he grunted, gripping her hips tightly. She was unbelievable, obliterating his control and he couldn't hold back anymore.

"When I slide my fingers in deep and wish it was you. I can feel how big you are, you're going to feel so good, Beau. Better than anyone else has." Her hot words, right in his ear. Her little pants and her wet heat sliding over him again and again took him right to the edge, threatening to hurtle him over before he got inside her.

"You're perfect Beau, I knew you would be. I can't…I'm going to…" she gasped, then cried out and he felt her spasming over him, a rush of wetness with her release. Her pussy pulsing over him sent him flying over the edge. With a groan, he came, hot jets coating him from the most intense orgasm he'd ever had as she continued to shudder over him.

Beau couldn't catch his breath, couldn't believe what had just happened with Taylor. *Taylor.*

Holy shit, that was amazing.

But she'd gotten him so worked up with her wet thrusts and breathy words that he hadn't even been able to get inside her before finishing. He hadn't been able to show her how good he was, hadn't taken her the way he had promised. He'd fallen short and his cheeks flushed with embarrassment.

"Let me clean us up," he said and disappeared into the bathroom before she could say anything. He wiped himself down and grabbed a towel, rinsing it with warm water. He debated putting a shirt on in case she saw him but stilled. She'd been spectacularly vocal about what she thought of him, maybe he should risk letting her see him. He took a deep breath, stepping out from the bathroom, readying himself for her reaction and he was greeted by her soft snores.

*

"Wake up, Tay."

His voice interrupted her dreams, pulling her into the land of people who were awake, and she didn't appreciate it one bit.

"Why?" she moaned, voice thick with sleep as she arched her back, stretching luxuriously like a cat. The soft material of the comforter rubbed against her bare legs, and she realized she was only in a t-shirt and panties. Then she remembered last night and oh God, now was *consequences* time.

She peeked out shyly from over the top of the comforter to find Beau standing over her, arms folded over his chest, his expression blank. Like they didn't have an amazing night together, like it hadn't been the best sexual encounter of her life and they hadn't even had sex. His gray t-shirt fit perfectly to his chest, a chest that she still hadn't seen but had her lips and tongue all over. He'd tasted so delicious she couldn't get enough.

"It's basketball game day," he said.

She frowned. "Won't everyone be too hungover to play?"

"Hell no. Now get your ass up," he said and left, his footsteps a little heavier than normal. For someone who had an orgasm recently he sure seemed grumpy. She shivered as the memory of him unraveling beneath her last night played through her head. Her body humming with renewed arousal, ready for more of him. Except it was only supposed to be the one time, that was the rule that she'd put in place and he had readily agreed.

There was so much more she wanted to explore with him, they had barely scratched the surface and now they wouldn't get a chance. She pushed aside her disappointment, it was for the best, otherwise feelings would start getting involved and Taylor didn't do feelings. The last thing she wanted was for him to get hurt or for them to lose the friendship they'd been building back up.

She dressed in red spandex shorts, a sports bra and a

loose black tank that read *Let's Get Physical.* Hmm she got physical last night, her nipples tightening as she remembered his mouth on them.

Great, is this how it was going to be now? She would continually think about how perfectly he played her body? And that she nearly gave in and begged him for that kiss she owed him? The thought sobered her up, no more dwelling, this was why there was just the one time. She just needed to focus on their friendship and on the plus side, at least their intimate experience would strengthen the fake relationship.

She went out into the living room and saw him watching TV and drinking some kind of protein shake thing. "Morning!" she called brightly, determined to behave normally with him.

"There's a couple of banana pancakes on the side for you," he said, glowering at the TV.

"Yummy, thanks." She grabbed the plate and then drizzled syrup over them along with some strawberries and blueberries. She enjoyed having actual food to eat, and fresh fruit and vegetables whenever she wanted. She would have to keep this up when it was all over. Her stomach dipped at the thought of him moving out. She didn't want him to leave, she liked having someone to come home to. She liked it being him.

"Whatcha watching?" she asked, thinking she could hear the theme tune to her new favorite reality baking show. He clicked the remote and cleared his throat.

"Sports," he grunted.

Seriously, what's crawled up his ass and died? He once said he knew all her tells, well she knew his too. She plonked herself down on the couch and snatched the remote from his hand, pressing the back button.

"Taylor!" he barked and grabbed for the remote, but

she held it out of reach. The familiar theme music filled the room followed by the image of the baking tent where all the tasty magic happened.

"Ah ha!" she shouted triumphantly, waving a pancake at him. "I knew you were lying! You've been watching this show."

"Big surprise, the overweight kid likes the show where they make food and eat it!" he snapped.

She frowned at him, taken aback by his temper and words. "Your previous weight has nothing to do with liking this show. You think the producers decided to make this show only for people with a specific body type? No, they didn't."

"Oh, you know for sure, do you?" he said petulantly.

"Yep, me and Paul Hollywood are like this," she said, crossing her fingers.

He squinted at her. "How do you know that name?"

"I love this show! And I want to watch it in peace so stop being defensive, you're not the 'overweight kid' anymore and you never were so just enjoy it," she said. They watched in silence while she ate her pancakes. *Damn they were good, he really is an amazing chef, definitely missed his calling.* She couldn't help moaning on the last mouthful, sad they were all gone. He glared at her.

"What is your problem today?" she asked when she couldn't take anymore.

"Nothing," he sulked, and she rolled her eyes. He continued to brood while she finished getting ready, not that she minded, he looked good all grumpy and lost in his thoughts.

They left the cabin, Beau driving them to the court the guys played at. For the whole journey he remained silent in the car, the mood subdued, until during a particularly moving Adele song, she let out a massive *woo!* She sent him a gleeful smile, trying to draw him out of his mood and into their game, but he just clenched his jaw.

"Okay, I give up, want to tell me what's got your panties in a bunch?" Was it their night together? She knew it was a mistake to cross that line, but her stupid hormones wouldn't leave her alone. *Consequences.*

His jaw clenched again; his knuckles white on the steering wheel but he didn't say anything.

"Come on Beau, tell me. We're friends again, right? And friends tell each other stuff," she said. More jaw clenching but this time she got the remix which included huffing and nostril flaring.

"Fine, don't tell me. But I swear on Dolly Parton that if yo-"

"Jesus Christ, I'm embarrassed, Taylor!" he burst out and she snapped her mouth shut. "We had one shot to do this thing, it's been building and building between us, and I came quicker than a teenager watching his first dirty movie! So yeah, I'm embarrassed, all right?" he said.

"Well, you shouldn't be. It may have escaped your attention, but I also finished very quickly. You got me so riled up and made me feel so good that-" She rolled her lips between her teeth; she hadn't meant to say that. She noticed his hand-flex on the steering wheel.

"For the love of God don't say things like that unless you want a repeat performance."

Her stomach flipped at the thought. Have him again? Yes please...*no!*

"I mean, it's not like you want a repeat performance, right?" he murmured.

Yes, yes she did. She wanted lots of them but that wasn't what they were meant to be doing here.

She swallowed thickly. "Do you?"

His eyes swiveled to hers, a fierceness banked in the

dark depths that had heat unfurling inside her. "Do you really want me to answer that, sweetheart?"

Fuck. Her lips pursed. "Maybe we should just forget what happened? We had some fun and now we know what it was like, it's out of the way and we can focus on getting our friendship back." Although there was truth to her words, she couldn't help but feel she just drew a line in the sand. She wanted to continue exploring their physical relationship. There were so many things she wanted to do with him but losing him wasn't one of them, and that felt inevitable if they continued.

He nodded abruptly and turned his attention back to the road and before long he was pulling up outside the basketball court. Justine and Blake were already there and as Taylor and Beau greeted them, Christy and Dean arrived. Everyone had the audacity to look fresh-faced and not hungover at all.

"Thanks again for last night everyone," Christy said, hugging Dean tightly.

"It was definitely memorable," Dean said, kissing the top of her head. "But now, it's a battle of wills: men versus women!" He added as he shoved Christy away from him dramatically and she rolled her eyes.

"I'm sorry, what century is this?"

"Oh hush it Taylor, it'll be fun. Come on, let's huddle up!" Justine pulled her and Christy into a huddle and glared over her shoulder as the men did the same.

"Right *chicas*, what do you know about basketball?"

Christy tapped her chin thoughtfully. "Mm—let me see—yup, nothing."

Justine cursed in Spanish. "What about you, Red?"

"Less than Christy." Another curse.

"Also, should you be playing?" Taylor asked, not wanting her to get hurt or damage the baby.

"I'm thirteen weeks pregnant not dying, and I need to play."

Taylor regarded her suspiciously. "Why?"

"Because, if Blake wins, he gets to pick the baby name. But if I win then I get to pick it and I'm sure as hell not gonna let that man win!" she said fiercely.

"Jesus, those are some big stakes!" Christy gasped.

"What the hell, Justine? Why couldn't you have picked something else, something we're good at? Shit, what are we gonna do?" Taylor moaned. Justine rubbed her chin and eyed the men, her brilliant, evil mind plotting.

"We'll have to use what our mamas gave us. New plan: seduction is our weapon," Justine said.

"For real?" Taylor gaped at her.

"Do you want Blake to name my baby Mötley Crüe? Or after a motorcycle? I can't wait to introduce you to baby Ducati Miller!"

Taylor sighed. "No."

"Then get sexy, now!"

"Some of us don't need to try," Christy's smug smile made Taylor snort with laughter.

"Just think sexy, Taylor, and go with your instincts. Aaaand break!" Justine clapped her hands together and they joined the men on the court.

"You ladies ready?" Dean asked, spinning the ball on his index finger, trying to intimidate them.

"Nearly, one question though. I don't wanna confuse my little lady brain on the teams so are y'all gonna be shirts and we'll be skins?" Christy asked, cocking her head innocently, gripping the hem of her shirt and lifting it over her head.

"Fuck no!" Dean yelled and pulled her shirt back down.

"Why have I seen her shirtless twice in the last twenty-four hours?" Taylor asked Justine who just winked at her and mimed *get sexy!*

"Okay ladies, I think I see where this is going, and I've got to say I'm a little disappointed in you. I think you just set feminism back fifty years at least with that little stunt. But if you wanna play dirty then we can accommodate," Blake said, then gripped the back of his shirt and pulled it over his head, tossing it to Justine.

"Wait, it's backfiring, no fair!" Justine whined and Taylor watched her run her eyes over Blake's torso lecherously. Dean laughed and removed his shirt, earning a curse and a glower from Christy. Taylor's eyes shot straight to Beau. His revelation last night of having no confidence had shocked the hell out of her. Had he *seen* himself? Holy hell. That's why she'd gotten a little loose-lipped in telling him exactly what she thought of him. She wondered what he thought of the things she said.

Her eyes stayed on him, and she was stunned when he smiled shyly at her and slowly pulled his shirt off, tossing it at her, hitting her in the face. She scrabbled with the material, desperate to get a view of him. There he was. *Finally!* Her eyes drank in the sight of him hungrily. And God, was it a sight to behold.

He was magnificent. Rope after rope of muscle cascaded down his chest and abdomen and oh crap, he *did* have the elusive eight-pack. Her hands twitched to press each of the muscles that popped in front of her, to feel him beneath her fingers again. She spotted the silvery stretchmarks stark against his tan skin, streaking across his shoulder to his biceps and some around the curve of his hips and stomach but that was all. She didn't care about those or the patch of skin he mentioned on his abdomen, they were actually very sexy. They were evidence of his journey, his weight battle fought and won, his *strength*.

Shit had she actually agreed they wouldn't sleep together again? As she stood here taking in the sight of him she struggled to remember why. Her mouth ran dry as she continued cataloging every inch of him. She finally met his stare and a strange smile played at his lips, one she hadn't seen before, almost devilish.

"Let's go, ladies. First to ten wins," Dean said.

"Is that it?" Taylor asked, unable to tear her eyes from Beau's chest, her tongue barely moving in her mouth it was so heavy.

"We're doing three rounds," Beau said, crossing his arms over his pecs, making her want to sink her teeth into the skin. God, she needed to calm down.

They took their places on the court, Blake giving Justine the universal signal for *I'm watching you* and then they began.

Chapter 19

The game turned into an epic clusterfuck.

Beau watched as Christy dribbled the ball up the court, Dean right behind her ready to snatch it away. Then Christy turned slightly and all of a sudden, she was rubbing up against Dean. Her ass pressed back into his crotch, once, twice, then Dean spun away leaving her unguarded as she raced up the court to shoot.

"What the fuck Dean, get the ball!" Blake shouted.

Dean faced the opposite way, his hands on his hips. "I, uh, just need a minute, guys," he shouted back.

"Unfuckingbelievable," Beau muttered under his breath, chasing after Christy but he was too late. Her tiny body leapt into the air to make a shot and the ball sailed through the net with a delicate *swish*. Beau fixed her with a sharp glare but she just gave him a coy smile and twirled a blonde curl around her pinkie like butter wouldn't melt.

"I see you, Christy. Damn cheats, all three of you!" Beau shouted, indignation firing his blood.

"Walk it off, man," Blake said, rubbing Beau's shoulders.

Beau shrugged him off. "I'm cool, I'm cool."

Christy high-fived Taylor who shot him a smug look before her eyes dipped to his chest which was damp with perspiration. He flexed a pec, the muscle jumping, and her gaze turned downright obscene. If the ladies were going to play dirty, maybe he could use his assets too. After the things Taylor said last night, and the looks she was giving him today, he felt the beginning of a newfound confidence in himself. The look she'd given him when he'd taken his shirt off was two parts *come fuck me* and one part *mine* and he loved it. Except she had put an end to any more sexy shenanigans between them.

The next example of blatant cheating came from Justine when she bent over in front of Blake to 'tie her shoelaces'. Her little skirt flipped up, giving Blake the perfect view of her panties. Taylor made the most of this distraction and scored.

Beau shook his head at Blake in disappointment. "Walk it off, man," he mimicked Blake's earlier words. Blake flipped him the bird.

The ladies won the first round but by the second round, the men were on to their tricks and had pulled back a victory. Midway through the final round, Justine had to bow out, feeling tired so Blake sat out with her in solidarity. Christy and Dean had been so successful at turning each other on that they had disappeared.

It was down to Taylor and Beau.

"You can do it, Taylor, you know what the stakes are!" Justine shouted from the side-lines while Blake fanned

Sweet Surrender

her with his shirt, trying to cool her down.

"So do you, Beau, don't let me down," Blake called.

Taylor dribbled the ball up the court and Beau chased after her, wrapping his arms around her, caging her in as he tried to block the ball. She stumbled but he caught her, pulling her against him. Her eyes glued to his chest, her tongue ran out over her lips like she wanted to taste him before she broke away to get the ball. He figured out how to get under her skin.

He came up in front of her, invading her space. "You like what you see, Taylor?"

She faltered, her eyes darting away.

"Is this what you picture when you touch yourself, sliding your fingers in deep and wishing it was me?"

She gasped at his words but the heat in her eyes didn't lie. She wanted him but she wouldn't give in. Looked like he had to take one for the team. She tried to get round him, but he blocked her, pulling her against him and batting the ball away.

He nipped her ear. "Shall we stop *pussy*footing around?"

"What do you mean?" Was she breathless from the game or from their closeness? He really hoped it was the closeness. He released her and grabbed the ball.

"One more basket, sweetheart. If I win, we get a do-over on our night together. If you win, we have it your way and we don't do it again," he said.

She snapped her teeth at him. "No way!"

"You scared?" He bent down putting them nose to nose. "Scared at how much you want more?" he purred, and she shoved away from him.

"Fine, let's do this and I *will* win. Now I have two reasons instead of one, you just made me more determined," she smirked, all sass.

They tore up and down the asphalt. Justine and Blake were screaming from the edge of the court. Beau managed to get the ball off of Taylor and ran full speed down the court, Taylor hot on his heels. He leapt into the air and her body crashed into his side, throwing him off-balance. He missed, the ball going wide of the basket. He was so stunned she managed to move him that he was too late. She grabbed the ball and was halfway back up the court. His pulse pounded in his ears, his heart in his mouth as he watched her shoot in slow motion and the ball sailed through the net.

"Yes!" she yelled, and then Justine was hugging her. High fives went round as Christy and Dean reappeared. Then she grabbed him and dropped a kiss on his cheek.

"Don't be salty, *Teddy Beau*, it's better this way," she murmured.

He remembered he was meant to be pretending to be her boyfriend which was why he pulled her into his arms and buried his face in her neck, not for any other reason.

*

Later that week Taylor burst into the cabin, slamming the door shut and scaring the shit out of Beau. He leapt to his feet, his heart in his mouth as he pulled her behind him, ready to take on whoever was coming after her.

"What's wrong?" he demanded, peering out the front door, the sun low behind the trees as it kissed the sky goodnight.

"Nothing, I'm good." She jumped in front of him, her eyes bright. "Get changed, I've got a date for us to go on." All smiles and excitement, she raced into the bedroom.

"Jesus Christ Taylor, you scared the crap out of me!"

he shouted, following her. He watched her skipping around the room as she grabbed clean clothes. He noticed that she got them from the dresser not the floor, sticking to her promise to be tidier. She quickly changed in the bathroom and then came out to find him still standing there. As she brushed her hair, he narrowed his eyes suspiciously. "Where are we going?"

She spritzed herself with perfume before turning to face him with that dazzling smile. "It's a surprise."

He frowned and she spotted his reflection in the mirror. She came and stood in front of him, the cloud of her scent wafting over him. "What's wrong with surprises, Beau?"

"You know I don't like them," he sulked.

She rolled her eyes and punched him playfully on the arm. "I know but it's a good surprise, I promise."

He didn't budge and her forehead creased until they were wearing matching his-and-hers frowns. His stomach clenched. He didn't ever want to be the reason she frowned.

"Don't you trust me?" she asked.

He stroked his thumb over the creases in her forehead, smoothing them away then tucked a curl behind her ear. "Of course I do," he replied softly, enjoying being able to touch her so freely.

"Great! Now get changed," she said, smacking his ass and tearing out of the room. *Tornado Taylor,* he thought with a smile and did as she asked.

"I'm ready, do I need anything?" He came out of the bedroom and felt her eyes sliding over him. He'd only changed into clean jeans and a V-necked sweater.

"Just your car keys but you can give them to me, I'm driving."

His eyes widened. "You've got to be kidding me."

"You said you trusted me," she pouted, and he wanted to pull her bottom lip between his teeth. *Did nibbling her count as kissing? Could he get away with a fake boyfriend nibble?*

"Fine," he sighed, dropping his keys into her outstretched palm. They left the cabin and got into his car. He watched as Taylor stroked the leather seats, over the dashboard and around the steering wheel reverently.

"Can you please stop fondling Beatrice?" *And start fondling me?* Watching her fingers stroke and squeeze was making his jeans extremely tight.

"Beatrice?" She snorted with laughter and then clamped a hand over her mouth, pulling a laugh from him. "I'm so looking forward to this," she said.

"Taking Beatrice for a spin or our date?"

"Both," she replied, smiling at him and he genuinely felt like they were headed out on a date together. Then she revved the engine loudly and his light and fluffy feeling disappeared.

"Oh God, I'm nervous," he groaned.

"About my driving or our date?"

"Both," he quipped, and she shot him a sharp look.

"I'm an excellent driver I'll have you know," she sniffed. A wave of nostalgia threatened to consume him as memories of teaching her to drive clamored for attention. Had she forgotten that? The arguments, the tears, the triumph when she finally got the hang of the stick shift. The way she'd thrown herself at him with glee and he'd tried not to sniff her hair and pretend she was his girlfriend.

"I know you are." His reply managed to convey all his memories and he felt a lump rise in his throat. Her gaze softened, her mouth opened then closed and she looked away again, breaking the spell.

They arrived at their destination in one piece, he only

had to pump his imaginary brake once as she parked at a random building in the next town over.

"I still have no idea what we're doing," he said, looking up at the building which gave him zero clues. She surprised him by taking his hand as they walked in and squeezing tightly, his pulse pounding at the contact.

"You'll see in a minute," she sang.

She led him inside and then he saw a sign for "Cathy's Couple's: Cooking and Baking Classes" and excitement fizzled inside him like he was a kid at Christmas.

"We're baking?" He tried to keep the eagerness out of his tone but failed miserably.

"Yup! Aren't I the best fake girlfriend ever?" She beamed at him but dropped her voice slightly when she said *fake*.

"Hands down the best fake girlfriend I ever had," he grinned at her. His brain trying to interject that so far, she was better than *any* girlfriend he'd had, real or fake, and he shoved the thought away. He wanted to pull her into a giant bear hug, squeeze her and never let her go, or press kisses all over her face.

She had done something really special and found an activity he would thoroughly enjoy. He couldn't remember the last time someone had done something special for him. His throat tightened as he savored the moment. With her beaming up at him, and the thoughtfulness she'd shown, and the pure amazing fact that they were here together, that they'd gotten to this point in their relationship. *I only ever want to be with her.* The thought cooled his blood slightly. *This isn't real, remember?*

"Come on!" She dragged him inside before he could dwell on his thoughts any longer.

Inside the room were six individual workstations that each contained a mixer, cake tins and utensils, ingredients, oven mitts and aprons. There were other couples already gathered at each station checking out their equipment. He and Taylor greeted everyone as they made their way to the empty station at the back of the class. Most couples said hi back but one couple in particular were really sizing them up.

Beau put his hand on the small of Taylor's back and dipped his head to her ear. "I think we've found the couple that are going to take this way too seriously."

"We're totally gonna kick their ass, aren't we?"

"Absolutely," he replied, kissing her forehead.

"I warn you, it's a beginner's class so don't get too excited about what we're baking," she said, nibbling her lip nervously.

He passed her an apron. "Sweetheart, I'm going to love it, no matter how easy it is because I get to do it with you."

She smiled back at him, taking the apron and then her expression shuttered slightly.

"Everything okay?"

"Yeah, I just don't want to get confused about what we're doing here," she said, pulling the apron on but struggling to tie the strings at her back and he desperately tried to ignore that it said *Kiss the Chef*. He knew what she meant. The lines felt like they were blurring but he knew that although he wanted to explore what he was feeling, he had to accept that she didn't. He took hold of her strings and spun her around, tying them.

"I'm not confused, I know what I want." He nipped the back of her neck and a soft sigh slipped from her. "And I want to beat that couple in front," he added, trying to keep the mood light and not wanting to spoil the evening. She laughed and shoved him away.

He put his apron on, his reading, *I Cook As Good As I*

Look. Taylor read the apron then her eyes ran over him, scorching, and he tried desperately to think of something else, he didn't want his apron tenting out in front of everyone.

A petite woman with dark hair and cherub cheeks came to the front of the class. "Hello lovers! I'm Cathy and welcome to Baking for Beginners!" She cheered and the other couples clapped, except for the one in front of them. Beau caught Taylor's stare and they rolled their eyes then stifled a laugh.

"Today we're going to be making a classic Victoria sponge cake along with six raspberry and white chocolate cupcakes."

"Fuck yes," Beau murmured, and Taylor snorted next to him.

"The couple with the best bakes will win two free spots in the intermediate class," Cathy added and there was a chorus of *oohs*.

"Is this bringing out your competitive edge?" Taylor hissed.

"Absolutely, I need you to bring your sassy A-game because we're gonna be trash-talking Romeo and Juliet in front."

She snorted. The sound warmed him, he loved making her laugh, always had. Cathy ran through what to do first and then they were let loose.

"Hand me the cupcake tin," Taylor said.

"Which one is that?"

"It's cute that you're pretending you don't already know but cut the macho bullshit because we need to win," she snapped and the couple in front turned to stare at them. Taylor smiled at them sweetly, and the couple spun back around, bumping into each other, and knocking their tins flying with a resounding *clang*. As they scrabbled around trying to pick them up they bumped their foreheads together and started arguing.

Beau put his fist in his mouth to stop from laughing. "That's my girl."

They worked closely together, dividing up the tasks, watching as the other couples devolved into arguments that would definitely carry on when they got home that night.

"I don't know about you but I'm feeling pretty smug right now," Taylor murmured.

"I know. We've got this, I believe in you," he replied.

"Do you think that's too much sugar?" Taylor asked. He peered over her shoulder. Tendrils of red hair that had long escaped the messy knot on her head now stuck to her neck. Without realizing what he was doing, he clamped his hand around her neck and dug his thumb in, massaging the tissue.

The moan that slipped from her lips was downright carnal, causing another couple to stare at them. The man in front saw what Beau was doing and the effect it was having and tried to copy him. But when he grabbed his partner, she dropped the cake batter all over the work surface, ruining it and then another argument escalated.

"I think we're showing everyone up," Taylor giggled.

"Good," he replied gruffly, possessiveness clawing his chest. He kissed the back of her neck and had the satisfaction of watching goosebumps rise on her skin. "Perfect amount of sugar," he said then stepped away, hiding his tented apron as best as possible.

A little while later they were putting the finishing touches on both cakes. Another domestic broke out with a third couple, and Taylor and Beau didn't even pretend they weren't watching.

"Definitely going to continue that fight when they get

home," Taylor murmured.

"I feel like Cathy needs to have a Singles' baking class for all the couples that break up in this one. I forgot how much fun we had people watching," Beau smiled.

"Okay, I'm done with frosting, what do you think?" Taylor said. He came up behind her, her usual scent of cinnamon combined with sugar making his mouth water. He looked down and saw she had piped adorable little love hearts on the cupcakes. He rested his arms either side of her against the workstation, bracketing her in.

"They look perfect."

She cheered then spun around. "I think we'll do it; we'll win!" she said excitedly, her eyes shining at him. She had a dab of frosting in the corner of her mouth and his eyes zeroed in on it, desperate to swipe his tongue out and taste it, taste *her*. *Finally*.

"You've got something..." his voice broke off as his hormones went into overdrive. Her eyelids dipped seductively, and her breathing quickened as his eyes captured hers and refused to let go.

"Taylor..." he began, his voice rough as stone. "Ask me..." he said and her eyes flared as she realized what he wanted. Her eyes dropped to his lips then back up to his, her pupils expanding but she didn't move. He could see a thousand thoughts flit across her face. "I won't take it, not if you aren't offering..."

Chapter 20

His words played across her mind. God she almost wished he would take it. That he would kiss her, take the decision away from her because it was toying with her constantly and she couldn't take much more. Her wants, her desires were warring with her head.

They stayed locked together for what felt like an eternity, like they were alone in the room waiting for the decision to be made. With a heavy heart, she swiped her tongue out and licked up the frosting, then turned back to the cupcakes.

She thought that things would turn awkward after their moment, but they settled back into easy conversation. He chatted away like nothing had happened and it warmed her that their friendship was there, underpinning them. Like now it would always come first.

Sweet Surrender

The thought was freeing in a way, so that if she wanted to give in to her desires and sleep with him again, hell even kiss him, that maybe they would be okay afterwards. Perhaps it was because they spent so long without each other in their lives that they already knew what the worst-case scenario felt like.

Cathy clapped her hands to gain everyone's attention. "Okay couples, time's up!"

She went around each workstation, sampling cakes and giving constructive feedback. Taylor noticed the couples who were still speaking were hugging, holding hands or touching each other in some way. She always had a natural instinct to touch Beau and had spent years fighting against it. Now she gave in, leaning back against him and smiling to herself as his arm circled her waist and he rested his chin on her head.

"There's no way these couples have done better than us," he whispered.

"Cocky much?"

"You know it. Me and you can do anything together." The confidence in his tone made her smile even wider and then Cathy was at their workstation. She sampled a cupcake and the Victoria sponge, when she went back for a second helping, Beau shot Taylor a triumphant smile.

"I think we've found our winners!" Cathy declared. "Your sponge is light, moist and perfectly baked. Same with the cupcakes and the frosting. Absolutely delicious, the flavor has just the perfect amount of raspberry without being overbearing. Congratulations you two, I'm impressed." They both shook Cathy's outstretched hand and then Beau spun Taylor around, cheering. Cathy gave them the information about the next class and the other couples reluctantly congratulated them on their way out.

"That was a perfect evening," Beau said when they got

home later that night. Sincerity shining in his beautiful eyes. He slipped his arms around her waist and pulled her into a tight hug. "No one's ever done anything like that for me before," he murmured then dropped a kiss against her hair. His sweetness made her heart ache, and she squeezed him tighter.

"Well it's not over yet, we've got a couple of weeks until the next class."

"We better get practicing," he said, pulling away before she was ready. She reluctantly dropped her arms then scolded herself for being upset. *She* was the one who had put a stop to any more physical activity between them.

"I'm gonna head to bed," she said, her voice a husky rasp.

His eyes flared at her and she had tried to fight it but there was no use denying how much she wanted him. If he gave her the signal, she would launch herself at him now. The domesticity of their evening had gotten her riled up like she couldn't believe, especially with all the touching, teasing and close encounters.

"I've got some meal prep to do so I'll be a while," he said, heading into the kitchen. *There's your answer.*

"Oh, okay well goodnight then," she said, the sting of rejection pricking at her.

"Yeah, night." He was already pulling out his containers and grabbing food from the fridge so she went into the bedroom and shut the door.

It didn't take long to fall asleep but dreams of him plagued her. Replaying their night together but extending it and creating new scenarios. Him on his knees, worshiping her. Her on her knees worshiping him, coming together to find their release. She moaned so loudly in her sleep that she woke herself up, her skin damp, her breath panting.

"Sweetheart, you're absolutely killing me," came his muffled voice next to her.

"Beau?"

"You're awake?"

She heard the covers moving as he turned towards her, she could see the outline of him in the dark, the pillow fort disbanded long ago. Then his hand was on her arm, his heat seeping into her, her skin too sensitive from her dream.

"I am now," she breathed. Her body ached for his touch, not the gentle touch of a friend but the urgent, insistent touch of a lover.

"Bad dreams?" he croaked, stroking up and down her arm to soothe her but it had the opposite effect. He knew exactly what she was dreaming about but this time she wasn't embarrassed. She wanted him to know, hell, she just wanted *him*.

"Only because they weren't real." She gripped his arm, pulling him closer to her.

"Taylor…" his warning echoed around the room.

"I know what I said. But now I know what I want, Beau." She took his arm, stroked over the bunched muscle of his bicep, down his firm forearm and brought his hand between her legs. He didn't move but his heavy breathing told her everything. "So give it to me. Please," she whimpered, and he pulled her back against his bare chest and then cupped her sex. They both groaned, his head falling into the crook of her shoulder. He took his hand away to pull his sweatpants down and she ripped off her tank top and shorts.

He tugged her back against him, skin to skin, his hips cradling her ass. Then his hand was back between her legs, stroking her. He slid a finger between her folds, circling her clit in dizzying strokes. Pleasure spiraled through her and she wrapped both her arms around his that ran down her body, trapping him to her. Covering his hand with hers, she pushed him to where she needed him to go, crying out when he hit that spot that made her world fragment and rearrange.

He held her tight, impossibly close, working his fingers inside her expertly. Like he could tell exactly the way her body needed to be touched. Like he had been doing it for years, so in tuned to her that knowing how to please her just came naturally. He added another finger, stretching her and she cried out, rolling her hips into his hand.

He hummed in her ear. "What am I doing, sweetheart?" His voice low, commanding a response and driving her need higher.

"You're touching me, stroking inside me," she gasped out as he pinched her clit, rolling it between his thumb and forefinger. His hips rocked against her ass, his hard cock hot silk against her skin.

"Does it feel good?"

"God, *yes*. Don't stop." She clenched around him as a little shockwave passed through her, a taste of what was to come. He wrapped his other arm around her collarbone, trapping her against him. His hot breath caressing her ear over and over until she was shaking.

"I want to feel it, sweetheart. I want to feel you give yourself over to me."

She whimpered as he buried his face in her neck, nipping at the tendon then kissing, sucking. He rolled her bud between his fingers, and she lifted her hips again and again until she screamed. Lights shooting off behind her eyes and her whole body shaking from the intensity of her orgasm.

He brushed kisses over her neck, shoulder and jaw and

she shuddered through the aftershocks. "That's my good girl," he murmured and just like that, she was revved up all over again.

How the hell did he do it? It was like he reached into her brain and hunted out all the sexual needs and fantasies that she didn't know she had and brought them into the light, exposing them.

He kissed her temple again and removed his fingers then sat up, pulling her boneless body into his lap. Her legs automatically wrapped around his hips and she came up against his erection. She took hold of him, stroking him through her wetness and his dark curse filled the room. Her fingers didn't quite meet as she held him, God, he was going to feel amazing.

"I know we're not concerned about a pregnancy but are you sure you want to keep going without a condom?" His use of *we* and the gentleness in his words took the sting out of the painful topic. "I've been tested, I'm all clear," he said, his voice straining slightly as she wriggled in his lap.

"So am I," she said, then put him at her entrance and released her grip on him. His hips thrust up and he pulled her down and repeated until her body finally accepted him. He paused, his forehead pressed against hers, giving their bodies a moment to get used to each other. He bent his head and slid his tongue across her nipple. She clenched around him and his breath huffed out, he leaned back on his arms and then he let go, thrusting up into her with hard pulses of his hips.

"Do you know what it's been like, laying next to you every night and listening to that sexy moan, knowing you're dreaming about me?" he grunted out as he pounded into her. She whimpered, words failing her as she clung to him, sailing towards another climax.

"Who's inside you?" he demanded, his hand cupping her ass and squeezing tight, grinding into her and her eyes rolled back in her head.

"You," she moaned.

"Who's fucking you, Taylor?" That same demanding tone that drove her wild. Making her want to obey and defy at the same time, just to see what he would do next.

"You are, it's only you. Making me feel so damn good." His hand dipped between them to stroke her while he kept her tight against him, not allowing her space. She couldn't escape the intensity, the *intimacy* he was demanding of her. Goddamn him, she gave in.

"Who is it?"

"It's you Beau. I only want you," she cried out, spasming around him. He held her down, held her still then groaned as he filled her, their foreheads still pressed together. He left her nowhere to go but just let her walls crumble down as he held her, their panting breaths the soundtrack of her surrender and nothing had ever felt this right.

"Fine," she muttered as her breathing returned to normal. "I guess we can keep doing that."

He chuckled. "Finally, we're on the same page."

*

Her consciousness tried to pull her out of dreamland, but she wasn't ready yet. Except she felt warm, wet and *really* good.

"I need you to wake up sweetheart, otherwise I can't keep going without this being all kinds of wrong." The gravel in his voice teased her nerve endings to a fever pitch and her eyes popped open. She was laying on her back in bed, the blankets bunched around her. A smile lifted her lips as she saw Beau at her waist, pressing kisses to her stomach, his arms wrapped around her, hands on her ass. Those damn glasses perched on his nose, giving her all kinds of feelings.

"That's a nice view first thing in the morning," she sighed, combing her fingers through his soft hair, tugging gently as he nipped her skin.

"Tell me about it," he growled, staring down at the panties covering her. "It's about to get a whole lot nicer. Up," he commanded. Her hips shot off the bed at his demand and her eagerness to have his mouth where she needed. He leaned back as he pulled her panties down her thighs and off and she got a glimpse of his arousal outlined by his boxers.

Just kissing her and the promise of what was to come was enough to get him hard and she loved how receptive he was. She noticed he didn't try to cover his body, he owned it now, confidence cloaking him and nothing was sexier. He lay back down, his mouth hovering over her, his hot breath teasing her.

"Put your legs over my shoulders."

She didn't hesitate.

"Good girl." He smirked at her eagerness but she didn't care, she just wanted what he was about to give her.

He slid his thumb over her damp slit and her breath hitched as he found her clit and she watched him focus his attention on her. He stroked over her a few times before he dipped his head. The first slide of his tongue had her back arching off the bed, pressing her firmly into his mouth. The second slide had a moan slipping from her. Then he pushed two fingers inside her, pumping in and out as he leisurely licked her. He fit his lips around her clit and hummed, the vibrations echoing through her body and she gripped his head, holding him to her.

"Greedy girl, aren't you?" he groaned.

"Yes, now give me more," she gasped. He pulled back and blew gently against her exposed skin, the cool air tingling over her.

"Beau…" she grunted. Part warning to stop playing with her and part desperate. He dipped his head again and this time slid his tongue inside her as his fingers rolled over her clit in tight circles. Her moans became louder, her hips rolling into his mouth with fervor. Just as she was about to have the orgasm of her life, he stopped.

"If you want that orgasm sweetheart, you've got to earn it," he said, untangling her legs from his head and standing up.

"What the fu-?" she began, dazed and confused.

"We're going for a run and if you're a good girl, you'll get a treat afterwards," he said, pulling on a t-shirt and covering up all those delicious taut muscles.

"Are you actually serious right now?" she squawked. He tugged on his shorts which did nothing to hide his erection. One she wanted to get her hands on, now. She reached for him but he stepped away then threw some clothes at her.

"You're mean. You're not a nice boy at all," she grumbled, and he huffed out a laugh.

"Now you know the awful truth. Come on, the more time you waste the less likely you are to get your treat," he said and with that he left the room. She watched him go, baffled at what was happening. He was *bribing* her? To go for a run?

"Asshole!" she muttered.

"I heard that," he called from the other room.

"Because I said it out loud!" she shouted back, her frustration making her furious.

"One more time and there'll be no treat afterwards. Trust me, Taylor, you want this treat."

Her body screamed for attention but she was also intrigued by what dirty delights he had in store for her. She got dressed, muttering under her breath, angrily shoving her legs into her shorts.

Ten minutes later she was running. Taylor didn't run but the delight on Beau's face had been so worth it. *Almost.*

As they ran through the town, she could tell he was running at a slower pace than normal so she could keep up and she tried not to find that super endearing. They ran into the forest and she had to beg him for a break from this damn torture.

"This....is.... hell," she wheezed.

His laugh echoed around them, bouncing off the trees. "Just a tiny bit further."

She glared at his back as he jogged off, a glare was all she could muster at this point. Plus she got distracted by the way his round ass bounced along in those running shorts. Her distraction caused her to trip over a tree root and at the speed she was going, a plummet to the ground felt inevitable. She braced herself for impact but it never came. Beau grabbed her, stopping her from face-planting the dirt.

"You okay?" he asked, looking her over. She stood up straight, wincing slightly as her ankle hurt.

"Come here." His arm went around her waist, the other hooked under her knees and lifted her into his arms. "There's a clearing just up ahead where you can rest for a bit," he said.

She snuggled into his chest. "A girl could get used to running."

A deep laugh rumbled from his chest and as they made

it into the clearing she gazed around, her eyes wide. Pine trees lined the edge of the clearing, their shed needles covering the ground in a soft, spongy carpet. The lake was so still, the water so clear it reflected the trees from the opposite bank on the calm surface. Crickets and birds sang in perfect harmony. Large rocks lined the edge on one side and Beau gently placed her on the smooth top, settling down next to her. They sat in silence, listening to the birds, watching the water, enjoying the tranquility of nature together.

"This is where I like to come for peace," Beau said after a while.

"Oh yeah? I didn't take you for a nature buff," she teased, bumping his shoulder with hers.

"I used to come here to get away from school. Girls using me, teasing me. And I figured I ought to get some fresh air in between *Star Wars* marathons," he joked. She frowned, remembering how the girls treated him, so callously. She figured his change of tone signaled it wasn't something he wanted to discuss so decided to go down the nerd rabbit hole with him instead.

"Did you ever pretend to be looking for Leia in these woods, like in *Return of the Jedi*?"

He stared at her for a moment, his mouth open. "How did you know that?"

"Please, it's so obvious, this is totally Endor!"

"You know about *Return of the Jedi*?" His excitement was palpable.

"Calm down, it's the only one I saw. But I do love me some Ewoks," she grinned at him.

"You kinda remind me of an Ewok you know?" He ran his hand through her hair, tugging at the strands.

"Hey!"

"What? I mean the hair, yes. And how cute but feisty

they were, definitely reminds me of you."

She pouted. "Yes, all women want to be compared to the stupid teddy bear things and not every male's fantasy of Princess Leia." She folded her arms over her chest, her pride stinging.

"Okay, firstly, they're not teddy bears. They're sentient furred bipeds who-" he cut himself off when she growled at him. He laughed and pulled her into his arms, kissing her neck.

"Secondly, Princess Leia has nothing on you, sweetheart," he murmured, kissing her neck again and nibbling the sensitive skin at the hollow of her throat. She tilted her head back, letting him explore, her eyes fluttering closed.

"That's better," she purred, sliding her hands around to cup the back of his head. He kissed his way under her chin then up the other side of her neck and along her jaw. Her breath hitched the closer to her lips he came until he stopped. He looked at her, waiting to see if she would ask him, his eyes practically begging her to beg him. She wanted to but she knew he would think it meant something and she didn't want him to place any significance on it.

She did want to please him though. She maneuvered herself in front of him and stroked her hand down his chest. He wasn't even worn out or sweating from their run, the man had stamina which only meant good things for her. She trailed her hand over his abs to his crotch where she felt him growing hard and pressing against the material of his shorts.

"You talking about *Star Wars* is definitely my new kink," he smirked. She smiled and stroked over the ridge and his eyelids fluttered closed, bliss creeping over his face when she squeezed his length. The sun shone down on him through the trees, warming his tan face, highlighting the shades of brown in his hair. Damn he was the most beautiful man she had ever seen. She glanced around and seeing no one nearby, she dropped to her knees, tugging at his shorts.

His eyes flew open. "Taylor, we can't!"

She laughed at his scandalized expression as she popped him free of his boxers. She closed her hand around his length and pumped up and down a few times before arching her brow at him in question.

"Do it," he growled.

Her pulse pounded, she loved it when he told her what to do. She slowly slid her tongue over the head of him and he grunted. "Again."

She submitted and ran her tongue down the length of him, pressing against the thick vein that ran along the underside. She dallied, taking her time with him.

"Quit playing, sweetheart. Suck it, now." His voice all rough and ready, his dark eyes glittering down at her with banked need. She took him into her mouth, hollowing her cheeks and was rewarded with a dark curse as his hands flew into her hair, guiding to where he needed her.

"I know you can take it all." He stroked her jaw and she angled her head back, relaxing her throat and he slipped in a few more inches. She hummed and watched as his head dropped back on a moan. His hips thrust and she tightened her lips around him, rolling her tongue.

"God Tay, you're amazing," he grunted as she sped up. His hands tightened and his breaths turned to short, sharp pants. She pulled back and focused on his crown, her hands working him.

"Shit, I'm going to...if you don't want..." He couldn't get his words out but she didn't mind. Loved that she had him like this, reduced to moans and grunts and unable to finish a sentence. This strong, powerful, commanding man was putty in her hands. She had unraveled him and it was a sight to behold. She sucked hard, sliding her tongue over the slit tip of him and squeezing the base.

"Taylor!" His hips stuttered and he burst onto her tongue in waves and she continued working him, pulling every drop of pleasure from him until he slumped back against the rock, completely boneless.

She smirked, satisfaction fizzling in her veins along with renewed arousal. She pulled his shorts back up and then fell against him, her arms winding around his neck. For some reason she needed to feel him close. He kissed her shoulder, then her cheek.

"That was…I can't…no words."

"I can tell," she laughed, taking in his slightly steamed up glasses. "That was your punishment for leaving me needy this morning."

His lips lifted in a smirk. "That was a punishment? Best one I ever had." His hand ran up and down her spine.

"You got the energy to run back?" she asked when he didn't move.

"Always but let's walk. Besides, now it's your treat. Come on." He took her hand, leading her out of the clearing. Half an hour later they were sitting in a booth at Ruby's Diner with a massive slice of cookie dough cheesecake and two forks.

She raised her eyebrow, skeptically. "This was my treat?"

He grinned at her as he speared his fork into the crumbling crust. "Is this not good enough?"

"Well, it's not gonna give me an orgasm is it?"

"Let's see, shall we and if it doesn't then I guess I'll just have to step in. But it's really good so…" he trailed off, waggling his eyebrows and she fought a smile. He shoved a forkful into his mouth, moaning in ecstasy. She watched him but hesitated.

"What's wrong?" he asked.

"I don't know. I just need a minute. I know it's only cheesecake, but I haven't had this since…" she trailed off, realizing she had said too much.

He frowned. "Really?"

She nodded, her cheeks heating. "I know it's stupid but I didn't want to eat it…without you." A tidal wave of emotion rushed through her and tears stung her eyes. *What the hell girl, it's just fucking cheesecake! But it's not, is it? It's all the times we had it together, all the conversations and laughs, the memories.* As her brain argued with itself, he reached over the table and rubbed her knuckles with his thumb.

"I only ate it without you so I could remember the times we had together, the memories. I felt like it somehow made me closer to you. So it's not stupid at all," he said, his expression unreadable. An emotion she couldn't pinpoint floated in the air between them. Affection? Nostalgia? Something more? Who knew, but it was making her uneasy.

"Distract me," she demanded, digging her fork into the biscuity goodness. "How are your folks? And your sister?"

He nodded. "Folks are good, they retired to Florida to be near Rachel and they're enjoying every moment of it. Especially as Rachel just had nephew number three. I really need to take a trip to see them, Uncle Beau has missed a lot recently. Those boys will be driving her crazy but they're amazing," he chuckled. Her stomach clenched at seeing his face light up talking about his nephews.

"Do you want kids?" Her question slipped out before she could stop it. He stopped eating, his fork hovering in front of his mouth. He swallowed thickly then shrugged.

"Yeah I do. Someday. I've never really thought about it, never met anyone who made me seriously think about it. Except you," he murmured.

"You know I can't have them."

"No Tay, that's not what I meant." He sighed, dragging his hand impatiently over his face, bumping his glasses. "You know adoption is totally an option, right?"

Her face heated, she didn't like talking about this, God knows why she even brought it up? He had this uncanny ability to see into her and have her spill all her thoughts and feelings to him, even her most private, guarded ones.

"I've not let myself consider it before. I don't want to get my hopes up just to have them dashed."

"Why would they be dashed?"

"Because who's gonna let me have a kid when I'm single and spend all my time in a bar and have a psycho stalker who-"

He cut her off. "You mean who's going to let the smart, caring, maternal, *selfless*, successful businesswoman with a strong sense of right and wrong and a great supportive family unit behind her raise a child?"

She looked down into her lap, unable to meet his eye after his lovely words. "Beau-"

"I'll come with you to enquire, if you don't want to go alone," he said softly. Her chest constricted at the thought of him being there with her through this journey. A small flame of hope flickering before she doused it.

"Ha! How long do you think our fake relationship is going to last, the next eighteen years?"

"Be serious Tay. You can do this. You can raise a child, you're the best woman I know with the biggest, fullest heart." He took her hand, rubbing his thumb over her knuckles again. She looked into his eyes, so full of hope and compassion and something else she didn't want to inspect too closely. She wondered if he was pushing this out of guilt, maybe he felt like he had to right a wrong.

"It wasn't your fault."

"I know that."

"We're not a real couple."

"I know that too Taylor, shit," he growled, his jaw clenching as he looked away. "But that doesn't mean I can't help you achieve something you want so damn badly. Something you would be incredible at."

She felt tears prick the backs of her eyes. No one had ever said she would be an amazing mom before. He patted her hand and went back to his cheesecake like he knew that was enough on this topic, knowing she'd hit her limit.

Her fork still held her helping of cheesecake and she brought it to her mouth. Her first bite since she was seventeen. She shoved it in, immediately moaning as the flavors hit her tongue. *Sugar, glorious sugar.* She inhaled the rest of the slice, licking her fork clean, tongue combing the tines before she remembered her manners. She looked up. His eyes were locked on her mouth, wide and burning at her.

"We're leaving now," he grumbled and dragged her out of the booth, slapping some money on the counter as they left. Taylor was glad Ruby wasn't around today to witness the scene, she would have a fuck ton to say about it.

They ran back to the cabin until she had to stop halfway, her ankle starting to hurt again. He heaved her over his shoulder and kept running, slapping her ass when she griped about it and then she giggled at his desperation to get her home. He put her down on the front porch so he could unlock the door. She ran her hands over his wide shoulders and broad back, eager to get him naked and have him inside her making her moan.

He unlocked the door and went inside already reaching for her but she stilled him, spotting the white envelope on the doormat. A chill ran through her veins at the sight of it, all her mail went directly to the bar, the last time she got a note like this it was from Dale.

"What is it?" he asked.

She picked it up, turning it over. The envelope was blank, unsealed. She steadied her shaking hand and pulled out the paper inside. There were a few sheets folded together in half. She unfolded the first one, taking in what she was looking at and gasped.

Chapter 21

Tension thrummed in his veins as all the color drained from her face.

"What?" he demanded, taking the paper from her hands. Then he saw it: it was a sketch of a forest but in the clearing, against a rock was a man and a woman. The woman was on her knees while the man had a hand buried in her red hair, his head tipped back in pleasure.

Beau's stomach dropped as he realized it was depicting their mind-blowing encounter just hours earlier. Only one person would be following them, only one person would be sick enough to draw a picture of their private moment then send it to them. Dale had been so quiet for so long that Beau had been certain he had gotten the message and left them alone.

"He's still watching," Beau said, scrunching the paper in his hand. She nodded, her hand covering her mouth.

He took the other pieces of paper from her and looked through them. They were all different sketches of the two of them together. Them at the gym, at the bar, playing basketball, even watching TV on the couch: the fucker could still see into the cabin.

"Christ, he's been watching us this whole time!" Beau shouted, rage consuming him at all their intimate moments being invaded.

"What's it say on the back?" At her voice so quiet, so small, his rage dulled and his need to protect her roared to life. He flipped the page over and ran his eyes over the angry red scrawl.

All these private moments and not a single kiss shared...

Beau growled, tamping down his instinct to tear the note to pieces when they needed the evidence.

"Fuck!" he shouted, some of his rage escaping. He pulled Taylor into a hug, needing to hold her, to know she was safe in his arms and craving comfort himself. She buried her face in his chest and sighed deeply.

"It's gonna be okay," she mumbled against his t-shirt.

A laugh huffed out of him despite everything. "I'm meant to say that to you."

She pulled back and looked up at him, shrugging. "I'm sorry I dragged you into this, it must be a nightmare for you."

"Hey, no! Do not apologize, it's not your fault, it's his."

She gripped his t-shirt, balling the material in her little fists. "I'm glad I'm doing this with you. As vile as the situation is I'm kind of grateful. I mean look where we are now, compared to a few months ago." A small, shy smile formed at her lips. "We've got our friendship back."

She was right, if anything this trouble with Dale had done the impossible by bringing him and Taylor closer together. Although it was true, he was annoyed she reminded him that they were just friends, even now, after everything. Surely they were at least friends with benefits? It felt so natural and he didn't want this to end. He wanted them to stop faking and start living this relationship for real. They were the best of friends, but he wanted more, he wanted forever.

The thought pinged around his mind like a pinball. He knew in his soul she was the one for him, had known it his whole life. No other woman had ever compared to her, no other woman felt as right as Taylor did in his arms. No other woman had ever known him like her. She was it. She was *his*.

The only part of his realization that terrified him was that he knew she didn't feel the same. He knew she was happy they were friends again, but more than that? She didn't do relationships, didn't do *any* serious attachments, so where did that leave them? It was too depressing to think about, so he shoved it aside and smoothed a hand over her hair. "I hate the guy but I think I'll always be grateful for what he's given me."

Her wide eyes, full of emotion, wrecked him. Making him want to get on his knees and beg her to let him inside her heart, let him love her and love him in return. But he couldn't.

"Let me call Blake," he said, pulling away. When Blake answered Beau proceeded to explain what happened. After a few grunts and some cursing, Blake said he'd meet them at the bar when Taylor's shift started.

Taylor went to shower and get ready while Beau checked the perimeter of the cabin and tried to rearrange the drapes so there was no way Dale could see inside.

When she was done, Beau got changed and they went to the bar together. He would stay all night; he didn't dare leave her alone tonight.

When Blake turned up, they all went into her office.

"What are these pictures?" Blake asked, pulling on forensic gloves. Taylor unfolded them and held them out. Beau held up his hand as Blake took them.

"One of them is…sensitive." Beau gave him a meaningful look. He wasn't worried about how it looked on him, it was Taylor's privacy he cared about. Blake nodded and looked them over, cursing when he saw the one of them in the forest. Taylor shifted next to him, and when Beau took her hand in his, she squeezed it in comfort.

"I take it you've not seen him during any of these…incidents?" Blake said, looking through the sketches again.

"Not since he last came to the bar," Beau replied.

"We couldn't get any prints off the last note he sent but maybe we'll get something from this and see if there's anything in his house we can match the handwriting to."

"Has he been home?" Taylor asked.

"Not that we've seen. He's still in the area, we got a hit on his credit card but we got there too late. We're pulling all the local CCTV to see if we can find anything. We will find him, I promise. I won't fail either of you," Blake said, an edge in his voice.

"I know you won't, B," Taylor nodded.

"Just keep doing what you're doing. He's already teasing us. He'll come out of the shadows and we'll get him," Blake said.

After Blake left, Taylor went right back behind the bar, throwing herself into work while Beau kept a close eye on her. When it became really busy he jumped behind the bar to help her out, pouring drinks, laughing with customers and keeping everyone happy. Eventually when there was a lull, he dragged her out from behind the bar and pulled her onto the little dancefloor, desperate to be close to her, to hold her.

"You need a break, and a smile," he murmured, wrapping his arms around her. She smiled up at him, her arms eagerly circling his neck. He began swaying them, a feeling of peace settling over him. Just as contentment at being with her washed over him, his doubts from earlier invaded his brain again. Could she have feelings for him? Could she want-

"Kiss me," she demanded, pulling him out of his romantic thoughts.

"What?"

"Kiss me. I'm asking you now. Have your reward or whatever, and kiss me," she said. Her hands linked behind his head and tried to pull him down.

He'd longed for this moment, where their lips would finally meet but something felt off. It wasn't intimate or the moment he imagined. The urgency in her eyes made him wary; it was all wrong. He tightened his muscles, stopping her.

"What's happening? Why now?" he asked.

She looked around them. "Because look how many people are here, it's public," she said. "Because if he's still watching then he'll see us and know it's serious." Guilt lay beneath her words.

Hurt crawled through him. She didn't *want* to kiss him. Wasn't desperate for his kiss even after all these years. She was just *using* him to hurt Dale. Using him like other women had used him in the past. The irony of the situation wasn't lost on him. He had tried to get her to do the exact same thing weeks ago, only he wasn't intimate with her then, his feelings weren't involved.

"So you only want to kiss me to make him jealous? You can break your rules when it suits *Dale* but not for me?" Her mouth opened to respond but he was too angry. "You want to *use* me?"

She reared back at his anger and he regretted how much hurt had slipped into his tone, not wanting her to know how it affected him.

Her brows knitted in confusion. "I hate to break it to you but what do you think we've been doing this whole time?"

He gritted his teeth. *That was different.* "But I thought-"

"You thought what?"

"Nothing," he said and pulled away. "I'll be back in a minute."

He raked a hand through his hair and left her on the dancefloor, heading to the bathroom. He needed a minute to pull his pride back together. To forget all the times someone had used him before. Telling himself that this was different, that Taylor was different. But this hurt more than any other time.

*

Taylor served her last few customers, looking over her shoulder again at Beau. Something was off with him. She had clearly upset him during their dance but she didn't know how. He'd said she was using him but Taylor hadn't intended to make him feel like that at all.

Yes, their agreement meant she was using him now, but he knew about it and had agreed to it. And hell, they were both benefiting from it, so what was the problem? The only reason she had asked him to kiss her was because she was desperate for this whole thing to be over so that she didn't have to keep looking over her shoulder for Dale any longer. So that she and Beau could continue on in peace…

Wait, no.

Once this was all over, she and Beau wouldn't be doing this anymore. A sharp lance pierced her chest and she rubbed it away, shaking her head to dislodge her thoughts.

There had been a second reason she suggested they kiss. She *wanted* him to kiss her. She wanted his kiss so badly but didn't know how to drop her walls and communicate it to him without it being such a big deal. If it was in a public place, then it took the significance out of this as the first kiss she had experienced since they were teenagers. That way, he wouldn't realize what he was beginning to mean to her.

If she kissed him, she would be breaking the only rule she ever had. *A rule put in place after the last time you kissed him,* her brain reminded her. None of this was helping. She was more confused than ever.

The point was, she had never meant to hurt Beau. She was surprised that even though she had hurt him, and that he was angry with her, he hadn't stormed out of the bar and left her. He was still here, like he had been the whole evening, supporting her. *Not* abandoning her like her brain had told her he would. Not abandoning her like Bobby and her deadbeat father had.

The bar eventually emptied and she closed off the register. Then she was locking up and walking back to the cabin with Beau. He was quiet and didn't try to take her hand. When they were inside he went into the kitchen to start his food prep for the next day. She hovered, unsure what to say.

"Uh, thanks for spending your whole evening at the

bar and keeping an eye on me." She wrung her hands as he turned his back to her.

"No problem, all part of the service." His tone was even but she could read him better than anyone, she could tell he was still hurt. He needed time to cool off. If she pressed him they would have a fight and that wasn't what she wanted.

"Okay, well, I'm going to bed," she said. He didn't reply so she left him to it. Hopefully when she woke up in the morning she would be wrapped in his arms and everything would be fine. She was already smiling at the thought.

But when she woke up the next morning, he was already gone. *You saw him last night, how do you miss him already?* Her phone pinged and she saw his name, a smile spread across her lips. *See? Maybe he misses me too,* she thought smugly. She opened his message but was disappointed when all it said was that Blake would be stopping by the bar to check on her. She thanked him and then got up and jumped in the shower to get ready. She had a long day ahead of her today: she was conducting interviews all morning before she started her actual shift in the afternoon.

She thought about Beau all the way through her interviews, barely paying any attention to them. Did he have many clients today? Were the Thirsty Bitch Brigade molesting all his thigh-quivering muscles? Did he have enough food to keep his energy up? Should she bring him some food? No, she couldn't leave. When she hired someone, she would be able to work shorter hours and head out for errands. Take him food if she wanted to. Take one of his classes. Pop out for some afternoon sex…maybe after she did his yoga class. He would get all hot and bothered helping her in and out of those poses, then they could steal off somewhere…

Finally, it was closing time and when she stepped outside and saw him standing there, her heart flipped in her chest. She felt icky since yesterday and hadn't realized how much she needed to see him. She threw herself at him and hugged him tight. His hands clenched around her, pulling her into him.

"I missed you," he murmured against her hair.

"I missed you too," she said, her heart banging against her ribs. When she stepped inside the cabin a sweet scent filled her nostrils, making her stomach growl. She narrowed her eyes at him. "What have you been up to?"

He gave her a crooked smile and gestured to the couch. "Take a seat."

By the time she shrugged off her jacket and sat down, tucking her feet under her, he was joining her.

"I'm an asshole," he said, and held out a plate to her that had a slice of cookie dough cheesecake resting on the surface.

"What?"

"I shouldn't have gotten upset yesterday. I understand why you thought that was the best thing to do, to kiss I mean. And I'm sorry my pride got in the way, I was forgetting what this was all about."

Her cheeks warmed and she looked down at her plate. "Did you make this?"

"Yep, it's my apology cheesecake. I know how much you like it, what it symbolizes for us and I also wanted to practice it before our next baking class." He ducked his head and she laughed.

He took a seat next to her. "I'm sorry, Tay."

She liked that he said the words, she hated when people said *I want to apologize* but didn't actually say sorry, thinking the statement was enough. "I'm sorry too, I didn't mean to hurt your feelings. Now shush, I need to try this."

He laughed and she cut a sliver and forked it into her mouth, her eyes closing.

"Mmm my god," she moaned, immediately shoving in another bite.

"Good?" he asked. She couldn't speak, not wanting to stop eating dessert-heaven, so she nodded. He smiled then popped a bit into his mouth.

"Oh God, I'm good," he groaned.

She snorted and watched him, smiling in amusement until he moaned again and licked his lips, his tongue swiping out. Then he closed his mouth around the fork, his lips pouting around the metal, his tongue sliding and her insides clenched, remembering what that tongue could do and what she was owed.

She watched Beau, completely oblivious to the havoc he was wreaking on her. She waited until he finished eating which really should have earned her a commendation for restraint from some kind of government body. Then she snatched his plate off him and dropped it onto the floor.

"What are you-"

She pulled him on top of her.

"Oh, I see." He grinned down at her. "I guess cheesecake for the win?"

"Shut up being smug and make me moan already. You owe me, remember?"

His eyes darkened. "I haven't forgotten, sweetheart."

He pulled off her top in one swift movement and peered down at her lacy bra, her small breasts trying to escape from the cups. He palmed her roughly, and stroked his thumb over her nipples, shifting his knee between her thighs. She bit her lip as he tormented her nipple, driving her need higher until she was trying to rub against him. Then he closed his mouth around the tip through her bra, the damp lace molding to her. He moved to her other breast and gave it the same treatment while tugging her skirt down.

"Wrap those gorgeous long legs around me," he commanded.

God, she loved it when he spoke to her like that, firing her up. She did as he said, hooking her ankles behind his back and he deftly flipped them so she was straddling him. Her core landed directly over the hard bulge in his jeans and she writhed against him while he kissed her chest, his tongue sliding over her skin.

"Please touch me," she moaned against his forehead. He pulled back and their eyes locked as he hooked a finger under her panties, finding her damp center and pressing hard. A gasp flew from her and his eyes heated another degree. He continued to press while using his other hand to remove her bra. Once her breasts were free, he sucked a nipple into his mouth and worked two fingers inside her, stretching her.

Her head lolled back and he sucked at the base of her throat, hard, biting and holding her in place as he rubbed that sweet spot inside her, driving her to the brink. He removed his hand and she growled in frustration, working at the buttons on his jeans, working him free so she could get him inside her quicker.

"Steady, sweetheart," he said, his voice gruff. He stood up and her legs dropped from him, toes digging into the plush carpet. He knelt down and slowly drew her panties down her legs and she braced herself on his shoulder as she stepped out of them. Then he leaned forward and pressed a kiss to her center. The kiss turned carnal as he slid his tongue over her clit, wrapping his arms around

Sweet Surrender

her and pulling her to his mouth, his palms squeezing the cheeks of her ass as he ate at her.

She cried out as she came, and he held her up before giving her ass a sharp swat that had her inhaling deeply as her body throbbed again. He grabbed her and bent her over the front of the couch and moved behind her, his hard cock fitting into the seam of her ass and rubbing gently.

He stroked down her bare back, over the curve of her ass then smacked her sharply.

"Oh, shit," she grunted into the cushion.

"That's for making me think about you constantly." His voice dark and rough, had her shivering and desperate for more.

Smack.

"That's for making me think about all the ways I could fuck you all damn day."

Smack.

"That's for making me think about how pretty you look when you're sucking my dick."

Smack.

"That one's for loving every single second of getting spanked like the naughty girl you are."

"Oh, God Beau, please," she moaned, not even sure what she was asking for, just feeling mindless with lust, his words driving her need even higher. He stroked over her skin, soothing away the sting and then he was at her entrance, pushing in.

He rocked his hips and eased into her slowly, not increasing his speed. She panted and clawed at the couch cushions, desperate for him to *move*.

"This is torture," she moaned.

He bent forward, his chest to her back, nipping her ear. "Why's that, sweetheart?"

"Because it's not enough!" she gasped out as he pinched her nipple between his fingers.

"Not enough?" He thrust inside her, swivelling his hips, hitting her just right but keeping the pace slow. Stars exploded behind her eyelids.

"Are you sure?"

"Hmm, God, yes."

"Because it sounds like you're enjoying this torture."

"Beau please!"

"Please what? Fuck you harder? Make you scream? Pound into you until we're both so mindless that we fall apart?"

"Yes."

"No, sweetheart. I like torturing you," he murmured.

And damn him but he did. Sweet, slow torturous strokes that drove her so out of her mind that when she finally found her exquisite release, she practically sobbed at the intensity but she wasn't done.

"Pull my hair." The command slipped from her, the first time she had ever asked for anything like that. She looked over her shoulder to see his reaction, how would he take it? His face was the picture of aggressive passion. He smiled at her, then wrapped his fist into her hair, her curls snaking themselves around his fingers in invitation, latching onto him.

"Say please."

"Please," she sobbed.

"That's my good girl," he purred, tugging her hair sharply and she rewarded him with a gasping moan. Then he finally pounded into her, exactly as he described, tipping her over the edge again. Giving her the best of both worlds and ruining her for any other man. He followed her over the edge, releasing her hair and she felt him pulsing inside her.

He collapsed onto her back, raining kisses down over her before tugging her into his lap. He hugged her tightly, both of them trying to catch their breath. Then she burst out laughing.

He pulled back, staring at her as if she were mad. "Taylor?"

"I was worried you would be boring in bed," she said, then laughed again. He just shook his head, a smile playing at his lips and pulled her in for another hug before feeding her more cheesecake.

Chapter 22

Taylor's perma-smile was starting to scare her interview candidates. She worked her jaw and massaged her cheeks, trying to ease the aches from her muscles before her smile slid straight back into place. She tried to fight it but why bother? If she was happy, she wasn't going to hide it no matter how much it bothered the twitchy frat bro sat in front of her.

She finished his interview very quickly, having already decided not to hire him the moment he greeted her with, "'Sup bro." *Ugh. My bar, my rules.*

She waited for the next interviewee to turn up, doodling little hearts and flowers over her notes and designing her next tattoo. Her phone pinged and she glanced down, her smile widening if that was even possible.

Beau: I miss you x

She began replying when she saw those three little dots appear and his follow up message came through.

Beau: If you could be a hidden design cake, what hidden design would you be?

She snorted to herself and started a new reply, her fingers flying over the screen and the door to her office opened.

"Take a seat," she called without looking up, too busy finding all the dirty emojis to send Beau followed by the cake emoji. The silence in the room had her frowning so she stopped typing and looked up. Gasping, she dropped her phone on the desk and jumped up. Her chair skidded back, scraping across the wooden floor.

"Hello baby. Did you miss me?" Dale purred.

When Beau spoke to her in that tone her whole body responded but when Dale did it, bile rose in her throat. He stood a few feet from her, his eyes wild, his smile sinister. His beard was long and unkempt, his clothes dirty and torn in places like he'd been on the run for a few weeks.

"Get out!"

He tsked. "I've been waiting so long to get you on your own, I wouldn't leave now."

Her eyes darted towards the door and he laughed, the sound hollow.

"Don't even think about it."

"What do you want?" She stepped out from behind her desk, not wanting to be cornered.

"You. And just to talk," he said, looking around the room.

"About?"

"When are you going to stop pretending there's something going on between you and that meathead? Like he would even be your type!"

His words gave her pause. He was right, Beau wasn't her normal type. She usually went for guys that were the complete opposite to him. As though her whole adult life she had avoided anyone who could remind her of him.

"His name is Beau and he means the world to me, so I don't need to pretend a goddamn thing." She folded her arms over her chest, confidence cloaking her because her words were completely true. Dale came closer but she refused to back up and show him she was scared. The stench of stale alcohol and cigarettes wafted from him and her stomach rolled. This was nothing like Beau's clean, fresh scent. God, how had she ever been attracted to Dale?

"I've been watching you," he taunted.

A shiver tried to roll down her spine at the reminder but she refused to react.

"How fun for you," she replied, all trademark sass and *don't give a shit* vibes. Reminders of the things he'd done to her, to her squirrels, barreled through her brain and she fought to stay calm. She adopted a bored expression and lifted her hand to study her nails, hoping he wouldn't notice how they shook.

"He doesn't mean shit to you, baby. You don't look at him like you looked at me, you don't even *kiss* him. He doesn't make you happy," he growled.

She fixed him with a cold smile. "I've only ever kissed two men in my life. One of them is him and the other sure as shit wasn't you," she taunted.

His face twisted with rage and his arms snapped out, trying to draw her to him, his lips puckering for a kiss, but she was quicker. She thrust her hand out and up, just like Beau taught her, the heel of her palm connecting with his nose. The sickening crack echoed around the room and Dale howled as blood poured from his nose.

Taylor used his distraction to make her escape, lunging for the door and yanking but it didn't budge. He had locked it. Her shaking hands fumbled, costing her precious seconds. Dale banded his arms around her in a bear hug, dragging her backwards. His putrid breath filled her nostrils as he slicked his tongue up the side of her face and she fought the urge to vomit.

Her pulse pounded, adrenaline spiked as fear tried to take over. She made herself focus on Beau's training. She shoved her panic away, and bent forward at the hips, using all her strength to flip him. Her muscles screamed but he flew over her shoulder, crashing onto the hardwood floor. She didn't pause, just ran straight for the door, unlocking it and throwing it open.

"Kayleigh!" she shrieked as she ran out. It was still early so the bar was empty and shit, she needed her phone. Dale was still rolling on the floor groaning, so she ran back to grab her phone and call Blake. Then Kayleigh was rushing in, concern on her delicate face.

"Taylor? What's going on?"

"Blake! I need you now, Dale-" She began when he answered but Dale lumbered to his feet and was running for the door. He barreled into Kayleigh, shoving her out the way and she cried out as she slammed into the door, dropping to the floor with a sharp crack of the head.

"Kayleigh!" Taylor cried, dropping her phone and running to her. She was slumped on the floor, not moving, and fear gripped Taylor. She rolled her over, crying out as she saw the blood coming from Kayleigh's head wound.

"Kayleigh? Can you hear me?" She patted her cheeks gently. Kayleigh groaned but didn't move.

"Help! I need some help in here!" Taylor shouted into the bar, surely there was someone here? There was a pounding of feet and then a man appeared.

"Oh my God, what happened?" he asked, his young face paling as he took in Kayleigh.

"I need some ice now!" Taylor snapped and off he went. She tried gently shaking Kayleigh but other than the odd groan, she wasn't getting much response. Taylor's stomach clenched with worry.

The young man reappeared. "I've called an ambulance, locked up the back and turned off the stoves. Here's the ice, we need to get her to wake up and to keep talking until the ambulance arrives. She's probably concussed, here's a bucket if she needs to be sick." He took a cloth and dipped it in the water, mopping over Kayleigh's brow and cheeks then dabbing carefully at her wound.

"Ka- uh, What's her name?"

"Kayleigh," she replied, dumbfounded.

"Pretty. Okay, Kayleigh you need to wake up now," he said, pulling her up so she rested back against his chest.

"Who are you?" Taylor asked.

"I'm Ben Morgan, I'm here for my interview," he said, his green eyes swinging to her. A couple of shades lighter than her own, more jade. His dirty blond hair flopped over his forehead. He continued wiping Kayleigh's face, talking to her and keeping her awake. Taylor couldn't believe Kayleigh had been injured because of her. Poor, sweet Kayleigh who wouldn't hurt a fly.

"Taylor?" Kayleigh groaned.

"I'm here," Taylor replied, taking her hand.

"I'm no doctor but I think she's definitely got a concussion," Ben said.

Kayleigh sighed and beamed at Taylor. "I love you!"

"Aw, I love you too, Kay," Taylor patted her hand, but Kayleigh moaned.

"No, you beautiful dummy. I *love* you," Kayleigh said

again.

Taylor's eyes flicked to Ben and he gave her a tight smile, and said, "Yeah, she doesn't know what she's saying, I'd ignore that."

Taylor nodded, and then the ambulance was here. Taylor and Ben moved to the side while the paramedics got to work.

"So, um shall we reschedule my interview, I'm free anytime?" Ben said, tucking his hands in the pockets of his jeans.

"Fuck your interview, you're hired. When can you start?" She'd watched him remain calm under pressure, think outside the box, and care for his future colleague. She'd seen all she needed to see. Anyone could be taught to pour a pint but the qualities he'd already exhibited impressed her more. His eyes flicked to Kayleigh and he worried a hand over his stubbly jaw.

"Really?"

Taylor nodded eagerly.

"I guess I can start next week?"

"Perfect! Wait, how old are you?" she asked. His face was young but his mannerisms spoke of someone much older.

"I'm twenty-six and a non-smoking Sagittarius who likes long walks on the beach and quiet nights in," he quipped then his smile fell. "Ah, sorry about that, my mouth runs away with me sometimes."

"Then we're gonna get along just fine. And you'll be fine with Kayleigh too, you're the same age so you'll probably have loads in common."

He looked at Kayleigh again, concern on his boyish face. "Yeah, we probably do."

Then Blake was rushing inside with Beau right behind him.

"Taylor!" Beau shouted when he spotted her, all frantic energy. He pulled her into his arms, holding her tight and she wrapped herself around him.

"Are you okay?" he asked, trying to examine her for injury.

"What happened?" Blake asked, taking out his notepad.

She hugged Beau again, not ready to let go. His arms flexed around her as she went into detail for Blake. The whole time, Beau's hand was running up and down her spine in soothing strokes. When she mentioned how she defended herself, Beau gripped her chin, tilting it up.

"I'm so fucking proud of you, sweetheart," he said fiercely, and his stare fell to her lips before he pressed a hard kiss to her forehead. Her eyes closed in bliss as she bathed in his pride, warming her like the sun. She finished explaining what happened with Kayleigh just as the paramedics interrupted to say they were taking her to hospital.

"Surely you can arrest him now? That's assault," Beau said.

Blake nodded. "Yeah now we can, just need to find him first. Um—and who are you?" Blake turned to Ben who had been watching Kayleigh quietly. Ben introduced himself.

"Are you prepared to give a witness statement?"

"Anything for my new boss," Ben smiled, and Taylor had a good feeling about him.

"Right, let's head to the station then. I'll get a man posted in the area to keep an eye on the bar and your cabin, see if this asshole shows his face again," Blake said, then ushered Ben out. Taylor locked up the bar then Beau drove them to the hospital.

"Are you really okay?" he asked. She took in his

clenched jaw, his knuckles white from choking the steering wheel, his clipped tone. The man was on edge.

"I'm a little shaken. I didn't know what he was going to do, Beau. I didn't know what his intentions were. But I stayed calm and did what you taught me." She thought that might calm him but judging by the rigid set of his shoulders he was getting angrier by the second. His nostrils flared dangerously; she needed to show him she was okay.

"I kicked his ass!" She whooped and Beau's eyes flicked to her briefly, and she did a series of karate chops shouting 'hi-yah!' like a fucking pro. When he turned back to the road she saw the twitch in his lips and had to settle for that.

"Thank you for showing me how to defend myself. You protected me without even being there," she said.

"When I think about what could have happened…"

"Don't," she shushed him and took one of his hands, lacing their fingers together. They rode the rest of the way in silence. When they got to the hospital, they had a long wait until Kayleigh was finally discharged. When she tottered out into the waiting room, Beau wrapped an arm around her shoulders, holding her up.

"You're gonna have a badass scar," he said, pointing to the stitches on her forehead.

"Kay, I'm so sorry about what happened," Taylor said, pulling her away from Beau and into a hug. When she had first started at the bar, Kayleigh had annoyed the hell out of her but now, she was the little sister Taylor never had, she was family. "Obviously take as much time as you need to recover."

"You want me to come back?" Kayleigh asked, her eyes wide and bright.

"Of course! Why wouldn't I?"

"Because I said...never mind."

"Besides, we have a new bartender to train up and I can't do it without you," Taylor said, squeezing her shoulders again. They drove Kayleigh home, getting her settled. Her parents immediately began fussing over her.

When they headed back to the cabin, Beau remained silent the entire time and Taylor kept shooting him questioning looks. Once they were back inside, he dropped down onto the couch, and she flopped next to him.

"When Blake messaged me, my heart stopped, Tay. I haven't known fear like that before. I thought I'd lost you."

"Hey, I'm fine, because of what you taught me, remember?" She placed a hand on his broad thigh, the muscles bunching under her touch. Man, why hadn't she paid attention to his thighs more, they were yummy.

"I know, it's just the thought of losing you..." His voice trailed off and he looked at her, his dark eyes deep pools of worry. She needed to comfort him, she needed to comfort herself. When she thought back to this morning and what could have happened, it made her think about things, what she could have lost, what she'd been missing.

Before she could talk herself out of it, she climbed onto his lap, her legs straddling his. Their faces a breath apart and his hands settled on her hips naturally. His eyes shifted over her face, questioning. Her pulse thudded in her ears, every sense heightened to excruciating degree and she leaned in to kiss him.

He pulled back and a low growl slipped from her lips when he denied her, his eyes flaring hotly.

"Ask me nicely, Taylor."

He probably didn't think she was serious. Goddamn

him, he was even controlling this too, testing her, demanding she do this his way, making her *work* for it. As though he read her mind he said, "You made me work for this, so now I'm making *you* work for it." His lips hovered over hers, his words breathy, tickling her, ratcheting up her need. His nose nuzzled hers, his grip on her hips tightened to a degree she thought she would bruise but she didn't care.

"Beg me," he breathed. She inched her body closer, arching a brow when she came up against his hardness. "Someone's overexcited."

He huffed out a laugh. "I just know how good this is gonna be."

"But what if it's not?" The hitch in her voice betraying her vulnerability.

"Are you actually worried about a kiss when we've had mind-blowing sex?"

"But our first kiss was…what if this isn't?"

"Our first kiss was *what*, Taylor?"

She pinned him with her stare. "Perfect."

His eyes darkened at her admission. "Well, I'm worried too," he said.

"You are?"

"Yeah. Worried that you'll only let me do this once when a million times wouldn't be enough."

Her heart stuttered in her chest at his words, at his sweetness.

"I haven't kissed anybody since Bobby, that day in the hallway," she blurted out. Anger flared in his eyes but was gone a moment later. He tucked a strand of hair behind her ear, cupping her jaw and stroking his thumb over her cheek. The way he was touching her, the way he was looking at her like she was the reason the sun rose every morning, she felt cherished. He had dismantled her walls little by little, working his way inside her.

"No pressure on me then," he said softly. "Now stop stalling, you know what I want to hear." The timbre of his voice grew rougher by the second, razing over her skin causing shivers to ravage her.

"Please Beau," she whispered. A sound she could only describe as a snarl slipped from him.

"Again." His hand circled the back of her neck, cradling her skull.

"Please Beau. Please, kiss me."

Finally he closed the distance, agonizingly slow, making her wait. His own exquisite brand of torture just for her.

His lips hovered. "So beautiful," he whispered, then kissed her cheek. Softly. Gently. His lips like silk over her sensitive skin. He kissed her other cheek, then each of her eyelids. Her forehead. Her throat became thick with emotion. Then he was kissing his way along her jaw, stopping just as he reached her lips. She moaned, the anticipation killing her. *Pure, undiluted torture.*

His lips whispered across hers, tingles crawling through her entire body as he did it again, continuing to tease her, making her hungry for more. When a whimper slipped from her, he gave her what she needed.

His lips pressed against hers firmly, his hand wove into her hair, holding her to him. Her stomach clenched as his tongue slid along the seam of her mouth and she opened eagerly.

He tilted his head for deeper access, stroking his tongue against hers, the kiss spiraling to a wild, animalistic place. A rumble echoed in his chest as she sucked his tongue and nibbled at his lips. A desperate noise wrenched from her and she tried to grind against his lap.

Then Beau slowed the tempo, pulling back and making her follow his lead. Dominating, setting the pace and she could only surrender and let him control it. Goosebumps raised her skin as his lips opened and closed over hers. Heartbreakingly tender. Ruining her, just like she knew he would. She was ready to tear his clothes off, she never wanted this to end. Never wanted to give up heaven now she found it.

No other man had tempted her to break her no kissing rule, because she knew no man could kiss her like *this* man. Beau knew what she wanted, their bodies spoke to each other, in complete harmony. They were one, their lips fused, only parting to change angle, to get closer. *Can't get close enough.* His tentative little licks into her mouth drove her wild, pushing her to breaking point.

She started trying to pull his shirt off but he stilled her hands, pressing his forehead to hers, his breath tickling her skin.

"No, sweetheart. Do you know how long I've wanted to kiss you? How many years I've thought about our first kiss? I'm not stopping already; we're going to do this all damn night if we have to." Then his mouth landed back on hers.

She sipped at his lips, drinking them down like the most expensive champagne. They changed positions, rolled onto the floor then he carried her to the bedroom, not breaking their connection once, and they kissed until they fell asleep.

It was the best night of her entire life.

Chapter 23

Taylor ran into the cabin, startling him from his thoughts and fantasies of the previous night.

"Did I miss it?" she shouted, throwing her purse down and leaping onto the couch, snuggling into his side. He could feel how wide his damn smile was as he peered down at her, her eyes sparkling with excitement.

"No sweetheart, I paused it. I was beginning to think you wouldn't be back tonight," he said.

"I know, Dean was feeling a little down. He's missing Christy loads but her book tour is nearly finished so she'll be back soon."

"Ready?"

"Set?"

"Bake!" they shouted together, and he hit play on the remote and the *GBBO* began. It was the final episode of this season and what a season it had been. Full of drama, scandal and amazing bakes.

"Amir is totally gonna win, remember his bread sculpture last week?" he asked, kissing Taylor's head, breathing in the scent of her hair.

"Psh, it looked good but it didn't have the right texture and consistency. Hazel has had two *Hollywood Handshakes*, she's definitely going to win," Taylor countered.

Further into the show Beau was getting annoyed over the harsh critique Amir was receiving. "The technical round is too hard; they can't prepare for it!"

Taylor snuggled into his side deeper and linked their fingers, resting them in her lap. "No, it's not. Just because someone hasn't ordered a margarita doesn't mean I don't learn how to make it, like, always be prepared?"

He snorted. "Like a boy scout?"

"Exactly! This is why Hazel is gonna kick his ass. Did you see her showstopper? That woman can make anything."

He chuckled, looking down at her and a weird feeling clenched his stomach. He couldn't imagine sitting here and having this debate with anyone else. He didn't want to be here with anyone else. He only ever wanted her. The domesticity of the moment had him picturing forever with her and a lump caught in his throat.

He loved her.

Who was he kidding, it had always been her, even when he hated her, he had loved her. Taylor was the woman he'd never forgotten, never moved on from and never gotten over. The one he couldn't live without because if he had to, he would be a fraction of the man he was when he was with her.

She pushed him, made him want to be better, be a better match for *her*. She was what his life had been missing. Being here with her, true satisfaction settled in him for the first time, like all the pieces of his life were slotting casually into place. She was his and he needed to know how to convince her they were better together this way.

He thought she might be starting to feel the same. Hope filled him when she had kissed him, he knew what it meant to her. Their kissing yesterday had been intense, emotional and it had fused such a deep affection and connection between them that he was sure she was falling.

"Yes!" Taylor crowed, breaking through his thoughts. His attention turned back to the TV and he saw Hazel being presented with the winner's prize: the cake stand trophy. Taylor leapt up from the couch and began a crazed victory dance that had Beau laughing until she was chanting *loser* in his face. He grabbed her, flinging her over his shoulder and carried her to their bedroom.

"Put me down, you Hulk!" she shouted, half laughing.

"Whatever you say," he said, dropping her onto the bed and immediately covering her body with his. His lips hovered over hers, letting her make the decision. She instantly arched up and met his, sliding her tongue into his mouth and he moaned at her tantalizing taste, making his pulse pound.

He took comfort from the fact that she didn't even hesitate to kiss him now. That definitely meant something. That he was the only person she kissed since she was a teenager reconfirmed his hope that what she felt was more than friendship and explosive lust. She sucked his tongue hard and his cock jerked in his sweatpants, eager to get inside her wet heat. He fumbled with their clothes, their mouths connected the entire time. When they were naked he rolled them onto their sides and slung her leg over his hip.

His hand trailed down the smooth, creamy skin on her stomach to his new paradise. She was already so wet and he grunted his approval, unable to use words anymore. He slid two fingers inside her, her panting breaths trekking over his face as he watched her eyelids flutter closed in pleasure, brows pulled together in satisfaction. He couldn't get enough of watching her, imprinting her on his brain so he would never ever forget. Her eyes opened and a seductive smile curled across her lips.

"It's rude to stare," she murmured, raising a sassy eyebrow. God, he loved her sass. He stroked over the spot that had her squirming then thumbed her clit, her gasping moans making him feel pretty smug.

"You were saying?"

She cursed and he laughed until she took control, pushing him onto his back and climbing on top, she bent and kissed her way down his stomach, paying extra attention to each of his stretchmarks and that only made him love her more. She made him feel something he'd never felt before; *beautiful.*

She shuffled down his body, her mouth hovering over his hard length. Her hot breath teasing the sensitive flesh.

"Do it," he commanded. She gave him a long, slow lick, flicking her tongue over the tip until he was lifting his hips and fisting the sheets. She teased and taunted him, tortured him like he had done to her until he couldn't take anymore and he flipped them, rolling her onto her back. He parted her legs, looking down at her spread wide for him.

He pressed himself to her entrance and watched as her body took him inside. He slid in and out slowly, whimpers and pleas falling from her lips. He bent his head and took her hard nipple into his mouth, sucking gently and her nails clawed at his back. Her every movement, every sound drove him wild until slow was no longer an option. He drove into her, their arms wrapped around each other, leaving them nowhere to go to escape the intensity.

He crushed his mouth to hers and she opened immediately. She lifted her hips to grind into him, he knew what she needed, always knew. But he couldn't bear to remove his arms from around her, never wanting to let her go. Instead, he swiveled his hips, hitting a deeper spot.

"Beau, my Beau," she chanted as she came and that was enough to send him over the edge. Her body squeezed and clenched around him, refusing to let him go. As they both came down from the high, their breathing returned to normal. She pressed a soft kiss to his lips and those three little words nearly fell from his. He managed to snap them back at the last minute. He'd told her with his eyes and his body how he felt but not his words.

His words would scare her.

*

It had been nearly a week since the incident with Dale and Taylor hadn't realized until she received a message from Ben confirming he would be at the bar shortly for his first shift. She had been too wrapped up in Beau, literally, to notice. She shivered at the thought of him, a warm fuzzy feeling snaking its way through her. They were insatiable at the moment, they couldn't be around each other for more than two seconds without ripping each other's clothes off.

He punished her yesterday morning when she got

smart with him over his morning breath which hadn't been anything other than minty fresh, but she liked poking the bear when she knew what the reaction would be. He'd given her three earth shattering orgasms with his hands and mouth before he declared she'd been suitably punished, and she was too weak to comment either way. Until she saw the smug grin on his face and tackled him until he surrendered to his own punishment.

The next day she'd been in the bathroom, brushing her teeth when he sauntered in. She could see the solid outline of his erection through his sweatpants, his stupid sexy glasses perched on his nose, taunting her. When he used his index finger to push them further up his nose, she was a goner. Her core had pulsed in anticipation as he swaggered over to her and the next thing she knew they were going at it on the bathroom floor.

This morning he'd been late for work, which was absolutely not her fault *whatsoever*, and he'd forgotten his lunch so Taylor was taking it over to the gym for him. When she arrived, he was in the middle of a yoga class, currently in downward facing dog and *fuck* did his ass look good. So biteable. The women in the class clearly thought so too as most of them weren't even in poses, they just watched him with an intensity that bordered on unacceptable. Maybe she needed to show them all that he was taken, that he was *her* man.

She blinked at the thought. Obviously the sex haze she was in was fogging her brain and making her plan a future she wouldn't have. He wasn't hers. He never would be.

She watched the session from the side-lines, enjoying the way he moved around the room, teaching others, correcting poses, so full of patience. He was always so calm and tolerant, until he was with her. Her favorite thing about Beau had always been his kindness, his goodness. She was always wild and rebellious but he grounded her. Now she'd discovered he had a secret carnal side to him, a dominating, taunting side that came out to play in the most wonderful of ways and lord he was giving. To everyone else he was the happy-go-lucky perfect gentleman. To her, he was down, dirty and raw, nothing held back. He was a surprise and he was perfection.

In short, he was a sex unicorn, and she didn't plan on letting him go anytime soon. Wait, *retraction*, she would be sad to let him go when this whole thing was over. But until then, she would continue to enjoy him.

The class came to an end and this time when all the women swarmed him for attention, Taylor was at the front of the crowd, throwing elbows and not feeling bad about hitting a horny Grandma. Before he took his lunch from her, he greeted her with a passionate kiss that drew catcalls from the women, Ruby being the loudest of course. Taylor wasn't ready to leave him yet so she waited until the women were finally done with him. Ruby sidled up next to her in another fabulous outfit of bright orange and purple spandex which left zero to the imagination.

"You marrying him yet?" she said.

"Actually yes, has your invitation not arrived?"

Ruby sucked her teeth at Taylor's sarcasm then swanned off shouting, "Lock that shit down now!"

Taylor laughed, shaking her head at the old bat's antics before she turned back to Beau. Finally everyone left and they were alone. Then he was dragging her into the nearest supply closet. Her mouth was on his, her dress pulled up and his sweatpants down in seconds.

"Goddammit woman, I've thought about you all morning, you're driving me crazy," he grunted as she wrapped her legs around his waist and he thrust into her, backing her into the wall and pinning her with his hips. He fucked her hard and fast, just how she wanted it, how he needed it.

"You feel so good, you always know what I need," she moaned. He pressed their foreheads together, their breath mingling. She felt the build up inside her, wanted to look away from him but couldn't, it was all too much.

"Beau, I don't think I can do this anymore, it feels too real," she whispered. She could no longer hold back the fear she'd been hiding. The words slipping out without her permission, but she was raw and exposed under his penetrating stare.

"That's because it is, sweetheart, it is real."

Her heart pounding as he fed her another soul-stirring kiss. God, she loved his kisses, how had she spent so much of her life without them? They both came with a shout and then they slumped to the floor. She sat on his lap, catching her breath.

"Coming to the bar later for lock-up?"

"Of course I am. Do you want me to come in sooner? You don't need to worry, I'm not gonna let anything happen to you."

"No, it's fine. Ben and Kayleigh will be there until closing," she said. She wasn't asking him because she was worried about her safety, she just didn't like the idea of not seeing him for all those hours. God, how pathetic was that? After more of those drugging kisses, Beau pulled away moaning.

"We need to go or we're never gonna leave this damn closet."

"Is that such a bad thing?" Her voice husky when she felt him hardening inside her again. He groaned and scrubbed a hand down his face, his expression stricken, and a laugh bubbled out of her.

"Fine but you owe me tonight then," she said.

"Deal, can't wait." He kissed her nose then she got off him and they righted their clothing. They went back out to the gym which was mercifully quiet.

"Did you drive here?"

She hesitated, knowing he would be pissed. "Uh, I walked."

"Taylor!" he exploded. "Anything could have happened to you!"

"But it didn't! I saw lots of people, the streets were busy. I'm safe."

His jaw clenched and she wrapped her arms around his waist, peering up at him. "Are you mad? Are we fighting like a real couple?" she cooed.

"No, why?"

"Because then we can have super-hot make up sex." She waggled her eyebrows at him and his nostrils flared.

"Take my car and go now, woman. Before I show you that supply closet again," he growled.

"How will you get home?"

"I'll run." Another kiss to the tip of her nose.

"Okay but eat lots today then, I don't want you exhausted after running back. You need your strength for later," she dropped her voice and stood on her tiptoes to nip his chin.

His eyelids slammed shut. "Jesus woman, take my car and go. Right. Fucking. Now."

She giggled and snatched the keys from his outstretched hand and placed a quick kiss to his lips. "I love it when you cuss like that, wanna know how it makes me feel?"

"Taylor…" His warning had her laughing, she was such a brat.

As she left the gym she turned back and found him

watching her, the goofiest grin on his face and it took all her strength to leave and not go running back to him. She had to remind herself that this relationship was part fake, part besties and part friends with benefits, but it wasn't real, no matter what he said about it.

She drove home and floated into the bar, so pleased to see Kayleigh back at work. She was a little jittery which was to be expected but Taylor also felt like Kayleigh was avoiding her. She gave her the space to fall back into the routine, not wanting to push her. Then Ben appeared and she introduced him to Kayleigh properly.

She watched as Kayleigh showed him how to make cocktails and change a barrel over. Ben was eager to learn, watching Kayleigh with rapt attention. The evening went by with Taylor anxiously watching the clock, waiting for the night to be over so she could be with Beau. She had always loved her job but right now it was the thing keeping her from him, so she hated every minute of it. She decided to close up ten minutes early, unable to wait a moment longer.

She said goodbye to Ben and Kayleigh, almost shoving them out the door. Beau would be here in a minute anyway. She cashed up the register, counted and bagged in record time and headed for the door, excitement driving her steps forward.

She opened the door to the bar and reached behind her to flick off the lights but from the corner of her eye she saw a shadow outside. She froze. Beau wasn't here yet, she'd just looked out her office window and seen him moving around the cabin.

Her instincts went on high alert and fear trickled down her spine. Her heart pounded as she tried to slam the door shut but a foot blocked it. Then the door flew open and Dale was barging inside, all menace and erratic energy. He slammed the door shut behind him and her pulse skipped as he headed towards her.

Taylor didn't wait, she spun and ran for her office. He came up behind her, hot on her heels but she was so damn close to safety. He grabbed her hair, yanking her backwards and she cried out as strands were ripped from her scalp. She stumbled and fell, landing hard on her ass, pain rocketing up her spine. She pushed the pain away and rolled over, crawling towards the door.

"You can try as much as you like but you're not going anywhere," Dale sneered. His tone empty and cold. He waited until she had nearly reached the door then he stepped in front of her, blocking her path. He peered down at her.

"What do you want?" she spat, her voice wobbling slightly because she was scared and just wanted Beau. Dale ran his eyes over her, lingering on her body in a way that made her stomach drop. Did he want to hurt her? Rape her? She had no idea. Until now she had thought he just wanted her back but no, this—this was different.

"I just want to talk." He shrugged like it was no biggie. She made a move to stand but he put his boot on her hand and pressed down. Her knuckles cracked under the pressure and she cried out.

"You need to stop trying to run from me, baby and accept that we're meant to be together," he said.

"I couldn't think of anything worse," Taylor grunted through the pain.

"Are you sure about that?" he asked. The glinting of metal in the light caught her eye and her fear hit a whole new level as she realized it was a knife.

"Now I have your attention, here's what's going to happen. You're going to get rid of that meathead you're pretending to give a shit about and call off that fucking

Sheriff. Then we're going to be together, we'll live happily ever after once we've left town. I know without any other…distractions…we'll get back the love we had."

He bent down, the movement putting more pressure on her hand and a pained whimper slipped from her. He stroked a hand down her body, cupping her ass and she squirmed to get him off.

"How I've missed you, baby," he purred and her stomach churned. "The only question is can I wait to have you?" She tried not to vomit at the thought.

Then she heard it. Footsteps on the wooden decking outside and whistling.

"I bet that's lover boy now," Dale hissed in her ear. "Should we invite him in, dispense with the first distraction now?"

She froze. This new fear was nothing like what she felt moments ago. "No! Let's just leave, get away, just the two of us. It'll be like old times!" she said, trying to keep the edge of hysteria out of her voice.

"That sounds perfect," Dale replied, using the blade of the knife to brush the hair back from her face and she tried not to flinch. "But I need to get rid of him. I saw him kissing you, he took what's mine and he needs to be punished." He pulled away and headed for the door.

"No! Beau, run!" she screamed.

"You bitch!" Dale shouted. Whirling on her, he kicked his leg out and her hand was too slow to protect her face. Pain ricocheted across her cheek and lip, stars winking behind her eyes.

"Taylor?" She heard Beau's voice but she couldn't form words. Then the door opened and he saw her. "Taylor!"

"Don't touch her!" Dale screamed, launching himself at Beau.

"No!" Terror filled Taylor as they both tumbled to the ground, the knife gleaming and then disappearing. She tried to get to them but her body was sluggish, her face on fire and everything hurt. The men were locked together. She could hear the sounds of flesh against flesh. Grunts filled the room. She hauled herself to her feet and shot forward on wobbly legs.

"Taylor, run! Get out of here!" Beau shouted. It was sweet that he was trying to save her, but she would never leave him. Her hand was fucked so she used her bodyweight, just like Beau had taught her and threw herself at Dale, knocking him sideways. She tipped, the movement catching her off-guard then Beau grabbed her, dragging her towards the door. Dale rallied and came at her from the side, knife raised, enraged that she'd betrayed him and tried to help Beau.

Beau twisted and leapt in front, blocking Dale's move for her. Beau ducked and swung, nailing Dale in the ribs but it didn't slow the motion of the knife coming down. Taylor couldn't move, frozen as she watched that knife slicing towards Beau's chest.

Two shots rang out and Taylor screamed as Dale lurched forward and collapsed onto Beau, both of them crashing to the ground. She spun and saw Blake in the doorway, expression deadly, smoke curling from the barrel of his gun.

Beau hauled himself out from under Dale. Taylor ran to him, checking him for wounds. When she didn't find any, she burst into tears and for once she didn't reprimand herself for the emotion.

"Shh, sweetheart. I got you, it's okay," Beau murmured, stroking her hair. "Nice timing man," he said, peering over her shoulder to Blake.

"My officer watching the bar didn't check in when he

was supposed to. I'm naturally a suspicious guy, turns out for good reason," Blake said. He holstered his weapon and went over to Dale's body, bending to check his pulse before he shook his head. "He's gone."

"I'm gonna be sick," Taylor said. She ran for the restroom with Beau hot on her heels, holding her hair back while she emptied the contents of her stomach into the toilet. Then he got some wet paper towels and dabbed her face, frowning at her injuries. He threw the towels in the sink and turned away from her.

"Beau, are you okay?"

He sighed and turned to her, a new expression of torment in his eyes.

"Everything is fine now," she said and he leveled a dark look at her. "What else do you want me to say? I told you to run and you didn't." she continued.

"You think that's what I'm mad at? That I didn't run when I had the chance?"

"Aren't you?"

"Fuck no. Besides, you didn't run when I told you to either," he said.

"I couldn't leave you with him!" she cried.

"Ditto!" he snapped back. They fumed at each other. He folded his arms across his chest all anger and raw masculinity and she just wanted to curl up in his arms. Arms that were bleeding.

"Oh my God, come here," she pawed at him and he shook her off.

"It's fine, he barely got me. Come on, Blake will have questions." He held the bathroom door open and followed her out. More officers had turned up and were cordoning off the bar. Blake broke away and headed over to them.

"I'll need you both to come to the station to give

statements. The paramedics are outside to take a look at you first." He squeezed Taylor's arm affectionately before patting Beau on the back in that manly way that signified emotion.

"Thanks for everything, B," she said, kissing Blake's cheek.

They didn't get home until the sun was rising and all Taylor wanted to do was go to bed. She headed straight in and Beau helped her under the covers then snuggled up next to her, pulling her into his arms, holding her tight and finally she felt she could breathe again.

Chapter 24

When Taylor awoke a few hours later, she felt like shit. Her head was pounding, her body ached, her lip was sore. She was alone and she didn't like it but she needed to get used to it. She got dressed and went out to the living room where she found Beau watching a rerun of *Bake Off*.

"How are you feeling?" he asked, reaching for her but she stepped aside.

"Like shit," she muttered.

"Kayleigh said she and Ben can watch the bar today-"

"No, I want to go in," she interrupted.

"Tay-"

"No. He won't take this from me," she said.

She didn't like how intensely Beau was staring at her, so she turned away and busied herself in the kitchen. She had come here for a reason but the churning in her stomach and jittery nerves were making it hard to focus.

"So uh, the plan worked. Yay for us," she cheered weakly, not feeling victorious in the slightest. Beau didn't respond. Just pinned her with that stare that she refused to meet because if she did, she wouldn't get the words out. "It's all over, I guess we can stop pretending we're in a relationship now."

He dropped his head. "Is that what you want?"

Her heart skittered in her chest, banging against her ribs. She took a deep breath. "Yes."

He nodded then stood up and stopped in front of her. "Just so there's no misunderstandings, I want to be clear where I'm at. That's not what I want."

Her heart leapt into her throat and after a pause she said, "But it's what I want."

His eyes probed her and she tried not to flinch under the intensity. "We're perfect, Taylor. We're goddamn perfect together."

"Beau, no. It's just the situation forcing us. It's made you feel-"

"I've been thinking about you since I was fifteen years old. I've never stopped thinking about you. About *us*. I've tried to forget you but dammit you are a woman who refuses to be forgotten."

She stared at him, open-mouthed, stunned into silence as he paced back and forth.

"I've fallen in love with you, and I tried so hard not to. Actually, that's a lie, I didn't try at all. Because I wanted it. I've fallen hopelessly, *embarrassingly* in love with you!" he shouted. "You make it too damn easy to love you, you know that? You're too funny, too sassy, too caring, too sexy, too…. everything. I see you and I *feel* it, sweetheart, every damn time I look at you. I feel it in my soul." He grabbed her hands in his, his forehead pressed to hers, desperate breaths leaving him.

"Beau, that's very sweet but…" Her words failed her. He was asking her for a chance at forever but she'd seen what happens, forever didn't exist. She saw that people got bored and they left. Nothing lasts. Beau had already left her once before, and the result of that had been devastating as a teenager but now… and who was to say it wouldn't happen again?

She saw what heartbreak did to a person, how someone leaving could hollow you out, making you a shell of your former self. If Beau ever left her, she didn't think she could recover and she had worked too damn hard on building herself up, earning her own respect, to do that to herself now. Not even for Beau.

Plus, Beau still had the option to have children naturally and she wouldn't take that away from him like it had been taken away from her. He deserved the chance to have his own family on his terms, not be constricted by hers.

She needed to do what she always did and get out first; she was making the right call.

"Beau, I love you…as my friend. My best *friend*," she said, her voice hoarse from trying to squeeze around the lump in her throat.

"So that's it, you're giving up on us? You're not even going to fight for it? For me? I didn't take you for a quitter, Taylor."

She pulled away. "I'm not quitting us, we have so much history and I love having you back in my life and I look forward to a future of keeping you there. But as my friend."

"You're scared."

She never could hide from him, he could always see straight through her. "I'm not scared, I'm being smart. *We* need to be smart, to protect this and protect what we've got back. That's what I'm trying to do."

A hand tore through his hair, fisting the strands and he worked his jaw. "That's your final answer? You don't think this would work even though it's working perfectly?"

She shook her head and saw the resolve harden his eyes.

"I'll get my things together. I'll be out by the end of the day," he said, his tone empty.

Panic clawed at her chest, her throat as she reached for him. "Beau, you don't need to leave so soon."

He brushed her off. "Yes, I do. I think it's best we don't see each other for a while."

She gripped his arm, terrified at his withdrawal. "No! I've just got you back after all these years, please don't take this away from us. That's not what I want."

"But it's what I want," he deadpanned, echoing her words. He turned away.

"Beau, look at me," she pleaded.

"I'll see you real soon, Tay." He headed for the door but turned to face her just before he left, his heartbreak shining in his eyes and it was like she'd been sucker-punched. He walked out the door and hysteria bubbled in her throat.

She tried to tell herself that everything would be fine. That their friendship would recover, that they'd been through so much and come so far that she wouldn't lose him now. Their friendship was too important, it was *everything*. He just needed some time.

All day she tried to busy herself with work now that the bar was no longer a crime scene. She tried to dredge up some sadness for Dale, but she was too numb.

Every time the door to the bar opened, she turned, expecting to see those broad shoulders and dark sultry

Sweet Surrender

eyes and when she didn't, disappointment choked her. When the day was finished she ran back to the cabin, hoping he was still there. Maybe they could make some kind of friends-with-benefits type of deal.

She burst through the front door and without even looking around she knew he was gone. The cabin was cold and empty, he'd taken all the warmth with him when he'd left. She ran to the fridge throwing the door wide open, expecting to see all his pots and tubs stacked up, but they were gone. His bag wasn't on the table, but he'd left the TV. The TV full of baking shows she didn't want to watch without him.

She went into the bedroom, the pillow fort was stacked on her bed, all his clothes were gone. *What about...*She spun to the dresser which still held all the photos of them together. He'd left the original one he brought into the cabin. Clearly he didn't want the reminder anymore, and she grabbed it, clutching it to her chest and burst into tears.

That night she cried herself to sleep.

A Month Later...

"Ye look like *shite* for someone who should be on top of the world," Dean said. For some reason that Beau couldn't be bothered to ask about, Dean was trying out a Scottish accent. Trying and failing.

"I'm-" Beau began.

"Are we just gonna blow past whatever the fuck accent that was?" Blake scoffed.

"Christy's been watching *Outlander* and got a thing for Jamie Fraser so I'm just trying it out," he explained, his tone defensive as Beau and Blake looked at each other and burst out laughing. Blake slapped Beau on the back as

Dean's prissy expression sent them into another round of guffaws.

Damn it felt good to laugh. He hadn't laughed for a month, ever since he left Taylor's cabin after handing her his heart and having it crushed.

It felt like a lifetime ago that he'd been waking up in her bed every day, touching her, *kissing* her. Now when he woke up, he lay there miserable, contemplating the point of even getting out of bed. If he didn't have clients, he wouldn't have bothered.

Dean was right, he should be on top of the world. Business was booming, he was ticking off another career goal met but couldn't enjoy it at all. Nothing had mattered after she told him they were just friends.

Fuck he was a mess.

He wanted to see her so bad, but he'd stayed away. He couldn't stay in town and be reminded of her every time he stepped outside his door. He'd escaped to Florida to stay with his sister for a few weeks and wasn't ashamed to say that when she opened the door to him and he saw her face, there may have been tears.

His nephews were the perfect distraction for him, keeping him busy and his mind occupied. But he missed Taylor so damn much he ached. He wanted to continue being her friend and part of her life but right now everything felt so raw. If he saw her before he was ready, he was genuinely scared he would throw himself at her and beg her to love him. Even if she just faked it again. And no one wanted that. He just wanted *her*, however he could get her.

Beau knew she was pushing him away because she was scared of what they were and what they could be. He knew she didn't want to lose what they had now and he understood that her whole life she had been abandoned by people who said they loved her. He knew she had doubts about real, lasting love. But damn, she had kissed him, that had to mean something, right? Didn't she love him just a little?

He also figured the fact that he wanted kids was a factor in her pushing him away, but it just made him love her more. He wanted kids but he wanted *their* kids, children they would raise together, that didn't automatically mean biological children.

When he moved out of the cabin it was like he left a limb behind or a vital organ, he couldn't seem to function without her. He longed to hear her husky dirty laugh, her sassy quips. He missed the smell of her, the feel of her, missed *Bake Off* evenings with her, even tidying up after Tornado Taylor. He couldn't escape his misery even in his dreams. He always found himself dreaming of her, of them together. Always woke up with his cock hard and his heart aching. It was all too much.

He had finally dragged himself back to Citrus Pines yesterday, figuring he'd wallowed on his sister's couch enough already. Tomorrow was Christy and Dean's wedding and the first time he would see Taylor after a month. Anticipation had his heart skipping in his chest. At least they would be surrounded by their friends so they wouldn't be alone long enough for him to scream *please love me!* at her as she walked down the aisle. *Awkward.*

Even though he wasn't in town, like a fool he needed his dose of Taylor and had employed Ruby as his spy, offering private yoga sessions for intel. He felt like he was really going to regret those yoga lessons but if he got word of how Taylor was then it was worth any inappropriate touching or propositions Ruby hit him with.

According to Ruby, Taylor was fine and not missing

him at all. Throwing herself into the bar and was coping well after Dale. Beau had been worried how she would handle the fallout, but Ruby assured him that Taylor had reached out to Justine for some sessions to help with dealing. He was so proud of her; his woman was so strong.

"-Tay's plus one," Dean said, pulling Beau from his thoughts.

"Wait, what? Is that for the wedding?" Beau demanded, his palms starting to sweat. *Was she bringing a date?*

"And now we know why he's such a Gloomy Gus," Blake said, a shit-eating grin on his face that Beau didn't appreciate one bit.

"Hey, I remember what you were both like when your lady loves didn't want you so let's cut me some slack, alright?" Beau snapped.

"You're absolutely right. I was a complete mess over Justine," Blake said, shuddering as he remembered the dark time.

"Same. Sorry dude. I know my sister, she'll come around. Unless you did something that I need to know about?" Dean's expression turned slightly feral.

Beau opened his mouth, ready to tell Dean that he was 'let's get married, adopt fifteen babies and grow old together' in love with Taylor but he was interrupted.

"Where is he?" A deep voice boomed through the house and then Will was standing in the doorway of Blake's living room, currently painted a bright shade of orange. "Come here you sorry sonofabitch!" he shouted, opening his arms wide and he and Dean hugged before Will greeted Beau and Blake.

Beau felt guilt prickle at him. It was meant to be Dean's last night of bachelordom and here he was being a mopey moperson with a broken heart. He needed to do better.

"You're meant to be my bestie, why did you greet him first?" Beau fake pouted, shoving a beer into Will's hand.

"Aw don't be jelly, precious, I just needed to make him feel special," Will teased before turning back to Dean. "How are you feeling man? Ready to run yet?"

"Hell naw, I'm excited. Can't wait to spend the rest of my life with her, it'll be our greatest adventure yet," Dean said.

Jealousy punched Beau straight in the gut. That's how he would feel if it was him and Taylor. He would give anything to be in Dean's position. Their life together would be exciting, she would keep him on his toes, he would love the opportunity to keep surprising her. It would be magical. *Magical?* Dude...*oh fuck off, it would be.*

Will shuddered next to him.

"What's wrong with that?" Blake asked.

Beau slung his arm around Will's shoulders. "My man here is a serial one and done. Not the marrying kind."

"It's true. Although marriage makes great business sense, it makes yucky personal sense. It ain't for me," Will added.

Blake shook his head. "Dude, I've only known you a few months and I love you but, that's bullshit. You just haven't found the one who makes all your pieces fit together. Once you find that, you'll change your tune, trust me."

A contemplative look crossed Will's face and he fell into silence.

"I think you broke him..." Dean quipped.

"Bullshit, I'm just wondering when you're gonna feed me?" Will replied, snapping out of it.

Beau laughed and as best man, it was his duty to

organize the pizza. Dean said he didn't want anything fancy for his last night as a single man, just the guys, pizza and beers. He wanted to be with his family before the big day.

They ate, drank, watched movies and rough-housed when Blake challenged Will to an arm wrestle which quickly escalated. Dean backed down, his excuse that Christy would kill them if he turned up tomorrow with a black eye, and they couldn't disagree.

They went to bed but Beau lay awake most of the night thinking about seeing Taylor tomorrow, his emotions at odds, feeling like he was about to have a big exam in the morning but also like a kid at Christmas. Fuck, he wished he pressed Ruby for more info. Was Taylor pissed he stayed away? Happy? Unaffected? Had she already found a new man? She did have a plus one to the wedding, what if she brought a date? His heart thudded at the thought before he decided to put her out of his mind and finally fell into a fitful sleep where she continued to torment him in his dreams.

Chapter 25

Anxiety burned in Taylor's throat but hey, it was a nice break from the constant misery she'd felt over the last month, ever since he left her. She was adrift, floating around day to day without her anchor grounding her.

Beau had come back into her life, burrowed under her skin and set up home before he left her all over again. She couldn't work out what was more painful, seeing him or not seeing him. She didn't care anymore. She just knew she missed him with every fiber of her being. Missed coming home to him, telling him about the crazy customers she had at the bar. Missed hearing about his clients at the gym, missed baking dates with him, being kissed by him, waking up next to him. She just missed *him*.

She tried to move on, but it was like he'd taken her joy with him when he left. She'd hit her life goal and bought the second half of the bar, but she felt no triumph. The only person she wanted to tell about it wasn't around, he'd abandoned her just like she was afraid he would. She wasn't even mad he'd left this time. She was just empty. So she continued floating around, her days without him insignificant, indistinguishable.

Even now, on her brother and best friend's wedding day, she felt little joy, just anxiety. Anxiety over finally seeing him and dammit why had she agreed to give this speech? She didn't know what to say about love so she Googled it and cobbled together a basic-bitch mishmash of words that even she knew had no heart in it. But what was she going to do now? It was too late.

"Okay, I'm ready!" Christy crowed, getting up from the vanity in her room. Taylor and Justine turned and both gasped then sighed.

"*Te ves hermosa,*" Justine whispered, placing her hand to her chest, her eyes filling with tears.

"What she said," Taylor laughed, holding out a hand to Christy and twirling her. Her blonde curls bounced on her shoulders, making the diamantes woven through her hair glitter in the light. Her dress was an off-the-shoulder, floor-length lace number, but the most amazing thing Christy wore was her smile which shone brighter than any accessory, and Taylor couldn't help but return it.

Christy glowed, happiness bursting from her. It was infectious, even dispersing Taylor's dark cloud. They hugged, gripping each other tightly. This was a huge moment in their friendship, the first to marry and start an actual adult life. Justine cradled her stomach when she stepped back and this time Taylor felt no pangs of sorrow, just supreme happiness for her friend. All was not lost for Taylor; Beau had got her seriously thinking about adoption and now she had a larger stake in the bar

Sweet Surrender

she had more stability. For the first time, there was hope for her becoming a parent.

"I love you both," Christy said, smiling.

"We love you too," Taylor squeezed her hand. "If you want to run though, we've got your back."

Christy laughed. "And miss out on the rest of my life with that man? Are you kidding me?"

"Just checking," Justine grinned.

After a pause, Christy's head dipped and Taylor saw her playing with the ring on her right hand, her mom's ring. "Can I have a moment?" she asked, her voice hesitant.

"Of course," Taylor said gently. Both Christy's parents had passed away so today must be extremely tough for her.

"I need to pee again," Justine sighed and headed for the bathroom. Taylor stepped out onto the patio, needing some air. She smoothed her hands over her navy wrap dress before combing them through her hair, forgetting she also had diamantes woven throughout the tight coils and accidentally pulling one out. She cursed, throwing the stupid thing on the ground.

"What did that sparkly thing ever do to you?"

His rough voice was music to her ears. God, she missed hearing it. She spun around and there he was, leaning against the wall of the house, his arms folded over his chest.

"Hey you," she whispered when she found her breath.

"Hey sweetheart."

Those words did funny things to her insides, they clenched, caving in on themselves as she drank in the sight of him, looking all suave and panty-melting in his suit. Her gaze roved him until she met those eyes that curved so seductively at the edges, promising her all kinds of wicked delights that she knew he could definitely deliver.

"Don't we scrub up well?" she joked to break the tension.

His eyes did their own leisurely stroll over her body. "My thoughts exactly."

"I missed you." It slipped out before she could stop it. Any anger she felt at him leaving town and ignoring her for the last month immediately evaporated the moment she saw him. She knew now how harmful grudges could be.

"I'm sorry about that, Tay. I needed the time to get my head straight. I'm all good now, though," he said.

What did that mean? Does that mean he doesn't love me anymore? Why did the thought of that suddenly make her feel like a knife had been plunged into her chest?

"How's the bar?" he asked, changing the subject.

"Real good. I, uh, bought the other half. She's officially all mine," she said, sheepishly. His smile was a thing of beauty, stealing her breath.

"That's amazing, Tay. I'm so damn proud of you." A huge, goofy grin overtook her face, one to rival the brightness of Christy's. He pulled her into a hug, his strong arms banded around her and she collapsed into them. So familiar and safe, like home. His scent, fresh and minty made a beeline for her, wrapping around her and dragging her down memory lane until her chest flooded with anguish and a longing she felt to the depths of her soul.

"Sounds like the guests are arriving, I better go. See you at the end of the aisle," he joked, pulling away and then he was gone, leaving her to meltdown over that hug and those words. She knew he was kidding, it wasn't *their* wedding but what if it was? What scared her was the fact that it *didn't* scare her. Holy shit, is that what she wanted?

Half an hour later she was walking down the aisle towards Dean who had an equally huge smile on his face, both dimples on full display. Beau, Blake and Will stood to one side and she could feel Beau's eyes on her but she couldn't meet them so she focused on Dean instead.

She hugged him. "Don't you look so handsome? I love you, big bro," she whispered.

"Dang it, Taylor. Don't make me cry on my wedding day," he grumbled before kissing her cheek. She chuckled and took her place, watching as Justine walked down the aisle, belly first, shoving out her tiny bump proudly for the world to see. Taylor laughed and shook her head as Justine took her place beside Taylor and they linked arms.

Then Christy was heading their way, glowing. She heard Dean's sharp intake of breath when he saw her for the first time and Taylor's eyes flicked to him. He was in awe, his face lit with love, pride and hope.

Taylor's stomach clenched as she watched the ceremony, not taking her eyes off them. Their love was tangible, flowing out from them. Reaching out to everyone, demanding to be seen, to be recognized. She turned her attention to Justine and Blake and saw the same expression on both of their faces. Pure, undiluted love and devotion.

Panic clawed in Taylor's throat. How could love be denied when the evidence of it was all around her? There was no way either of these couples would ever leave each other, not if their lives depended on it. Just like her and Beau in the bar that night with Dale. Neither of them had run and left the other, both facing down a madman with a knife in order to protect the other, unwilling to abandon or give up.

"You may now kiss the bride!"

She blinked the ceremony back into focus to see Christy fling herself at Dean who caught her, laughing before they had the steamiest kiss ever seen at a wedding. Her eyes moved to Beau of their own accord. He was already watching her with an intensity that she couldn't explain. Then they were all heading back down the aisle, posing for pictures and off to the bar in Justine's car.

"You think I'd sit upfront because I'm the eldest," Ruby grumbled from the backseat.

"Hush it, you're lucky enough to be here after you made me ask for a plus one just *days* before a wedding," Taylor replied. Ruby's bickering helped distract Taylor from the knot that had formed in her chest. The realization she had made a colossal mistake, and with no idea how to fix it, or if it was even possible.

They arrived at the bar and quickly set to work getting it ready for the guests and the bride and groom, putting out flowers, champagne, the works. Ruby followed her around, making sarcastic comments and baiting her until Taylor snapped at her.

"What the hell crawled up your ass, girl?" Ruby sulked.

I think I'm in love and I don't know what to do because I royally fucked it up and now he's over me! Taylor wanted to scream but she didn't, instead she glared at Ruby.

"Well shit. You finally figured it out, didn't you?" Ruby cackled and Taylor promptly burst into tears. Goddammit, Beau had turned her into an emotional wreck. Ruby sighed and dragged Taylor to her office for privacy.

"I don't know what to do," Taylor sniffled in-between sobs.

"I don't understand, where's the problem?" Ruby asked, looking around her.

"I'm scared."

Sweet Surrender

"We're all scared all the time, Taylor."

"Why are you being mean, just be nice for once please!" Taylor wailed and Ruby sighed heavily.

"Because nice won't get you what you need right now. I know you're scared, I *know*. But you've got to move past that."

"That man is making me want all the things I said I never wanted. So now what do I do?"

"You take the risk! Without risk, there is no reward." Ruby said then paused. "Did I ever tell you about my Roger?"

"No?" Taylor sniffled.

"Most arrogant man I ever met in my life, I hated him. He pursued me doggedly for years, so damn annoying. He wore me down eventually. Made me love him. Then the bastard went and died and left me. God, I hated the SOB for that, for leaving me all alone. But if I knew the outcome ahead of time, I wouldn't have changed a goddamn thing. Because it was so worth it. Love is always worth the risk and that boy has loved you his whole life. Just like you've loved him. You're just too dang stubborn to see it."

"But I can't give him children naturally and he wants that, he deserves that chance."

"That's not for you to decide, it's for him and I think he's probably figured that out by now considering the way he stared at you throughout the ceremony, so I wouldn't say it's an issue. Stop finding excuses not to be happy."

Taylor hiccupped. "What if he gets bored and leaves me?"

Ruby put an arm around her and pulled her close. "What if he doesn't? What if he stays and you get everything you never knew you wanted?" Ruby stroked her hair and cupped her cheek. "This risk is worth the reward. Trust someone who lived it and knows."

They were quiet for a moment and then Taylor heard the guests arriving, but Ruby didn't immediately let her go.

"Thanks Ruby."

"I love you like you're mine, you know that right?" Ruby asked, softly.

"Who are we kidding, I am yours!" Taylor sobbed, squeezing her tight.

"Good, now hurry up and tell that boy you love him and adopt my grandbabies already."

Taylor laughed. "So demanding."

The knock on the door had them pulling apart and Justine's head poked in.

"Taylor? It's speech time."

Taylor groaned, anxiety bubbling in her throat again. "Oh God!"

She grabbed a glass of champagne, her notes and made her way through the crowd to the stage. Her heart pounded in her chest, ready to crack her ribs and escape as she looked out over the faces filling the bar. Christy and Dean were right at the front, their arms around each other, still beaming and Taylor's nerves increased all the more. She raised her notes and began reading, her voice shaky.

"Love. William Shakespeare once wrote that love…" she trailed off. She couldn't bring herself to read this speech full of quotes by famous people and bland, unfeeling, *un-Taylor* words. Not after what she witnessed, what she felt today.

Christy and Dean looked at her expectantly, but she watched Beau, her eyes latching on to his and giving her everything she needed.

"Love is a funny thing. You can't see it, you can't hold it, so how do you know it exists? You have to trust and have faith. Then you see the signs, the symptoms of love. The lingering looks, the affectionate touches, the willingness to put another person's needs first and then you realize love snuck inside you. You *can* feel it, you *can* see it, it's there and when it's gone you're just…empty."

Beau's eyebrows winged up, that crease forming between them, and a small smile quirked at his lips.

"Love is about being there, truly turning up for the other person, every day, no matter what. Not abandoning them when things get hard, when they're pissing you off or hell, in a life-or-death situation."

The crowd chuckled and Beau's smile widened, bringing about her own.

"It's your soul finding its counterpart, its other half in that person and pulling you back together to make a whole. So perfect, it'll fulfill you both for life with more to go around to your friends and family, and maybe one day, children. It's giving up everything to protect that one person. It's having the courage to take the risk, to trust once more, to *love* once more."

Beau looked away and into the crowd and when he met her eyes again, his expression was unreadable, and she faltered. She turned her attention back to Christy and Dean to get through the rest of the speech.

"And when you meet your love that you want to spend the rest of your life with, you hang on to them tight with both hands. And the rest of your life can't come quick enough."

Christy and Dean grinned at each other.

"Watching you both today, something became crystal clear. The rest of your lives are going to be full of love, respect, adoration and friendship, and we should all be so lucky. To Christy and Dean!" Taylor finished, raising her glass. The crowd repeated the words back to her followed by raucous applause.

Taylor stepped down from the stage on shaky legs and was rushed by Christy and Dean. After hugs and kisses she finally begged for a break. She immediately scanned the crowd, looking for Beau, eager to speak to him. Then she spotted him in the corner talking to a gorgeous woman who was standing too close for Taylor's comfort and jealousy snapped at her. Maybe she was reading too much into it, they were only talking, for God's sake.

She met Beau's eye and waved at him. Even though he definitely saw her, he didn't return the wave and turned back to the woman, laughing at something she said. Taylor's heart plummeted, embarrassment heated her cheeks and she turned away. Although Kayleigh and Ben were working the bar, Taylor jumped in to help them out and to give herself something to do.

A couple of hours later she found herself face to face with the woman Beau had been talking to the entire time.

"Hi," she said softly.

"What can I get you?" Taylor asked, trying to keep the *unfriendly* out of her voice.

"White wine, please."

Taylor moved away to get the drink, cataloging the woman's completely fictional faults to make herself feel better. When she placed the drink in front of her, the woman smiled again.

"Can I ask…so you dated him, right? Any advice to help a sister out?" she asked shyly.

Taylor grinned shrewdly. "I thought you'd never ask…" A thousand fake insults flooded her mind that she had used to chase off his previous dates. Lies about his manhood – *perfect*. Lies about his breath – *perfect*. Lies about him being a criminal... but they all died on her tongue.

She loved him; she could never say those things about him knowing how amazing he was. Even if he wasn't *her* man, he was still her best friend. She wanted him to be happy, even if that meant she had to witness it and hear about it for the rest of her life.

"He's...a really great guy, you're very lucky," she choked out, giving the woman her most sincere smile and escaping to her office before another round of the weepies hit her.

Chapter 26

Beau came back from the bathroom to find Elizabeth waiting for him. She smiled at him and headed his way.

What the fuck? Why is she still here?

"Would you like another drink?" she asked, sidling up next to him.

"What?" he replied, dumbfounded. He expected her to have been chased off by now with some bullshit lie from Taylor as usual. He had been counting on it. That Elizabeth was still standing in front of him only fanned the tiny flame of hope that had sparked to life during Taylor's speech. Just because she had stared at him the whole time while giving a heartfelt speech about love didn't mean she loved him. But not chasing off a potential love interest for the first time *ever? Hello Hope, my name is Beau.*

He needed to find Taylor, now.

"Excuse me," he grunted, blowing past Elizabeth. He couldn't see Taylor in the bar but spotted her office door was shut and made a beeline for it. He burst in, seeing her looking out the window, her knuckles brushing across her lip in a gesture he knew like the back of his hand. He slammed the door behind him.

"What the hell, Taylor? I went to the bathroom and when I came back, she was still there?"

She looked at him like he'd grown another head. "What?"

"I was counting on you! What are you playing at? Why didn't you tell her that I have bad breath?"

"Because you don't."

"That I'm a criminal?"

"Because you're not."

She was taking the wind out of his sails with her small voice and wide green eyes shining up at him with untold emotion.

"Tiny dick?"

She shook her head, a small smile hovering where he wanted to kiss. God, he missed her kisses. He'd been living off the memory of them alone for the last month and he needed the real thing soon or he would go insane.

"Complete asshole?"

"You're the best man I know."

His head dropped forward, resting his chin on his chest. "You're killing me here, sweetheart." His feet moved before he could stop them, eating up the space between them until he was in front of her. "Then why is *she* still here?" he growled.

"Because I want you to be happy."

He closed his eyes against her vulnerability before it clawed its way through his chest.

"Because I love you," she said simply and his eyes

snapped open, capturing hers. "I couldn't say the words when you needed them. You're right, I was scared, but I'm saying them now. Tell me I'm not too late?"

He didn't even hesitate, just pulled her tight against his body and crushed his mouth to hers in the sweetest kiss he'd ever had. Because he'd *finally* won. She surrendered and he had finally won *her*.

She opened on a moan and he swept his tongue inside, tangling it with hers, lust plowing through his chest as her grip tightened on his shirt, hands fisting the material. *Paradise.*

She pulled away. "It's always been you, I was so stupid, how did I not see it? We've wasted so much time!" she cried, tears slipping over her lower lids and trickling down her beautiful, splotchy cheeks. He kissed each one away, shushing her worries.

"Don't say that. We've got our whole lives to go yet. We have all the time in the world to love each other. You have my whole heart, forever."

She nodded but nibbled her lips, his eyes going directly to them, wanting to replace her teeth with his.

"What is it, sweetheart?" he asked, stroking her back, his fingers trailing her spine through the thin material of the dress that had wreaked havoc on him all damn day. He couldn't wait to peel it off her later.

"I'm still scared," she said, her voice low.

"Tell me."

He held her tight and soothed her as she whispered her darkest fear to him. That she wasn't enough for him, that he would get bored, that he would leave. And when she finished, he stared down into those eyes shining like polished gems and he laughed. Her brows slammed together, and he tried to stop laughing.

"I'm sorry. I'm not laughing at your fear at all. Wait,

maybe I am? But sweetheart, I've known you for a really long time and not once have I ever, *ever* been bored. Do you honestly think either of us would let this get boring?"

She wrung her hands together then squinted up at him. "No?"

"Exactly! There'll be some tough times, I can't lie about that because all relationships have them but boring? Sweetheart, you couldn't be boring even if you tried. In fact I should be worried you'll get bored of me!"

She tapped her chin contemplatively. "Hmm, true." She shot him a cheeky grin.

He growled. "It's that kind of behavior that results in a spanking."

She eyed him wickedly. "Promise?"

He barked out a laugh and kissed her again, melting into her body. He would never tire of kissing her.

"So how do we stop it from being boring, what do we do when we know all of each other's stories and memories?" she asked, peering up at him.

"That's easy, sweetheart. You make new ones."

*

They came out of her office, figuring that they could at least try and wait until they weren't at their best friend's wedding to have makeup sex. Hand in hand they strolled through the bar over to their friends.

"Is this what I think it is?" Christy squealed, pointing to their clasped hands. Taylor looked up at Beau, her soul blooming to life, full of happiness and love. They nodded.

"Best wedding present ever!" she shrieked.

Dean shook his head. "Really? On my wedding day this is now the mental picture I'm gonna have? You two shacking up together."

"I'd suggest you don't think about it," Beau said with a wink. Will and Blake burst out laughing at Dean's scowl.

"This makes me so freaking happy!" Justine bawled, then reached into Blake's back pocket and pulled out a twenty-dollar bill, slapping it into Christy's waiting hand.

"Whoa, I thought bets were our thing?" Taylor moaned to Christy.

"Um, Taylor?"

Taylor turned to see Rebelle stood behind them, wearing the dress that Taylor had sneaked into her laundry bag.

"You came!" Taylor wrapped her arms around Rebelle, and felt the woman stiffen at her touch, probably not expecting to be hugged.

"Yes. Thank you for the outfit," she said, for Taylor's ears only.

"It looks great on you."

"Thanks." She smiled shyly before glancing around and dropping her voice. "I was wondering though, did you still need help at the bar? I was thinking maybe I could pick up a shift or maybe two a week?" Rebelle took a deep breath and Taylor saw her looking at Justine, Justine gave her a slight nod and a thumbs up.

Hope lit Taylor's chest at the idea of bringing Rebelle into their fold more but before she could answer a large shadow eclipsed them both.

"Hey there, pretty lady. What's your name?" Will's confident voice boomed out. Taylor glared at him for not reading the room better and she thought she heard a growl coming from Blake. But Rebelle didn't even look at him, didn't react like anyone else had entered their conversation.

The silence stretched on as Rebelle ignored him, keeping her gaze fixed solely on Taylor and Taylor tried to pull their conversation back to fill up the awkwardness, gobsmacked that Will had just been so spectacularly rebuffed. "Uh, I've just hired someone but I can take you on a couple of nights a week?"

Relief lit Rebelle's delicate pixie features. "I would really appreciate that," she said, still ignoring Will who hovered awkwardly next to Taylor, watching Rebelle with rapt attention.

"Great, why don't you pop by next week and we can sort it all out?"

Rebelle smiled softly. "Great, see you then, and thanks."

She waved to the group and then she was gone.

Will turned back to them. "Who was that? I need deets immediately."

A louder growl from Blake echoed through the group. "Don't even think about it."

Justine stilled him with a hand on his chest. "Stop it honey, she's a grown woman." Justine turned to Will. "Ignore him, he's a little overprotective of her, she's like a sister to him."

Things descended into chaos when Will said he would be staying in town for a couple of weeks and couldn't wait to bump into Rebelle, it was like a red flag to Blake's raging bull.

"I'm stealing you away," Beau murmured in Taylor's ear, pulling her onto the dancefloor and into his arms. She wrapped her arms around his neck and stroked her fingers through his hair. She spied Ruby over his shoulder and smiled brightly when Ruby made a heart shape with her hands. Then Ruby made a ring with her thumb and index finger and poked her other index finger through it, mimicking sex and Taylor burst out laughing. *Thirsty old lady.*

"What?" Beau asked, trying to look over his shoulder.

"Nothing," Taylor said. He narrowed his eyes but let it go. They swayed together staring into each other's eyes and she could have sworn she saw the rest of their lives play out in his and it was beautiful. She knew it in her bones that this man was it for her. Had always been it. There had never been anyone who even came close and as she examined her heart she knew without a shred of doubt that no one ever could. He was hers. Her love. Her *person*.

"Isn't this the part where you talk about how you had me first? Kissed me first?" she joked, she knew his MO.

He frowned. "But I didn't get your first kiss."

She smiled at his dejected tone. "True, but you'll have the next kiss, all my next kisses and you'll have my last."

"Very good point," he murmured, dipping his head to take one right now.

She couldn't wait to kiss this man for the rest of her life.

*

Two years later...

Anticipation held Taylor's stomach in a vice-like grip and she constantly felt on the verge of vomiting. She paced back and forth across the living room of the home she and Beau shared. She could feel his eyes on her, sweeping over her and assessing but she couldn't stop. She was a wreck.

"What if we haven't child-proofed enough yet? Our house is so freaking dangerous, why did we not do more?"

"Sweetheart, calm down. The home study was fine, we

got the green light from Ali months ago which means we did enough. But if you're still worried then we'll wrap them both in bubble wrap or buy those big plastic bubbles and they can live in those forever and be bubble children."

She stopped wringing her hands long enough to glare at him. "When did you get so sassy?"

"I learned from the best." He smirked and came over to her, dropping a kiss on the tip of her nose. Dammit, she couldn't stay mad at him when he was so sexy and supportive. Ugh, he was too perfect sometimes, her Mr Goody Two-shoes.

She looked around the room and saw that none of their furniture had sharp edges, it was all well-spaced so no one would bump into anything and there was no way anyone could grab any cables or stick curious fingers in dangerous sockets.

Taylor's eyes locked onto the mantel-piece above the fireplace that held all their pictures, including the one of their wedding day. Taylor in her pink wedding dress, Beau holding her in his arms, his matching pink bowtie on display and both of them grinning from ear to ear. There was space next to that picture for a new one, one they were waiting to take: their first family picture.

Beau was right, they had prepared so she shoved that fear aside, having a brief moment of excited euphoria until her next fear consumed her. Taylor immediately began wringing her hands again and peered up at him. "What if they hate us?"

"Sweetheart, I love you. More than life itself and I would walk through fire for you, I've faced a madman for you. But I need you to stop. We've met them, many times, and we have a great connection with them. They don't hate us, we wouldn't be allowed to adopt them if they hated us. I know you're worried, I am too. But no one could hate you," he said, clasping her hands tightly in his.

"You so did," she pouted.

"No, I didn't hate you at all, remember?"

A small smile split her lips. "Fine, I believe you, but only because you're right, I am super awesome."

He laughed, those deep brown eyes of his glittering with amusement and he tucked a strand of hair behind her ear. "There's my girl."

"You're awesome too, I guess," she conceded. He dropped his head and covered her mouth with his. She opened automatically, like she always did, and hummed with pleasure. His tongue rolled and stroked against hers so slowly, patiently like he hadn't a care in the world. How did he stay so calm at a time like this?

Outside she heard a car door slam and Beau shoved her away from him. "They're here!" he yelled, running to the window and peering out; and she smothered a laugh. *Clearly nothing like as calm as he pretended.*

An ache pierced her stomach as her anxiety crept back in and she took a moment to stare at him, memorizing him and this moment before their lives changed forever. She sent a silent prayer of thanks to the heavens or whoever was responsible for bringing this man into her life. She didn't know what she had done to deserve him, to deserve such a fairy-tale ending but she made sure she was thankful every damn day.

"They're coming!" Beau shouted, snapping her back to the present and they both ran to the front door and swung it open. They gripped each other tightly as they watched their social worker, Ali, shepherd two small children up the porch and then they were standing in front of them and it took every ounce of Taylor's willpower not to burst into tears.

It was Homecoming Day.

"Welcome home Mi Sun and Dal!" Ali said, ushering the two children inside. Mi Sun stepped inside first, confidently and clutched her stuffed pink rabbit tightly to her little chest and Taylor bit the inside of her cheek to stop the tears. Her heart full to bursting seeing Mi Sun carrying around the stuffed toy that Taylor gave her on their second visit with them.

Dal was a little more cautious. He was older and a little less trusting but he had dropped his guard slowly over time. He looked down at his sister and frowned slightly at her bold nature, choosing to stay close to Ali who had been their caseworker for nearly a year. But Taylor spotted the action figure that Beau had given him dangling from his grip. She smiled, remembering the hours Beau had spent in the toy store agonizing over whether Dal would prefer Superman, Batman, Spiderman or Luke Skywalker and nearly having an emotional breakdown.

"How can I raise them when I can't even pick a toy!" he'd cried, and Taylor had tried really hard not to laugh at his dramatics. Okay that might have been insensitive, but he was being ridiculous. He would be the best dad in the whole world, he just didn't know it yet. Taylor looked over at him and saw he was also struggling to hold back the tears.

Adoption had been a long process, painful, exhausting but so rewarding and there was no one on earth she would rather have done this journey with. Hell, it was because of Beau that this journey was happening at all, she never would have had the courage to do it. Wouldn't have wanted to do it without him, her soulmate.

They had been in the process for well over a year now

and had been devastated when they weren't matching with any candidates. But then they were matched with Mi Sun and Dal, and everything changed. Their parents had migrated to America from Seoul soon after Mi Sun was born, and both died in a tragic car accident last year leaving the two children without a family. They had been placed with a wonderful foster family who Taylor and Beau had met many times during their visits but finally Mi Sun and Dal were home, where they belonged.

Ali helped them get the kids settled in the house and then panic rose in Taylor's chest as Ali made a move to leave. Ali had been the rock they had leaned on so hard during the last year that Taylor was surprised Ali still wanted anything to do with them. And now she was going to leave and what…that was it?

"Well, that's that. Congratulations again on your Homecoming Day. I'm so thrilled for both of you and Mi Sun and Dal. You've got my number and Dal has it too to keep in touch and I'll schedule the first post placement visit. Let me know if you have any queries or concerns before then and feel free just to check in and give me updates," Ali said, pushing her glasses up her nose.

"Are you sure you want to go?" Beau gasped out, likely feeling the same fear as Taylor.

Ali chuckled and took their hands in each of hers. "You're going to be fine. I have every faith that you'll become a truly wonderful family. Don't be scared, you've got this! And I'm not gone yet," she replied, shrugging.

"Thank you so much, for everything. I don't think we can ever repay you," Taylor gushed, gratitude overwhelming her.

"You already have! I can see how happy you're all going to be. Now, take care and I'll see you in thirty days." With a final wave, she got into her car and was gone, leaving Taylor and Beau gripping each other tightly on the porch.

After a moment Beau turned to her. "We're parents." Awe filled his words.

Taylor nodded, tears slipping down her cheeks. "Yep, we're parents."

He wiped away her tears, not realizing his own were streaking down his cheeks and he laughed as she wiped his away. Then they took a deep breath and went back inside the house which now felt full with just the addition of these two tiny bodies.

Dal was on the floor playing with a train set that Beau had pulled out and Mi Sun came over to Taylor and wrapped an arm around Taylor's leg, peering up at her, holding the pink rabbit aloft.

"Pinky hungry," she mumbled around the thumb lodged in her mouth and Taylor's heart exploded in her chest.

Don't cry, don't cry, don't cry.

"Let's go find him something to eat!" Taylor replied brightly before taking Mi Sun's hand and heading toward the kitchen.

*

Beau paced the porch as he waited for Ali to finish conducting her review with Mi Sun, who they now called Mi-Mi at her insistence, and Dal, hoping and praying that Ali wouldn't come out and say *That's it, we're taking them away from you, this last thirty days have been hell!*

They had been the best thirty days of Beau's entire life. Watching Taylor bloom into the most amazing mom as they both fell into a routine with Mi-Mi and Dal. Mi-Mi was bold and confident for a four-year-old and sure of what she wanted, not afraid to speak her mind, just like Taylor. Dal was more reserved, but observant. He watched and gathered information quietly, he'd taken longer to relax which was still impressive for only being with them for thirty days so far.

He couldn't imagine losing them now. Watching Taylor bond with them both and feeling that love build inside himself for his two children. It was a connection and love that would grow over time but he couldn't imagine loving them any more than he did right now.

Beau and Taylor had only introduced them to Grandma Ruby and Christy and Dean so far, deciding they didn't want to overwhelm them with more people during an already overwhelming time. But provided today went well they would take the pair to play basketball later with the gang and introduce them to their other aunties and uncles.

Taylor came up behind him and wrapped her arms around his waist, placing her head in the space between his shoulder blades and he felt her calm flow through into him.

"We'll be fine. I'm confident. We've done good," she whispered. He placed his hands over hers and nodded. Then the front door opened and Ali came out, her expression carefully blank and Beau's stomach dropped. He put his arm around Taylor's shoulders, needing her comfort, her balance to calm him.

"Well, how did it go?" he asked, his voice rasping.

Ali frowned and he felt Taylor quiver next to him and prepared himself for the worst. That Mi-Mi and Dal were unhappy and needed to be removed. How would Taylor cope, how would he get her through this?

"Mi Sun has some concerns..." Ali began. Beau swallowed thickly and gripped Taylor tighter, fear riding him. "She says Pinky isn't getting as many carrots as she feels he should." Ali fixed them with a wide smile and Taylor burst out laughing but Beau's legs turned to jelly with his relief.

"Ali!" he groaned.

"What are you both worried about? It went brilliantly, they're doing amazingly well. Even better than I had hoped, and I had no doubt that this visit would go well. You two need more faith in yourselves," she tsked.

Beau wrapped his arms around Taylor, gripping her as he realized this was it. The first test was done and they had passed, with flying colors. Ali chatted to them some more and said she would be back in another thirty days, that was the way the process went until all the legalities were wrapped up which could take a few more months and then she left.

"My heart was in my mouth," Taylor groaned, burying her face in his sweatshirt.

"Tell me about it," he replied and dropped a kiss to her head, resting his cheek against the pillow of wild, red curls that smelled deliciously like cinnamon.

"But I'm proud of us, we've done good. Now let's go and celebrate!" She cheered and ran into the house, then he heard Dal giggling and Mi-Mi shouting and raced after them.

They went to the basketball court and Uncle Dean and Aunty Christy made a beeline for them before they were introduced to Uncle Blake, Aunty Justine and babbling baby Harley.

"Are Will and Reb-" Justine began but was cut off by a loud shriek from Harley.

"No, I think they're in Georgia right now at the new shelter opening, they should be back soon so we're going to introduce them to Mi-Mi and Dal then," Beau replied.

After the introductions were made, the teams were formed. Dean and Christy versus Justine, Beau and Dal with Blake and Taylor sitting on the side-lines with Harley and Mi-Mi.

Dal shuffled his feet as he stood there listening to Dean explain how to play before Beau swung Dal up and onto his shoulders.

"No fair, I didn't realize you were gonna join up to make one super player!" Dean pouted. Dal giggled as Dean reached up to ruffle his hair and Beau smiled watching the bond form between them.

The game began with Beau and Dal dominating. Beau dribbled the ball up and down the court then passed it to Dal to slip into the basket. Blake heckled and cheered from the side-lines while Taylor and Mi-Mi picked grass to feed to Pinky.

Beau and Dal were an unstoppable team winning the game and then they all went to Grandma Ruby's for celebratory food. That night as Taylor and Beau sat on the couch watching some Pixar movie the kids loved, Beau looked at them both, fast asleep after an exhausting day and love filled his chest.

"Thank you," Taylor murmured.

He swung his eyes to her. Her skin glowing in the light from the TV, her eyes shining. "For what?"

"My family," she replied.

His brows dipped as his throat thickened with emotion. "Thank you for mine." He leaned across the two sleeping children to press a soft kiss to her lips.

Her eyes popped open. "Did you feed the squirrels earlier?" she mumbled against his lips.

He pulled back, smiling. "Yes, they'd eaten all the food from the day before, they're getting greedy. I swear I saw one the other day that was the size of a small bear."

Sweet Surrender

"They're storing the food for all the babies we're going to have!" she squealed with excitement, the children stirred but didn't wake up.

He rolled his eyes. "I didn't realize I married a crazy squirrel lady."

"You did, and now she wants you to take her to bed." She tossed her red mane over one shoulder and shot him a look that spoke volumes.

They switched off the TV and put the kids to bed before heading to their own room. As Beau lay in bed, watching Taylor undress, his eye caught the new tattoo she sported on the back of her neck that had their children's names. He raised his hand to rub his own tattoo, his *first* tattoo just behind his ear of the letter *T*. He'd gotten it right after Taylor admitted that the *B* behind hers, her first tattoo that he went with her to get, had always been his initial all along.

Taylor turned to him, thoughtful. "You were right, you know. I know it's not been long but this," she gestured between them, "will *never* get boring."

He chuckled. "I know, I'm always right."

"Ha! You wish, mister," she snorted.

"Are you disagreeing with me?"

She stomped over to him, hand on her hip, all confidence and sass, just how he liked. "You bet your fine ass I am!"

"Good, it's that kind of attitude that resorts in a spanking," he purred and snapped his arm out, pulling her on top of him.

"Promise?" she breathed as she pressed a kiss to his lips, nipping at them.

"Always."

The End.

Acknowledgements

Thank you so much for reading Taylor & Beau's story, I really hoped you enjoy it and please consider leaving a review on Goodreads, Amazon and any socials you have. Reviews really help indie authors and we need all the help we can get from awesome readers like you.

Huge thank you as always to my alpha's, beta's and critique partners Mimi, Anna P, Anna L, Carley and Michelle – I love you ladies so much and couldn't do this without your amazing support, feedback and 20 minute ranty voicenotes!

Massive thank you to my editor Caron for getting this ship shape and for highlighting just how appalling I am with comma's and how many times I used the word THICK. This has now greatly reduced haha.

Finally thank you to my ARC readers, seeing your amazing reviews come in gives me such a boost. Imposter syndrome is a needy, aggressive bitch and each lovely review from you helps tell it to shut the hell up xx

About the Author

Lila is a thirtysomething writer living in Derbyshire, England with her *cough* parents *cough*. She loves romance, sharks, cats and has an ~~un~~healthy obsession with Henry Cavill.

Sweet Surrender is her third novel in the Citrus Pines series, head to Amazon to check out books one and two if you haven't already read them! Lila is a huge fan of the romance reading and writing community so why not say hello, she can be found on Instagram, Facebook, Pinterest, Tiktok, Goodreads and contacted via her shiny new website www.liladawesauthor.com

Printed in Dunstable, United Kingdom